The Hurst Chronicles

Reader Newsletter

Sign up for the no-spam Hurst Chronicles newsletter and be the first to hear about the next books in the series as well as reader offers and exclusive content, all for free.

Sign up now at Hurstchronicles.com

Sentinel

Robin Crumby

Website: HurstChronicles.com
Twitter: @HurstChronicles
Facebook: Facebook.com/HurstChronicles

Disclaimer

Sentinel is a work of fiction. Names, characters, businesses, places, events and incidents are either the products of the author's imagination or used in a fictitious manner. Any resemblance to actual persons, living or dead, or actual events is purely coincidental.

"For when I bring them into the land flowing with milk and honey, which I swore to their fathers, and they have eaten and are satisfied and become prosperous, then they will turn to other gods and serve them, and spurn Me and break My covenant."

Deuteronomy 31:20

CHAPTER ONE

The early winter storms had been raging for days. The noise was deafening. It wasn't just the howling wind; it was also the giant rollers sweeping in from the English Channel from the South West. Surging past the Needles and the western tip of the island, the waves were sent crashing against the weathered groynes and battered sea defences at the base of the castle walls. Spray flew high into the air before being carried away by powerful gusts.

Hurst Castle had seen storms worse than this. Every winter for nearly five hundred years, Mother Nature threw her worst at the man-made structure. The castle squatted resolutely on this most remote and desolate location, at the far end of a shingle spit that connected the fortress to the mainland and, like an unwanted guest, nature made her resentment known on a regular basis. Little by little the raised causeway that ran along the top of the shingle defences was being slowly washed away. It was only a matter of time before the castle would be completely cut off from the mainland, reachable by boat across narrow tidal channels that ran between the salt marshes around Keyhaven.

Jack slammed shut the wooden door to the lighthouse that he had made his home over the long months since arriving here. It needed another lick of paint, its surface blistered and peeling.

Buffeted by another gust, he wrapped his coat tighter around his trunk, shielding his face against sheeting rain. He hurried towards the shelter of the castle wall, relaxing a little as the wind dropped and he could hear himself think again. The drawbridge was already down and the two guards who were taking shelter in the covered entrance straightened a little upon seeing Hurst's leader striding towards them.

"Morning, lads. Anything to report?"

"Not really," said Tommy, rubbing his cheek, trying to remember anything of note from his shift. He glanced jealously at Scottie who had just appeared, cupping a hot brew. "Other than a couple of false alarms around midnight, we've mostly been chasing shadows as usual."

"Did you manage to get some sleep, Jack?" asked Scottie, blowing the steam off his coffee. "Stormy night, eh?"

"Me? Oh, I slept like a log, thank you," laughed Jack. "But I'm used to it. Remember, I spent half of my life at sea. Bit of wind and rain never hurt anyone. Did the patrols find anything?"

"Oh, nothing out of the ordinary," shrugged Scottie. "We got the call from the *Chester* that there were a couple of radar blips heading out of Lymington harbour, but by the time we got a team out there, they were either turned round or had vanished into the night."

"Sergeant Flynn said they were probably in a dinghy or rowing boat. Virtually impossible to pick up on radar," added Tommy.

"Same pattern we've seen for weeks. People trying to make the crossing to the island in the dead of night. Not much we can do about it," lamented Scottie.

Jack nodded, scratching his beard. It needed a trim. He normally relied on Terra for haircuts, but she still hadn't returned from the island. He hadn't given up hope she was still alive. It was common knowledge that she was being held captive by the former inmates of Parkhurst Prison and their leader Briggs. He thought fondly back to the times she had grabbed hold of his head and started chopping away at his locks with a blunt pair of scissors, despite his protestations. Like shearing a sheep, she had said. He smiled at the memory.

"Makes you wonder how many are getting through the net," reflected Tommy.

Jack sniffed at the wind. There was something foul in the air this morning. He turned his back against a forceful gust as the three of them moved back within the shelter of the entrance.

The Solent was now under the watchful protection of the Allies. For the first time since the outbreak of the Millennial Virus, order was slowly returning to this coastal region. Its many waterways, creeks and harbours were scrutinised day and night by a radar operator sat in near permanent darkness, staring at a screen on board the *USS Chester*. Anchored in the Solent, the American missile destroyer worked hand in hand with the Royal Navy's growing fleet of patrol boats and fast launches, co-ordinating the defence of the island. Hurst Castle was again a critical outpost defending the western approaches. Built by Henry VIII as part of a chain of forts and castles along England's southern coast to guard against attacks by the French and Spanish navies, today Hurst had resumed its military role. Like a passive sentinel, Hurst remained alert, day and night, ready to do its duty.

Thus far, there had been little to do. Chasing shadows in the night, seeing ghosts and echoes. Urgent radio calls from command would request they check out an unauthorised vessel attempting to make the crossing under cover of darkness. They had a powerful searchlight set up on top of the lighthouse, but with limited fuel for the generator, they rarely had it running. They relied on handheld lanterns and high-powered Maglites to scan the darkness from the shoreline or from a R.I.B scrambled to intercept.

"We need more men," said Scottie. "It's a huge stretch of coast to monitor with such a small force. We need more boats on patrol, 24/7. It's like trying to find a needle in a haystack. As things stand, we've got no chance."

"Well, it's not like we're the only line of defence," corrected Jack. "Even if they run the gauntlet and make it to the island, all the beaches are defended with barbed wire, obstacles and armed guards."

"They're turning that place into a fortress. Next thing they'll build a wall. Then what?" asked Tommy.

"If that's what it takes to keep the island virus-free and control the population flow through the quarantine zones, then so be it."

The attacks had started several weeks ago. Most came in the dead of night. At first, they were disorganised, sporadic incursions, initially dismissed as desperate people trying to reach the sanctuary offered by the newly formed Camp Wight on the island. More recent attempts suggested a systematic probing of the Allies' defences. To what end, Jack had no idea. Forces unknown were orchestrating events, keeping the defenders chasing shadows, scrambling interceptors only to find the small vessels they were sent to find had disappeared or were returning to safe harbour.

There came the sound of footsteps echoing around the battlements as someone raced across the courtyard towards the guardhouse. The three men turned to see Sam trying to catch his breath, one hand on the stone wall nearest him.

"What's up, Sam?"

"It's the *Chester* on the radio, Jack. Command wants us to take the *Nipper* out and intercept."

"Surely not in this weather?"

"Probably another false alarm," suggested Tommy.

"They wouldn't ask unless it was urgent, Jack. Apparently there's a ship about five and a half miles south-east of Portland Bill heading this way. Command said that, from the size of it, it's probably a coastal steamer or small tanker. They need us to intercept, make contact and find out their intentions. We're to take Sergeant Flynn and a squad of marines, just in case."

"Can't they send the helicopter?" asked Tommy. "It would be much quicker."

"Not in this." Sam gestured skywards. "The winds are gusting storm force."

Jack looked back outside and squinted at the rain clouds. The storm was strengthening. It would be lunacy to take the *Nipper* out. She was a thirty-five-foot coastal fishing boat, broad in the beam and more than capable of operating in all conditions. Nevertheless, Jack was experienced enough to know that a good skipper never underestimated a storm.

"I'm assuming they don't have any other patrols in the area that could check this out?"

"Apparently everything is returned to port on account of the weather. We're the nearest."

"Okay, Sam. Can you let Sergeant Flynn know, grab the oilskins and safety gear and get her ready? We'll call the *Chester* for an update when we're on the way. I don't want to go out in this unless we have to."

Jack grabbed two sets of oilskins from the coat rack in the

guardhouse and hurried down to the lighthouse to find his rucksack. He hastily repacked the bag with binoculars and a revolver before joining Sam at the jetty a few minutes later, where the *Nipper* was sheltering from the storm. The engines were already spluttering noisily and the mooring lines were being held on a slip. As soon as Flynn and the three other men and their packs and weapons were on board, they cast off.

It was approaching high tide and together with a storm surge, they had plenty of water to get out through the mudflats and shallows to reach the main channel. As they rounded the spit and turned west into the teeth of the gale, they met the full force of the wind and waves sweeping towards them. The Needles channel was narrow where water funnelled over rocks creating an overfall. Coupled with an eastward flowing tide and a westerly wind, it made the half-mile out to the deeper water of Christchurch Bay bumpier than usual. In front of them, further out to sea, lay a maelstrom of wild, heaving water.

Sam came back inside the small cabin and braced himself against the next set of rollers surging towards them. The waves were building in size and power, towering over the small fishing boat. The four marines were below decks looking decidedly green around the gills. One man was retching into a bucket he was clinging on to. He had both arms wrapped around the receptacle, like his life depended on it. Up the steps to the wheelhouse, the wiper blades on the windscreen were fighting a losing battle to clear the spray as it swept in on the wind. Looking behind them towards Hurst Castle, the sea had become a roiling mass of white horses.

Jack kept both hands on the wheel, working hard to keep the *Nipper*'s bow in to the wind and waves. Their engine was straining to make headway and he estimated their forward progress no better than two or three knots. He picked up the radio again and tried to contact the *Chester*. The first attempt had proven unsuccessful, their transmission lost between waves more than twenty feet high.

They had been told to steam south-west and meet what was likely to be a steamer or small tanker making for the Solent, now some three miles beyond Portland Bill. The vessel was unresponsive to all attempts to contact it and moving very slowly. Jack reckoned that they should be no more than a mile or two away from it. Right now, visibility was so poor they could pass within one hundred yards and not see anything.

The radio crackled into life and they heard an American voice, faint but intelligible. Jack snatched the receiver from its cradle.

"*Nipper* here, *Chester*. Receiving you loud and clear. We're entering the sector. No contact to report. Can you confirm bearing to intercept?"

"You're right on top of it. Should be dead ahead of you now. Less than a mile. Just off your port bow," said the radar operator.

"Copy that," said Jack. "Right, stay alert, keep your eyes peeled."

Sam grabbed the binoculars and started scanning the horizon, adjusting his stance to compensate for the pitch and roll of the boat. Each time the bow of the *Nipper* collided with a wave, the forward momentum seemed to slow as the propeller fought hard to drive them forward again. Jack was worried the engine would overheat and they would be left without power to drift onto the rocks. He'd seen it happen before. A powerboat washed up on the shingle beach at Milford, holed and broken. He sincerely hoped that this wasn't another wild goose chase.

Sam nudged him in the ribs and pointed to an enormous

shape that had appeared from nowhere off the port bow. It took Jack a few seconds to make sense of what he was looking at.

The ship was a tanker in some distress. It sat broadside to the waves, heavy in the bow and listing a little to starboard. It had taken on a lot of water and seemed to be without power, drifting along the coast towards the island.

Jack circled to the ship's stern and scanned the bridge, walkways and railings trying to spot any crew members, any signs of life. Across the ship's stern was written *Santana* and its registered home port of Panama underneath. Sergeant Flynn joined them in the wheelhouse. As they nudged closer, Jack handed over his binoculars for Flynn to take a closer look. A huge wave swept over the bow of the *Santana* and the whole ship seemed to lurch towards them. Jack rammed the engines in reverse and withdrew another fifty yards, suddenly concerned that the whole ship could roll on its side if it was hit again with similar force.

"Better call it in," said Flynn. "Let's find out what they want us to do."

CHAPTER TWO

Jack navigated the *Nipper* around to the port side and remained on standby at a safe distance. Coming out of the wind shadow, they again faced the full force of the wind and waves and he wrestled with the wheel to keep the boat's bow nose on to the weather.

"*Chester,* this is the *Nipper* again. We've located the tanker the *Santana.* She's listing approximately ten degrees and has taken on a lot of water in the bow. The stern is still riding high but she appears deserted. No lights or any sign of power at the current time. They're unresponsive to all attempts to contact. What are your instructions?"

"Copy that, *Nipper.* Standby."

There was static on the airwaves as the message was relayed to command and a discussion ensued off-air before the radio operator came back on.

"Our logs show that the *Santana* is listed as a coastal tanker, registered out of Panama, last known to be operating from Kuwait to France and Belgium. She's 515 feet in length and normally has a crew of fourteen. Can you confirm whether she is laden or unladen?"

Jack glanced at Sam and Flynn. Judging by how low she was

in the water, their best guess was that she was carrying a cargo.

"We're not one hundred per cent sure, but we think she's fully laden. But it could just be that she's waterlogged."

There was static again as they waited for a decision. The *Nipper* was too small to tow her to safety and attempting to board her in this weather would be lunacy. Their best option would be to wait out the storm and get a tug boat out the next morning in calmer weather.

"Your orders are to board her, mount a salvage operation. Restart her engines. As soon as the weather clears we can get a tug out to you to tow her into port."

Jack grimaced at Flynn. He didn't like it, but they didn't have a choice. A cargo of oil was priceless and certainly worth the risk, but boarding a ship in weather like this was no small feat. It would require all his skills to even get them close. The rest was up to the marines. He just hoped they had trained for this. The last thing he wanted was to lose someone overboard. It would be a death sentence. There would be little chance of rescue.

He knew Lieutenant Peterson would have considered the risks carefully. For such a prize, the marines' lives were expendable. Unfortunately, that also meant Sam and Jack were in danger too. He looked across at Sam as he was preparing the safety lines, helping the marines organise themselves. He could tell from the deep breaths and frozen expression that he was terrified, but was hiding it well from the others.

Flynn and his men stood ready on the *Nipper*'s deck in the shelter of the wheelhouse, bracing themselves against the heavy roll. Another wave smashed into the bow sending spray high into the air, showering down on top of them. Flynn had a grappling line and was intending to hook the railing and climb on board. On his back, he carried a rope ladder some twenty feet long.

Jack brought the *Nipper* back to the leeward side of the enormous tanker, keeping his distance. Each time the tanker met another wave, it rose thirty feet above them before sinking into the trough. Their plan required exceptional timing. Jack was to get them right in close, a gap of no less than ten to fifteen feet to avoid a collision that could crush the tiny *Nipper*. As she rose high against the *Santana*'s superstructure, Flynn would throw the line and, with a large degree of luck, he could climb on board.

Flynn waited by the gunwale. One of the other marines held tight to his belt leaving his hands free to operate. Jack gunned the engines and they surged towards the towering hull, bringing them alongside. The two vessels lurched towards each other, see-sawing higher and higher before plunging towards them. Jack shouted "Now!" at the top of his voice and Flynn swung the grappling hook. He threw it high towards the railing but the gap closed and with a loud clang, the line fell short, plunging into the sea between the two ships. He shook his head, hauled in the line and waited to try again.

The gap between the vessels closed again and briefly, there was contact, a dangerous scrape of metal on metal, tearing a hole in the *Nipper*'s toe rail before Jack could get a last-minute response from a sharp turn of the wheel. Flynn tried again, taking careful aim. This time he found his mark and pulled hard to secure the line. As the ship rose again, he clung to the rope and was lifted off his feet, soaring higher until his body slammed into the hull. They watched nervously from below as he clambered hand over hand, hauling himself up the rope. After what seemed an age, he got one hand on the railing, pulled himself up and flopped on to the deck, safely on board the *Santana*.

As soon as he had caught his breath, he took the pack off his back and removed the rope ladder. After securing it fast to the railing on both sides, he unfurled the ladder and waited for the first marine to make the climb. Jack closed the gap to within a few feet and waited for the hull of the *Santana* to plunge towards them once more. The marine timed his jump to perfection and made it safely on to the bottom third of the ladder, pulling himself clear of the waves and straddling the rail. The next marine stood ready. Jack noticed him visibly shaking, terrified of the leap of faith he had to make. When the moment came, he jumped just too late as the *Nipper* lurched to starboard. He clutched for the bottom rungs of the ladder but fell short, disappearing into the waves behind the *Nipper.*

Jack cupped his hands to his mouth and shouted "Man overboard" as loud as he could.

Sam looked round anxiously. He ran to the back of the boat, snatching a life ring and threw it towards the flailing arms of the man in the water.

The marine was not wearing a life jacket and struggled to stay afloat, groping for the line attaching the ring to the boat, as he drifted away. Sam took up the slack, ready to pull him in.

The marine floundered, fully clothed, desperately trying to keep his head above the water. He drifted towards the ring, fighting for breath. He reached for the life ring, swallowing another mouthful of seawater. It was just within touching distance, yet the current was sweeping him past it quickly now. Another wave surged through and the ring jerked back towards the *Nipper*, leaving the man floundering before he disappeared from view.

Sam bellowed toward the wheelhouse: "Jack, we need to circle round to pick him up."

Jack hesitated, looked forlornly up into the darkening sky. It was a terrible choice. They wouldn't get another chance at boarding. He glanced up at Flynn who was gripping the rail, helplessly watching his man drift away. Flynn looked down blankly and shook his head. He was right, without a life jacket and fully clothed, he would not last long. There would be a low chance of even finding him again. Certainly, not in this weather. Even if they could, there was no time to mount a man-overboard rescue and get the rest of the team on board the *Santana.*

The two remaining marines steeled themselves to the task, taking extra care before readying themselves to jump. To Jack's relief, they both made it up the ladder without incident, leaving Jack his turn.

He handed over the wheel to Sam.

"Get clear but stay in the lee of the ship just in case we can't restart the engines and need taking off again."

Sam nodded, patting Jack on the shoulder for reassurance. Jack waited for the *Nipper* to roll back and stood ready, mid-ships, waiting for the distance to close and the ladder to level off in front of him. Taking a deep breath, he lunged forwards, groping for a handhold. His right foot slipped sideways on the wet rail and he fell.

For a few terrifying milliseconds, his arms flailed in mid-air, reaching for the ladder. He thought he might fall short until the *Santana* rolled away from him and, to his huge relief, the bottom of the ladder appeared out of the water. He grabbed hold of it with his left hand, smashing his body against the steep sided hull. He swung his right arm up, searching for a good handhold. If he couldn't climb up before the next wave swept through, he knew it would be over quickly.

With all his might, he heaved himself up the ladder. Soaking wet, he made slow but steady progress as the ship rolled back to starboard. He looked up and saw one of the marines reaching down to grab him. The outstretched hand was almost within touching distance, just a few more rungs. He felt the aspect of the ship begin to change again and the angle of his climb revert to the vertical and then the ladder seemed to swing in mid-air. He clung on, not daring to climb. Voices from above were shouting, imploring him to keep going. Beneath him, he saw the *Nipper* head away from the *Santana.* There was no way back. The only thing he could do was climb or die.

When the roll of the ship swung back the other way, he summoned every ounce of remaining strength and reached high, hand over hand, until he felt a strong arm gripping the sleeve of his jacket. He was manhandled soaking wet on to the deck, panting. His eyes closed as he said a small silent prayer, whispering "thank you".

"Come on," said Flynn. "We don't have much time."

CHAPTER THREE

Jack followed Sergeant Flynn and the three marines as they climbed a series of stairwells to reach the doorway to the bridge. Peering through the reinforced glass there was no sign of the crew. They cranked open the water-tight door, weapons raised. With a curt nod, he waved them inside. The three men were well trained and systematically swept the room, covering the angles and corners before each calling clear, one hand raised. Jack stayed close behind Flynn as he stepped inside, peering round him to see what lay within.

The bridge was relatively modern with all of the latest navigational aids. It was a different world from the merchant ships Jack had known as a young man. Back then, there was a more traditional look and feel to a bridge. Binoculars, brass fittings, dials, compasses, teak and green screens. This felt like stepping into the control room of a nuclear plant. Everything was automated and electronic. He felt completely out of his depth surrounded by all this technology. All of the screens were blank, although there was a panel of lights blinking in the corner. One of Flynn's men put his rifle flat on the counter and conducted a number of system checks, moving from console to console, calling out what each gauge was telling him.

"Main power systems are all off-line. Backup power generator is in stand-by," he said flicking the handle into the on position. There was a reassuring hum as the screen nearest him lit up. "Oil pressure, water pressure, fuel, hydraulics, pumps, everything looks normal. Hard to say what happened here, sir."

"So, where's the crew?" asked Flynn.

"Beats me. Maybe they abandoned ship when they lost power."

"Unlikely, all the lifeboats are still on-board. Unless the crew was rescued. Makes no sense."

Jack noticed some dark liquid spilled on the floor and reached down to touch it, lifting his fingers to his nose. It was coffee. He looked around behind a computer terminal and noticed a grouping of bullet indentations in the bulkhead. He called Flynn over and they inspected the marks, inserting the tip of his finger into each one, noticing other holes in the ceiling.

"Small arms fire. Nine-millimetre most likely. Perhaps there was a hijack or scuffle."

"It's possible the crew never left. They could still be on board or dead. We'll need to search the ship and make sure. Osler, Mathews, you two check the crew quarters and engine room. Stay together and report back anything suspicious. No heroics mind."

The two men nodded and set off on their search. One man was armed with a revolver, the other had a standard issue SA-80 assault rifle.

"Lucas, you stay here and focus on getting the engines and pumps back on line. Whatever it takes."

"Yessir."

"Jack, let's you and me search the hold and forward compartments. We're not taking any chances with infection. If we find anyone alive, we quarantine them until we reach port."

Jack nodded his agreement and followed Flynn through a doorway that led down a steep ladder, gripping the rail as the ship rolled heavily again to starboard. Below the main deck, they opened up a water-tight doorway and entered the corridors that ran alongside the ship's hold.

The air down here was stale and the temperature several degrees cooler close to the waterline. Stepping into the next compartment, Flynn switched on a powerful Maglite. It was pitch black inside. Their heavy boots clanked noisily on the metal walkway. Below them, they could hear water sloshing around. As they moved closer to the bow they saw water ahead of them. The forward compartments were completely submerged.

Satisfied that there was no one left alive down here they were turning around to head back when the radio crackled into life.

"Sergeant Flynn. Mathews here. We've found survivors in the crew quarters. Looks like someone locked them in here and sealed the door."

"Standby, we'll be with you in a few minutes. On our way to your position now."

The two men exchanged surprised looks, Flynn's eyebrows raised. They hurried back the way they came. As they reached the next bulkhead door, the ship lurched violently again to starboard and they were both thrown against the wall. Jack helped Flynn up. He was nursing a bruised shoulder where he had fallen, grimacing in agony.

The ship remained at an unnatural angle. Perhaps her buoyancy was compromised and her seaworthiness slowly deteriorating, thought Jack.

"She's not going to take much more punishment. She's taken on too much water already. If we can't get the engines started and the ship turned into these waves, she's not going to last much longer."

"I hear you. We need to get the pumps started or we're done for."

It took a few more seconds before the *Santana* returned to an even keel, fighting slowly to right herself. It was hard to tell down here, but Jack thought the conditions might also be getting worse. Either way, they were reaching a critical point. He wondered whether he would be better off helping Lucas on the bridge. Perhaps his many years of experience below decks in engine rooms could still prove useful.

Outside the doorway to the crew quarters, Osler and Mathews were waiting in silence. The door was sealed shut from the outside with a rope securing the handle from being opened.

Flynn reached down to his waist and unsheathed an enormous bowie knife and started cutting away at the rope. Jack grabbed his hand.

"Wait, how do you know the crew is not infected? Maybe that's the reason they were locked inside."

"Good point," said Flynn, coming to his senses.

At the sound of their voices, there came a metallic clanging from inside and the faint sound of voices shouting for help.

There was a rumble from beneath them as the dull rhythmic whirr of the engines began cycling up and a voice on Flynn's hand-held radio confirmed that power was coming back online. The lights in the compartment flickered and then steadied as they switched from backup power. There was an audible cheer from behind the locked door.

"I say we leave the crew where they are and concentrate on saving the ship. If we can get her back to safe harbour, we can deal with this lot then."

Back on the bridge, Lucas had a thin smile on his face. "Report?" demanded Flynn.

"Sir, I've got all primary systems coming back online, both engines look fine and I think I've figured out how to get the pumps in the forward compartments working again."

He reached across to another terminal and typed in a few commands before sitting back and watching the panel lights switch from red to green.

"Good job, Lucas. What are you waiting for? Let's get her turned into wind."

Another huge wave hit the ship broadside and again she rolled heavily. Jack grabbed hold of the console nearest him as the bridge tilted alarmingly. Looking down over the deck towards the bow, the massive surge of water had engulfed the forward sections, submerging the foredeck for a few seconds. Jack gritted his teeth, fearing the worst.

She was heeling nearly fifteen degrees to starboard. Any further and she might just broach. Once hatches were submerged, he feared a chain reaction would begin that would result in her flooding. From his days as a merchant seaman and senior engineer, he knew that the stresses placed on the ship's structure would be enormous. The bow was already partially submerged and the damage from the force and weight of each new wave on the integrity of the hull would be beyond imagination. He willed the *Santana* to fight.

The bow seemed to hear him, surging upwards, resisting the enormous forces holding her down, sending water cascading over the side again. With a slow lurch, the ship started righting itself.

"We've got to get her turned into wind," said Jack. "She can't take many more of these broadsides."

They looked up from the screens, dreading the next series of waves surging towards them. It was taking far too long. How much longer did she have?

"She's turning, sir," enthused Lucas, watching the compass reading begin to change one degree at a time.

"It's too slow," worried Jack. "Can we give her any more power?"

Flynn nodded and Lucas increased to full power, hearing the electrical hum change and increased vibration judder beneath their feet as the engine revolutions surged towards ninety per cent.

Another enormous roller was approaching, its crest breaking and foaming. As they sank down into the trough, the wave looked set to break over them.

"Brace yourselves," shouted Flynn, as the huge wave smashed into the hull of the *Santana* which juddered, as it fought to absorb the force of the impact. There was a terrifying sound of metal screeching. Jack imagined the hull flexing under the incredible stresses, its bulkheads bulging, rivets popping below the waterline.

Jack remembered stories of vessels broken clean in half by Atlantic storms. If the hull was ripped open amidships, they would stand little chance of saving the ship. They were so close to the safety and shelter of the Solent and yet, right now, they might as well be in the middle of the ocean. They were on their own and nearly out of time. If only they could turn the ship faster.

The digital compass dial began to rotate a little quicker. Each digit change improved their chances of survival but remained painfully slow. Their eyes flicked from the compass to the approaching wave. Jack grabbed hold, his knuckles white, braced for the next onslaught. The unrelenting wave smashed into them, but this time, caught them a glancing blow. The angle of impact was reducing. The tearing of metal and the groan of the ship's hull seemed more muted.

Fully three minutes after they had started their turn, the partially submerged bow began to take the full impact of each approaching wave, weathering the storm a little better. Was it Jack's imagination or were the pumps also beginning to have an effect? The ship was still very low in the water, but her seaworthiness was perhaps a little improved. With any luck, they could still wait out the worst of it before heading into port.

In all the excitement, Jack had completely forgotten about the *Nipper* and Sam. Looking to the right, he caught sight of the little fishing boat's keel as she launched off the top of a crest, surfing down the backside of the wave, her bow submerged for a second under a torrent of water. The *Nipper* looked tiny down below but somehow seemed to be more than a match for the atrocious conditions. He thought he could see Sam in the small cabin fighting hard to keep her bow on to the waves, frantically turning the wheel from side to side. Knowing Sam, he'd have a big grin on his face, adrenaline pumping through his veins.

He grabbed the radio and hailed the *Nipper*, waiting for Sam to pick up.

"Sam, there's nothing more you can do now. We've got things under control here. I'd get the hell out of here and head for home."

"You sure you don't need me? Was just beginning to get the hang of this."

"No, we're all good. Just be careful on making the turn. Timing's everything. Don't get broadsided. Turn between the waves ok? Once you're stern on, you'll surf all the way home."

He watched with some trepidation as the *Nipper* waited for its chance. As a massive wave raced through, he saw Sam put the wheel hard over. He had fifteen seconds to make the turn before the next wave. He didn't make it. He was three-quarters way through when the wave hit.

Jack watched helplessly as water cascaded over the stern, flooding the deck and surging around the small wheelhouse, disappearing inside. Jack held his breath for a second, losing sight of the *Nipper* behind the crest of the wave as it was submerged beneath a torrent of white spray and foam. Just when he thought she must have been rolled, the *Nipper* reappeared. Her positive buoyancy made her pop up again like a cork. With a sigh of relief, he saw Sam complete the turn and head away from the *Santana*. Flynn cheered and they all congratulated Jack, who was still clenching his fists but trying to master his breathing again.

"Right, what can I do?" said Jack as Flynn pointed him towards the console with the pumps.

"Keep your eye on those readings and shout if they change. Let me check in with the *Chester* and give them the good news. If we can just ride out this storm, then we can take her into port when it eases a little."

"Can we claim salvage on the cargo, Sarge?"

"Very funny, Lucas. What, you think you're a pirate do you? If you're lucky, I'll treat you to a cup of tea. We're not out of the woods yet. Let's keep focused on the job at hand, okay?"

"Yes sir," chimed the marines in unison.

On Jack's screen, an alarm sounded followed by a warning message and a flashing icon indicating that one of the pumps had failed. Lucas rushed over, nudging Jack out of the way.

"Uh oh. What did I do?" asked Jack.

"No, it's nothing you did. The bilge pumps are working

beyond their normal parameters. Thousands of gallons of water to pump out and looks like it's just shorted out. Let's give it a minute and try resetting it, shall we?"

"Can we still make it with the pumps we have left?"

"There's built-in redundancy on these things, so even if one fails the others can take up the slack. It'll slow things down but providing the hull's still watertight and the rivets and bulkheads hold together, we should be fine now. See how she's riding the waves now rather than nose-diving into them? Another couple of hours of pumping and we should be ok."

"That's a relief. Didn't fancy dying today," stuttered Jack. His whole body was shivering from the soaking wet clothes clinging to his body, now that the adrenaline had begun to subside.

"That makes two of us," said Flynn grimacing, rubbing his bruised shoulder.

CHAPTER FOUR

Peering out of a small iron-framed window made of single-paned glass, Riley was trying to make out the island in the distance across the narrow waterway. There was a gap between the window frame and the stone wall that allowed a steady draft of cool damp air, whistling in with each gust. When the wind strengthened again and rain lashed against the alcove windows on the first floor of the castle, she shivered involuntarily.

It had been a comparatively mild start to the autumn months thus far. After weeks of seemingly incessant rain throughout June and July, the skies had finally cleared, giving way to several weeks of sunshine. It was only late September, but it was beginning to turn colder. The south-westerly storm currently venting its fury was the first tell-tale sign of the approach of winter.

Since the arrival of the first detachment of soldiers, things had started to change at Hurst. The mood was different somehow. The peace and harmony of the survivor community were irrevocably altered. There was now a restlessness, a sense of foreboding. It was almost as if the presence of soldiers, far from making the occupants of the castle feel safer, actually made life more dangerous.

The more horticultural amongst them were grateful for all

the rain and they had ensured that they stored as much water as possible. A system of water butts and gutters funnelled rainwater to a large storage tank beneath the castle. Riley wondered whether this was the first of many storms to come. The previous winters had been mercifully mild here, but no less grim. Living in a castle so exposed to the elements, everything remained dark and dank throughout the long winter months. Jack said it had been like this living on a merchant ship; nothing ever really got dry. Everything always smelled damp.

How many months had she been at Hurst now? She had lost track after the second year. Riley had been part of the second wave to arrive, part of another group living outside Everton at a large farm. They had been forced to abandon the farm when resources had run scarce following an unexplained illness that had affected their herd of cows. Without a vet, all they could do was put the poor beasts out of their misery and move on.

Perhaps she would spend the rest of her days here. There were worse places to live out your time. She had grown to love the castle; its history, its austerity. It was a constant, unchanging monolith, impervious to man's desperate fight to survive. There was a sense of permanence here, of continuity through the ages.

She had come to think of the other survivors as her family. They had been through so much together. It would be hard to leave all this behind.

Hurst's remoteness and inaccessibility by road were becoming problematic. They had made some running repairs to the roadway over the hot summer months but without heavy earth moving equipment, concrete and diggers to reinforce the sea defences, the next storm system, in all likelihood, might punch a hole clean through. It had happened many years before, when storm force winds had battered the shingle spit. Even now, the roadway was increasingly impassable to all bar farm tractors and four-wheel drive vehicles.

After a busy few months, the fields that surrounded Keyhaven were awash with colour. Corn, wheat, and maize grew long. In the Spring, they had dug row upon row of vegetables, now rewarded with carrots, potatoes, and turnips. Nearer to the farm buildings were lush pastures, dotted with sheep and cows huddled together in the shelter of an old stone wall. Most of the team's days were spent tending to the animals. Their herd of dairy cows was a rich source of milk, yoghurt and an assortment of cheeses stored in the cool cellars with mixed results.

As a fisherman, Jack had often reminded Riley how grateful she should be. They were blessed with a whole ocean full of fish, right on their door step. They only had to row out a weighted net to the buoy in the main channel and on the incoming tide would be rewarded with an extraordinary haul of mackerel, skate, or bass. The pots they hauled up daily never failed to catch a large crab or lobster. Jack said that the ocean was slowly healing itself after years of overfishing. In a few more years, he predicted a return to fishing hauls not seen since Tudor times when the Solent was teeming with a multitude of now rare species.

Unlike other survivor camps, Hurst's food supplies were fairly secure. Water and fuel remained their biggest challenges. Even with butts collecting rainwater from every gutter and rooftop, it was never enough.

She was sure there were other places where life was a little easier. Rumours told of a new world on the island. Electricity, running water, virus free. It all sounded a little too good to be true. Besides, they had a job to do. A renewed sense of purpose that required discipline in their defensive role, guarding the western entrance to the Solent. She had to admit, the plans for reconstruction had instilled in her, in all of them, a new hope for the future.

The door slammed behind her and Tommy appeared, his sweater soaked through. His hair was lank, sticking to his brow, flattened by the rain.

"Hey Riley, have you seen Will or Scottie?"

"Nope, not since lunch. What's up?"

Tommy said he had been out repairing a slow puncture on the Land Rover. It was about the fifth time they had fixed it and spares were in short supply. He looked out of breath, waiting by the door, panting noisily.

He noticed the fire almost burned through and the empty basket for logs beside it and slapped his forehead. "Liz asked me to bring more wood in. Completely forgot."

"You'd forget your own head if it wasn't stuck on."

"Liz told me forgetfulness is the only way she can get through the day without screaming at me. Don't know what she was banging on about, though."

He made to leave before turning round. "Oh, Zed was looking for you. I think he was heading down to the beach at the far end. Take a raincoat, eh, it's filthy out there."

"Will do, thanks, Tommy. Tell Scottie when you see him, he never brought me that cup of tea."

"If I find him, he's helping me fix that blooming tyre first before it gets dark. He can bring you tea later when he's done his chores."

"Go on then," she smiled. "Off with you."

The door slammed shut again and Riley let out a deep sigh and lowered a red-jacketed book with gold embossed letters onto her lap. She was reading *Tess of the D'Urbervilles* for the third time. It was one of her favourites. There was something about Tess and fatalism that chimed with Riley.

Zed would make fun of her when she railed against the world, of "blighted stars" or "troubled hearts". Riley was fond of speaking of fate, how things were the way they were, because that's how they were meant to be, and there was little anyone could do about it. Zed said that you made your own luck. That nothing was pre-determined. He said there was no plan, no divine intervention. Riley refused to believe in a universe that was somehow indifferent. Most of all she believed in herself. "Bless thy simplicity" taunted Zed when she spoke of fate.

Since their escape from the clutches of the Sisterhood at the Chewton Glen Hotel, a veil of sadness had settled on Riley. Leaving Stella behind had been a body blow. They had only known each other a short time but the circumstances of their meeting, Stella's vulnerability during her pregnancy, had developed in Riley as an emptiness since their return to Hurst. It was a void she found difficult to bridge. Stella reminded her so much of the younger sister she had so tragically lost to meningitis when she was a student.

She had grown adept at disguising this sadness from others. Heaven knows, everyone had suffered loss and hardship over the last few years. This was certainly nothing unusual that warranted special treatment. Every survivor of the Millennial Virus had their own stories of loved ones lost, mistakes made, opportunities missed; but somehow Riley's thoughts always returned to Stella. She could not explain it rationally to others, but she felt strangely responsible for her. It was Riley who had found her at the hospital while searching for Will. Stella had been abused, beaten and experimented on by the men there. If it hadn't have been for Riley, who knows what would have happened to her, in the name of science? She had returned her safe to the bosom of the Sisterhood, and yet gratitude had been short lived when the

Sisters had blamed the Hurst team for the fire and the escape of Joe and the others. They would at least care for Stella, support her through her pregnancy, of that she was sure.

She stood up and determined to take a turn round the battlements, find Zed and try and shake off these dark thoughts.

She found Zed taking advantage of a break in the weather to stretch his legs and walk round the castle walls before it got dark. At the far end of the complex, he took a seat on the battlements, his legs dangling over the side. He was watching with some amusement as Corporal Ballard put his Royal Marines through their paces, doing push-ups and sit-ups till it was too dark to see. One of the party was standing to one side with his head between his legs, throwing up on the grass, exhausted by their physical exertion.

Zed was scanning the horizon, his hair flattened by the wind, squinting into the distance. There had been a lull in the storm. The enormous waves were breaking on the Needles, sending spray high into the air. Those that raced towards the shingle beach smashed against the shore, sending pebbles flying over the top of the causeway. It was bracing sitting up high, a witness to the full force of nature and the sea. Riley wondered who else was fool enough to be out in weather like this.

Riley admired the soldiers. They were disciplined, professional. Out here, rain or shine, whatever the weather, day or night. Considering the rest of the world was falling apart, people like Flynn and Ballard gave her hope. They were driven by an unfaltering set of beliefs. A life in the military had taught them to be resilient, to make do with what they had, to respect the chain of command. Perhaps it wasn't much, but it meant something to Riley. It chimed with her memories of childhood and being sent away to a boarding school at an early age when her father was sent overseas for work. With her mother working to make ends meet, she was told it was for the best. Her father had been a disciplinarian and had little time for sentimentality or homesickness. He had been intolerant of weakness, unforgiving of failure. It had influenced her life choices greatly.

She could hear Ballard barking orders at the dozen men who were running relays back and forth. It made Riley tired just watching them. The wind masked her footsteps as she approached and it was only when she coughed that Zed spun round a little startled.

"Sorry, am I interrupting?"

"Not at all. Just watching our friends from the military. Pull up a pew and come and join the fun."

She sat next to him, their elbows touching in silence. Zed glanced across at Riley and noticed her eyes welling with tears.

"Hey, what's up?" said Zed putting his arm around her, pulling her in. She leaned her head against his shoulder and sniffed.

"It's silly really. Just can't stop thinking about Stella, that's all."

He squeezed her tighter. He was trying to think of the right thing to say. He probably didn't dare tell her what he was really thinking.

"Listen. She's in good hands, right? The Sisters will take good care of her, be there for her when the time comes, when the baby is born. Talk about support network, just think about all those women clucking and cooing over the baby."

Riley smiled. Zed could always cheer her up when she was feeling down. It was why she sought him out, despite their differences. He had a big heart, buried deep beneath that thick skin of his. She wondered whether anything ever got to him.

"I suppose it's just..." her voice trailed off. "I feel responsible for her. It was me who got her out of that hospital, away from those monsters, returned her safe to the Chewton Glen. I know it was her choice to stay with her people, but part of me wishes we had forced her to come with us here. Liz and Greta could have looked after her. Jean is good with young children."

"She chose to stay, Riley. We tried to persuade her to come with us, but she was adamant that she should stay put. You must respect her decision."

"But where are they? We've been back to the Chewton Glen three times since and, by all accounts, they never came back. We've searched the whole area and still no sign. No one has heard or seen anything of them for months."

"If you ask me, they're long gone," admitted Zed with a resigned sigh.

"Maybe, maybe not. The nurse said they would come back as soon as it was safe to do so."

"They are a large group so they probably ventured further afield, Christchurch, Ringwood, even Bournemouth. Chances are they are all fine," suggested Zed, trying to make light of it. "Maybe they found a better set up, easier to defend, more plentiful resources. Who knows?"

"Do you think we'll ever see them again?" wondered Riley with a note of anguish she was trying to suppress. She didn't want to blub in front of Zed. She was too stubborn and proud for that.

"I honestly don't know. If we kept looking, headed further west, then maybe we'd find them. But it's not worth the risk. Even with our new friends riding shotgun," said Zed gesturing towards the soldiers.

Riley knew he was right, but it didn't make it any easier to accept. She blamed herself, whether rationally or irrationally.

"Do you ever think about Stella's baby?"

"Can't say I do, no. Was never much one for infants. I was on overseas trips when both my two were born. I was never exactly the hands-on parent."

"If Stella's immune, do you think the baby will be immune too?"

"Professor Nichols said that immunity is most likely hereditary. That anyone who survived the first outbreak, their children would inherit whatever immunity their parent had."

"Makes sense. Maybe the next generation will have better luck. Maybe there will be no need for a vaccine. The virus will just die out and that will be the end of it."

"Maybe. Or maybe this is just the beginning of the outbreak?"

There was a moment of silence as they both looked out into the distance, listening to the roar of the waves.

"Come on," said Zed, nudging Riley in the side. "It's getting dark. Let's leave these guys to it."

Zed levered himself up and brushed white dust from the seat of his trousers, before helping her up. Riley looked back along the beach, pulling the coat tighter around her body. Far off in the distance, she noticed the beam of a torchlight dancing along the shingle in the falling light.

It was getting too dark to use the binoculars. She couldn't make out the shape to determine whether it was male or female. Zed put two fingers to his lips and whistled loudly to get the attention of the soldiers below. One of them looked up and signalled to Corporal Ballard who called a halt to the drill, looking up curiously at Zed. Zed didn't attempt to shout down, his voice would have disappeared on the wind.

He pointed in the direction of the approaching figure along the beach that stretched away towards Milford village and silently relayed the warning by hand signals, as he had taught Riley and the others on the scavenging trips into town. Ballard acknowledged and the men grabbed their weapons and lay in wait.

By the time the person reached the end of the shingle causeway and the small slope that ran down to the roadway running round the castle walls, the soldiers were hiding out of sight. Riley and Zed had run round and stood in the shadows.

"That's far enough. Who are you and what are you doing here?" challenged Ballard.

A woman's voice, that Riley recognised but couldn't place, flatly answered: "I'm unarmed."

She was plainly dressed in a long dark blue rain coat that stretched from top to bottom to protect her slight frame from the elements. A hood covered her head and face. Her nose and mouth were all that was visible. The woman calmly raised her hands high into the air as one of Ballard's men approached with a rifle pointing at her chest. They kept their distance, following their training, nervous about contamination.

"What do you want?" repeated Ballard.

"I'm looking for someone. A young girl. I'm told she came here. Her name is Jean."

The soldiers looked at each other, shaking their heads, unfamiliar with the name. Riley stepped forward, still puzzling over the voice.

"Who wants to know?" challenged Riley.

The woman removed her hood and Riley was astonished to recognise Sister Imelda, one of Sister Theodora's enforcers from The Chewton Glen hotel. The last time they had seen each other was in rather strained circumstances. Riley had been accused of starting the fire that had killed so many innocents. Even now she could picture Stella clutching her face after being struck by one of the guards for daring to intercede on behalf of the group from Hurst. Only Zed's intervention with a shotgun had saved the day.

"I never thought I'd see you again," said Riley putting her hand to her mouth, shaking her head, her eyes heavy with tears.

Zed stepped forward. "You've got a nerve coming here."

Riley put her arm out and held him back, shaking her head slowly from side to side.

Rain drops started landing all around them.

"Is there somewhere we can talk?" asked Sister Imelda looking up at the sky.

CHAPTER FIVE

They had come from miles around. Emerging from their shelters and makeshift homes like refugees from a war zone. Children dragged their feet, some with improvised footwear. Dressed in rags and blankets, their shoes were several sizes too big for them. It was poor protection against the wind and the rain. With them, they carried spare clothes, food and water in plastic bags. On wheelbarrows, shopping trolleys or on the back of push bikes were stacked all their worldly possessions. A rag-tag band of travellers picking their way along the road between the carcasses of rusting vehicles and discarded suitcases, too heavy to carry further.

They kept the women and children towards the middle of the group. On the outside of the walking party were keen-eyed adults armed with sticks, golf clubs or baseball bats, anything they could find to defend themselves from the other travellers who coveted their possessions. At their head was a stocky middle-aged woman with a flowery headscarf and double-barrel shotgun slung over her arm. Without warning, she raised her arm and the shambolic group came to a disorderly halt. They looked around warily at the warehouses and industrial buildings with broken windows that lined the road leading to the old harbour-front at Portsmouth.

At the heart of this motley crowd of washed-up humanity, Heather and her brother Connor craned their necks. They were trying to see what was going on over the shoulders of those in front of them. Heather pressed a finger to her lips and pulled her younger brother towards her, cautioning him to be quiet. Despite his exhaustion, his piercing blue eyes looked sharp and alert, framed by a filthy grime of accumulated dirt, smeared across his cheeks and forehead. She pulled at the sleeve of the woman in front who whipped her head round and scowled at Heather as if the children were an inconvenience to be tolerated. She softened when she looked them up and down noticing how pathetic they both looked, trembling with fear or cold, it wasn't clear which. She relaxed into a thin smile, mouthing the word "Checkpoint" in barely more than a whisper.

This was the third time their group had been stopped. They were so close now. Portsmouth harbour and Gunwharf Quays were just ahead. Ferries waited to take the fit and healthy to the island. Hope had got them this far. A small wave of weary excitement carried them onwards towards safety.

As they got nearer, it was clear that they were by no means the first to come this route. Dozens of people were collapsed at the side of the road. They pleaded for food or water from those that passed by, their hands outstretched towards them like garden nettles reaching for sunlight. They had nowhere to go, no energy left to move, carried here by a tide of hope that had suddenly dissipated. Many they passed were clearly sick, racked by coughing fits, weak from fever.

Momentarily, Connor staggered and brushed against an outstretched arm that grabbed at his sleeve. Heather reacted quickly and hauled him back, terrified. The woman in the headscarf looked round and bent lower to his level shaking her head.

"Stay away from that lot, lad. Don't let them touch you," she cautioned. "They're sick, can't you see? That's why they're still here. The soldiers turned them away."

Heather nodded and dragged him back to the middle of the group, holding his hand tightly. Despite her best efforts to shield him from the horrors of this new world, he had seen far too much suffering for a boy his age. He spent much of the day whittling down sticks with his pen knife or staring off into the distance. She wondered how much he really understood. She knew it had been hard on him. He was still only nine.

It was said that they were taking only those fit enough to work. Men, women and children. Every able-bodied person would be given safe passage. Those that worked, would be fed and watered, given shelter. Or at least that's what they had been told.

They weren't taking everyone. She knew not to get her hopes up. The same rules applied to children after all. The quarantine rules were absolute. Only the healthy could make the crossing. Her worst fear was that they would be split up. That they would take her but not him, or vice versa.

They had grown up fast over the last few months, living on their own. They had no choice. They had learned to look after themselves, find food, a place to live. When their mother had died not long after the outbreak, a kindly neighbour had driven them south towards the coast to the caravan they shared with some friends on Hayling Island. It wasn't much, but it was home. They counted themselves lucky to have a roof over their heads, at the heart of a small community, where people looked after each other.

Both of the children were painfully thin. She had heard one of the grown-ups use the words "borderline feral" to describe her brother. She hadn't understood what they meant at first, but when she realised, she had wanted to slap her so hard for calling her brother names. It reminded her of the big words they used at the doctors or dentists. It was a secret language adults used to conceal their true meaning. To talk about someone rather than to them. She didn't like being treated like a child; she never had. She was four years older than her brother, no longer a child; old beyond her years.

After living off scraps for so long, catching the occasional rat or rabbit had meant a feast. They would spit-roast them over a small fire, picking clean the bones. Both of the children were now adept at trapping, skinning and gutting a variety of woodland creatures. They had occupied their days gathering berries, mushrooms and catching all manner of fish with rod and line, bringing home their haul in a trolley they had found and repaired in the sailing club boatyard. Life at the caravan park had been hard, but leaving their adopted home behind in the hope of something better had been harder still.

They had been walking for what felt like days. It had rained without stopping. Hour after hour as if God was trying to wash the earth clean and start again. It reminded Heather of the Bible story of Noah's Ark and the great flood. Perhaps that's what this was. The pair of them going to the island, two by two, as the world cleansed itself.

She wondered why the virus only affected humans. Would a new order emerge in their absence? One day they would all be allowed to return home when the virus had died out, just like when the waters had subsided after the flood.

Between her and Connor, they were wearing all the clothes they possessed, soaked to the skin. On their backs, they carried school rucksacks with a half-eaten packet of biscuits, some water and a couple of cans. They had been saving the tinned pineapple for a special occasion, when they were safely on board the ferry, if they made it that far.

The rumours about the island had reached the caravan park two weeks ago. Several of their group had volunteered to be the first to try. They never came back, nor sent a message back to the group as had been agreed. That didn't seem to deter the rest. They maintained the belief that the first group had made it to the island. Many were undecided, unsure whether to risk what they had, to gamble on finding something better. In the end, Rowan, their leader, had said that they couldn't last another winter at the caravan park. It was their duty to follow the others.

Heather trusted Rowan. He had a gentle face with a warm smile that hid a steely resolve. He had always been so kind to them both. He brought them fire wood and looked in on them from time to time. Once, she had heard Rowan talking to one of the other men, a young guy who was no more than eighteen. He used to stare at Heather until she blushed and looked away. Rowan told the youth in no uncertain terms to stay away and they had fought, pushing and shoving each other. After that, he told Heather to keep the door to the caravan locked at night and to ask before opening, just to be safe. He couldn't always be around to look after them and furnished her with a small pocket-knife with a serrated blade and taught her how to use it. It never left a leather pouch on her belt, just in case. You could never be too careful, Rowan had said.

He had told Heather that they would all have a fresh start on the island, that there was no sickness there. It sounded too good to be true, but Rowan said he believed it and she trusted him. Why would anyone lie about something like that? Besides, whatever lay in wait for them on the island could hardly be worse than facing another bitter winter in the caravan park with no heating and no power. Could it?

They reached the next checkpoint and waited in line for their turn. A supermarket lorry was partially blocking the way ahead. The barricades were reinforced with rolls of barbed wire and upturned furniture and crates. She noticed improvised firing positions for those tasked with defending the line. On top of the articulated lorry, there were sandbags positioned to form a nest with a machine gun barrel poking over the top. The silhouette of a soldier against a dark grey skyline, drinking from a canteen, stared down at the approaching group. Connor gripped his sister's hand tighter and she squeezed him back as a fit of coughing shook his slender frame.

The soldier waved their group forward, pointing down the road towards another checkpoint in the distance as the next stage in the processing of refugees. The soldiers barked orders, impatient and irritable, passing instructions up the line.

"No guns or knives beyond this point. Last chance to surrender any weapons. Anyone found concealing anything will be kicked out. You've been warned."

One by one, they stepped forward and submitted to a body search, holding their arms out wide to left and right, manhandled and prodded. Someone in front was questioning why they had to hand-over the guns.

"You don't need weapons on the island. You'll have us lot protecting you from here on. Come on, we don't have all day."

Each surrendered item was inspected and handed to a pair of gangly youths who sorted them into piles. Shotguns and rifles were taken through a doorway into a makeshift armoury. Knives and swords were thrown into a skip piled high with metalwork.

"Look after that, will you. It's a family heirloom," demanded the woman in the headscarf, handing over an antique double-barrelled shotgun with ornate engraving on its stock and barrel. The soldier studied it for a second, admiring its artistry.

"Very nice," he nodded. "Don't worry, I'll look after that one myself. Jerry, take that will you?"

"I'll get it back, right?" she asked.

"Of course you will, darling. When this is all over, you come find me," laughed the soldier, revealing two missing teeth.

The final approach to Gunwharf Quay and the old Wightlink ferry terminal was bedlam. It was only mid-morning but already hundreds of refugees were waiting for their turn to cross. They were crammed under cover to avoid the downpour or huddling under canvas shelters, tarpaulins stretched taught. Heather had overheard two soldiers saying that more had come than they had expected. Many too sick to make the journey came anyway. Whispers of treatment lured them from their sick beds. Anyone with obvious symptoms, such as fever or coughing, was instantly escorted away to a quarantine zone, to avoid infecting others.

The group from the caravan park tried to stay together, but the children were waved forward first and given priority. They exchanged concerned looks with the rest to calls of "good luck" and smiles of encouragement. Reluctantly they joined the long line of refugees queuing for their turn.

"See you on the other side," shouted Rowan cheerily from behind them.

There was no shelter for those waiting. The incessant rain hammered down, seeping into every crevice and corner of clothing. A bout of shivering racked Connor's slender frame. She stooped and rubbed his arms and back, trying to summon any remaining warmth from his emaciated arms. He was all skin and bone, badly undernourished but alive. That was the main thing.

She cradled his grubby chin, lifting it from its hiding place in the folds of his hood and smiled at him. "Nearly there now Connor. Not much further."

He blinked back at her, his eyes tired, close to tears. After months of solitude and silence, being in such close proximity to hundreds of others was uncomfortable; intimidating, to say the least.

The group in front of them, mostly women and children, shuffled forward and those behind pressed against them, surging towards the boarding ramp some two hundred meters away.

In front of them was a solitary soldier in camouflage fatigues with a gun in his holster like a cowboy, thought Heather. He was unshaven and edgy, looking over his shoulder, waiting for his commanding officer to return. He was soaked through, rain dripping from his nose. An interminable wait to be relieved. The radio on his belt crackled and he stepped in front of the line, raising the palm of his right hand to make them stop. Heather pushed back her hood to expose her left ear, craning her head to listen. It was hard to hear anything over the howling wind and rain.

"Say again, Hotel Quebec. Didn't catch that." He sounded exhausted, worn down by the flood of humanity he was responsible for keeping under some semblance of order. He screwed up his face and turned his back against the rain and wind, hunching over, trying to hear better. The voice from the radio was hard to make out, but Heather caught snatches of the response.

"Repeat…compromised…our position is being overrun…we need reinforcements…don't wait."

The next few words were unintelligible. The soldier stood shaking his head, shielding his ear with his free hand. He looked around distractedly, at the people in line nearest him and back towards the ferry, searching for something and not finding it. There were already what seemed like hundreds of people aboard, dozens more of them crowding the ramp, pressed together, impatient to get off the mainland.

In the distance came a low indeterminate rumble. Everyone stopped their conversations, listening to the sound, trying to discern its source with puzzled expressions. They didn't have to wait long. The rumble was swiftly followed by a loud explosion, much closer this time, which shook the windows of the nearby portacabin and ticket office. The line of refugees ducked down as one. Some grabbed their children, pulling them closer, covering their heads protectively.

At first, Heather was confused. It reminded her of the sound the rubbish truck made when it emptied the bins from outside their house on a Monday morning in Winchester. It was a noise so familiar and yet completely alien now.

The growing panic in the soldier's face suggested he realised it was something more serious. Perhaps they were under attack? He seemed flustered, fumbling with his radio. He was depressing the transmit button with growing alarm, adjusting the settings to check the handset was still working.

"Say again Hotel Quebec. Your last message was garbled. Hello? Is anyone receiving this?"

Another soldier came running back towards him from the portacabin and they hurriedly conferred before lowering the red and white vehicle barrier, blocking the way to the ramp and the ferry beyond. He started waving away the refugees motioning them back towards the gate.

"I'm sorry, we can't take any more. That's it for today. You'll have to try again tomorrow."

The people at the front of the line pleaded with him to take them, but the soldiers looked distracted, no longer interested in the waiting line.

Heather looked beyond the barrier, watching the renewed urgency of the crowd by the ferry walkway who were now pushing and shoving at the people in front to hurry them inside. Those around Heather were beginning to panic, so close to safety, their hopes were being quashed unexpectedly at the last moment. The soldier looked back at them, surprised that they were still there.

"I said clear the area. That means you, and you," he said flustered, unholstering his weapon. "Go on, get out of here. You heard, go on."

Another explosion, much closer this time, certainly beyond the barricades. It was answered by the crackle of small arms and the staccato rhythm of a machine gun firing in short bursts. Inside the ferry terminal complex, a growing chorus of screams and gasps rose from those around them. A couple of women to their right seized their chance and ducked under the barrier, making a run for the ferry ramp.

The soldiers lunged after them a fraction of a second too late, clutching for their collars and coats. Those they caught were manhandled forcefully back towards the line. The rest of the group was emboldened now and ducked under. Heather and Connor were forced on by the sheer weight of those behind, pushing forward. Twenty people were now beyond the barrier, making a run for it. Heather seized her brother's hand and ran.

A gunshot rang out close at hand, followed by shouted warnings to get back behind the barrier. Several of those closest to him and certainly within range, stopped in their tracks. The two children ran on, oblivious. This was their chance. They weren't going to let it slip away.

The soldier shook his head, took a deep breath and closed one eye, aiming squarely at Heather. She saw the weapon pointing in her direction but ran on, terrified. She stumbled in alarm as a wild shot rang out, close enough to split the air next to her ear. She clutched at her left temple, expecting to feel pain. Whether deliberately or not, he must have missed.

"Have you gone completely mad?" shouted the Sergeant behind her. "They're just kids for God's sake."

"Sorry, sir. I wasn't thinking," he cowered apologetically. "I panicked. It won't happen again."

Heather and Connor dodged between bodies and lost themselves in the safety of the crowd, panting and laughing. Looking back beyond the terminal building, they could see smoke rising from the direction they had come. The loading area had been transformed into a scene of chaos as those left behind scrambled for cover. She scanned the crowds trying to find Rowan and the others from her group, but they were gone. They were on their own again.

CHAPTER SIX

As the Isle of Wight ferry cleared the jetty and harbour wall, they passed Spice Island and Portsmouth old town to the left. Heather and Connor found a quiet corner near the ferry's stern, where a bulkhead shielded them from the worst of the wind and rain buffeting the ship. The lower deck was empty of vehicles but abuzz with noise and excitement as the hundreds of refugees lucky enough to have escaped the mainland chaos inched closer to safety. Looking around, very few men appeared to have made the crossing.

Back towards Portsmouth, they watched the once majestic sight of Spinnaker Tower disappear slowly in their wake. A tattered Union Jack flew from a flagpole on top of the tower, which was decorated with graffiti to an impossible height, where gangs had dared to climb ever higher. Clear of the harbour channel, the ferry swung southwest towards the island, smashing into the teeth of an unforgiving headwind, gusting gale force. The sea behind them had become a maelstrom of white water and spray, horizontal rain sheeted down. They struggled to make out the mainland now, a dark outline of Southsea castle in the distance and the enormous shape of Spitbank Fort looming close at hand, shrouded in mist. Heather knew there should be other

Solent forts visible like this one but could not make them out.

A soldier wearing a poncho stepped between the groups, scanning the refugees' faces. A rifle was slung over his shoulder. Only his eyes and nose were visible. A hood hid his forehead in ghostly shadow. It suddenly occurred to Heather that he might be looking for them. She turned away, taking no chances, keeping her face hidden, motioning to Connor to do likewise. They had learned to keep a low profile to avoid unwanted attention wherever possible. The soldier moved on, oblivious to their presence.

The crossing was bumpy and at times uncomfortable, buffeted by the wind. The *St Clare* ferry was a twin-hulled catamaran and certainly not designed for heavy weather. She laboured over the short distance without further incident. Craning her head around the corner, Heather saw the island ahead of them and the ferry port of Fishbourne. The village of Wootton Bridge lay beyond. For the last half mile, the *St Clare* was joined by a Royal Navy patrol boat, bashing into the chop. On board, Heather was surprised to notice a man in bright orange oilskins clinging to a bow-mounted machine gun which he kept trained towards the ferry as they bounced up and down. They were clearly taking no chances today. Once in the shadow of the island, the wind and waves dropped quickly and the howling wind fell to a more melodic whistle as the gusts hurried through the ferry's superstructure.

With a soft bump, the bow of the ferry nudged the first of the wooden mooring posts. Plunged deep into the mud and river bank, the columns were draped with tyres and rubber defenders to protect visiting ferries against collisions, particularly in difficult docking conditions like today. The skipper had made this passage a dozen times in the last couple of weeks alone and expertly controlled their approach, using his bow-thrusters to counteract the force of the wind and current. Once secured fore and aft the hydraulic pistons groaned into life, forcing the ramp down to meet the hard of Fishbourne.

A welcoming party of solemn-looking soldiers waved the three hundred or so new arrivals off the ship. They were escorted forward in strictly controlled groups of thirty at a time, heading up to be processed.

Heather squinted at a cluster of medics standing chatting by one of the welcome channels. Each processing point was covered by a small marquee pitched to keep the rain off the heads of those sitting scribbling numbers and names on clipboards. She could just make out a whiteboard displaying a message that read "Welcome to Camp Wight". Underneath was the number 438 which looked like it had been rubbed out several times already as more people cleared the quarantine area.

The medics wore green overalls and disposable white face-masks, held in place with elastic ties. They stood ready to assess each new arrival and send them on to army trucks waiting to take them to the refugee camps said to be less than a kilometre away near Ryde. Heather and Connor patiently waited their turn to disembark, shuffling forward, keeping up with the other refugees. Behind them, soldiers swept the passenger deck, shouting "clear", making sure there was no one left on board.

Heather had made this crossing many years before with her parents. Gone were the lines of cars and caravans packed with smiling children's faces daubed with chocolate and ice-cream. She remembered bored-looking officials waving cars forward, wearing day-glow orange jackets.

Now things looked very different. Surrounding the tarmac area were twenty-feet high fences topped with rolls of razor wire.

She wasn't sure whether the fences were to keep the new arrivals in, or others out. She suspected they were to stop refugees making a break for open countryside. It was common knowledge that everyone had to be declared fit before progressing to the camps beyond. Trapped in the fence and on the razor wire, she noticed long strands of what looked like fabric, newspaper, and cardboard, flapping noisily with each gust of wind.

There was an unsettled buzz about the place. Perhaps they had heard about the trouble back on the mainland and feared there might be troublemakers or infected as part of this group. The soldiers nearest them looked on edge, shouting instructions between them, never taking their eyes off the new arrivals.

The front-line soldiers directly handling each refugee wore bio-hazard suits. One by one each person was ushered forward to be manually checked for symptoms of the virus. Connor gripped Heather's hand tighter.

"I feel sick Heather."

She turned to face him, trying to hide her alarm. Talk about bad timing. She noticed he was shivering with cold. They had been in wet clothes all day and he probably had a fever coming on.

"Don't be silly, Connor. Here, take my coat. There, that's better. Just you wait. Once we get beyond here, you'll see. They'll have hot chocolate, cake, and biscuits just like Rowan told us. I promised you didn't I?" She forced a smile, but inside she was terrified. They were so close. They had come so far.

"I'm scared," blurted Connor, fighting back tears.

"You'll be fine. Come on," she said putting her arm round him and rubbing his arms to get his circulation going again.

The group in front of them were next and one by one they were called forward.

"Name?" barked the woman behind a desk with a clipboard with dozens of scribbled details in uneven columns. The doctor in the bio-hazard suit grabbed hold of the refugee, a teenage girl Heather recognised from the boat, with long brown hair and kind eyes. The medic grabbed hold of her lapel, feeling her throat and glands, opening her eyes wide, checking the skin tone, rudimentary screening for signs of the virus.

"Stick your tongue out and say 'ah'."

The young girl tilted her head defiantly, but complied. The medic nodded and another person bustled up and thrust a thermometer in her ear canal, pausing while the digital readout settled at 98 degrees.

"Clear. Go ahead and join the line to the right. Next?"

Heather and Connor were next after the girl. The teenage girl was watching the pair of them with a smug grin. She shrugged her shoulders as if to say: "what's all the fuss about?" Heather watched her go, envious. Her stomach was doing somersaults, fighting down bile. It wouldn't play well to be sick on the soldier's boot. She distracted herself by concentrating on her brother, squeezing Connor's hand. He was shaking like a leaf, with cold or fear; she couldn't tell.

Heather pushed Connor forward and made him go first. She needed to keep an eye on him, make sure he was keeping it together. When asked for his name by the person with a clipboard, he responded in barely above a whisper, noticeably trembling in front of the medic. The doctor softened his tone a little, aware of how nervous the boy was.

Connor's fever was obvious, even to an untrained eye, but the medic was a professional and stuck to his task, going through the motions to make sure. Heather watched nervously as his gloved hand pressed against the redness around his eyes where he had been crying, lifted his head to inspect bulging glands and clammy skin around his throat. He thrust the thermometer into Connor's ear and waited for the loud beep. He cleared the memory and retested.

"One hundred and two," he announced to the clipboard lady with barely a note of regret.

Two soldiers moved forward, taking up position, one hand on each of Connor's emaciated shoulders. Her brother looked up forlornly at the soldier for any sign of sympathy but was met with impassive detachment, devoid of any hint of humanity or empathy. It was plain that this was a situation played out all too often. In her state of exhaustion, Heather's mind drifted, feeling herself floating above the situation.

Rowan had told her that cases of the virus were on the increase again as people left their hiding places seeking out the sanctuary of the island. It was ironic really. Bringing so many people together had proved a catalyst for a fresh outbreak. Not exactly what the Allies had intended. Yet their safeguards had so far prevented the virus from reaching the island.

"Heather?" Connor implored his sister for help as she snapped out of her reverie. The hand on his shoulder tightened as he struggled to reach his sister with an outstretched hand.

Heather felt her back stiffen as she interceded on her brother's behalf, pleading with the soldiers.

"Please. You don't understand, we've been together all this time. He's never been sick before just now. We haven't been in contact with any strangers. I'm telling you, he's not infected. It's probably just a chill. I promise. Look, I would be the first to know. Please?"

The soldiers paused, blinking uncertainly towards the medic, suddenly unsure what the correct procedure was. The doctor, a young woman judging by her size and shape beneath her biohazard suit and mask, shook her head, disinterested. She looked down at her clipboard again, oblivious to their plight.

"He's got all of the classic symptoms. Elevated temperature, swollen glands, clammy skin. We can't take any risks. The rules are the same for everyone. Move along. Next person in line."

Heather lunged forward, grabbing her brother's hand and trying to pull him away. "I won't let you take him. He's my brother."

As soon as she stepped out of line, the demeanour of the soldiers changed. Any semblance of pity evaporated.

"I'm warning you," said one of the soldiers, wrestling to grab her arm and pull her back out of the way.

"You're wrong," she writhed to release herself from his grasp.

A soldier standing a few meters away unholstered and cocked his pistol and took careful aim at Heather's chest.

"This is your first and final warning. Step away or you will be shot."

Heather froze, tears welling in her eyes. Beyond the fence, the commotion had attracted the attention of the other refugees who were loading up onto an army truck. Its canvas cover was pulled back while the last of the passengers was being helped on board. A man shouted back at the soldiers together with a chorus of dissent.

"Hey, pick on someone your own size. They're just kids."

The soldier with his pistol drawn grabbed hold of Heather again by the sleeve and pulled her away, dragging her towards the gate and the waiting truck.

It broke Heather's heart to have to leave him behind, but there was nothing she could do now. Connor held his hands out towards his sister as she was escorted away. He was inconsolable, tears streaming down his cheeks. She tried one last time to make a break, to give him a hug goodbye, but the soldier tightened his grip, dragging her towards the truck. When she looked back again, he was gone.

CHAPTER SEVEN

Terra woke to the ringing of a hand-bell from somewhere outside, just audible in the lull between successive gusts that had been battering her window all night. She stretched and yawned, snaking her arm across the bed. It was still warm where his body had lain.

She grabbed a man's shirt several sizes too big for her and draped it around her shoulders, leaving it unbuttoned at the front. Standing at the window, the rain was still sheeting down outside, running rivulets down the glass. Beyond the courtyard, the crumbling walls of Carisbrooke Castle stood proudly, towering over the chapel and former Privy garden, now planted with all manner of vegetables for the kitchen. She could just make out Briggs' right-hand man Victor gesticulating wildly at one of the farm workers. She puzzled at the nature of the confrontation. The local man put down the two large buckets he was struggling with, his head bowed deferentially. Victor cuffed him roughly round the ear and sent him on his way, shouting after him. He stood there for a moment, shaking his head, before striding back towards the main building. He faltered mid-stride, noticing Terra standing by the window. He touched his cap, and she self-consciously pulled the shirt tighter round her body.

Victor held her gaze, then continued on his way.

She finished dressing, wriggling into some tight blue jeans, thick socks and walking boots for the day ahead. She slipped a cashmere shawl over her head and adjusted her hair in the mirror. She still looked tired, she thought, rubbing foundation into her cheeks and applying some bright lipstick. The cashmere felt luxurious next to her skin. She brushed her shoulder-length auburn hair into some semblance of order and then tied it back. She was growing tired of her natural colour. She wondered whether it was time for a change. Turning her head from side to side, she thought perhaps brunette. Maybe cut her hair shorter, but not too short.

Briggs always ensured they had the best of everything here. She only had to say the word and one of his henchmen would see to it, scouring the surrounding area for a particular brand or hard-to-find item. Her dressing table was covered in jewellery, necklaces and precious stones, perfumes of every description. She smiled in spite of herself, picking up several items before choosing an antique platinum ring, set with a sapphire, and diamond stud earrings. Her wardrobe would have made a Hollywood A-lister blush. Dresses for every occasion. And yet, by day, she risked his displeasure by rebelling, wearing comfortable clothes fit for the season and an outdoor life. He would rather she stayed indoors, a trophy to enjoy when he saw fit. She had grown accustomed to his eccentricities and misogyny, but refused to conform. He was a man used to getting his own way and these small battles and disagreements seemed to excite him somehow.

She had been at the castle for nearly five months now. Brought here against her will. Kidnapped during the attack at Osborne House. She had suffered the ignominy of having a sack thrust cruelly over her head, then being bundled into the back of Briggs' vehicle, despite her screams. That all seemed like such a long time ago. She had bent over backwards to earn his trust, to fit in, to ingratiate herself, to become part of his inner circle. Briggs seemed to think she was important somehow, that her loyalty could be bought with trinkets. It would take more than that, much more, she mused. She had grander designs, but for now she would play along, play the part she had been given.

Downstairs, the place was deserted and she breakfasted on her own. A simple meal of fruit and cornflakes. She was just clearing away the plates when she heard voices outside in the courtyard and the front door slammed open in the wind, as half a dozen men shuffled in, in high spirits.

The door to the dining room was thrown open to reveal Briggs laughing, slapping Victor on the back, striding towards her, a shotgun over his arm. Briggs was dressed like a country gentleman in a shooting jacket and tweed. They handed the weapons to one of their party. Behind them were two others carrying a brace of pheasants, heading for the kitchen where they would no doubt be hung for a few days.

Terra composed herself and smiled her broadest smile. Victor's mask seemed to slip seeing Terra, until he glanced back at Briggs and resumed his charade of good humour. Briggs strode over to her and ostentatiously bent down and gave her a kiss on the forehead. He put his arms round her shoulders and half squeezed, half throttled her, until she pulled his hands away. He turned to wink at one of his henchmen. Victor looked disinterested and poured himself a cup of coffee.

"How did you get on?" asked Terra, leaning forward, resting her head coquettishly between both hands.

"Not bad, not bad. I bagged a couple of fat-looking

pheasants, Harry got one. This muppet here couldn't hit a barn door," he said pointing at one of the others who shrugged his shoulders. "We almost had a deer as well, but Harry scared him off," said Briggs, pointing across the room as Harry protested his innocence, trying to laugh it away awkwardly.

"Where did you find pheasants round here?"

Briggs pointed at Victor. "Ask him."

"One of the kitchen workers told me about this place not far from here. His father was a groundsman many years ago. Kings and queens used to visit this same wood to shoot. Very old, lots of history. Before guns. Bows and arrows even. It's in a valley, sheltered from the wind. Full of pigeons and grouse. It was, how do you say, a real turkey shoot? No one has been there for months. Very overgrown, very beautiful. Perhaps Terra, you would like to come with us next time?"

Terra blushed at the idea of accompanying the men. They spent the better part of their days engaged in sport, playing golf or shooting. She opened her mouth to respond but was cut short.

"And this bloody idiot shot one of the dogs," reprimanded Briggs, all humour suddenly gone from his eyes.

Terra looked genuinely shocked. "Oh no. Which one? Please tell me it wasn't Keira."

"Which one's Keira? The black lab?"

Terra nodded.

"Then it was Keira. I'm so sorry, gal. I know you loved that dog," said Briggs with what sounded like genuine remorse. "She was flushing out the birds for us. I told you, didn't I? Don't fire at ground level. Aim high. You could have killed one of us. As it was, it was lucky it was only a dog."

He corrected himself. "Sorry Terra. You know what I mean. I had to put her out of her misery."

"I'm really, really sorry," said Harry, the guilty party, "Believe me, I feel terrible."

"I'll find you another one," said Victor. "There's a fresh litter at the farm just up the road. Someone was telling me yesterday. I'll get you one of the puppies. It's the least we can do."

Harry was one of the more sympathetic men that Terra had warmed to during her time at Carisbrooke Castle. If she was to forgive any of them, it would be him. He was different from the others. He was an ex-con, same as most of Briggs' men, but an educated man, someone she could have a proper conversation with. About music, culture, history. About the way things were. His fall from grace had been the result of a nasty drug habit during his years working in the city, which had spiralled out of control and taken him down a dangerous path. A comfortable middle-class existence destroyed in short order. To feed his addiction, he had systematically embezzled money over nearly five years before getting greedy and pushing his luck one too many times.

Stealing from the banks and big business was one thing, but when you stole from dealers and career criminals, you had to expect repercussions. Briggs' protection was a small price to pay for being able to sleep at night. No one dared touch him after that. Harry had promised Briggs a generous share of the fortune he had squirrelled away. The authorities had never found the money. At least he had the foresight to convert his paper fortune into portable wealth - gems and stones - not trusting the financial system. It was said that his stash was buried in a location near Guildford known only to Harry. Fat lot of good that would do anybody now, thought Terra.

Briggs wandered over to Harry and put an arm round his shoulder. "If I was you my friend, I would give Victor a hand getting one of those puppies. Make it up to Terra, yeah? There's a good chap."

Harry avoided Briggs' stare and nodded. His shoulders tensed as Briggs massaged his neck with his enormous leathery hand. He released him and patted him on the back, straightening his collar and smiling.

"Right, I'm off to get changed out of these wet clothes. Terra, when I'm down, I have some stuff I need your help with. A few letters to write going to the mainland this morning."

"Sure. Whenever you're ready," she smiled.

As soon as Briggs was gone and the others were engaged in conversation over a late breakfast, Victor sidled over to Terra and motioned for her to follow him to the drawing room.

Once the door was closed, they stood by the mantle piece as Victor tried to coax new life from a fire that had been lit first thing but left unattended. The three logs had already burned through to ashes.

Keeping his voice low, he glanced up at Terra who was waiting expectantly. "I have news for you." She opened her eyes wide in anticipation.

"I just got back from the *Maersk Charlotte*. The Allies are accelerating their plans. Things are happening much quicker than they expected. There are many more refugees arriving at the embarkation points than they can reasonably manage."

"What difference does that make to us?" spat Terra dismissively.

Victor looked at her puzzled. "Isn't it obvious? It means they need more equipment, more machinery, more manpower. It's a seller's market and the middle man stands to make a small fortune."

"And that just happens to be you, right?"

Victor shrugged his shoulders and looked suitably smug. He

wandered over and stood by the window, drinking his coffee. She didn't trust him as far as she could throw him. He made an unlikely ally, yet they shared a common goal. Terra waited for him to continue but he remained silent as she grew increasingly impatient.

"I don't understand. What does that have to do with me?"

"You and me are partners Terra. This is good for us. Don't tell me you've forgotten our little pact already?"

"Of course not. But it hardly seems an equal partnership. I'm stuck here like his personal pet, while you drift around touring his empire, building alliances. I don't see how what I'm doing helps the cause."

"Patience Terra. Your time will come. He is beginning to trust you. That's what's important. And not without a lot of reassurance from me, I would have you know. Don't think he doesn't question whether he's doing the right thing. You may not recognise it, but the plan he's executing is yours. He trusts your judgement. He took your advice, he's playing a waiting game. Slowly infiltrating the Allies' set up ready to subvert their plans. That was smart Terra. Very smart."

He turned around and fixed her with his cold expressionless grey eyes. "You should be proud. This is your doing. When we're ready and all our pieces are in place, they won't know what hit them. They will fall like dominos."

"And you really think that's what I want? To see the Allies fail? More death and destruction?"

"Isn't it? Think carefully. Look into your heart, Terra. What is it you really want? There is a price to pay, yes. There is always a price to pay. One person's gain is another person's loss. That is life. After we do this, you and I will be sitting pretty. We can take what's ours, what we deserve. People like us Terra have always been second in line. Always the bridesmaid, never the bride, is that the right expression?"

She nodded. "I don't know why I ever listened to you Victor. What if you're wrong? You really think that this rebellion has any chance of succeeding?"

"Sure. Every day, we win more and more support. More people arrive from all over the South coast. You think people want the Americans here? They are like a cuckoo. They take what does not belong to them. Squatting at Osborne House, bossing the locals around, while they sit in state sipping champagne and eating smoked salmon? We need to drive them out, send them back where they came from. This island belongs to the locals. It belongs to us, Terra. It's there for the taking. Trust me."

"So you keep saying, Victor. I get it. How much longer do I have to keep up this charade?"

"Not much longer. We're close now. Your time is coming Terra. Your moment to shine. It will be spectacular. Trust me, it'll all be worth the wait."

CHAPTER EIGHT

On board the *Santana*, much to the relief of an exhausted Jack and Sergeant Flynn, the helm nursed the stricken ship towards the narrow western entrance to the Solent. Alert to the danger, the team at Hurst had run power lines to the light house to guide the ship through the treacherous narrow passage. Passing the Needles in the fading light, Jack watched the beam from the light reach out across the water, illuminating the headland and rocks to their right. They were close enough to hear huge breakers surging through the gap between the jagged rocks, rolling towards the shingle spit beyond.

For the last two hours, Jack had been watching the control panel for the bilge pumps like their lives depended on it. If one more of the pumps had failed, the *Santana* would have been in desperate trouble, facing huge seas, taking on water from who knows where. Yet, through good judgement and a large helping of luck, they had made it. The remaining pumps had held. The ship was almost back on an even keel, barely listing more than five degrees. She was still heavy in the bow but seaworthy again. Jack felt a surge of pride. Adrenaline had kept him going these last few hours. Entering the home straight, he gave in to an all-consuming fatigue.

Ahead of them, *HMS Marker* was holding position just off Fort Albert in the lee of the island, sheltering from the wind. Her navigation and steaming lights were visible against the darkening shape of the headland. The voice hailing them on the radio was Captain Armstrong's.

"*Santana*, this is *HMS Marker*. We're on standby to escort you on to Southampton docks. We'll send a pilot and his team across to relieve you."

Flynn acknowledged the instructions, his voice thin and brittle.

"Congratulations, Sergeant Flynn. You had us worried for a while there. Your team has done an outstanding job."

"Thank you, sir. We have Jack and Sam to thank for getting us on board in the first place. We couldn't have done it without them."

"Quite right. Thank you Jack. Let's hope it was all worthwhile. With any luck, the *Santana* is carrying enough refined petroleum to keep Camp Wight's equipment and vehicles running for several more precious months. According to her logs, her standard cargo was something close to one hundred thousand gallons. Judging by her waterline, that looks about right. All thanks to you."

"Just doing our job, sir," croaked Flynn, clearing his throat and patting Jack on the shoulder.

"Standby, maintain current course and speed. We're coming alongside you on your port bow."

HMS Marker closed the gap between the two ships, until her boarding party waiting amidships were in line with the rope ladder swinging invitingly above them at head height. Four men hurried up the ladder and Jack was surprised to see Lieutenant Peterson was among them. What could possibly be important enough to get the American out here at this hour and in this weather?

"Welcome on board Lieutenant, quite a welcoming committee. We weren't expecting the royal treatment."

"Hello Jack," said Peterson, taking his hand as he straddled the guard rail. "We've been following your progress from the *Chester*. We had your back. Our guys were on standby just in case things got too hairy. Sounded like you had things under control. Sorry about your man, Hughes was it? There was nothing we could do. We talked about scrambling the Seahawk, but in weather like that, chances were slim we'd ever find him. We'd only put more lives in danger. My condolences."

"Let's hope it was worth the risk. So, what brings you out here in person?"

"I wanted to be the first to speak with the *Santana*'s crew."

"Why?"

"Think about it Jack. How long's it been since we were in contact with anyone from outside this area? They might be able to tell us something, about what's going on in other countries they've visited."

"What makes you think they've come from overseas? For all we know they could have been drifting like that in the English Channel for weeks. They may know no more than we do."

"Just a hunch. Who knows, they may have made it across the Atlantic."

"What I want to know is why they were locked up in the first place?"

"Yeah, I can't say I'd given that much thought. But now you mention it, how about you tag along and find out what their story is?"

"Must say, I'm curious. It's certainly piqued my interest."

"Be my guest. It won't take long. Then we'll get you back to dry land. Can you get Flynn and his men to provide some backup? You can't be too careful, right?"

Jack waved Flynn over. The Sergeant snapped his fingers and his men grabbed their weapons and followed Peterson and Jack back down towards the crew quarters and the sealed door, which was still lashed shut with some webbing.

Peterson leaned in close, putting his ear to the door, his eyes flicking around, concentrating hard, listening for any sounds. He shook his head and then used the gold ring on his right hand to hammer on the metalwork and called out in a language Jack didn't speak but recognised as Spanish. From inside, there came voices and the sound of men getting to their feet. Peterson banged again, louder this time and gestured to Flynn to untie the webbing securing the door. He levered it open a crack, peering inside, cautioning the men to stay back as he pointed his weapon into the space beyond.

The stench from within made them step back, covering their mouths with their sleeves. It was a heady mix of sweat, urine and faeces that flooded the corridor. Inside was a dark hellhole that had been the crew's prison for who knew how long. Those still alive squinted towards the light, their arms raised with pained smiles on their gaunt faces.

One by one, Flynn waved them forward, stepping over the sill of the doorway, until they stood with their backs to the wall in the corridor, facing their rescuers. Flynn's man kept a gun on them at all times, but by the looks of them, they didn't have the energy left for heroics. They looked broken and beaten. Each of them had dark hair, heavy beards, and tanned skin. Jack's best guess was that they were South American, possibly Mexican.

When they were in an orderly line, heads bowed, Flynn stepped aside and let Peterson pass.

Peterson spoke quickly in fluent Spanish. There was an edge

to his questions, repeated until one of the men shook his head and muttered a single word response. It was clearly not what Peterson was looking for. He renewed his inquisition with added fervour, anger spilling over into his body language as he towered over them. He slammed his hand in to the wall just above one of their heads, frustrated by the lack of cooperation. They cowered, shrinking against the officer's aggression.

The crew member who had spoken looked up for the first time and Jack noticed a flicker of recognition and alarm spread across his face. He put his hands in front of his body in a defensive posture, shaking his head and whispering something as he kissed the cross hanging from his neck.

"Lock them back in until we get to port. I'll deal with them later. No one speaks to them without my permission. Got it?" spat Peterson as he glared at Flynn before striding away.

"Yes, sir."

Jack looked on, puzzled, and whispered to Flynn.

"Did you catch any of that? Speak any Spanish Sergeant?"

"I did Spanish at school years ago. Something about 'El Diablo'. He kept asking him where it was. He kept repeating the same phrase over and over."

"I got the distinct impression those two had met before."

"Not sure how that's possible, Jack. You really think the *Santana* followed the *Chester* here?"

Jack shrugged his shoulders. He couldn't explain it rationally, but his intuition told him there was more to this than met the eye.

Once the crew quarters were sealed again, Jack and Flynn returned to the bridge, where Private Lucas was walking the pilot through the status of the *Santana*'s primary systems. Peterson gave the order for Lucas and the rest of the salvage team to be relieved and escorted them to the rail where, one by one, they climbed down to the deck of *HMS Marker* keeping pace beside them.

Armstrong was waiting below them on the foredeck of the Royal Navy patrol ship to personally congratulate them. He shook hands with Jack and Flynn. Jack stood unsteadily, holding on to the rail, exhausted. It was some twelve hours after the original call had been made by the *Chester*.

"Good job, gentlemen. Outstanding work. There's a brew and biscuits inside. Go and get cleaned up and we'll drop you back at Hurst."

"What's going to happen to the crew?" asked Jack.

"Oh, they'll be put in quarantine, interrogated when we get back into port. Why, what's on your mind Jack?"

"Just curious, that's all. Something doesn't add up, them being locked up like that and the ship disabled."

"Not really, it was probably pirates. If you ask me, they were boarded, imprisoned as they searched the ship. Then, for whatever reason, they lost power and the pirates panicked and high-tailed it out of there. It was a standard tactic in the Gulf of Aden to kill power if you were boarded by Somali pirates, knowing sooner or later they would give up and go home."

Jack wasn't so convinced, but agreed it seemed like the most plausible explanation. He was still trying to make sense of the exchange between the South American crew and Peterson. Who or what was this 'Diablo' they had argued about?

"Right you lot, off you go."

The men nodded wearily and headed through the hatchway. Armstrong caught Jack's arm. "Hold up Jack. Do you have a minute?"

"Sure. What's on your mind?"

"Listen, I wanted you to be the first to hear." He paused as a crewman handed each of them a steaming cup of milky tea and left again.

Armstrong seemed hesitant, nervous about something.

Jack noticed for the first time the pepper grey hair at Armstrong's temples. He reckoned Armstrong was in his early forties. He had met the sort so many times before. A career naval officer who looked down his nose at non-commissioned types. Fleet Auxiliary servicemen like Jack were something of a joke to people like Armstrong. A lifetime of privilege had bestowed upon the naval officer certain airs and graces that got right up Jack's nose. Despite all the hardships they had both been through, Armstrong had lost none of that inbred haughtiness and sense of entitlement he'd seen so often in naval officers. It was almost laughable.

Jack wracked his brain trying to think what possible news Armstrong could be about to share.

"Is it Terra?" pre-empted Jack hopefully.

"No, Jack, I'm sorry, no news there," he frowned. "No, it's about Hurst."

"What about Hurst?" he batted back to the younger man.

Armstrong looked over Jack's shoulder, following the contours of the island to the faint outline of the Needles rocks growing smaller in their wake.

"If it's all right with you, I'm just going to cut to the chase. We've known each other long enough. I owe you that."

There was a pregnant pause while Armstrong fiddled with his wedding band.

"As you know, the security situation is deteriorating. We've all seen the same increase in attempts to reach the island. We think this is just the start of what's to come."

"Captain, we spoke about this at length at the last council meeting only two weeks ago. We planned for this. There were contingencies made. This mass migration was always expected. As word spreads, we knew more and more people will be drawn here. So what's changed?"

"Well, here's the thing. We're successfully channelling the bulk of the refugees through our clearing zones in Lymington, Southampton, and Portsmouth. So far, that's working, we're just about coping. The island remains virus-free. The quarantine controls are working, even allowing for numbers far exceeding our models."

"I'm afraid I'm not following you. So where's the problem? What does this all have to do with Hurst?"

"I'm coming to that, hold on."

"Perhaps you don't realise, but we are working day and night. We've done everything we've been asked to do."

"I know Jack, no one's questioning your commitment. But the creation of Camp Wight has created a humanitarian disaster-zone right on our door step. We all have to deal with the consequences."

"If you're suggesting that we're not pulling our weight? If this is some sort of lecture Captain..."

"Not exactly Jack, no," he interrupted.

"Because if it is, then with all due respect, I don't want to hear it. I should remind you that it's us who are on the front line. We're the people who find bodies washed up on the beach every day. We have to deal with all the crazy people trying to make the crossing to the island on anything that floats: dinghies, rowing boats, lilos, rubber rings. It's lunacy. For every person we turn back or rescue, ten more make it across. We're doing our best here. We have twenty-four hour patrols, but in the darkness, without proper equipment, it's virtually impossible to catch them all."

Armstrong held his hand up in an attempt to placate Jack who felt his hackles rising at the thought that their efforts were going unappreciated.

"And that's my point," said Armstrong with some finality. "With Portsmouth under the control of the Royal Navy and the Americans in charge at Southampton, we believe a predominantly civilian operation at Hurst is no longer feasible."

"Surely that's why you stationed two squads of marines there in the first place? Isn't that enough?"

"I'm afraid the Americans don't share your optimism, Jack."

"So what are they proposing then?"

Armstrong sighed and delivered the killer punch Jack had been dreading.

"They are proposing a full militarisation of Hurst. All civilians will be evacuated to the island in the coming weeks. They have allowed for a phased withdrawal to give your team time to make the necessary plans."

"That's not going to be popular," grimaced Jack. "People have worked for more than two years to build that place into a sustainable community, a place they can call home. You realise that, right?"

"I'm afraid there's nothing much we can do about that. It's for the greater good Jack, I hope you can understand. This is bigger than Hurst. The security of the island is paramount. Your people will be treated fairly, housed and accommodated on the island."

"Let's not kid ourselves, Captain," sneered Jack. "We all know what happens on the island."

"I'm not sure what you mean."

"Oh you know. Martial law, forced labour."

"I don't know where you heard that. I can assure you it's not true."

"We've all heard the rumours. Everyone on the island works, they get assigned to groups that fit their skill sets and experience. Those that work get to eat. Those that don't fit in get reassigned to the mainland. Are you seriously telling me that we'll be allowed to stay together, that the children will not get sent somewhere else?"

"I'm sure they'll do their best to keep you all together. They're not insensitive to the shared interest of families and friends. Anyway, there are whole villages in the south and west of the island that are being reserved for key workers."

"Is that what we are? Key workers?"

"You know what I mean, Jack. I can put in a good word, see what can be done. But listen, you're right. On the island, people work. It's no holiday park, it's a new start. It's a massive operation that's only going to get bigger as our focus expands to the mainland."

"And what if we refuse to leave Hurst?"

Armstrong looked surprised momentarily, caught off guard. He seemed to stiffen a little at this veiled threat to his authority. He recovered his composure almost immediately. His reputation for political astuteness was well known and respected amongst the council. Jack knew he was playing a dangerous game.

Armstrong leaned in and lowered his voice.

"Jack. We both know that no one can force you to do anything. Your voice on the council is highly regarded as is your team at Hurst. No one is going to do anything to jeopardise the special relationship we have with you. But that said, if you're not able to secure the western approaches, then one way or another, steps must be taken, with or without your cooperation."

Jack clenched his fists tighter, waiting for the officer to continue.

"Listen, we both knew that sooner or later it would come to this. Hurst is isolated. It's an outpost. The more people that flock to the South coast, the harder it will be to maintain security there. The only place where we can guarantee everyone's safety is on the island. I wouldn't be surprised if, in a few months, we'll need to evacuate everyone. Living there will be untenable. As resources dwindle, it will get a little harder every day. Your team will need to scavenge further and further inland for supplies. Jack, you must realise that you have a choice. It doesn't have to be like that. Right across the water your team can be safe. A fresh start for all. You must see that."

Jack sighed, an air of weary resignation creeping over him. Despite the enormous sense of pride he felt after everything they had achieved, he had learned the hard way that Hurst was vulnerable. Even with soldiers stationed at the castle, sooner or later, they could expect more attacks. Armstrong was right, it was only a matter of time.

"This is going to be hard to hear for many of them. How long can you give us?"

"Not much. We're out of time Jack. I have another squad of marines coming over today. In the short term, they have some additional hardware and equipment to make the castle more secure. They'll take charge, oversee the handover. Free up your team to farm, scavenge and all that other good stuff you do. Can I count on you Jack? I need your full cooperation for this to work."

"Captain, whether we like it or not, we are all in this together. You can count on our support. But if your people think they're going to be welcome at Hurst, think again."

"That's something we'll just have to accept. I suggest we get the Hurst team together as soon as possible and let them know. As soon as they see the next squad of soldiers arriving and the equipment they're bringing, the grapevine will go into overdrive, believe you me."

The two men leaned on the railing looking out in to the growing darkness where Hurst's crumbling walls were still visible against the skyline. Jack drained his cup and closed his eyes for a second. It had a been a long day and the warm glow of success was now tinged with foreboding. How on earth was he going to break this news to the others?

CHAPTER NINE

Riley and Zed led Sister Imelda through the castle gates to puzzled looks from passers-by. The sight of a stranger, arriving alone, so late in the day, not to mention dressed in a nun's habit, seemed totally incongruous. Passing the canteen where people were beginning to gather for dinner, there was a subdued buzz of conversation and whispering. Riley held the door open and they retraced their steps back through the Tudor gate, across the courtyard and up the outside staircase towards the reception room upstairs in the Gun Tower, where she had been reading earlier.

Tommy stood aside and made way for them to pass. He was laughing about something or other with a youth who seemed to have become his companion of choice recently, supplanting his old friend Sam. He had changed out of his wet clothes but still looked weather-beaten, his face raw and salt-streaked. As if noticing the stranger for the first time as they climbed the steps, Tommy called out.

"Aren't you going to introduce me?"

The party stopped and looked down at him over the railing.

"I'm sorry Tommy," apologised Riley. "This is Sister Imelda from the Chewton Glen Hotel. You know, the group Jean was with before coming here. Can you do me a favour and go and find her for me? We need to speak to her."

Sister Imelda inclined her head respectfully as Tommy studied her, blinking. He clicked his fingers remembering, as a big grin spread across his face. Joe's salubrious stories about his time at the hotel had proven quite popular with the younger men.

"Nice to meet you, Sister. It's..." he paused as if searching for the right word, "an honour to have you here."

He was looking her up and down. "Well, if you ever need a volunteer to escort you home, I would be happy to oblige," said Tommy playfully.

Zed stifled a laugh.

"Excuse our friend," interrupted Riley. "He's not the sharpest tool in the box."

Sister Imelda didn't seem to know how to respond, unsure whether he was making fun of her. She stared at him suspiciously before taking her leave, bowing her head and following Zed down the dimly-lit corridor. He held the large oak door open for the pair of them. Stepping inside it was noticeably warmer, lit by candles and the warm glow of a crackling log fire. Riley offered the Sister a seat but she declined, preferring to remain standing.

There was an awkward silence while they waited for the Sister to collect her thoughts.

"Perhaps you can enlighten us as to why you are really here, Sister?" asked Riley suspiciously.

"I'm grateful for you receiving me at this late hour. I had hoped to arrive a little earlier, but the journey took longer than I had expected," she adjusted the folds of her skirt, looking up at Riley. "I've come here to see Jean. There's something I need to talk to her about."

"I very much doubt that Jean will want to talk you, though," mumbled Zed testily.

"To come all this way, alone, just before nightfall, it seems incredibly risky."

"My escorts camped at a safe house in Milford for the night. I thought it better that I came alone."

"I see. So, where have you been hiding all this time?" said Riley.

"We've not been hiding, we simply had our hands full," said the Sister, eyebrows raised. "After what happened at the hotel, we couldn't stay there any longer. There were too many bad memories, too much sadness."

She looked down at her hands, straightening the folds of her habit, before continuing. "I heard you came looking for us."

"I came looking for Stella. How is she?" Her face brightened at the thought of her friend. "Did she have the baby already?"

"Stella is fine. She's being well looked after."

"And the baby?"

Sister Imelda's face softened into a smile. "Adam," she said inclining her head. "She had a beautiful little boy."

Zed was nodding, looking very pleased with himself, as if he'd won a private bet. Riley sighed, doing her best to ignore him. She wished so much that she could be with Stella right now.

"When can we meet him - the baby?"

"I'm afraid that's out of the question," said the Sister dismissively. "After everything that happened, Sister Theodora would never allow it."

"I hardly think that's up to the Sister, do you?" added Zed, waving away Riley's protest.

"Where are mother and baby now?"

"Somewhere safe, look, I'm sorry, I didn't come here to talk about Stella, I came to speak with Jean."

"All in good time. As I'm sure you can imagine, we might be more inclined to accommodate your request if you could facilitate ours. Sort of, you scratch our back and we'll scratch yours," offered Zed, his eyebrows raised.

There was a loud knock at the door which opened, without waiting for an answer. In the darkness beyond, Riley recognised the shape of Tommy and two others she assumed were Jean and Joe. Zed nodded and waved them in.

Seeing the Sister in the flesh again, Jean froze in the doorway. The colour seemed to drain from her face. Jean remained fixed to the spot, hiding behind Joe, reluctant to go any further.

The Sister swept towards Jean in a swirl of wool and wooden beads. She clasped both of Jean's hands and ushered her gently into the room, turning to face Zed and Riley.

"May I speak with Jean alone?" she implored.

"I'm sorry," said Riley, "I think Jean would rather we stayed."

Jean nodded, reaching for Joe's hand and looking anxiously at Riley for support.

"Very well," said Sister Imelda, turning to address the young girl. "Jean, we've all been very worried about you. What possessed you to run away? To help those men escape? I will never know. I can only assume that Seamus and the others talked you into it."

"Jean should never have been allowed to spend time with that man in the first place," started Joe before Riley pleaded with him to let the Sister continue.

Riley noticed Jean's discomfort, staring at her shoes and wringing her hands. She was refusing to look the Sister in the eye.

"You do realise that seven women died in that fire. Countless others suffered life-changing injuries they'll never recover from. People are naturally suspicious that you ran away that night. What were you thinking? I don't suppose you were thinking at all, were you? You stupid child."

"Okay, I think that's enough," intervened Riley her palm raised. "She knows that what she did was wrong."

"Wrong? It was nothing short of murder."

"You can't seriously be suggesting that Jean started the fire on purpose?"

"That's exactly what people have been saying. And it's only fit and right that Jean is brought back to stand trial for what she did. We need to get to the bottom of what happened and why. Only Jean knows the truth."

"That's not going to happen," said Joe, stepping forward in between Jean and the Sister. "There's no way Jean is being taken anywhere against her will."

The Sister held her ground, snorting in disapproval.

"It hardly surprises me that you, of all people, won't allow it. You are as much to blame as Jean is."

Riley tried to defuse the mounting tension between the pair.

"Look, we've been here before. Last time you accused all of us of being involved and we gave you our assurances that we had nothing to do with it. I've told you before and I'll tell you again, we had nothing to do with the fire or with the men's escape. For a start, your group locked us in a room for the night, for goodness sake."

"We accept that you all had no direct involvement. Which just leaves Jean, no one else could have done this."

"And it hasn't occurred to you that the fire was just an unfortunate, terrible accident?"

"This was no accident. We have proof."

"Proof? What proof? You have nothing," said Joe testily.

The Sister waved him away, refusing to listen to any more of their excuses. She wagged her finger at Riley.

"I can see I'm wasting my time with you. Who's in charge here anyway? If you refuse to listen to reason, then perhaps someone else will."

"You really are a piece of work, aren't you?" interrupted Zed. "Who do you think you are, breezing in here and bossing everyone around?"

"Do I really need to remind you that we took you in, saved your life, nursed you back to health? Is this how you repay that kindness?"

"Perhaps you're forgetting that you locked up this man. Suggested Joe was a danger to others. Treated him like an animal, a 'breeder'? Accused us all of murder. Is that really what we should be grateful for?"

Joe seemed uncomfortable with Riley speaking on his behalf, shrugging as if to say that it wasn't all bad. Riley batted away his levity.

"I think we're done here, don't you?" said Riley as she turned to face the young girl. "Jean, you don't need to listen to another word. Let's go."

"I'm not leaving until I've spoken to your leader," said the Sister, crossing her arms, finally sitting down. "Perhaps you would let him know I'm here."

"I'll let Jack know. But you're wasting your time."

"We'll see about that, won't we?" sneered the Sister.

Riley and Zed rose from their seats and with one last scornful look at the Sister, slammed the door behind them.

They headed downstairs to the canteen in search of Jack. Down here, the smell of cooking was over-powering. A heady and not altogether pleasant smell of stewed vegetables. It reminded Riley of school sports halls and boys' changing rooms. Three long wooden tables were set out with bench-seats on either side. Elbow to elbow were sat more than fifty men, women and children, giving in to their hunger, slurping stew in near silence. Scottie looked up at their approach, his face shrouded in steam. He looked concerned, trying to get a sense of how the meeting had gone. Riley shook her head in disappointment.

She scanned the room but Jack was nowhere to be seen. She learned from Sam that he was still on his way back to the castle after this morning's salvage mission. He was expected within the hour. He had asked Sam to gather everyone together. They had Captain Armstrong coming to address them, some important announcement.

"An announcement?" mused Zed. "I wonder what the old man has gone and agreed to now?"

"I dread to think," puzzled Riley, rolling her eyes.

CHAPTER TEN

Back on dry land, Jack limped through the castle gates and into the shelter and relative peace of the courtyard. His hip was still hurting from where he had slammed into the *Santana*'s hull when climbing aboard during the storm.

Ahead of him was the canteen and dining area, freshly rebuilt, its timbers repainted in navy blue. Above the doorway, there remained the scorch marks from the inferno that had torn through here during the attack. It was a fitting reminder of those who had lost their lives defending the castle, many of whom had been gunned down in cold blood. He still blamed himself that he hadn't been here to oversee the defence of the castle, that their preparations had proven so inadequate. He had promised himself that would never happen again. He would never let down his guard.

Walking into the canteen, he nodded from the doorway at Zed who was sat with Scottie, Joe, Will and a few others. In the middle of the table was a large bowl of ripe apples from an orchard they maintained not far from here. This year had been one of the best yet, yielding a bountiful supply of fruit. What they couldn't immediately eat, they stored for winter. Liz's hands and lower arms had been stained red for days afterwards, along with the others who worked in the kitchens pickling, bottling and preserving jams on an almost industrial-scale.

On the side sat a large pot of coffee. Jack helped himself to a cup, stirring in two heaped spoonful's of sugar.

He wandered over to the nearest of the tables and caught the end of one of Joe's raucous stories about his time at the hotel, cursing the Sister under his breath. Jack stood behind him, smiling warmly as the laughs died away and his audience fell silent. It took Joe a few more seconds to realise that Jack was standing behind him. The look on their faces suggested his appearance must have been a little alarming, hair wild, streaked and rigid with salt spray.

"Sorry, Jack. Didn't see you there. Jeez, you look like you've had quite a day. That storm was something eh? How did you get on with the salvage?"

"We made it back by the skin of our teeth," sighed Jack with his hands on his hips. "It was touch and go for a while until we got the engines going again and the bilge pumps restarted. Listen, I don't want to break up the party, but *HMS Marker* is just mooring up at the jetty and Captain Armstrong and a section of marines will be here in a few minutes. He's asked us to gather everyone together."

"So we hear. This all sounds a bit ominous," worried Scottie.

Jack grimaced, "I'd love to tell you more, but we don't have much time. Can you rustle up the rest of them?"

Scottie nodded and raised his bowl, draining what was left of the stew. He nudged Will and the pair of them got up and headed in opposite directions to find the others.

Jack cast his eyes over the faces of those already gathered. There were a few people staring at him, perhaps sensing his discomfort. He reminded himself that they would all be watching him, trying to guess the nature of his announcement. It was up to him to reassure his people and set their minds at rest. To be straight with them and not obfuscate what had to be said. He was just organising his thoughts, trying to figure out how to break the news, when Riley appeared at his elbow.

"Jack, can I have a quick word?"

"Can't it wait Riley? We have Captain Armstrong arriving any second and we need to get set up."

"Actually, it's kind of urgent. We have another visitor who's demanding to see you. I'm afraid she's refusing to leave until you talk to her.

Jack raised his eyebrows, waiting for her to continue.

"One of the Sisters from Chewton Glen just arrived out of the blue. She's up in the snug, waiting for you. Wants to talk about Jean. Holds her responsible for the fire they had at the hotel. She's proposing to take her back to stand trial. We said no, but she's pulling rank."

"Well, she'll have to wait, Riley. Can't you see I'm busy?"

"Listen, I told her you wouldn't be interested," said Riley, holding her hands up defensively.

"Hold on. That's not what I said. I'd be happy to receive her in the morning, but I'm too busy this evening. If the Sister has reasonable grounds to believe Jean had something to do with the fire, then it's only right and proper that we hear what she has to say. We have a duty to help."

"Jack, she didn't do it. You know Jean, she wouldn't hurt a fly."

"Riley, I look forward to hearing all about it tomorrow," said Jack distractedly, noticing people arriving from all corners of the castle, jostling into the dining area, where there was standing room only.

Jack sensed a degree of unease amongst his people. The room was abuzz with whispering and lowered voices. His gut told him he was doing the right thing by telling them the truth without delay. The rumour mill at Hurst was brutal at the best of times. Despite his best efforts to keep everyone informed, it was only natural, he supposed, that people should be suspicious, particularly since the arrival of the soldiers. He wondered whether he should let Armstrong do the talking. Let him break the bad news. He rejected that idea. They should hear it from him. They were his people.

Corporal Ballard and his men trudged in, their uniforms soaked through from their evening exercise in the rain. They hadn't had a chance to change and stayed together, steaming at the front of the room, self-consciously keeping themselves to themselves. Ballard looked as clueless as the rest about why they were all here.

Zed was keeping watch by the door and wolf whistled to let Jack know that their guests had arrived. Armstrong knocked on the door and was ushered through by Zed, followed by another officer Jack half remembered from Osborne House and six uniformed soldiers from the barracks at Portsmouth. The military men acknowledged each other and shook hands in silence.

Armstrong joined Jack at the front of the hall. He leant in and asked Jack to kick things off and then hand back to him. Jack hushed the room, appealing for quiet, waiting for the last conversations to die out.

"Good evening, thank you all for making the time. I think you all know Captain Armstrong here. He and I spoke earlier about some developments at Camp Wight. I wanted to update you about what's been going on and the next steps the Council are proposing."

He glanced across at Armstrong, who invited him to continue.

"You'll all be aware that we're witnessing a massive surge of refugees entering the Solent area. The vast majority are here to secure passage to the island. Many are being turned away. They're only taking the fit and healthy. Those that don't make it across, are staying in the area, putting increased pressure on local resources and that's already having an impact on us here. The orchard has been stripped bare, animals are missing from the fields, winter stores have been raided by travelling groups. The Council believes it's only going to get worse. So we're looking to move to the next phase. Captain, perhaps you can explain further?"

"I would be happy to. Thank you Jack. First of all, I wanted to acknowledge the outstanding job you've all done. Hurst Castle has played a vital role in protecting the Western approaches to the Solent from unwanted visitors. Your vigilance has been absolutely critical to our success so far. I know it hasn't been easy. Only today, one of our men paid the ultimate price. I suspect you've all heard about the daring rescue that happened earlier. Jack, Sam and Sergeant Flynn successfully boarded a stricken tanker, disabled by the storm and being blown ashore. They managed to restore power, restart her engines and get her safely back to port. They are all heroes. Sergeant, I know Private Hughes will be sorely missed."

The Sergeant acknowledged his commanding officer with a thin smile and patted the nearest marine on the back, who had been close to Hughes.

"You will all have noticed that the number of people trying to reach the island is growing week by week," continued Armstrong. "So far, the island remains virus-free. We have had no new cases of infection for several weeks now. But that's only because our quarantine procedures have, so far, proved effective. There are no exceptions. No one gets in unless they are free of infection. If even one infected person sneaks through, it would put us back to square one. A fresh outbreak on the island would be unthinkable."

There were murmurs of approval from the crowd who were listening intently, arms crossed, curious about what was coming next.

"Up till now, this has been primarily a civilian operation at Hurst Castle, but the acceleration of our plans and the sheer tide of humanity heading to the coast mean that we need to step things up."

He paused, taking a deep breath before continuing.

"The council has decided that we need to move to the next stage. We're placing Hurst under full military control."

The room seemed to erupt with surprise and hostility, as if they had all been holding their breath. There were dismissive gestures and cruder insults thrown Armstrong's way as he appealed for calm. Jack attempted to quieten them down but his complicity made him an additional target for the ire of those around him.

Tommy was the first to question Armstrong. "Just what do you mean by 'full military control'?"

Before Armstrong could answer, Scottie volunteered: "Well if it means wearing khaki, count me out," to the sniggers of those around him.

Jack smiled in spite of himself, appealing for calm before answering on the Captain's behalf. "This means a phased withdrawal of all remaining civilians from Hurst. They are going to start bringing more soldiers across over the next few days and weeks. In due course, we'll all be relocated to the island."

"No way," shouted Tommy. "You can't do that. This is our home."

"That's right," joined in Scottie, jabbing his finger in Armstrong's direction. "We built this place from nothing. You can't just take it away from us."

Others joined in protest, shouting and gesticulating angrily at the Captain. The new arrivals from the barracks at Portsmouth looked restless, alarmed by the febrile atmosphere. They were watching Sergeant Flynn closely for any indication of threat, unsure how to respond to the hostility in the room. He cautioned them to remain calm, indicating that this was somehow under control, despite appearances.

Jack intervened again on behalf of the Captain.

"Listen, we're all on the same side here. We're part of the same team. If the council believes further militarisation is necessary to ensure the safety of the island, then so be it."

He glanced back at Armstrong, who had his arms crossed. "I'm assuming this is a temporary escalation?" he said in a voice lacking conviction.

The Captain opened his mouth to respond but had second thoughts himself, unsure of what to say.

"Sod that," said one of the younger guys, advancing boldly towards the Captain. Corporal Ballard stepped into his path, towering over the youth, who stood eye-balling the soldier, chin up. Tommy put his arm on the youth's shoulder and tried to lead him away. The younger man dipped his shoulder and pulled away from his grasp.

"Back it up sonny," warned Corporal Ballard, shaking his head. "Be a good boy will you and run along?"

Jack appealed for quiet again, growing increasingly impatient. The Captain took him to one side.

"This isn't helping, Jack. They must understand that we wouldn't ask for this sacrifice unless circumstances demanded it. We are all grateful for their hard work, but right now, we need their efforts to be redeployed elsewhere. I suggest you speak to your leaders in private and listen to their concerns. I can come back another day when things are a bit calmer. Maybe answer their questions?"

He patted Jack on the shoulder and motioned for Sergeant Flynn and Ballard to follow him out to escort him and his men back to *HMS Marker*, waiting at the quay. As the door swung closed, Jack noticed Zed shaking his head, saying something derogatory to Riley, no doubt. He knew Zed did not approve of the presence of soldiers here in the first place. Another squad would only make matters worse.

Without their officers, the marines looked uncomfortable and made their excuses, escorting the new arrivals to the far end of the castle where they had set up their own quarters. Jack watched them leave, smiling weakly at those who turned his way.

He muttered under his breath: "You haven't heard the last of this, that's for sure."

CHAPTER ELEVEN

The following morning Riley was woken by the distant hum of an approaching helicopter. She checked her watch, an old wind-up Timex with a leather strap and a chip in the glass. It was just after seven. Seemed a bit early for normal visiting hours. The hum grew louder and louder until it was all-consuming, echoing off every stone, making the glass in the windows rattle.

There was an unfamiliar shape covered by a blanket in the corner of the room. Rubbing sleep from her eyes, she watched its first stirrings, before remembering Sister Imelda's arrival the previous evening. Let sleeping dogs lie, she thought. She was in no mood for further confrontation. She knew from her previous encounters with the Sisters that they were unlikely to admit defeat, to soften their approach. They saw the world in black and white, right and wrong. There was little scope for interpretation, for shades of grey. She didn't relish another round of intransigence and condescension this morning, though she knew she couldn't put her off forever. Sooner or later she would need to get the Sister that audience with Jack.

Riley pulled on some leggings, a loose-fitting t-shirt and a grey fleece, peering out the window, trying to catch sight of the source of the noise.

The Seahawk helicopter from the *USS Chester* circled the castle and skilfully came into a hover in the landing area beside the dock. Riley and half a dozen others emerged from the castle gate, shielding their eyes and tucking shirts in. A few exchanged excited looks and shrugged shoulders. The sight of a helicopter round these parts remained somewhat of a novelty.

Inside the helicopter, next to the pilot, Riley could make out Lieutenant Peterson, staring off into the distance. His lips were moving as if he was having an animated conversation with someone over the radio. All of a sudden, he removed the headset and threw it against the windshield in frustration. The pilot attempted to placate him, palms raised but was met with hostility and got an earful for his troubles. Peterson noticed Riley and the crowd of on-lookers and seemed a little embarrassed by his behaviour. As the whine of the helicopter's twin turbo-shaft engines and its four rotor blades began to slow, he cracked open the passenger door and jumped down onto the grass with a disarming smile.

As always, the American was well turned out. Freshly pressed uniform, clean-shaven, hair cut short. The crew of the *Chester* always looked well fed, showing few signs of the malnutrition and poor diet that affected most other survivors. But then, it was said that they had the best of everything on the island. If you believed the stories, awaiting those who made the passage was a land of milk and honey. A world free of famine and suffering. Most importantly, it was free of the virus. The crew were the poster children of the new world. Athletic, healthy-looking and fresh faced. It made Riley wonder how they managed it. The initial wave of gratitude following their arrival had made way for growing resentment and latent hostility amongst the locals. There was something of a swagger about them, but a lack of transparency made everyone, including Riley, suspicious.

Peterson nodded at Riley, greeting her with a curt "Mam", and continued past her to the gate. Tommy was on the early shift for guard duty again and motioned him towards the canteen area, where Jack and Armstrong were already waiting. The sliding door from the main cabin was thrown back and four other passengers emerged from the helicopter, yawning and stretching from the short flight from Portsmouth or wherever they had come from.

Riley spotted the cheery smile of Captain Anders from the *Maersk Charlotte* who was waving at her, clutching a leather holdall stuffed with items. He rarely came empty handed. Behind him was the tall and gangly figure of Professor Nichols, the man tasked with the search for a vaccine, along with two other men she didn't recognise. One was in combat uniform with the insignia of a full Colonel on his right arm. She glimpsed the distinctive badge he wore which displayed a rose surrounded by a crown flanked by what looked like laurel leaves with the Latin motto *Manui Dat Cognitio Vires*. Written above were the words, "Intelligence Corps". Riley wondered which rock he had crawled out from under. The other new arrival looked very familiar, but she couldn't place the face. He was mid-forties, weak jaw, collared shirt with cravat, chinos and brogues. The way he smiled at everyone and shook their hands, reminded her of a politician, like visiting royalty.

Riley was curious to know more and followed the group through the entrance and courtyard, trying to listen in on their conversation, but their voices were low and muffled. They went through into the canteen and closed the door behind them.

"Who's all that lot then?" asked Scottie, his arms crossed, trying to peer through the window.

"Beats me. But the guy at the back I recognise. Wasn't he our local MP or something?"

"It wouldn't surprise me. After Armstrong's little speech last night, your guess is as good as mine," said Riley wearily.

"There's no way Jack will just let them take this place away from us. He wouldn't. I don't care how many soldiers they have. Over my dead body," suggested Tommy.

"Let's hope it doesn't come to that. Who were those other men with Peterson?" asked Scottie.

"Anders you know," said Riley. "He's the guy from the *Maersk Charlotte* who always comes bearing goodies. If you need anything, he's your man. Professor Nichols is the scientist guy Jack was talking about. Him and his team are leading the research into the virus. The military guy I've never seen before. Did you see the insignia? He's military intelligence."

"Now there's a contradiction in terms right there," laughed Scottie.

Zed joined them, bringing three cups of coffee and winking at Scottie. "What I wouldn't give to be a fly on the wall, eh? What do you reckon they're talking about in there?"

"Evacuating us civilians to the island, probably. Knowing Jack, he'll not put up much of a fight. For the 'greater good' or something. Rolled over and handed this place on a platter to the military, without so much as a whimper. Everything we've worked hard for, gone. Just like that."

"He doesn't have much choice though does he? What are we going to do, fight them?"

The door opened and Jack stuck his head out. "Zed? Riley? Can you come in and join us? There's something they want to talk to you two about."

He disappeared back inside, leaving Riley and Zed frowning

at each other. Riley shrugged her shoulders and followed Zed into the dining hall. Inside Armstrong, Peterson, Anders, Flynn, the Professor and the two others were finishing up their conversation. Flynn raised his eyebrows at Zed playfully, watching him coming in.

"Thanks for joining us," said Peterson, interrupting the others.

"Quick introductions. Zed and Riley, I think you know these gentlemen," pointing round the table at Anders and Armstrong. "The other two you may not know. This here is Colonel Abrahams and at the end you will recognise local MP, or should I say, former Member of Parliament, David Woods."

The two strangers stared at Riley and Zed without acknowledgement. Riley was wracking her brains, trying to remember what she knew of David Woods. Right wing, strong views on immigration, always railing against Europe. It struck her as ironic really. She wondered whether his stance had softened in the face of the migration crisis on their doorstep. The boot was on the other foot now the surviving British population were in transit, trying to reach the island.

"Colonel Abrahams is working closely with Professor Nichols here to make sure he gets the resources and manpower his research team needs. Colonel, perhaps you can elaborate and explain why we're all here."

"Happy to," he said tersely. "Either of you ever heard of Porton Down?"

He watched both of them shake their heads. For Riley, it rang a bell, somewhere she had been on holiday years ago as a child was her best guess. Zed's expression was blank. If he did recall anything, he was giving nothing away.

"Nope? Okay, well Porton Down was an old Ministry of

Defence facility up near Salisbury. They specialised in research into biological and chemical warfare. Highly classified, top secret stuff. It was one of the sites that the government stockpiled vaccines and stores in case of an attack or outbreak. Stands to reason that they should still have equipment and resources that we could use. We've been unable to establish contact with the team there, but we're hoping the facility is still operational."

"The reason the Colonel knows so much about the place," said Armstrong, taking over, "is that he was stationed there for a number of years. Knows the place like the back of his hand. Still has some contacts and clout there."

"Our plan," continued the Colonel, "is to lead a reconnaissance mission up there. Make contact with the Porton Down team and report back on their status. With any luck, they'll be able to help us out. If we really get lucky, they'll have resources and research which could accelerate things tremendously."

"That's great to hear, but what does it have to do with the two of us?" asked Riley puzzled.

Peterson looked straight at Zed. "Care to take that one?"

Zed remained poker-faced, a picture of innocence.

"So there's nothing you would like to add here?" Armstrong cocked his head, waiting for Zed to answer, but he was either not following or playing dumb, Riley wasn't sure which.

"Very well." He unfolded a printed sheet with redacted information on it.

"Zedekiah Joseph Samuels, intelligence analyst at the Ministry of Defence, '94 to 2007. Three years with counter-terrorism division, four with DSTL, specialist in chemical and biological weapons programmes. This ringing any bells for you yet, Zed?"

"That's me, but I seriously think you're clutching at straws. I was an analyst, very low level," claimed Zed, without blinking.

Armstrong lent forward, squinting at the scanned document. "Says here you left the MoD rather suddenly and joined a US biotech start-up, PharmaT Ventures. There was an investigation into the nature of your departure. Rumours that PharmaT was bankrolled by the Israelis. Nano-technologies, cutting edge research. All seemed to be hushed-up. Couldn't find any further details in our records. Seemed to have been scrubbed. Someone might say whitewashed."

"PharmaT had contracts with the US Army. One hundred per cent legitimate. There was no hint of impropriety."

"So why the threat of action by the MoD?"

"Oh, just a grudge playing out from a superior officer. He questioned my motives for leaving. Left a hole in his organisation or something."

"Still, all seems a bit fishy if you ask me, leaving like that. In a bit of a hurry, were you?"

"I'd done my time. Was ready for something different."

"Sorry, you're saying this man was a spy?" chuckled Riley, turning her head towards him. "You certainly kept that quiet. I thought you were a teacher for God's sake."

"I was a teacher, Riley. The MoD job was years ago," he glanced at her for support before looking back at the others defiantly. "Listen, this was all a long time ago. What possible use could all that be now?"

"Let's stop kidding around," cautioned Peterson. "I think you know where we're going with all this."

"Trust me, I really don't," said Zed, raising his eyebrows in disbelief. Riley was watching him very carefully, certain now that he was not telling the whole truth.

Armstrong grabbed the sheet of redacted copy from Peterson.

"We know you also spent time at Porton Down. You were part of a special team based there for two years. Colonel Abrahams remembers you by name, for heaven's sake. I had one of my men pull your file from the archive at Portsmouth. They still have paper copies of MoD service records you know, right up to the outbreak. There's no point denying it. Why would you lie about this?"

Zed said nothing, staring at each of them in turn. His shoulders seemed to slump, relaxing a little, before letting out a big sigh.

"Okay. Listen, it's true that I spent a short spell at Porton back in the Nineties. So what? If I thought anything from back then could help, don't you think I would have mentioned it?"

"What about Project Wildfire?" asked Colonel Abrahams, dumping a brown folder on the table top with a reassuring thud. "You don't think that has any relevance?"

Zed was speechless. It had been a long time since he'd heard that name.

CHAPTER TWELVE

Riley and Zed had been asked to wait outside the canteen while the others discussed next steps in private.

"So when were you thinking of telling us you were James Bond?" sneered Riley, shaking her head.

Zed laughed awkwardly. "You've got it all wrong Riley. I was an analyst, not a field operative. I worked behind a desk, okay?"

"So you say."

"Riley, I'm telling you, I wasn't jetting around the world hunting down terrorists. Mostly I just worked from home, did what I was told, went wherever I was sent."

"Doing what then? Or can't you tell me?"

"I wrote reports. It was intelligence gathering for the Ministry of Defence. I had a security clearance that meant I could review sensitive documents."

"But on what?"

"All sorts of stuff I could never talk about. Well, I don't suppose it really matters any more, but still. I was on the MoD's books as a special investigator. I was one of their go-to people for biological and chemical weapons research programmes."

"Do you mean like WMDs? Iraq war? That sort of stuff?"

"Exactly. Pretty much every rogue nation had an illegal

weapons programme that contravened various international conventions. Our job was to figure out what they were working on, how advanced they were in their research and, if necessary, to call in a strike to shut it down."

"I thought that was all fiction. Are you seriously telling me that in this day and age countries were still working on weapons of mass destruction? Unbelievable."

"Sure, of course. You'd be surprised how many nations had clandestine programmes, including the UK, although no one would ever admit to it officially."

"So those conspiracy theorists were right all along?"

"Not exactly. But a lot of stuff went on that never made the papers. Most of what I worked on was classified. We investigated all kinds of weapons programmes, anything from biological agents, small pox, anthrax, designer viruses, you name it. Once we had identified the locations of their research and production facilities, boom, a drone would be despatched to take them out. Or, if they couldn't risk a direct strike, say in China or Russia, then a cyber-attack would be launched. Remember Stuxnet? There were plenty of malicious worms and computer viruses designed to target specific machinery and systems used in the supply chain. We were pretty good at it."

Riley was staring at him open-mouthed.

"I'm seeing you in a totally new light. So just to be clear, your role in all this was desk-based? You're telling me you were never sent into the field to hunt down enemy operatives?"

Zed laughed, enjoying her renewed interest in him.

"Listen, I had some standard MoD training for people in my line of work. Just routine stuff like counter espionage and self-defence. I think they were worried we were going to be recruited by the Russians or Chinese, blackmailed into betraying state secrets or something. But no, I never got anything that would have been really useful like weapons or combat training. I keep telling you, I wasn't a soldier. I didn't do field work."

"Pull the other one, Zed. I was always suspicious why you seemed to know so much about how things worked: the military, agriculture, medicine, infrastructure."

"I was a science teacher. I paid attention, okay? My training gave me good instincts, taught me how to think, how to reverse-engineer how stuff works. If you have that curiosity then you figure things out. Most people you meet just didn't care how an engine worked or how crops were grown in the field, why diseases spread in some countries but not others. I suppose I became a student of human nature and what makes people behave in the ways they do."

"I get it, you're smarter than the rest of us," she said, shaking her head dismissively. "So tell me, what is this Porton Down place? And why have I never heard of it?"

"It was one of the MoD's military research facilities. They did all kinds of testing to prepare the country against likely threats. You name it. E coli, anthrax, nerve agents. Top secret stuff mostly. They were the ones who always got a bad rap for testing stuff on animals, primates, guinea pigs. Remember the protests? Activists picketing scientists? They only knew half of what was really going on down there."

The door opened and Jack came out, looking Zed up and down. "Well, you certainly kept that quiet, eh Zed? Still waters run deep. Intelligence analyst? Who would have thought it?" he said, slapping him on the back.

"It hardly seemed relevant, Jack. We all had lives before coming here. It doesn't change who we are."

"Come on, they want you both to come back in."

Riley and Zed followed Jack and stood by the wall waiting for their turn for questions. Peterson finished a private conversation, tapping the folder in front of him. He leaned in closer and whispered something inaudible in the Colonel's ear before looking up and smiling at Riley and Zed.

"The Colonel was just filling me in on Project Wildfire. Perhaps you would care to add some colour?"

"My memory is a little rusty but from what I can recall, Wildfire was a DSTL research programme born out of the second Iraq War. Officially, they never found any Weapons of Mass Destruction and politicians and analysts like me took all the blame for overestimating Iraq's capabilities. But I can assure you that the intelligence reports ahead of the invasion were confirmed. The grounds for war were undeniable, they just couldn't release that kind of operational intelligence, especially as it related to ongoing programmes. It simply became more convenient to publicly claim that no weapons were found. It was less dramatic that way."

He looked out of the window, as if retelling this story was in some way distasteful, painful even.

"Saddam was already at an advanced stage. He had stockpiled warheads and delivery mechanisms, the infrastructure of a fully-functional chemical and biological weapons programme. Tens of thousands of litres of anthrax were found, but that was only the tip of the iceberg. We had evidence they were working on something more deadly. A clear and present danger to the West if left unchecked. We concluded that within three to five years, he would have been ready to launch an attack on Israel or one of his other enemies in the region. If those weapons were to be smuggled to the West or fall into the wrong hands, then the death toll would have been unimaginable. Or at least that was the fear. When the Allies located Saddam's research and production facility in Baghdad, all of the data and samples were removed for safe disposal and incineration. Off the record, the live samples they found were never destroyed. Instead they set up Project Wildfire to continue the research."

"Why Wildfire? What was so special about this Iraqi programme that the Allies wanted to maintain it. Surely the technology and research in the West were much more advanced?"

"Yes, and no. The Iraqis were not acting alone. They almost certainly had help from the Russians or Chinese. Amongst all the different programmes we uncovered, there were some that were less conventional, shall we say."

"Less conventional than anthrax?" sneered the Colonel.

"Theoretically, they were attempting to weaponise the flu virus, but for so many reasons it was flawed. They were obsessed with the idea of designing a virus to specifically target the West. It was entirely impractical. In reviewing their research, our own teams at Porton and other DSTL facilities dismissed their ideas as unworkable, their scientists as crackpots."

"What happened to the Iraqi team who were working on this?"

"It was rumoured that they were the subject of extraordinary rendition to the US. They were unquestionably debriefed in the UK but what happened next is still a mystery. Perhaps they were flown on to a secret facility in the States where they would continue their research. But I never believed that. Last I heard, Project Wildfire was mothballed, shut down."

"Officially, that's correct," said the Colonel tapping the cover of the report. "Project Wildfire was cancelled, its funding withdrawn. But I'm not so sure."

"What makes you suspicious Colonel?" asked Peterson.

"When I was at Porton Down, there were all kinds of active programmes that even I didn't have access to. They were compartmentalised for security reasons. Most teams worked in isolation, unaware of what others were working on in the labs next door. We were sworn to secrecy, warned never to discuss our work. It is entirely possible that Project Wildfire just went underground. The only people who would know for sure are still at Porton. If they're even still alive."

Peterson leaned forward, staring directly at Zed.

"Zed, we're putting together a special recon mission and we want you to be part of it. We need a team to go to Porton Down. You'll accompany Colonel Abrahams and Professor Nicholas, make contact with whoever is in charge there, assess the situation and the status of their own research and report in. Either we bring back the equipment and samples we need to continue their research back on the island, or we share what we know with Porton Down, pool our resources and evacuate their team. They'll be safer at Newport. I'm sending Sergeant Jones and his Seal team with you to provide security and guidance if things get hairy. They're trained for these types of missions. You'll be in good hands."

"But Lieutenant, Porton Down is miles away. The roads through the forest are dangerous, impassable even. How do you propose we get a team of this size there and back? Let alone transport all their equipment back to the island."

"We'll fly you up there. But depending on what you find when you get there, we'll need you to requisition vehicles to bring back the equipment and any personnel with you. Our plan is to meet you near Totton, just outside Southampton, where we'll have boats ready to transport the men and equipment to the island and on to the hospital."

"Why me?" asked Riley. "What do you need me for?"

"Because Jack tells me you're one of the best he's got."

Riley looked back wide-eyed, enjoying the compliment. Peterson pulled out a handwritten sheet with her name at the top. "With all that testosterone on board, we need someone who can keep those men in check. It says here you have medical training in first aid, specialist counselling and physiotherapy for veterans with post-traumatic stress and other mental health issues. You are also weapons-trained. We're not sure what we're going to find at Porton Down. You would be an asset to the team."

He smiled as she raised her eyebrows, a grin spreading across her face.

"Well, God help us then."

"That's the spirit. Listen up," said Peterson leaning forward with some animation. "This could be our Hail Mary shot. Porton Down may well be the breakthrough we've been waiting for."

They all nodded wearily. They had all heard optimistic claims like this before. They had grown cynical over the years.

Jack relented. "It's a risk, but one we need to take."

"Hail Mary indeed," whispered Riley, as they turned to leave, nudging Zed in the ribs.

CHAPTER THIRTEEN

After a couple of miles of tarmac, the open-top army truck carrying Heather and the other new arrivals turned off the main road to Newport on to a muddy farm track. They were headed towards a cluster of farm buildings in the distance, following a convoy of three other identical trucks. It was standing room only. Forty or fifty of them were tightly packed together, holding onto anything within reach. The truck lurched violently to one side, bouncing over a mound of earth. Heather was thrown against the elbow of a gangly adolescent who pushed her away. She clutched at her midriff, temporarily winded.

Since her separation from her brother Connor, she had been crying softly into the damp hood of her jacket. What were they going to do to him? What did they do with the infected, if that's what he was? Would they care for them, feed them? Or just leave them to die, like animals? She was sure he wasn't properly sick. If he had it, then she would have it too, and she had none of the symptoms. She had to believe it was just a cold, or, at worst, a fever. Why wouldn't they listen to her?

When their mum had got sick two years ago, they had both been exposed to the virus. If they were going to catch it, they would have caught it back then. Rowan had said she might be one of the lucky ones who were immune. She had to believe that Connor would survive. She clung to that hope and it gave her strength.

She couldn't see any of the others from her Hayling Island group on the trucks and feared they were still stuck in Portsmouth when they closed the barrier to the ferry. There was a chance she would be taken to the same place as the other group from the caravan park, assuming they had made it this far. For the first time in many months, she felt completely alone and vulnerable. She looked around the faces in the truck, their bodies tightly pressed together, damp and steaming as their clothes began to dry out. She recognised the same indefatigability and humanity stripped bare. These people were beaten but not broken. Their spirits and good humour kept them going. They had survived this far and the prospect of salvation on the island carried them further. They were silent and hopeful, so close to safety.

Heather looked ahead down the track as the convoy slowed, approaching another checkpoint leading towards a newly constructed compound. Two soldiers emerged from what looked like a garden shed, dumped at an angle next to the roadway that offered some shelter from the wind and rain. Dark clouds hurried across the sky above their heads, but at least it had stopped raining. The guards were dressed in long, army green raincoats with rifles slung over their shoulders. They saluted the driver in the first truck and checked his paperwork before lifting the barrier and waving them forward through the open gateway. Either side was a hastily dug chain-link fence some twelve feet high that stretched around the compound, with wooden posts sunk into the grass and mud every three meters or so.

Ahead she could see row upon row of large green tents and beyond them a dozen timber-framed buildings set on newly-erected concrete foundations. It reminded Heather of a school summer camp she was sent on when she was eleven, to Normandy or someplace in the north of France. She remembered rock climbing, canoeing, water slides and swimming in freezing cold rivers and lakes, eating marshmallows and burgers round a camp fire, laughing with school friends. She smiled at the memory, wiping her nose with her sleeve. The whole compound looked like it had just been completed. Huge piles of building waste and freshly dug earth stood waiting to be cleared near the road and farm buildings.

They pulled up near a simple stone-built farm cottage set with four symmetrical windows either side of a door in its centre. Ivy climbed its walls from planters set in front. A stern-looking officer with grey hair and a red armband walked down the line of trucks, banging his hand against the side.

"Everybody out. Let's be having you. We don't have all day."

A woman in a beige Tilley hat, who might have been the farmer's wife, unhooked the board at the back of the truck and held her hand out to help the new arrivals down onto the hard. Heather waited patiently as the others shuffled their feet, moving slowly towards the tailgate. When it was her turn, she jumped down, grimacing as her boots splashed in a muddy puddle that was pooling under the truck, soaking her jeans in freezing water.

She brushed the worst of it off before it could soak in and joined the line of people queuing for supplies. Each was handed a blanket, a small bottle of water from a pallet wrapped in polythene and an energy bar from boxes stacked high, one bar per person. They trudged into the field and were split up into groups, six per tent. When the woman with the headscarf noticed Heather all alone, she pointed her and another older girl towards a family group huddled together with their arms around each other outside one of the tents. They were shepherded inside the canvas structure, its entrance flaps folded back to reveal an empty interior with a waterproof ground sheet stretched across the floor and an unlit paraffin lamp swaying from the centre. There was no furniture, no beds or mattresses. A pile of flat sheets of cardboard had been left inside for comfort against the cold hard earth. It wasn't much but it would be dry and warm after being exposed to the elements for the last few hours.

When it was her turn, she followed the older girl in front into the tent and picked up a long sheet of cardboard ready to sit on. The older girl snatched it from her hand and pushed her aside.

"Hey that's mine. Find your own."

Heather sat down on the cold earthen floor, running her hand over the bumps and grooves through the plastic. She glared at the girl nearest her who was making herself comfortable on the folded cardboard, wrapping her shoulders and head in the folds of a blanket. She looked about fifteen or sixteen years-old and physically much bigger than Heather.

The family of four were keeping themselves to themselves in the corner, watching their fellow occupants warily. Heather caught the kindly eye of the mother. She was cuddling her sons one on each side, rubbing their arms and backs to warm them. She noticed Heather shivering all alone and waved her over.

"Why don't you come and sit with us, dear. You'll get warm quicker that way. This is my husband Paul and these two are Joey and Rick."

Heather smiled at their kindness and moved across next to the smaller of the two boys. She scowled back at the older girl and unhooked the straps of her rucksack, placing it against the tent wall. She sat back against it, making herself as comfortable as possible in the close confines of the tent, wrapping the blanket round herself as she fought the cold.

"How old are you?" asked Joey. He looked to Heather to be about the same age as her.

"Thirteen. You?"

"Same. Where's your family?"

"Joey, don't you know it's rude to ask questions. Why don't you eat your snack and settle down, try and get some sleep?" said the mother.

"Honestly, it's ok," replied Heather disarmingly. "I don't mind talking about it. I came here with my brother, Connor, but he didn't make it through quarantine. They took him someplace else."

"What about your parents?"

"Mum and Dad were separated," she said with a shrug. "He was working away from home and then he moved out, or rather Mum kicked him out and we lived with her for a while. But then, she was one of the first to get sick in the first outbreak."

"What happened to your brother, was he infected?"

"He had a fever, but it wasn't the virus."

"Well, I wouldn't worry too much. As soon as his temperature drops and he's better, they'll soon realise it was just a cold," said the father, who sounded confident, like he might be a doctor or nurse.

"What about your father, do you know what happened to him?"

"No, not really. We thought he might come and find us, but he never came. We left notes and messages at our old home and with friends and neighbours."

"Maybe he's still searching for you. The whole world's been upside down. People are scattered all over the place. So where have you been living all this time? Has it just been the two of you? You and your brother?"

Heather looked down at her hands and wiped some mud on her jeans.

"It was really hard to begin with. Our next-door neighbour back home in Winchester looked after us, but when it all started breaking down, we drove down to Hayling Island, to a caravan she used to rent in the summer. We've been living there ever since. We came to Portsmouth this morning with our group, but we got separated."

"Well you're here now. I can't imagine what you've been through. You poor love. Come here and sit closer, you look freezing. Paul, why don't you go and try and find a hot drink or something? Nice cup of cocoa, that's what you need, dear."

"That would be great. Me and Connor have been talking about cake and tea all day."

Her voice caught in her throat, remembering her brother, thinking about what he must be going through, surrounded by people dying, pleading for help. She imagined him rocking backwards and forwards with his hood over his head, clutching his arms around his knees, like he did when he was scared. She used to read him extracts from 'The Hitchhiker's Guide to the Galaxy' which they carried with them. Connor used to love the story of the Ravenous Bug Blatter Beast of Traal who thought he became invisible if he closed his eyes or hid his head. It always used to make her laugh seeing him adopt this defensive pose, clenching his eyes shut. She used to comfort him by wrapping her arms round his chest from behind, enveloping him, like their Mum used to do. It seemed to comfort him and remind him of home. She so wished she could hug him right now.

"Come here and let me give you a hug, you poor brave girl. You can stick with us OK? We'll look after you, won't we boys?" she nodded at Joey and Rick who were smiling at her. They both looked completely disinterested. The prospect of another mouth to feed prompted a shake of the head from the father.

"Family's all we've got. We look out for each other, don't we boys? You're one of us now. OK?"

Heather nodded at her and felt her tired limbs begin to relax. She looked back at the adolescent girl who was lounging back on the cardboard, with the blanket covering her head and shoulders. She could just make out her eyes glaring at Heather, jealous of all the attention she was getting.

"Go on Paul. Get this girl a hot cup of something. Off you go now."

The father reluctantly got to his feet and brushed aside the flap of the entrance, sending a shower of raindrops down on his head. He marched up the path, muttering to himself, heading towards one of the wooden framed buildings which had smoke pouring out of the chimney on its roof.

A few minutes later, he returned with three cups of tea, in the company of a kind-looking man with an oval face and trimmed beard. He was carrying a clipboard under his arm. The man waited a few moments for the father to go inside and hand out the tea before knocking in a cheery "Shave and a Haircut" musical rhythm on the tent pole. He stuck his head inside with a grin like a Cheshire Cat, crouching down on his haunches. Heather found his good humour deeply irritating. In fact, considering the poverty of their situation, she considered his levity faintly disrespectful. He wrote down their full names, dates of birth and explained that he needed to ask them each a few questions. He started with the family, asking the adults about where they had come from, their education, their jobs, any training they had had, hobbies or skills, noting everything down in what looked to Heather like illegible scrawl. When it came to her turn, the questions were a little different. They wanted to know her parents' names, relatives, where they lived previously, and what she had studied at school before moving on to the other children.

When the bearded man had left, the two adults looked at each other, puzzled.

"What do you think that was all about? What will they do with all that information?"

"Well, we can't stay here forever. This is just a quarantine zone. A holding area. Anyway, who would want to stay here? Davy was saying..."

"Who's Davy when he's at home?" interrupted his wife.

"Lives three doors down. Anyway, stop interrupting. Davy was saying that we'll all be reassigned to work parties. They'll keep family groups together. There's a medical centre at Newport, so we'll probably go there on account of my training, as an anaesthetist. There's a fully functioning hospital there, so makes sense. Or else there are smaller medical centres and hospitals scattered around the island, so who knows, we might go there too."

"Do you know what's going to happen to people like me, with no family?" asked Heather.

"I heard that any unaccompanied children are being sent to a boarding school not too far from here in Ryde."

"That doesn't sound so bad, does it? You'll be with other children your own age. They'll look after you better than being stuck here with the rest of us," reassured the mother with a smile.

"But I want to work too. I don't want to go back to school. What use is learning about the world? Why does any of that stuff matter anymore?"

"Of course it still matters. If we're going rebuild then it'll be up to your generation. You're the future. You'll need to learn practical skills. How to fix stuff when it's broken, how to build houses, make tools, grow vegetables, that kind of thing."

"I suppose. But we won't have to learn languages or useless stuff like geography or history?"

"You probably don't realise it now, but all of that stuff is still important. It teaches you about the world, how to think, how to communicate. Okay, maybe learning French is less relevant right now, but your generation needs to understand what's gone before, to pass that knowledge on to future generations. Without that continuity, then thousands of years of progress risks being lost. Who's going to tell stories about Henry VIII or the Battle of Hastings if all that history stays locked away in libraries? Now more than ever, you'll need to learn to be self-sufficient, not to rely on others like we used to. We need to make what we've got last for a long time. The world is changing. We need to make sure that our future is secure. That there's enough food to feed everyone, that we have medicines to treat the sick, that we have fuel and water. All those things we took for granted."

"You said that everyone on the island has to work, has a job to do. What about us children?" asked Joey.

"I did say that. Thank you for actually listening for a change," nodded their father. "You two will have to go back to school, but you'll have chores to do too. Cleaning up, fixing things, the sort of jobs you used to do at home before all this. You're going to have to learn all about the world around you. How to hunt and fish, how to cook and clean, how to change a spark plug in an engine, how to defend yourself. How to splice rope, how to treat injuries and a million and one other things to help you survive and thrive."

"Will we get pocket money if we do real work?" asked Rick, the younger boy.

"I'm sure you'll get something," said Paul, ruffling the boy's hair. "Sweets or cake most likely. Don't you worry about that!"

They all stopped talking simultaneously as a strange sound, like an air raid siren, grew in volume until all the children covered their ears, wincing in mock pain. The noise continued for almost thirty seconds before slowly dying again. Voices could be heard throughout the camp shouting instructions.

"Lights out. You there, put that light out. Curfew."

The father checked his watch.

"It's only seven thirty."

"What are we meant to do now?"

"Rest, sleep if you can. If it's anything like today, they'll wake us at the crack of dawn. I wouldn't be surprised if we move out tomorrow. Reassigned to wherever they're sending us next."

Heather wriggled further under the blanket and lowered her heavy head on to the rucksack she was using as a pillow. It was wrapped in a filthy towel, but she found it more comfortable than the scratchy canvas against her skin.

"Good night," whispered Heather. The father mumbled a response, but from the snuffles, it sounded like the boys were already asleep.

She rolled on to her side and said a silent prayer for Connor. It felt good to be part of a family unit again. Like being part of a group, there was safety in numbers. People to look out for you. It reminded her of her father. She wondered whether he was still alive. Who knew? Maybe one day he would come for her. That's what she had always told her brother.

At bedtime, their father had always told them stories and Connor had insisted Heather kept up the tradition. She would repeat the half-remembered stories her mother or father had told them. About trips to faraway places, holidays by the seaside, about fantasy worlds, myths and legends. A world that seemed so distant and alien from her current situation. They had both revelled in the tales of kings and queens, princes and princesses, magical kingdoms, goblins, elves and dwarves.

In the distance, from one of the other tents, she heard someone humming a sad mournful tune. Heather blinked a tear from her eye as it ran down her cheek, falling on to the towel. The last few months, scraping a living out there, had been hard. She could admit that to herself now. She didn't have to pretend to Connor any more. She allowed herself to hope, to dream for the first time in too long. Going back to school seemed like an absurd notion, like eating with a knife and fork, or using conditioner in her hair. Yet, she wanted to believe that life could return to the way it was, that somehow everything would be alright again. She shook her head, refusing to accept that such a life was possible, before slipping into a restless sleep, tossing and turning on the hard, cold earthen floor.

CHAPTER FOURTEEN

Armstrong was true to his word and returned to Hurst Castle around lunchtime the next day, to address the remaining unanswered questions. Jack had consulted with his team and heard them out. There had been a robust exchange of views. No one liked what had been proposed, though by the end of the session they seemed resigned to their fate.

Leaving their adopted home and all they had worked so hard to build was a bitter pill indeed. Whilst the island undoubtedly promised them all a new start, no one looked forward to starting again from scratch. A phased evacuation to the island now seemed inevitable. The consensus seemed to be that the sooner it happened the better. Jack for one had volunteered to stay behind until the bitter end to oversee an orderly withdrawal. Several others raised their hands, offering to keep him company, putting off the inevitable.

By the time Armstrong joined the group, there was little left to be said. There were a few clarifying questions, assurances sought, details agreed. The two leaders shook hands and Armstrong thanked them all for their understanding.

Jack wandered outside to get some fresh air. It had been claustrophobic in there. He felt overwhelmed by a sense of foreboding. He was not one for holding grudges, but would not forget in a hurry that he had been backed into a corner, pressured into a decision he accepted, but didn't necessarily support. "For the greater good" was the expression used a little too frequently for his liking.

His head was still pounding from the vodka Anders had plied him with the night before. They had stayed up into the early hours playing cards in the lighthouse round Jack's kitchen table, putting the world to rights. The two men enjoyed each other's company. Anders was someone he trusted implicitly.

"You need to be careful Jack," cautioned Anders. "Pick your battles."

"But they ask too much. The Americans don't seem to care whose toes they trample on to get what they want."

"Listen Jack. We've been friends a long time. I've always stood up for you, supported you. You know that. But the mood on the Council is hardening. There is little scope for compromise here. The Allies are under a huge amount of pressure. The security situation in Portsmouth is deteriorating."

"I heard. They've been forced to deploy more resources to shore up each of the embarkation points and deal with the sheer volume of people surging towards the island. They simply don't have enough men trained to deal with a situation like this," said Jack accusingly.

"You can't fault their ambition though," said Anders. "But it seems that the pace of change has left them exposed."

"How so?"

"For starters, the first of the new recruits they've drawn from civilian ranks are still weeks away from operational effectiveness. The burden will fall hardest on the Royal Navy. The Americans have no more men to spare, they have their hands full already."

Jack nodded, stroking his beard, pondering the situation.

"Ironically," continued Anders, "they can ill afford to spread their resources even thinner by sending more men to Hurst, but they simply have no choice. In the end, the two squads they've sent here are a token gesture only to placate Peterson. He's been vociferous in his demands."

Badly under-strength, the two squads that had arrived from Portsmouth were made up of a rag-tag bunch of part-time soldiers and support staff who were being slowly whipped into shape by Corporal Ballard. They made up for their inexperience with an impressive collection of weaponry from the burgeoning armoury at Portsmouth naval base.

The two old friends stood on the rooftop of the Gun Tower, watching the soldiers struggle ashore, cradling a series of awkward loads between them. Two crates, labelled with a cryptic string of letters and numbers down one side, were hauled up to the roof top and unpacked. A few minutes later, an impressive looking M134 mini-gun was bolted into place by two engineers to admiring glances from those gathered to inspect it.

From this high vantage point, Ballard said it would have a sweeping field of fire covering both the Needles passage and the surrounding beach and mudflats. At the far end of the compound they also mounted a GPMG 7.62mm machine gun to cover the spit, alongside boxes of what looked like belted ammunition. Next to be unloaded came a mortar which Jack recognised from his navy days and a multi-purpose Javelin missile system which Anders said could be used against all manner of armoured vehicles, not to mention ships, helicopters, even tanks.

As the men brought more equipment and stores ashore from the jetty, the whole place seemed to bustle with military activity.

"With all the additional fire power, they're turning this place into a fortress again."

"That's the general idea. If they can secure the Western entrance, then they lock down the whole Solent into one big controlled exclusion zone. No one enters or leaves without explicit authorisation from command."

"I hear they're fortifying the beaches on the southern side of the island. It's all beginning to sound like something out of a World War II movie, with tank traps, machine gun nests, the works."

"That's the price of freedom, eh? Do you think, in time, you will miss this place, Jack?"

"Of course, Anders, this is our home. It would be like someone taking over the *Charlotte* and telling your people to leave."

"Perhaps. But, I think, like moving house, once your people are set up on the island, they will look back with fond memories. Trust me, in time, life will be better over there."

"Time heals most things, my friend. I hope you're right," he conceded with a sigh. "Armstrong tells me we will be well looked after. He says there are villages set aside for key workers far away from the refugee camps. Down in Ventnor or Shanklin, where there are beautiful views and farmland. He says it would be our own little slice of paradise. Still, it will never be quite the same as Hurst."

"Who knows, maybe this move will be for the best?"

Anders paused, chewing his lip, as if remembering something.

"And what will happen to your prisoner when you move? Surely, you can't take him with you?"

The relaxed smile on Jack's face seemed to evaporate at the question, like a cloud passing in front of the sun.

"I promised that man he would rot in his cell for the rest of his life. For what he did to my people, it's no less than he deserves."

"I hear Peterson has made repeated requests that you hand him over to their custody, but you have always refused. I don't get it, why keep him here? Surely it keeps the wound open, prevents it from healing? It seems a reasonable request."

"Because I don't trust Peterson. I would worry that there's an agenda. That he would be traded as part of some prisoner exchange. I know the Lymington hospital group have made enquiries but it's never going to happen. I'd rather see him executed than handed over."

"What about if he was exchanged for Terra? Would that persuade you?"

"Perhaps. For Terra, I might make an exception."

"I should like to meet this Damian King. I have heard so much about him. He is one of those figures that almost seems larger than life. I know he's repeatedly refused to talk about his part in the rebellion. Refused to take responsibility for what his men did here. But why?"

"Oh it's not such a mystery. He likes playing with people. That's why. He knows that it's important to me, important to all of us, that he shows remorse, that he repents in some way. He calls this place "The Tower" and likens himself to Sir Thomas Moore refusing to accept the Reformation. Calls me Cromwell to bate me. It's all a game to him, like it's one big joke. It's weird, like he's channeling the Tudor history of this place to give himself strength. I had to read up on my history just to follow some of his references. Did you know that Charles the First was kept prisoner here during the English Civil War? I only found that out because he kept asking to be called Charles."

"I like that. A man who knows his history is to be feared. Some say Damian King was a lawyer before all this, which might explain why he runs rings round his inquisitors."

"I wouldn't say that. He gives as good as he gets. He delights in probing for weaknesses. It's like a sport. To him, all emotion is weakness. Something to manipulate. He likes to twist the facts, play games. I've learned over the weeks since I've been meeting with him to give nothing away, to react to nothing he says. It riles him. If truth be told, I have no idea what he really thinks or believes, he's too cunning to give much away."

"Sounds like you've met your match. That you admire this guy perhaps?"

"I wouldn't go that far. To me, he's still the butcher of Hurst. Plain and simple, he's a murderer with sociopathic tendencies. But I'll say this, he's stimulating company, that's for sure. He has a brilliant mind. Reminds me of a commanding officer I once had. He was ex-military, steely-eyed. Great politician, always knew the right thing to say. Always seemed to be one step ahead of everyone else, as if he knew what was about to happen. Winterbottom was his name."

"It seems such a waste to have a man with his skills locked up in a dungeon. Doesn't the new world need men like him?"

"Not like him. He's twisted. So much bile, so much hatred bottled up inside. Believe you me, he's much better locked up. If he ever got loose again, he would turn this new world upside down. Even now, I'm convinced his influence extends beyond these walls, as if he's still pulling the strings."

"But how's that even possible? He has no contact with the outside world. Unless there's someone working with him, perhaps one of the soldiers. Is there anyone you don't trust?"

"I've had my suspicions. Changed the guard several times,

stuck with people I know are loyal. And yet, despite my precautions, he still knows more than he should."

"Intuition? Maybe he's just bluffing, trying to trick you into telling you what he needs to know."

"If he is bluffing, then he's very good at it."

"From everything you've told me, I wouldn't put it past him. If you would allow it, I would like to meet him."

Jack hesitated, but dared not refuse the request of his good friend.

"On one condition," insisted Jack. "That you tell him nothing about the outside world or what's been going on. I have carefully controlled what he learns from us about the Allied plans for Camp Wight. Agreed?"

Anders nodded his consent and the two men took one last look around the sweeping panoramic views of the island and Solent before bending double and climbing through the access hatch that led down the spiral staircase to the first floor. They descended the stone steps to the courtyard below and weaved through narrow passageways and sharp turns to reach the dry cellar where they were now keeping the prisoner.

Outside the makeshift cell was a guard sat engrossed in a paperback book. His page was lit by a shaft of sunlight from above that penetrated the darkness, casting a dull square on the stone paved floor. From inside they could hear a man whistling brightly. It was the tune to "It's a Long Way to Tipperary". Jack smirked and shook his head.

"He's in good humour today," said the guard, getting to his feet. "He was telling jokes earlier. Trying to get a reaction. I did as you asked Jack and ignored him."

"Well done. Don't engage with the prisoner. Follow the rules and you'll be fine."

"Yes Jack."

The whistling stopped abruptly and the prisoner called out in welcome.

"Ah Jack. My old friend's come to visit me and he's brought someone new. I don't recognise those footsteps. Come on, don't be shy."

The guard lit the Tilley lantern, passed it to Jack and unlocked the door to let them both inside, closing up behind them.

Jack held the lantern high above his head and located the prisoner in the far corner, sitting on his mattress wrapped in a grey blanket, a privilege he had granted him in return for good behaviour and his co-operation. The hours here were long and interminable, books and playing cards made all the difference. It had been weeks since he had seen daylight.

"If I'm not mistaken, you must be Captain Anders from the *Charlotte*."

Anders looked taken aback. "How did you know my name? Have we met before?"

"Just a wild guess. There's not much goes on round here that I don't know about. To what do I owe this pleasure?"

Anders flicked a glance at Jack who had not reacted in any way. Jack had seen it all before with the prisoner. Nothing surprised him anymore. Jack raised the lantern, noticing something different about the prisoner. He moved the light closer to illuminate his face and features.

There was heavy bruising around his left eye and his mouth was crusted in dried blood. Jack leaned closer, studying the prisoner's injuries through the glasses perched on his nose.

"Who did this to you?" asked Jack tersely, flicking his head back towards the door as if considering hauling the guard in here to give account of himself.

"It's hardly the first time," sneered the prisoner. "A couple of your boys paid me a visit earlier today. Mistook me for a punch bag. South African guy with a chip on his shoulder. Still getting his own back from his time in the hospital. Can't blame him really, Copper gave him a pretty good going over. He's got an understudy now, some young guy. A few bricks short of a full load that one. Very expressive with his fists."

"I'll have their heads for this. I'm sorry. I can assure you they acted on their own, they weren't here on my orders."

"Oh I believe you Jack. Not your style. You never were the violent type," he said with particular emphasis. He turned towards the new arrival. "So Captain Anders, how's my old friend Victor? I gather you two don't see eye to eye anymore."

Jack cautioned Anders with a glare.

"That's right. Jack doesn't like me talking to his friends. He's worried I might extract information. Learn what's really going on out there. Jack likes to think he's in control. Keeping me in the dark. Doesn't like me manipulating people. Isn't that right Jack? That's why he keeps me locked up in here."

"I keep you locked up in here because you killed twelve of my people."

"Hardly. It wasn't me who pulled the trigger, was it?"

"Make no mistake, you gave the order. Your people executed them in cold blood. They were unarmed, women and children."

"Let's not go over this again Jack. I told you, Copper was acting of his own volition. That guy is out of control. A ticking time bomb. He's the one to blame, not me. Anyway, this is all ancient history. Time to move on. Let's talk about something more interesting. How are things at Camp Wight, Captain?"

"I wouldn't know, I'm hardly a regular visitor," volunteered Anders before checking himself.

"I thought you and Jack were on the Council. You meet monthly with Armstrong, Peterson and the others. Isn't that what you told me Jack?"

"I told you nothing of the sort," said Jack, turning to Anders again. "He's fishing for information as usual. Don't fall for it."

"You're very uncooperative today Jack. Not your usual talkative self. Taking your forthcoming move to the island a little hard are we? Can't have been easy to hear. Still, it was only a matter of time before you had to move out, make way for people who can do the job properly. Amateur hour is over."

"Quite."

"And you Captain, what did you get in return for your cargo of humanitarian aid? Will you get a castle to live in?"

He waited expectantly for Anders to respond, shrugging his shoulders at his silence.

"Hmm. No, not your style. I don't detect much of an ego in you. Airs and graces not your thing? By the smell of you," he said, turning his nose up as he sniffed the air, "you like a drink. Your waistline suggests a healthy appetite. Still wearing a ring on your finger, but I'd warrant she died years ago. All those years away at sea were hard on her, no? She wanted children but you didn't. You were never around."

There was a flicker of anger in Anders' eyes.

"Those long dark winter nights on her own must have been hard. How did she die Captain? Was it suicide? No, more likely a long-term illness. Cancer? It was cancer wasn't it? Still, I suppose you made it back in time for the funeral. She would have appreciated that. It was the least you could do. Diverting to port and flying home when you heard the news. Her family never forgave you though, did they Captain?"

Anders kept silent throughout, trying to avoid betraying his thoughts or emotions, listening to the prisoner drive a ten-ton truck through his personal life.

"Just ignore him Anders. He's got a fertile imagination. Doesn't care what he tramples over to get a rise out of someone."

"I can't help it. You see, I see things. I can read you like a book. It's all there," he said waving his hand down Anders's clothes, studying him assiduously. "Even after all this time, the tells are as visible today as they ever were. Jack tries so hard to dissemble. He thinks that he can mislead me. Trick me into believing things that aren't true. Even now, you think I'll come round. Roll over and betray my own people. It isn't going to happen Jack."

"You're not half as clever as you think you are. Your arrogance is your weakness."

"Don't flatter yourself. It's not like I have a choice you know. Talking to you is slightly better than silence, but not much. I've grown to enjoy our conversations, Jack. I think of you as a friend. What would I do without you?"

"Your life means nothing to me. You're only alive because we cling to an outdated sense of justice."

"Justice?" laughed the prisoner. "That's rich coming from you. Whatever happened to guilty until proven innocent? Where was my fair trial? What you have here at the castle is medieval justice. Confess and we'll grant you mercy. Ha! That's more like a kangaroo court. Don't talk to me about justice, you don't know the meaning of the word."

Jack realised he was tensing again, feeling his chest tighten as his hackles rose.

"Come on," he motioned to Anders. "I think visiting hours are over. We've all had quite enough excitement for one day."

Jack noticed that Anders's bottom lip was quivering almost

imperceptibly. As he turned his head towards the door, Anders' eyes were glinting, full of tears. Jack had seen it before. The prisoner knew how to push people's buttons. He had a knack for winding people up at will.

Before he left, Jack reached down and snatched the blanket from around the prisoner's shoulders, shaking his head.

"I'll take that, thank you. I warned you, didn't I? Behave yourself or your privileges will be revoked."

"Take it," he sneered. "Good luck with the expedition up north Jack. Hope they find what they're looking for."

As the door slammed behind him, Jack had to wonder where on earth he was getting his information from. It was too good to be guesswork.

CHAPTER FIFTEEN

That afternoon, the storm had completely blown itself out to be replaced by a dull grey sky. Zed and Riley had said their goodbyes to the team and waited for the chopper that would be taking them north towards Salisbury and the military research facility at Porton Down.

They had been told to keep quiet about the reasons for the mission but the Hurst grapevine had circulated rumours of Zed's past. People seemed to look at him with new-found respect, as if his former role distinguished him somehow, elevating him beyond his more humble status as a secondary school science teacher.

Riley still had a hundred questions and Zed's good humour was wearing thin.

"Have you ever been on a nuclear submarine?"

"What? No, what do you think? What part of 'worked in an office' do you not understand?"

"Have you ever killed someone with a poisoned umbrella?"

"Stop already. And no, I never had an exploding watch either, or drove an Aston Martin, or skied off a cliff or owned a PPK revolver, alright?"

"I bet you're good at poker. Ever had a casino account?"

"Okay, I did have a membership card for a casino in central London once, years ago. That hardly makes me a spy though does it?"

"Hmm, I thought so."

"That's it. I'm not answering any more of your stupid questions."

Riley was enjoying getting a rise out of Zed.

"What are you going to do about the Sister? You can't put her off forever," said Zed, trying to change the subject.

"Oh I left her in Tommy's capable hands. Jack's agreed to have a chat with her later. Listen to her demands. Joe knows all about it. He'll sit in with Jean and make sure she gets a fair hearing. I've told Jack already that Jean had nothing to do with the fire. First they accused us of arson, for goodness' sake. It was an accident. I don't get why they won't just accept that. Why the witch hunt?"

They both looked round as they heard the distant sound of a helicopter.

"Right, this must be our ride. Equipment check?" said Zed.

Riley stood up and gave him a twirl with her arms stretched wide. As instructed, she was wearing a black waterproof jacket, hooded top, several layers underneath and dark cargo trousers and boots. This was what she called her "ready for anything" outfit. A large Bowie knife was strapped to the side of her rucksack which she shook to make sure there were no rattles. The bag contained extra clothing, a sleeping bag, some dry snacks and a water bottle. She wasn't carrying a pistol. Zed had told her not to bother. They would be well protected by the soldiers. Zed reciprocated and allowed Riley to inspect him and check his equipment was properly secured. He had insisted on bringing his double-headed axe with him.

The Seahawk landed briefly, long enough to slide the door back and allow them both to climb on board. Inside was a squad of six US Navy Seals, Professor Nichols, and Colonel Abrahams together with a pilot and navigator upfront. Two of the Seals nearest the door didn't move and stared at Riley as if they didn't approve of civilians, let alone a woman, making the trip. They stared down at Riley before reluctantly shuffling their backsides up on the bench seat. The Seal team leader, Sergeant Jones, leaned across from opposite and slammed the sliding door shut again, nodding at them both by way of cursory welcome.

As they took off, Riley enjoyed stunning views of the castle and Hurst spit. Gaining altitude, they headed north over the salt marshes towards Keyhaven, dipping forward as the helicopter accelerated. The noise inside the aircraft from the turbine engines was so loud Riley could barely hear herself think. Sergeant Jones pointed at the oversize headphones, with a microphone attached, hanging on a peg above her head. Suddenly, the active noise-cancelling headphones eliminated the ambient sounds and she could hear the pilot relaying course and speed back to a controller on the *Chester*.

"Good luck gentlemen."

"Copy that. We'll report in as soon as we reach Porton Down."

Over the intercom, Riley heard what she assumed was Colonel Abrahams' voice and it took her a second to realise that he was asking her a question. She looked up and saw him waving at her.

"Good to have you with us Riley. Have you met Sergeant Jones and the rest of the team?"

Riley shook her head and held out her hand to shake Jones's.

"You can call me Sarge, or Pete if you prefer. Me and my

team will be your escort for today's mission. Don't worry, you're in good hands. We do this kind of thing a lot. I'll introduce you to the rest of these reprobates when we get boots on the ground. Just stay close to me."

"Thanks, but you don't need to babysit me. I can look after myself."

"No question about that. I've heard all about you and Zed. You have quite a team at Hurst. I've met a few of them now. Jack, Sam, Terra."

He looked away, nervous he might have said the wrong thing. Sergeant Jones had been part of the hostage rescue team that had tried to save Terra at Osborne House, but Briggs and his men had disappeared into the night with a handful of hostages. "Bad business that. Sorry for your loss."

"Don't be. Terra and I never saw eye to eye. Anyway, I thought Briggs was still holding her and the others hostage. Human shields I heard or waiting to trade them for something. Or was that just a rumour?"

"I heard that too. Let's hope you're right."

Riley was amused by his overconfidence but liked the fact that he was avoiding being patronising or condescending. In her experience, military types tended to look down on their civilian counterparts and saw them as baggage, or worse, treated them like children who couldn't possibly understand. Perhaps he had read her sheet and knew she was different, an important asset to this team.

"How long will it take to get there?"

"Shouldn't be more than an hour. Colonel Abraham has been kind enough to brief us on the facility and best places to land."

"Do you have any idea what state the facility is in? Do you think it's still operational?"

"Yes mam. We believe that the facility will be operational. They would have been hit by the virus, same as the rest of us. But we understand that there's an underground complex and sufficient stores to sustain a team there for this length of time, so fingers crossed we'll find what we need."

"Have we been able to contact them at all?"

"Not yet. Either their radio is out or the range was too great. Hard to say. We're still trying. When we get closer, we should have more luck. Make sure they're expecting us. It wouldn't do for them to get the wrong idea. The last thing we need is friendly fire as we try to land."

"How do you know they're going to be friendly then?"

"We don't, but we'll give them a wide berth as we circle and see if we can't establish contact before we land. We're hoping they'll remember Colonel Abrahams from his time at Porton Down."

She relayed their conversation to Zed and he took the headphones from Riley and spoke to the Seal team leader. Riley tried to lip read but couldn't follow what they were saying. Zed spoke at length in response to Jones's questions before falling silent again. Riley pointed at her ear and gestured for him to explain. He exposed one ear and shouted back "Just getting to know each other, that's all."

Riley looked out of the window again to pass the time, as they flew over the New Forest. Autumn was her favourite time of year. She loved the change of seasons. Considering how days and weeks mattered little any more, other than marking time, the seasons were what counted. The change in the colour of the landscape was spectacular. Riley loved the bird's eye view of the forest stretching out beneath her in all directions and the patchwork of colour. She remembered from Biology classes years ago that as the chlorophyll in the leaves broke down, their green colour disappeared, morphing into yellows, browns and oranges, in a gorgeous display of autumnal technicolour.

She rested her head against the fuselage, remembering her last trip into town, the sackful of horse chestnuts she had brought back for the children, enjoying their squeals of delight as they played conkers in the courtyard. It had been one of her favourite schoolyard games growing up. The prize-winning conker she had when she was twelve. Her father had taught her how to drill out the centre and fill with wood glue. "Don't tell your mother," he used to say. "It'll be our little secret." He had died not long before the outbreak, probably for the best. The weak and infirm had stood little chance of survival. If the virus didn't kill them, then the lawless aftermath did. Only the strong had survived.

Riley must have dozed off for a few minutes, lulled to sleep by the vibrations. She woke up with her head slumped against Zed's shoulder. He pushed her upright again and she scowled at him with one eye open. Outside, they were flying low over open fields beyond the Forest. They were slowing down, losing altitude.

The Seal team members straightened in their seats and started running through equipment checks, relaying final instructions. She noticed Zed nodding, they were landing in five minutes. She fiddled with the strap to her rucksack between her knees, suddenly nervous about what they might find at the facility.

As they came in to a hover, slowly circling the buildings beneath them, she heard the pilot's voice over the noise in the cabin, enunciating clearly, presumably hailing the controller at Porton Down. He repeated the call several times without response. Riley grabbed the headphones off Zed, desperate to listen in to any exchange.

There was no sign of movement beneath them. They were beginning to think the base was deserted. The pilot tried one more time and much to the relief of all those on board, a voice from below greeted the helicopter.

"Seahawk AH-57, you are cleared for landing. Be advised landing zone is hot. Say again; landing zone is hot. After set down, send passengers to the main building as quickly as you can. Our team will be ready to meet you."

Riley wondered to herself what a hot landing zone was. Either way, it didn't sound good.

Looking beyond the high fence surrounding the facility, she noticed dozens of people emerging from the tree line. Then from all around, others appeared from hiding places, craning their heads, looking up at the helicopter as it circled. Many of them started running towards a large gap in the fence, heading towards the landing area. Perhaps they thought they were being rescued?

The pilot looked animated, relaying instructions to Sergeant Jones as they came in to land. A soldier leaned over Riley and pulled the heavy sliding door open, peering down at the ground. As soon as they touched down, he leaped out and helped the others down as quickly as possible, pointing them towards the building ahead of them. Riley glanced round the back of the helicopter as they advanced as a group, soldiers on either side shepherding them forward, and saw hundreds of people running towards them.

"Keep going," shouted Jones, waving them on.

Behind her, Riley heard the distinctive heavy beat of the rotor blades as the power was applied before lift-off, just before the crowd reached the landing zone. As the helicopter banked away, they became aware of the shouts and footsteps of the chasing mob. Glancing round, she shuddered seeing them closing the gap so quickly, their eyes wild, improvised weapons held in front as they ran headlong in their direction.

Professor Nichols was the weak link. An arthritic knee ensured he could manage no better than a slow shuffle, helped along with an arm across his back.

Ahead of them set to the right of the main block was a large reinforced sliding bay door which Riley imagined must lead to a loading area. A siren sounded and an orange light started flashing above the door as it slid slowly open. Two soldiers emerged and took up kneeling positions either side, taking aim at the approaching crowd.

"Come on, come on," encouraged a tall bearded figure standing just inside as the lead member of the group reached the doorway.

One of the kneeling soldiers fired a short burst above the heads of the approaching mob and the lead figures faltered mid-step, suddenly unsure of whether they should go any further. One of the crowd, who might have been their leader, was gesticulating and shouting something. Among a hail of expletives, Riley could make out the word 'cowards' as she raced forward.

As soon as the last of their group was safely inside, the soldiers double timed it back to the entrance and a large electric motor sealed the heavy bay doors closed. Momentarily, before their eyes adjusted, it was pitch black inside. Some emergency lighting overhead blinked on, bathing the group in a dull orange light.

"Welcome to Porton Down. We've been expecting you," said the tall bearded figure with a patch over one eye, staring at them suspiciously, his finger covering the trigger on his revolver.

CHAPTER SIXTEEN

Inside the semi-darkness of the loading bay, the Porton Down team stood facing the new arrivals in silence, waiting for their commanding officer to arrive. The two soldiers who had covered their approach were breathing heavily. They looked out of shape and pale from too many hours living underground, thought Riley. They were eyeballing the visitors warily, unsure what to make of them.

Sergeant Jones and his men set down their back packs and broke out their rations, glugging water greedily from their canteens. Jones offered Riley his bottle but she politely declined, reaching for her own. Professor Nichols and Colonel Abrahams were catching their breath, their backs against the reinforced door, whispering between them.

Riley looked around the covered hangar and noticed a large number of trucks and armoured vehicles in various states of disrepair. Engine parts were scattered around the front section of a Humvee. It was being cannibalised to repair other more serviceable engines. Many of the trucks' windows were fitted with reinforced grills to protect their windscreens against stones and bricks thrown their way. Their front sections had welded metal plates and reinforced bumpers capable of clearing obstacles and deflecting bullets.

High above them, just beneath the corrugated roof, a door opened and three uniformed men strode purposefully along a raised walkway that led from the guard tower that overlooked the landing area. Before the door swung shut again, they could hear the distant hubbub of a crowd who had refused to clear the area, unintimidated by impotent threats of violence, their raised voices shouting insults. Their challenge to Porton Down's willingness to defend itself was met with a burst of heavy machine gun fire. Those who had ventured too close to the loading area scattered, screaming.

The uniformed men descended the steps two at a time. One carried an SA-80 rifle, the others had side arms. The group came to a halt in front of Abrahams and the Professor.

"Colonel Abrahams, I presume? My name is Major Donnelly," he said, saluting the superior officer. "May I present Lieutenant Stephens and Staff Sergeant Heggarty."

Abrahams advanced towards him and the two officers stiffly saluted, before introducing the rest of the team, each coming to attention.

"Your arrival caused quite a commotion outside. It's been a while since we had visitors by air. The sound of the helicopter seems to have emboldened the local population. They haven't had the nerve to enter the base en masse in daylight hours before. They must think you're part of some rescue mission."

The Major had a large scar down the right side of his face which seemed to stretch his cheek taut, dragging the corner of his mouth upwards. It was almost like he was smirking at them, but Riley recognised this type of facial injury from her time counselling veterans. For the others, it took them a while longer to get used to his disfigurement, each realising in turn with embarrassment that they were staring. Otherwise, the Major certainly looked lean and in good shape. His military-issue light brown shirt was rolled up at the sleeves revealing thin angular arms and elbows. His manicured hands looked more like those of a scientist than a soldier.

"We're grateful for you receiving us at short notice. I trust you got our message?" asked Abrahams.

"We did. Although, at first we weren't sure what to make of it. I understand you were stationed here a few years ago. Is that correct?"

"I served under Major Tomlins who was base commander about a decade ago. I was here for eighteen months as part of my rotation."

"Yes, Tomlins, my predecessor. Good man. Bad business, all that."

Abrahams looked at his shoes and grimaced. "He was a friend of mine. I graduated from Sandhurst at the same time as his brother. The family were devastated, two young girls. I kept in touch for a couple years after he died, but lost contact. I think she moved away. America wasn't it?"

"That's right. Anyway," he said clearing his throat, "I'm sure you haven't come all this way to reminisce about old friends. How can we help you today?"

"Major, we're here to requisition whatever supplies and men you can spare us. You see, Professor Nichols here has set up a research facility on the Isle of Wight and is assembling a team of scientists to further research the Millennial Virus in the hope of developing a vaccine. Right now, we're looking for all the help we can get. Lab equipment, samples, hardware, data. From my time here, I know that you have everything we need."

The Major nodded slowly but was giving nothing away. His face was a mask of indifference.

"Well, I'm afraid you've made a wasted journey then. I'm not sure we can be of much assistance."

"Major Tomlins, I'm well aware of the purpose of this facility. There's no point dissembling. We haven't knocked on the wrong door by accident. We're working in close partnership with the Royal Navy and our Allies from the *Chester*."

"Colonel, with all due respect, and please don't take this the wrong way, there's a chain of command. I have no authorisation to accommodate you and your men. The work of this facility is classified. Without top-level clearance, there's nothing I can do for you."

"I don't know if you've checked outside recently, but who do you think you're protecting? Out there there's anarchy and chaos. The Ministry of Defence is no longer functional. The government, Prime Minister, the whole chain of command has fallen. We're as close to a functioning government as you'll find. You have a duty to your country to offer assistance."

"Colonel, I don't need a lecture about duty. This base has maintained operational efficiency despite daily attacks. We've had little or no support from the MoD or anyone else, but we've stuck to our task."

"No one's questioning your commitment, Major. The work your team does here is invaluable. We're sure a collaboration, a pooling of resources, would accelerate the search for a vaccine."

"Really? I think you'll find you're overestimating the capabilities of this facility. We're a relic of a by-gone age. Our equipment is outdated. Most of it is barely serviceable. We've had years of budget cuts and a lack of investment. I seriously doubt we can be of much use at all. These days we're more a storage facility and archive than anything else. We were mothballed years ago."

Riley had been watching Zed coming to the boil like a pressure cooker. He had been clenching his fists, listening to the Major's lies, shaking his head. She wondered what Zed knew.

"Why do you insist on maintaining this charade?" spat the Colonel. "Do you really think we'd be here if we didn't know what Porton Down is? We know what research you do here."

"I'm afraid you're mistaken. We might be able to loan you some test tubes and samples, but that's about as far as it goes."

Zed stepped forward, unable to contain himself any longer. "We all know what you do here. Fact: Porton Down has the largest stockpile of deadly pathogens, nerve agents and other chemical and biological weapons anywhere in Europe."

The Major turned to face Zed as if noticing him for the first time, his eyes narrowing disapprovingly.

"I'm sorry. And you are?"

"May I introduce Zed Samuels. He was a contractor to the MoD for several years." said Abrahams. "He was part of the Chemical, Biological, Radiological, Nuclear CBRN team, as a special investigator. Spent some time here on secondment to the Defence Science and Technology Laboratory."

Zed took over from Abrahams. "What about all the testing programmes run out of Porton? No one knows more about biological weapons than you do."

The Major was playing dumb, still refusing to cooperate.

Zed turned to face the Professor and Colonel Abrams.

"The bulk of the work I did on Project Wildfire was based here."

"I'm sorry," interrupted the Major, "Project Wildfire?"

"Wildfire was a covert feasibility study to determine whether it was possible to weaponise the flu virus," answered the Colonel.

"You've got to be kidding," laughed Riley in disbelief. "Why would anyone want to weaponise the flu virus? It would be unstoppable."

"Exactly," said Zed. "But we knew other countries were conducting similar research, so it was only a matter of time before someone figured it out. Wildfire was considered a strategic priority. Its budget and operational detail hidden, its mission was to develop both the virus and an effective vaccine."

The Major glared at Zed. "You're seriously mistaken if you think we're somehow responsible for all this. You think we'd have sat on our hands if we had stockpiles of a vaccine and did nothing, watching people die all around us?"

"No one is accusing Porton of that," reassured the Colonel. "By all accounts, Project Wildfire was decades of work. There must be reams of data in your archives. The MoD spent millions of pounds working on this, off the books, of course. If it had been leaked that the UK government was secretly developing biological weapons, well, I'm sure you can imagine the headaches that would have caused."

"You have a moral duty to cooperate Major," added the Professor.

"Please," said Riley imploringly. "We really need your help."

There was a moment of silence as the Major stared at Zed, his bottom lip stiffening, as he seemed to weigh his options.

"I suggest we continue this conversation somewhere more private. I would need to check if such a programme ever really existed and whether anyone is still alive who worked on it. It's not something I'm familiar with. Most of the research programmes were shut down following the outbreak. We have a skeletal staff now. Our resources are limited as I'm sure you can understand. I suggest the four of you come with me and the rest stay here. Staff Sergeant, can you fix these men up with some hot food and somewhere to rest up?"

The Major invited Zed, Abrahams and the Professor to follow him.

"What about me?" said Riley.

"I'm sorry," apologised Abraham. "This is all classified information. It's best if you stay here with Sergeant Jones and his men."

With a shrug of his shoulders, Zed hurried after the rest of the group as they headed towards a security door with a keypad next to it which gave access to a long subterranean corridor stretching off into the distance. The Major entered a six-digit code and waited for the door to hiss open. Riley watched them leave and turned to face Jones.

"I guess I'm stuck with you lot then."

"That's cool, you can hang with us. Stick with the grunts. We'll keep you company," winked Jones and gestured her over to sit with the rest of the soldiers, who made space for her.

CHAPTER SEVENTEEN

It was a long walk through countless dimly-lit corridors, sparsely decorated concrete and brick walkways that led further and further into a maze of underground tunnels and rooms. There were very few people down here and the whole base seemed deserted. They stopped at another electronically operated security door with a small glass window reinforced with wire mesh that revealed a more modern interior beyond. The Major grabbed a security card that was attached to a piece of elastic secured to his belt and swiped it through the device. The screen turned from red to green and with a groan the security bolts top and bottom sprang open and the door slid back.

Inside, Zed could see a series of labs off to the right. To their left was a conference room and office suite beyond. The Major waved the group inside and followed them through to the conference room.

"Take a seat gentlemen. Jenkins, can you get our guests some coffee?"

He waited for his aide to leave before closing the door and taking a seat at the head of the large oval table set with more than a dozen swivel chairs. The room was austere with plasterboard painted white and piles of paperwork, lever arch files were stacked high on shelves that ran the length of one of the walls.

"Colonel Abrahams, Mr Samuels, Professor Nichols," he said addressing each of them in turn. "Before I can discuss any operational details about our work here at Porton, I'll need each of you to identify yourself. Do you have ID of any description about your person?"

"You've got to be joking," sneered Zed. "Last time I carried an MoD card was nearly a decade ago."

"Major, surely you can look us up on a database somehow?" asked the Professor.

"I'm afraid not, our protocol says that I can only..." started the Major.

"Protocol?" laughed the Colonel. "With all due respect, screw protocol. As the ranking officer, I'm giving you a direct order. Either you give my team access or I will have you relieved of your command. Is that clear?" insisted the Colonel.

The Major swallowed hard, eye-balling his superior.

"Very well," he conceded. "In the circumstances, I can bend the rules a little. Identify you another way. Make sure you are who you say you are. If you can write down your full names, ranks, serial numbers, departments you worked for, and any security clearances, then we can see what we can do."

He passed round some paper and pens and Zed, the Professor and the Colonel spent a couple of minutes writing down as much information as possible. Dates, locations, reporting lines. When they were done, the Major scanned the lines of text, nodding silently. He excused himself, closing the door behind him.

"Do you think he's going to help us?" asked Zed.

"If he doesn't, I'll have him arrested," said the Colonel tersely.

"This place hasn't changed a bit," said Zed, looking round the room. "It's like time has stood still down here."

"Don't be fooled by appearances, gentlemen. This is a state of the art facility. If they don't have the answers, I doubt anyone else in the country will. This is our best hope."

"I hope you're right," said the Professor.

After what seemed like an age, the Major came back in with three printouts of their MoD-issued photo IDs. He seemed satisfied that the three of them were who they said they were and visibly relaxed. He took a deep breath before continuing.

"Very well. What I'm about to tell you is classified. Porton Down and the work we do here has been one of this country's best-kept secrets. If word ever got out about what we've been working on over the years, it could be very damaging. Worse still, if there was any suggestion that the government somehow caused the outbreak or failed to respond appropriately, you can only imagine the wild rumours and conspiracy theories. It would be unthinkable."

"We all remember the 'foot and mouth' scandal back in 2001," added the Professor. "The rumours that circulated about an accidental leak? It set public relations back years, decades even."

"My point exactly. Security around our research, even now, is absolutely critical."

Each of the visitors nodded their consent, before the Major continued.

"You asked earlier about Project Wildfire. Officially, that programme was shut down a long time ago along with several others like it. In reality, it was simply de-prioritised, kept on the back-burner just in case. When we got wind of other countries attempting to develop a weaponised flu virus, we reactivated our own programme. Project Wilderness was the upgrade to Wildfire. Since the most recent outbreak, we've redoubled our efforts. Sooner or later we figured that someone like you would come calling."

"Are we the first?"

"You are the first and only visitors we've had in some time. We lost contact with the MoD shortly after the outbreak. Since then, we've been on our own. At first we assumed that it was just a communication breakdown, but as time went on we realised the MoD was crippled."

"Major, perhaps I wasn't clear. The MoD, along with the rest of government, the police, the NHS, it all fell apart. There's nothing left. If you're waiting for a relief operation, then you'll be waiting for a long time. When was your last contact?"

He shook his head. "We've not heard anything for months now. We figured it wouldn't be long before they got things back up and running."

"So your men seriously have no idea what's been going on topside?"

"Colonel, these people have families, spouses, children living off-base. They're well aware of the outbreak. All leave was cancelled. We needed them to stay focused on their jobs and their research."

"So your team has been underground in this facility for over two years then? No one has come or gone in that time, is that correct?"

"We mounted two expeditions to the Army base at Aldershot but neither of them returned. They simply vanished not long after leaving Porton. We assumed the worst."

"Probably ambushed along the main road," added the Colonel. "We've heard reports of survivor camps and skirmishes throughout this area. Convoys being attacked, making attempts to relocate our forces very difficult. It's why we flew our team up here."

"Just keeping this place operational has been a challenge. We're fine for drinking water. We have all manner of recycling and filtration systems to capture rainwater and pump groundwater. Food is the problem. We're already dangerously short of almost everything. This facility was only designed to survive a level-one attack for up to six months. If we don't get a relief mission in the next few months, we can't continue. We cut rations again by a third two months ago. In the last few weeks, we've become increasingly dependent on scavenging missions into local towns. Well, you've seen what we're up against now. We can't even maintain a functioning perimeter. We're trapped underground, living like," he stammered, searching for the right words, "like rats."

"Major, we're evacuating as many of our remaining forces as possible to Camp Wight on the island. It's a new start, free of the virus. We could take you and some of your team to Professor Nichols' research facility near Newtown. You'll have everything you need."

"That's all very well, but how on earth would we get my whole team all the way to the Isle of Wight? There are hundreds of us. We would need a whole fleet of Chinooks. It's unthinkable."

"What choice do you have? You can't stay here forever. Camp Wight has everything you need to continue your research. It's a secure facility, with accommodation and food for thousands. Eventually our plan is to mount a clean-up operation of the mainland. We would hope to be in a position to get your team back here, perhaps in a couple of years. In the meantime, you're going to need to relocate. It's not safe here anymore, you must see that."

The Major sighed, accepting the inevitability of their

situation. They could only hold out so long here.

"I'd need to discuss this with the other officers. It would be a massive operation to safely relocate this many people and their lab equipment somewhere else. Even if we could replicate their set-up on the island, it would put our programme back by months."

"Don't you think that's a small price to pay? Better your team is relocated than left here to die."

"Perhaps, but my team say they are so close to a breakthrough. Just a few more months would see if they're right."

"How far has your team got with its research?"

The Major hesitated, as if he was pulling back from transparency.

"I'm sorry Colonel. I wish I had better news to share. It's been a frustrating time so far. So many blind alleys and dead-ends. Why don't I get the guys actually working on this full time in here and they can give you the run-down?"

He disappeared for a few minutes until they heard the footsteps of a small group returning. They knocked and entered. It was clear that the two men in lab coats accompanying him had not been outside for many weeks. Their skin was pale to the point of translucence. One of them had a straggly beard and lank grey hair that reached past his shoulders. Zed thought it smelled like neither of them had taken a shower in a week.

The Major introduced them both before handing proceedings over to the Colonel. Professor Nichols sat beside him unpacking a small black laptop computer from his rucksack and set out a notepad and pen ready to take notes.

"Thank you for joining us. As I hope Major Donnelly has already explained, it's a matter of national importance that you share everything you know about the Millennial Virus with the Professor."

The two men glanced at the Major before answering. He nodded his approval.

"Why don't you jump right in and give us a status report?"

The scientist introduced himself as Doctor Hardy and spoke rapidly in a sing-song voice that Zed found irritating beyond belief.

"We don't have an effective vaccine if that's what you really want to know. But we've come a long way. We already know so much about the virus, its origins, genetic profile, and its history."

"How long have you been working on this?"

"Oh, we've been tracking the virus since the very first outbreak."

"And when was that exactly?"

"Back in Singapore in September 2000."

"That long ago? That's far earlier than we were led to believe. Why was that not more widely reported?"

"Well, like any virus, we're talking about a moving target here. Each year since, there's been at least one different strain. The first outbreaks were minor, reported in CDC and WHO bulletins, the kind of thing you'd only find in medical journals, amongst a long list of other viruses. The most recent outbreak was much more virulent. Here we call it MV-27, or just MV for short."

"MV-27? So I am right in saying that there have been twenty-seven identifiable strains of this virus already? Why did the press never get hold of this? We were led to believe that the virus struck out of the blue. Or was that just the excuse that explained how poorly-prepared the country was to deal with a pandemic virus of this scale?"

"They were as prepared as they could have been. The NHS had run drills and tested the readiness of public health infrastructure, but in the end, none of it did much good. The plans were based on reasonable assumptions, early detection, sufficient time to prepare. The virus was unstoppable. None of the antivirals or generic flu vaccines we had stockpiled worked all that well. The only people who survived either avoided contact or had natural immunity."

"I'm assuming that exposure to some of those low-level strains has helped boost immunity in the general population, which suggests a sudden shift or mutation. Was there a catalyst or specific event that prompted the outbreak?"

"Possibly, we're still learning."

"Do you have a detailed history? Are there reports we can get access to?"

"Absolutely. We've gathered everything we could find that was available worldwide prior to the breakdown. Published papers, briefing documents sent to hospitals, WHO and CDC reports, patient histories, archived materials, everything."

"Fantastic, that's why we're here," said the Professor. "How many people do you have working on this right now?"

"Well, there's a core team of twelve scientists. Plus around another twenty or so in support roles, lab technicians, that sort of thing."

"And despite all those resources and years of data, you still have no breakthrough, no prototype vaccine?"

"Well, we've certainly had a few modest breakthroughs. We're getting closer by the day, but no eureka moment. It's only a matter of time and hopefully a bit of luck."

"Tell me about the current focus of your research?" asked the Professor.

"Before the outbreak, we were collaborating with three other facilities running similar research programmes in the US and Europe. We were able to exchange data sets and build a comprehensive study. That body of data was critical to the early breakthroughs we made."

"So where is that body of data now? Do you still have access to it?"

"Yes and no. Sadly when our internet connection went down, we lost access to anything held in the cloud. Fortunately, due to the sensitive nature of the data, we kept a secure copy of most of it onsite. So anything downloaded and stored in Porton's network is still available. But anything else, sadly, is now beyond our reach, unless someone can restore power to the DSTL data centre."

"Unlikely I'm afraid. Without detailed plans, there's no way of knowing where that data centre is, let alone getting a team there with the equipment to extract the data or get the power back on."

"So tell us more about MV-27 itself?" requested the Colonel, leaning forward.

"We've looked closely at both the human and viral side of the equation to track mutational changes over time and extrapolate clues as to where the virus might go next. We're big fans of computational biology here. We've been able to sequence the MV-27 genome and compare it with other similar flu viruses.

"Excellent. And what did your models tell you about its mortality rate?"

"Not good. They show a predicted mortality rate of over 60%."

There were audible gasps around the room.

"But that's unprecedented," said the Professor. "It's worse

than we feared then. A virus with high transmissibility and lethality. A perfect storm. Even Spanish flu only had a mortality rate of two to three percent. Our own model suggested that close to fifteen per cent of the population would have natural immunity to the Millennial Virus."

"Yes, that was our assumption too. Don't forget that survivor numbers are still being flattered by the presence of those who simply avoided infection so far. Many of those survivors sadly have no immunity. Sooner or later they will succumb to infection. It's only a matter of time."

"Unless we can evacuate them to the island. Do you have any safe way of testing for immunity?"

"Not exactly. There is an antibody we've identified, MRV-13, which is somewhat effective. In most cases we know MRV-13 attaches itself to the invading organism and stimulates a massive immune response. But we're a long way from solving the puzzle."

"Have you developed a test for this antibody? MRV-13?"

"With a blood sample and a lab, yes. But nothing we can yet take into the field. We'll need to develop a portable testing kit for this to work outside the lab. But again, it would take massive resources to manufacture and distribute, certainly more than we can do here ourselves."

"Camp Wight could help," suggested the Colonel. "We have the capability to scale this when the time comes. We have manpower, resources, and the will to make it happen. We're already putting in place the infrastructure to mass produce a vaccine that could be distributed nationwide, even worldwide, in due course. How long do you think it would take to create the portable testing kit?"

"The testing kit is relatively simple. The vaccine much

harder. But hey, with unlimited resources and a bit of luck we can do anything," laughed the scientist awkwardly.

"How long are we talking?"

"Say five to ten."

"Weeks or months?"

"I'm sorry, I misunderstood. I was talking in years. We might get lucky, but it's reasonable to expect..."

"What if we broke all the rules? Trebled the size of the team. Threw ethics out the window. I don't know. Could you, for example, accelerate the clinical trials process? Skip animals and move straight to testing on human subjects?"

"We're already doing that. We moved to human trials some time ago," said the scientist with a raised eyebrow. "We simply ran out of ferrets."

"Ferrets?" said the Colonel with some surprise, "I thought you guys used mice?"

"No ferrets are the test subject of choice for respiratory infections like the flu virus. They are model organisms for studying the pathogenicity and transmissibility of human and avian influenza viruses. We used mice too."

"Are the human subjects volunteers?"

"Not exactly."

"In my experience, Doctor, subjects are either volunteers or they're not."

"For the last few weeks, we've been despatching snatch squads to capture test subjects from the local communities living outside the perimeter fence."

"No wonder they're not very happy with you. How do the clinical trials actually work then? What are you testing for?"

"We inject the subjects with the live virus, leave for twenty-four hours and then begin testing various anti-viral treatments."

"And just how effective are those treatments?"

"Er, right now," the scientist paused looking a little embarrassed. "Less than five per cent effective?"

"Meaning 95% of the subjects without immunity die after you infect them?"

"That's correct. We've tried everything we can think of. We've targeted the virus itself and also the virus-infected cells. We were exploring the theory that if we can kill off those infected cells, we could counteract the infection."

"Interesting. I know a similar approach proved effective against H1N1 in 2009 and H3N2 in 2016."

"Those with high levels of the antibody have a survival rate of 99%. Even those with moderately high levels have an increased resistance. We've mostly tested on the older, less mobile subjects. Those we can catch more easily."

"Did you establish a control group, or use a placebo?"

"No, in the interests of time, we took certain liberties, tried to speed things up a little."

"You mention the age of the subjects. Is there any discernible pattern to those with immunity? I don't know. Lifestyle, ethnicity, age, gender?"

"I wish there was. We've found nothing so far. It sounds like you have a hypothesis there, Professor."

"Just a hunch really. Thinking back to the research published around the time of the initial outbreaks, there was evidence to suggest that infection rates were higher in younger age groups who had not previously been exposed to low-level strains of the virus and had no immunity. Our other assumption was that diet and lifestyle played an important part. Advances in inoculation programmes too. We worked on the theory, a while back, that something may have triggered the outbreak. An environmental catalyst, perhaps. If we could find ground zero, patient zero even, it might give us a clue."

"I can take a look in the records we gathered from the Singapore outbreak in 2000 and see what we can find."

"Zed, you worked on Project Wildfire. What are we missing? Are there any parallels?"

"Maybe. Nothing concrete. But it strikes me that you need to look further back, much further back. Beyond MV-1, perhaps beyond Project Wildfire."

The two scientists were staring at Zed for the first time with a mixture of incredulity and amusement. The Colonel encouraged him to continue. Zed noticed their scrutiny, feeling suddenly self-conscious.

"Okay, just go with me for a minute. At the end of the Second World War there were rumours that the Nazis were working on a killer flu virus. Nothing was ever proven."

He noticed Doctor Hardy rolling his eyes and exchanging looks with one of the other scientists who clearly thought he was a crackpot. He ignored them and continued.

"When the Allies reached the Rhine and moved on to Berlin, many of the escape routes were blocked and several Nazi facilities north-east of Berlin were captured intact by the Russians. Some of the scientists were spirited away to continue their research. Since then, it's been an arms race for who could get there first. North Korea, Russia, China, the US, France, the UK. They all had active weapons programmes. The Iraqis were the latest in a long line of rogue states trying to develop weapons of mass destruction. They were still years away. They lacked the technology and the know-how, but eventually, who knows? Wildfire was making some notable progress but then it got shut down suddenly and I got reassigned to another project. Your guess is as good as mine. Maybe they succeeded and the whole project was hushed up. Or perhaps it was an abject failure and they pulled the funding."

"Zed's right. We need to look further back. If the outbreak was pre-dated by dozens of other smaller outbreaks. If MV-1 itself was actually the first publicly-identified strain of this virus, then we're just scratching the surface. We're missing the bigger picture. Is that possible?"

"Sure why not? Don't you think it's suspicious that only a few years after Project Wildfire was shut down, a global pandemic nearly wipes out humankind as we know it? Sounds like somebody succeeded in their research," nodded Zed.

"But what would anyone gain from creating a virus that wipes out life as we know it? No one wins, everyone loses."

"Isn't it obvious?" claimed Zed. "The country that controlled the virus could theoretically programme it to target certain groups, countries, regions. What if the North Koreans or Chinese made a virus that only affected those in the West? Is that even possible Professor?"

"Yes, I don't see why not. It would be high-risk. Could backfire, mutate and kill everyone. It's certainly high-stakes poker."

"Gentlemen, I don't think this," the Major paused searching for the right word, "speculation, is getting us anywhere. Conspiracy theories about Nazis and clandestine Iraqi weapons programmes are not very helpful. My team are scientists, not fantasists," said the Major dismissively.

"But this could very well be the missing piece of the puzzle, Major. The first incidence of the virus. Patient zero. Their symptoms, treatment, secondary infection, survival rates. All of that data could prove decisive."

The Major raised his eyebrows and shrugged wearily.

"It would mean diverting precious resources away from the vaccine, but very well, we've tried everything else, I suppose it's worth a shot. Doctor, can you get your team to pull whatever you can find on Wildfire and see if it can't shed any light on what we're dealing with now. Meanwhile let's get the Professor set up with access to the archives. We're looking for anomalies, regional spikes, the earliest reports of cases. If we could pin-point the country, the city, the district, even the hospital, family or individual, then that could prove illuminating."

"Very well," said the Professor. "In the meantime, I'd like to speak with some of the test subjects you've identified as immune and ask their permission to conduct some further tests."

"Oh don't worry about asking permission. They do as they're told, or else," joked the Major. "You see the ones who survived, those that test positive to the antibody, know that they are valuable. Their status guarantees them certain privileges, enhanced rations, the best of everything. Being immune gets you a lot of things round here. If you like, the immunes are the new master race, at least for the time being. What we all wouldn't give to have what they have?"

"Let's get to work gentlemen," said the Colonel. "We meet back here in four hours with whatever we can discover."

CHAPTER EIGHTEEN

Riley sat in the canteen on an uncomfortable wooden bench seat opposite Sergeant Jones. Her arm was still sore from where they had taken a mandatory sample of her blood for testing and injected her with a first shot of retrovirals to boost her immunity. She was picking at the food on her own plate, watching the men eat. They had their elbows on the table, hunched over their food, slurping soup noisily, talking with their mouths open.

She noticed the posters on the wall behind them, amused by their irony. A map of Pompeii, inset with pictures of an amphitheatre, the Forum, Roman columns, statues and the tragic casts of human figures in indescribable pain. Couples clutching each other in a desperate final embrace, children curled into balls, hands clawing against superheated gas from pyroclastic flows and ash clouds. Perhaps the poster was a memento of an organised trip or family excursion. Riley wondered which was worse: to die suddenly in a volcanic eruption, or to survive the virus, to scrape a living only to die of hunger or disease years later? At least it was all over quickly for the victims of Pompeii.

The room was windowless on sub-level one of the underground complex. They had been told there was a total of seven sub-levels. A system of tunnels and bunkers that could sustain a large group of scientists in the event of an attack. A notice board in the foyer gave hints of what life must have been like here. Riley was amused to see items from a happier time. Toys for sale, football players wanted, bus timetables, lift-shares, memories of the way the facility would have run. Social clubs, a swimming pool, gym and cinema. In their brief tour of the facility, Riley had seen room after room stacked with equipment and stores of every description. If you had to choose a place to survive the end of the world, Hurst was good, but this was about as perfect as it got. Mind you, she wouldn't swap Hurst Castle for anything. She would much rather the sea air and views than being trapped underground. She wondered where they were getting all their power and water from. Perhaps they had a high-tech solution for that too. Solar stills, nuclear power, who knew what they had in the sub-levels here.

Even on sub-level one the air smelled musty and stale. Large ducts pumped filtered air from the surface to these lower levels. The walls were bare concrete, the lighting stark and unsympathetic. A defective strip light bulb caught the eye further down the corridor, as it blinked on and off.

She looked down at the untouched plate of food in front of her. It was mostly reheated tinned food. It all tasted artificial, but Riley had had worse. It didn't seem to bother the Americans. Perhaps they were used to eating this type of stuff on board the *Chester*. At Hurst, they took for granted that they ate fresh fish most days, not to mention the vegetables and fruit they grew themselves. Down here, it felt like a prison. She wondered what it would be like in sub-level seven, so far beneath the surface, airless and without natural light.

One of Jones's men passed down some dried biscuits and a

paste that might have passed for guacamole once upon a time. The rehydrated gunk remained stubbornly granulated despite the best efforts of the kitchen staff. Riley scooped a knife-full and spread the guacamole thickly on a biscuit. It tasted sour and gritty. She spat it out again.

"What's the matter? Food ain't up to Hurst's standards?" ribbed Jones, his mouth half-full.

"How do they eat this stuff? It's disgusting. You eat this on the *Chester*?" asked Riley.

"Hell no, not any more. We get the best of everything now, straight from the island. Fresh meat, vegetables, you name it. We get deliveries every couple of days. I hear your people are heading out to the island pretty soon."

"Not if I have anything to do with it. Hurst is our home. We won't leave it without a fight."

"Well, let's hope it doesn't come to that. The island ain't so bad. It's got everything you need. If you needed convincing, don't take my word for it. There are thousands of people lining up to get a piece of that. Your team has a VIP pass and you're refusing to take it? I don't get it."

"We've spent two years making Hurst what it is. Everything you see there is down to us. When we arrived it was just a museum with a coffee shop. Look at it now. It's surrounded by farmland, animals, it's a thriving hub. A gateway to the Solent. No way some jumped up Royal Navy officer is going to come and throw us out like it doesn't mean anything."

Jones laughed, sizing her up. Amused by her bravado and spirit.

"Hey, I get it Riley. If I was in your shoes, I'd probably be the same. But sooner or later you'll come round. Like the people here at Porton Down. It's just not safe to stay at Hurst forever."

Riley shrugged and pushed the plate of food away from her. One of the marines opposite leant across to grab the plate and paused.

"Mind if I finish that?"

"Be my guest."

The swing doors to the canteen opened and Zed poked his head round, scanning the room, looking for Riley. She waved him over and he poured himself a glass of carbonated water from a drinks dispenser and sat down, nodding towards the soldiers.

"How's it going 007?" she said, nudging him in the ribs as he sat down.

"Very funny Riley," he sneered, grabbing one of the biscuits and scooping some guacamole from the bowl. "Turns out Porton Down has been tracking the virus for years. They have a massive archive of data going back to 2000."

"So you were right then. The Major was lying all along."

"Not exactly, he was just doing his job. Like I was doing mine when I couldn't say anything before about what I did at the MoD."

"Yeah, I haven't forgiven you for that."

"Hey Riley, give me a break. We all have secrets right? What's yours eh? I'm sure you have a past. We all do."

"Not like yours Zed. I wonder what else you haven't told me?"

"You know all the rest. I'm an open book. The wife, the kids, where I grew up, the schools I went to, where I lived before the outbreak. You know everything."

"That's alright Zed. I forgive you. It was just a surprise that's all. Finding out the person you think you know has another side to them. I always knew you were an asshole!"

"Thanks Riley. Touché."

Jones leaned forward and in barely above a whisper asked Zed: "You think we can trust these guys? I mean, are they on the level? Something about them makes me suspicious."

"The Major sounds like he's pretty straight. So far, he's playing ball. Sharing intelligence, making his team available to the Professor. Oh, and I found out why there's an angry mob camped outside baying for blood."

"Oh yeah? You mean they needed another reason?" laughed Jones.

"Turns out they've had snatch squads capturing volunteers for their clinical trials. I think I'd be pretty unhappy about that."

"Reminds me of that other hell-hole," smirked Riley. "The hospital in Lymington. The place where they were holding Will and Adele."

Jones looked confused. "I don't think I've heard about that."

"Oh, ancient history now. Just another group who were experimenting on innocent people in the name of science. Some people never learn."

"Come on Riley. I'm sure they're not all bad," suggested Jones. "If it's a hospital, then it means there are doctors and nurses there. Dedicated professionals trained to save lives, not to harm or kill. Give people a little credit. So what if they break a few rules and cut corners? The needs of the many outweigh the few, isn't that what they say?"

"And so begins the descent into anarchy and chaos. Thousands of years of civilisation collapsing all around us. Don't you see?"

"Hey, nice to meet you," shouted one of the marines brightly. "I'm Anarchy and my buddy here is Chaos."

"You think this is funny? This is just one big joke to you guys," said Riley accusingly, failing to see the funny side of it.

"This is the beginning of the end. Don't you realise that?"

"Lighten up Riley," said Jones. "Don't be fooled. We're all on the same side here. Or at least we were last time I checked."

The other marine chipped in: "This ain't the end lady, this ain't even the end of the beginning. The beginning of our future."

"Don't take it personally. It's just the survival of the fittest," Jones said, slapping his team mate on the back. "Plain old evolution, ain't that right?"

"You're wrong. This is a tipping point for humanity."

"Right, and we need to pivot to survive," said Jones leaning forward intently.

Riley slammed her fist down on the table and closed her eyes for a second.

"No. You're wrong. I won't accept that this is a race to the bottom. Where only the fit survive and the rest are damned. Don't you see that it's up to all of us to stand up for what we believe in? We need to make a stand for what's right, what's decent."

"Listen, in my world, we follow orders or people die. If somebody says a mission objective is important, then we get it done. My job is not to question whether something is right or wrong. There's a chain of command. People smarter than me get the right to make that call. Sometimes you operate without context. Life's never that black and white. We operate in a world of shades of grey. I leave that other stuff to those with all the facts. My job is to get in, get the job done and bring everyone home again, alive."

Riley gave him a weak smile. "How very convenient! You never have to choose. That means you never have to lose sleep at night, wondering about morality or justice."

"Back off Riley. I make tough calls every day. Who lives, who dies. But I sleep like a baby, every night," sneered Jones, irritated by Riley's high-handedness.

"Well, I suggest you should crawl back under whichever rock you came from then."

"I'll do that. Why don't you go back to something you're good at, like whining, and leave us grunts in peace?"

"Come on Riley," whispered Zed, "before you start a fight."

Zed pulled her up and half-pushed her out the door, despite her protestations. Outside the canteen, he slammed her up against the wall.

"Have you completely lost your mind?"

Riley wriggled from his grasp and stared back at him defiantly.

"You do realise that we're a long way from home. We happen to need those guys if we're going to make it out of here in one piece."

He paused, staring into Riley's eyes. They were still burning bright from the confrontation with Jones.

"How did you think we were going to get back? Without these guys we have no chance. There are a thousand bad guys between us and home. We try stealing a car, hitching a ride, we wouldn't make it five miles from here. This is bandit country. The Wild West. We wouldn't stand a chance. We either get on that helicopter out of here, or we're not going home. So you may want to rethink your charm offensive with the Americans."

"Okay, Okay. I get the point. I'll try to be nicer to them. But only till we get home. I'm not sucking up to those guys for a moment longer than I need to."

"Right now, we need them a whole lot more than they need us."

There was a low rumble that shook the complex as dust and loose plaster from the ceiling fell all around them. They crouched down, covering their heads, noticing another group down the corridor doing the same. She caught the eye of one of the Porton Down men who feigned a smile and said: "That happens from time to time."

"What was it?"

"Probably some of the locals making their presence felt. Since we lost control of the perimeter fence, they do that sometimes. Every morning we drive them out, fix the fences and every night they creep back in under cover of darkness. But don't worry, we have a small army guarding the entrances. This bunker complex is completely secure. We're quite safe."

"Where have I heard that before?" whispered Riley to herself.

CHAPTER NINETEEN

Zed wandered back from the labs with his mind scrambled. The blood sample he had given when he arrived had proved the subject of much discussion amongst the scientists. The test for the virus had proved negative as expected, but had revealed that he had a very rare blood type, AB minus. They had seemed surprised this had never been diagnosed before which prompted perplexing follow-up questions about whether he suffered from incidents of cognitive difficulties, such as memory lapses, or attention deficit disorder. When he looked understandably concerned and asked for an explanation, the scientist seemed to clam up.

"It's nothing to worry about. We're just pursuing every lead, trying to understand why the virus affects people in different ways. You should count yourself lucky."

He certainly didn't feel lucky. Back in the stuffy confines of the conference room, Professor Nichols was sat with Doctor Hardy, one of the Porton Down scientists, staring at the pale white screen of a laptop. Either side of them on the table top were piles of print-outs and sheets covered in data points, graphs and analysis. He stood behind the two men, listening to their exchanges, struggling to understand their technical jargon.

Despite his scientific background, it was like listening to a foreign language at first, but the more he tuned in, the more he found he could follow along, without necessarily understanding every word.

"Is there anything I can do?" he said, hands on hips.

The two scientists paused in their discussion and looked up at Zed as if a child had just asked their parent whether he could drive the car.

"I wish there was," said the scientist with a hint of mockery. "There are only a dozen people in the country qualified to interpret this data and three of them are in this facility. The rest are likely dead. What did you say your specialism was before all this?"

"I was an analyst. Ministry of Defence. Specialist in biological and chemical programmes."

The professor smiled supportively and relented. "Listen, be our guest. What harm can it do? The summary report is in the green folder on the top of the file. Below that are the clinical trials and the analyst reports. Stay clear of the computer print-outs. Even I can't make head nor tail of those."

Zed took a deep breath and sat down at the end of the table and opened the folder marked "MV-27 contact report". It was dated the previous month and contained over a hundred pages of analysis, patient histories, trial data, recommendations for further research and summary conclusions. He was pleasantly surprised to find he could follow the narrative.

He immersed himself in the data, vaguely aware of the two scientists arguing about something. He had always been good at shutting out extraneous noise and focusing on the task at hand. It had driven his wife and children crazy. The ability to absorb himself in his work had been both an asset and a liability. A rich source of contention between husband and wife. His daughter joked that when Daddy went into his study to work, even the end of the world couldn't distract him. He had a nasty habit of missing mealtimes and bedtimes absorbed by whatever project he was working on.

Zed settled in to his reading, dimly aware of others coming and going. Riley popped her head round the door trying to attract his attention before a guard shepherded her back to the canteen area. He read the first three reports without pausing for breath. There were so many links with Wildfire, triggering a series of flashbacks, half-remembered conversations, wild theories, and unsubstantiated claims from nearly a dozen years ago. It was like re-activating a part of his brain that had lain dormant all this time, things he hadn't thought about in years.

There was something nagging at the back of his mind but he couldn't put his finger on it. He wondered whether the scientists were so close to the data that they were missing the bigger picture. He tried to remember his training. Look at the facts and what they're telling him. Take a step back and start again. Why was this happening? What could have caused the outbreak? Where did the virus originate from? Why was it so effective?

His instinct told him that there were few coincidences in this world. The Millennial Virus was effective, by design. Was it possible that someone had bio-engineered the virus and if so, how? Could they have spliced together two different known viruses? Was that even possible? He knew many countries had tried and failed. Was it reasonable to believe that someone had succeeded?

"Professor, sorry to interrupt. You said before that the Millennial Virus shared characteristics with many other common viruses but had several unique features?"

"That's right. The influenza viruses A, B, and C belong to the family Orthomyxoviridae. Influenza A viruses are by far the most prevalent. IAVs are further classified into subtypes depending on their surface glycoproteins..."

"I'm sorry Professor. You've lost me. In plain English, please?"

"My apologies. Theoretically, yes, it would be possible to bio-engineer a virus and mix parts of one with another to improve its efficacy, if that's what you're really asking. As far back as the 1970s, a couple of researchers, called Lamb and Choppin I think it was, proved that there were overlapping coding sequences that formed part of the influenza cloning and replication process and that mRNA splicing was occurring in the host organism. The amounts of cellular mRNAs and proteins evolve differently during the infection process. Attempts have been made before to alter the ratio of spliced to unspoiled mRNA. If a virus was bioengineered in this way, it might be conceivable through trial and error to splice together segments from other viruses in what would amount to a Frankenstein virus."

"And what if someone was to introduce segments from other deadly viruses, I don't know, let's say Ebola Zaire, Rabies or Smallpox, then what?"

"The question you need to ask is why? Why would someone want to engineer a virus with the potential to wipe out human life as we know it? Consider for a moment that a country had developed a designer virus capable of targeting an enemy. How would they stop the virus from spreading back to their own country and killing themselves? It would be a bit of an own goal wouldn't it?"

"I suppose, but humour me. Just for the sake of argument, what if there were environmental limiters that could ensure a virus could only survive and propagate in the target population centres, with minimal risk of spreading back to the country that created it?"

"Again, theoretically possible, but unlikely. We know from historical data collected prior to the collapse that all continents had been infected. It was everywhere. Africa, Asia, Europe, North and South America. It was present in all climates, all ethnic groups, all age groups. There was nowhere to hide."

"But leaving aside the 'why' for a moment, let's just imagine that a megalomaniac determined to unleash this deadly virus on the world, with little care for his own people or the consequences. Could it be done?"

"Yes, of course. Anything's possible."

"Then shouldn't we be looking at this with that theory in mind?"

"Zed, with all due respect, these people are not twiddling their thumbs. They have teams investigating all angles, all theories, however wild and implausible. They're conducting research without limits. Even if something is immoral or unethical, they chase down every lead. Trust me. But sorry, there I go again, shutting people down. Listen, don't let me stop you. If you have a hunch then follow your instincts. It's certainly an avenue of research we have been pursuing, just without much success."

Zed thanked the scientist and went back to the reports spread across the table. Leaning back in his seat, he closed his eyes, trying to organise his thoughts. He remembered a document that had been smuggled out of North Korea almost a decade ago that suggested the leadership was prioritising the development of a virus capable of targeting the West. The regime had determined that the native population could be vaccinated and protected.

But that was a long time ago. His team had dismissed the report as propaganda and disinformation. One of a number of similar attempts to mislead the West into believing a level of North Korean sophistication and technical expertise far beyond Europe and America. Still, Zed was an experienced enough investigator to know that the most unlikely explanations should never be thrown out. They had a habit of coming back to haunt you.

There was a commotion on the other side of the room as a scientist in a lab coat barged his way into the room clutching a computer printout.

"Major, I found this top sheet in the archive. It was restricted access. One of the clinical teams was working on a project several years back that was attempting to insert third party DNA strands into the H5N1 avian flu virus with limited success."

"That's right, they could never get them to bind properly. I remember the study now. Can you bring us the paperwork and get Miller working on it? There might be a clue in there somewhere. Worth a shot. We've only got an hour before we're due back in the large conference room. I suggest we start summarising what we've found so far and try and build a coherent plan with some next steps."

Zed blew out his cheeks. It didn't leave much time to get through the stack in front of him, let alone the countless others he would need to wade through to try and make sense of this. He knew there would be thousands of similar studies and reports. This was just scratching the surface. He didn't doubt that if he kept looking he would find something. He always did. Something overlooked. Something that didn't quite fit. Disconnected pieces that might form part of the jigsaw. It had been his job years ago and he was good at it. Some said very good. But there was a limit to what could be achieved working on his own. He just wished he had the rest of his team with him. He needed more staff.

He thought back to the early days of Wildfire and their interrogation of an Iraqi scientist. Chemical Sally, they called her. What was her real name? He couldn't remember after all this time. Then there was another, Nassir al-Hindawi, who was said to have masterminded Saddam's weapons programme. The Allies had captured one of his senior scientists who became part of a classified CIA rendition operation. The Americans had allowed a team from the MoD to sit in on one of the debriefing sessions where they were interrogating him about his research. Zed was trying to remember what they had learned. A flu virus had been discussed, he was sure of it. Collaboration with a foreign power. Funding certainly, resources and knowledge provided. There his memory failed him. Russia possibly. Anyway, what mattered more was that some of their attempts had focused on the flu virus. Saddam Hussein had been obsessed with biological weapons since the early Eighties. There had been incontrovertible evidence of their use in the Iran-Iraq war. Human experimentation, the use of anthrax against Iranian prisoners, field testing of bombs laced with camel pox against Kurdish rebels. It didn't take a huge leap of faith to believe the Iraqis were secretly working on other viruses. He stifled a laugh, remembering that two of the Iraqi scientists had studied and worked in the UK at Edinburgh University and the University of East Anglia. Perhaps the virus was conceived right here in this country. The irony of it was too much.

At the appointed hour, the Major collected Zed and the others from the meeting room where they had been working and ushered them through to a meeting room large enough to accommodate close to sixty staff. Around a dozen men were sitting at the back of the room waiting for the rest to arrive. Several others were standing near the back. Riley and Sergeant Jones looked disinterested, their arms crossed.

Zed stood next to the wall where he had a good view of the white board and projector screen. He listened distractedly to the Major's briefing, his thoughts elsewhere, churning over the reports he had been skimming.

The Major was saying something about pulling more scientists and researchers on to the project, focusing as much resource as could be spared on MV-27. He invited Colonel Abrahams to take the floor and after a brief introduction and shake of hands, the Colonel cleared his throat and surveyed the room.

"We're initiating a phased evacuation of this team to the Isle of Wight. The first convoy will leave here in the next 48 hours. We're calling this Operation Newtown. You will be given further instructions by your commanding officers. We'll leave a skeletal maintenance and defence team to keep this facility operational should we need it again. You only need to take the bare essentials, everything else will be provided for you at the other end. You'll be reassigned to Professor Nichols' team who have a research facility set up at St Mary's hospital."

He paused while several of his audience exchanged concerned looks, digesting the news.

"I'm sure you're all wondering why you need to be evacuated from a secure military facility," continued the Colonel. "Porton Down was designed to remain operational in the event of an attack or outbreak, for up to six months. You don't need me to tell you that we're now operating well outside those parameters. Even with rationing, we estimate supplies will last another few weeks at most, after which you'll be dependent on scavenging trips in to the local towns. For those of you who haven't been topside for a while, let's just say it's not a nice place to be. The locals have not taken kindly to your snatch squads. And, without wanting to alarm you, there's an angry mob up top, rampaging inside the fence. Right now, they're trying to find a way in. That's not going to happen any time soon, but we know full well that there will come a time when we'll need to make a break for it."

Riley noticed that the Major was looking anxious at the implication that his staff were in any way in danger or that his soldiers were incapable of defending the base. As soon as the Colonel paused for breath he jumped in.

"Let me reassure everyone that you're all entirely safe down here and we have sufficient men and firepower to allow you all to continue the important work you're conducting, long into the future. But the Colonel is right, it's only a matter of time before we exhaust our resources and that could be sooner than we think without resupply. I have therefore agreed to the Colonel's plan to begin a phased withdrawal. We'll start with the mission-critical personnel and scientists. You all need to start packing what we intend to take with us and be ready by the end of this week. Our plan is for the first convoy to leave this weekend. That leaves us roughly fifty hours to get organised."

The Colonel nodded and looked around the room, his eyebrows raised expectantly for questions. Sergeant Jones lifted his hand and approached the large map stuck on the wall that covered the south of England.

"Sir, my orders are to escort you and your team back to the island. Once I can get a message to command, we'll have a team make its way to here," his finger tapped on the map on the outskirts of Southampton. "Eling on the Test River is our designated RV point. We'll have a flotilla of small craft ready to ferry you the rest of the way. We'll also have a helicopter providing air support once we're clear of the New Forest. Major, how many men and vehicles can you spare us to make the first trip without compromising security?"

The Major redirected the question to a staff sergeant standing near the back.

"We have a dozen vehicles, trucks and jeeps, but most of them are not going to be serviceable until we get new parts and have a chance to make repairs. I reckon I can have the two Humvees, the big APV and a Land Rover ready for this weekend if we pull our fingers out. In terms of manpower, all told, we have forty-five soldiers and a whole armoury at our disposal. I'd say we could release a squad of men to go with you without causing too many problems, assuming we can shift things around."

"Excellent," said the Colonel. "That should be more than enough for the first convoy."

"What do we know about the terrain and civilian groups we're likely to encounter between Salisbury and Southampton?" asked Sergeant Jones.

"Nothing to write home about. Small survivor groups living in hospitals, hotels, that sort of thing. One or two forest encampments," replied the Major. "We ceased all reconnaissance trips several months ago and concentrated on the immediate area. Towns and cities were off limits, so we stuck to pubs, private houses, farms mostly. It was safer that way."

"And the roads? Highways? Are they passable?" asked Jones.

"We systematically cleared most of the local roads round here," said the Staff Sergeant pointing to the map. "We cleared the A338 as far south as Laverstock outside Salisbury, and North right up to the junction with the A303. But the A303 itself and the A36 are a total mess. They're virtually impassable without heavy lifting equipment. There are lines of abandoned cars and vehicles that will be rusting through, hand brakes locked on and a lot of dead and diseased bodies to deal with. Best avoided. The men would need to work in bio-hazard suits."

"I concur. We should stay off the highway," added Jones. "Stick to smaller roads that go cross country, through villages and farmland where we can stop if necessary and resupply. It's thirty miles or so from here to the RV point as the crow flies, so we should be able to do that in a day if the roads are fairly clear. Two days tops. Staff Sergeant, you want to introduce me to your quartermaster? We're traveling pretty light. We could use a little extra firepower."

"Be my guest Sergeant. We have a whole armoury at your disposal. Assault rifles, handguns, heavy calibre machine guns, grenades, C4, RPGs. You name it."

Zed noticed that Sergeant Jones had a big grin on his face. "Riley, you want to tag along and see what we can find?"

"Sure, wouldn't say no."

The Staff Sergeant blocked Riley's path and cautioned: "I'm sorry. I never said anything about handing out weapons to civilians."

"You're kidding right? You don't know Riley?" asked Jones rhetorically. "Don't be fooled by the lack of uniform. She's one of my team."

"My mistake," said the Staff Sergeant stiffening perceptibly, looking her up and down. "Follow me, please."

Riley stood a little taller with her new-found status and patted Zed on the shoulder as she passed him. "Good luck with your reading pile."

"Thanks. When you're done, you want to come and give me a hand?"

"Sure. I'll bring you back something from the armoury, eh?"

"Call me old-fashioned, but give me cold steel any day."

"You and that axe," she snorted.

CHAPTER TWENTY

"I've told you a hundred times, Jack. Jean had nothing to do with the fire," insisted Joe.

Jack slumped back against the chair's head rest and held his hands up with a resigned sigh. He was attempting to placate Joe as much as was possible, considering the emotion of the situation.

"Anyway, whatever happened to 'innocent till proven guilty'? You've always taught us the importance of the old ways Jack. Believing the best in people, rather than fearing the worst. There's no way that girl would get a fair trial if we allowed her to be taken back to the Sisterhood. Do I really need to remind you that it was the Sisters who locked me and the others up like animals? They called us breeders for goodness sake. Does that strike you as a group that cares about justice? They've already made their minds up, wouldn't you say?" said Joe shaking his head, his arms outstretched.

"Really Joe? You're calling the Sister a liar? I'm sorry, I find that hard to swallow. All I'm doing here is trying to get to the bottom of this. To understand the facts. To hear the evidence against Jean and see if she has a case to answer. It's the right thing to do, Joe. You must see that."

"If Jean says that she wasn't involved, then that's good enough for me," asserted Joe. "She's sixteen for goodness' sake. She's still a child."

"Look Joe. What would you have me do? I can't very well refuse her now can I? The Sister is waiting downstairs. She deserves to be heard. If the boot was on the other foot and one of the Sisterhood's people was suspected of a crime, then I'm sure they would do the same for us. We have a civic duty to help them, to facilitate justice. You have my word that she will get a fair hearing."

"You don't know these people. You can't guarantee that."

"It's my best offer. If it helps, I'm happy for you to sit in, if that's what Jean wants. She has a right to representation. She's technically a minor. It might make it easier for everyone."

Jack looked at his watch and realised that the Sister had been waiting nearly an hour for him. He couldn't delay the inevitable any further. He shouted for Tommy who was waiting patiently outside.

"Can you show the Sister in? And Joe, I'll be ready for you and Jean in a couple of minutes."

He sat back in the chair with weary resignation, waiting for the door to close. He puffed out his cheeks. This was all he needed; a lecture from a nun, of all things. There was a knock on the door and Tommy showed the Sister in. The Sister waited for the door to close before turning to face Jack.

"Please, have a seat Sister."

"I'll stand if you don't mind."

"Very well. Now, what can I do for you?"

"Thank you for seeing me Jack. I've heard you're a fair man, a good man. One of the few," she paused, her hands grasped together in front of her, looking down at him. "Look, I know you're busy and I don't want to take up too much of your time. I have been sent here by my superior, Sister Theodora, to bring Jean Mathews back to the Sisterhood, to stand trial."

"Yes, so I hear. And before I get Jean in here to hear the charges you're making against her, I wanted to ask you how you see this trial working? What will happen to her if she's found guilty?"

"She'll get a fair hearing, I'll see to that. And I can assure you that I wouldn't be here if I didn't believe she had a case to answer. She'll get a chance to tell her side of the story. To be tried by her peers. She can choose someone to represent her and argue her defence. Then, when all the facts are known, the jury will vote and the Sisters will decide her punishment."

"And what's that likely to be? What sort of punishment would the Sisters consider appropriate? For example, I'd have a hard time releasing her into your care if you were to tell me that she'll face corporal punishment?"

"We're not savages, sir. She'll be strongly encouraged to atone for her sins, to devote her life to God, to join the Sisterhood, to live a holy life."

"Very well," said Jack, his eyebrows raised. "Well, unless there's anything else, I suggest we get Jean in here and give her the opportunity to hear the evidence against her. Tommy?" he shouted, waiting for him to come back in with the others.

Jean was reluctant at first to come into the room, pulling back against Joe, who was holding her by the shoulders. "Come on, it'll be fine. I'll stay with you Jean. You've got nothing to worry about."

The pair of them came through and visibly kept their distance from the Sister. Jean looked terrified, staring at her feet, trembling uncontrollably as Joe rubbed her shoulders, trying to comfort her.

"The purpose of this meeting," started Jack, "is to hear the Sister's case against Jean. Jean, you will then have the opportunity to respond. We can then determine whether you should be taken from here to stand trial. Is there anything you want to ask before we begin?"

Joe shook his head. Jean was already close to tears, waiting for Jack to continue.

"Sister, when you're ready, please can you tell Jean what she's being accused of."

"Thank you Jack. The facts of the matter are that, on the night of April 17th, a fire raged out of control at the hotel and caused the death of seven of our residents, not to mention fourteen others who suffered second and third degree burns. Some of those survivors have life-changing injuries. We contend that Jean deliberately started the fire on the second floor to create a distraction, so that this man here," she said pointing to Joe, "and three others like him, would have the opportunity to escape from where they were being held."

"And what actual proof do you have that Jean was responsible?"

"Well, it doesn't look very good for her does it? Look at her," she said pointing in Jean's direction. "The guilt is written all over her face."

Jean started to cry, hiding her head in her hands, sobbing lightly.

"What do you have to say for yourself Jean?"

"It's not true. Joe, tell them it's not true. You know me I would never do something like this. I've never hurt a fly. I'm good, I am. Tell them."

"Look, I've known Jean for the last few months. She's just a child. She doesn't have a mean bone in her body."

"And I've known Jean since she was a little girl," batted back the Sister. "I know perfectly well what she's capable of. She's been in trouble before. She is easily led by people like this. By men. But I also know that she would never deliberately harm another. She would never have intended this to get out of control and for people to die for her cause. But there's no question that the fire was started deliberately. Jean, there's no point denying it any longer. You were seen on the stairs by two witnesses, Lucy and Abbie. We know it was you."

"You're wrong. You're all wrong. I wasn't there," she implored, her voice breaking. Joe stepped in front of her, as if physically trying to shield her from the accusations. He turned towards her, tenderly holding her face in his hands.

"I know you Jean. I know you helped us escape but you would never have risked something so reckless. Did Seamus put you up to this?"

Jean pressed her face in to his shoulder, sobbing. "It was Seamus, I'm telling you it wasn't me."

"But that's impossible, Jean. Seamus was with me all the time. No, I refuse to believe you would ever have intended anyone to get hurt. This was an accident."

"Jack, you must see," said the Sister turning to address him. "The girl had a motive, there are witnesses. She was trying to help her new friends."

Joe seemed conflicted. He was trying his best to protect Jean but it was no longer her word against another, there were witnesses. In his mind, that changed everything.

"We need to know the truth, Jean," implored Joe.

"The fire would have spread quickly," added the Sister. "A candle left unattended in an upstairs room, placed against heavy curtains. It's said that they would have smouldered just long enough, before catching alight. Long enough to allow the culprit to flee the scene. You were trying to distract everyone's attention, while you freed the men. Tell the truth child."

"No, it wasn't me."

"But it got out of hand. The fire spread too quickly, from room to room, to the dormitories where those poor girls were fast asleep in their beds. They never woke up. They died from smoke inhalation, Jean. There wasn't a mark on their bodies. Whether you intended it or not, you killed them and you need to face up to what you've done."

"No, no, I never did it. Joe, you've got to believe me. Please Jack. They'll kill me if I go back with them."

"Perhaps you can tell us where you were that night, Jean," asked Jack. "Without an alibi, the evidence is weighted heavily against you."

"You told me you were with Seamus at the time. So it couldn't have been you. That's right isn't it? Jean?"

Jean was shaking her head, looking up into Joe's eyes, a pained expression, her head tilted.

"You must tell us the truth now. This is important."

"I don't want to go back there, please don't make me. I never meant for any of this to happen. It was an accident. That's all. There's not a day goes by that I don't think about those poor girls who died."

The Sister turned to Jack, resting her hands on the table in front of him, with an air of victory.

"Are you satisfied? We have a confession. An admission of responsibility."

"Wait a minute," cautioned Jack. "That's not what she said. She said it was an accident. That she regretted what happened to those girls. Jean, are you now saying you did have something to do with the fire?"

Jean looked into Joe's eyes. "I'm so sorry Joe. I did it for you. Please don't judge me, I love you. Don't let them take me. I'd rather die than go back there, please."

Joe stood in front of her, blinking, not sure what to make of her words, his eyes filling with tears.

"I think we're done here, don't you?" said Jack. "Joe, I expect you'd like some time alone with Jean. If it's alright with the Sister, I'd like to suggest you accompany her, make sure she gets a fair trial. Can you guarantee that?"

"I give you my word. They'll both get a fair trial."

Joe looked confused.

"You're not suggesting I had something to do with this?"

"Absolutely, you're as guilty as she is," said the Sister triumphantly. "An accomplice to murder, corrupting a minor. You'll both stand trial together."

She turned to face a wide-eyed Jack. "Thank you for your cooperation. You've done the right thing."

CHAPTER TWENTY-ONE

Down by the quayside in Newport in the dead of night, Terra watched from the warmth of a heated passenger seat as one of Briggs' men worked by torchlight. He was removing the winter covers from an impressive-looking cabin cruiser, wrestling to unlock a large padlock securing the main cabin so he could stow the lifejackets and bags below.

The *Sheridan* was what Terra sneeringly thought of as a "stink boat". A luxury motor boat probably used, in her former life, for day cruises or fishing trips around the Solent area. Terra's family had always been somewhat sniffy about any pleasure craft without a sail, as if motor boats lacked the grace and dignity of a yacht. Her father had shouted insults at their owners as they raced across their path, leaving their small sail boat to roll violently in their wake. In her experience, power boats were driven by uncouth tattooed men dripping with gold jewellery who butchered the Queen's English in their own inimitable estuary dialect. To make matters worse, the vessels normally had humorous names like *On The Rocks* or *Lady Buoy*. The *Sheridan* was probably named after a hotel the owner had stayed in on holiday in Florida or Marbella.

Their vessel was broad in the beam but fast enough for

smuggling people or contraband right under the noses of the Allies. She also had a shallow draft which made her useful for narrow tidal estuaries and smaller harbours. Her cabin was modestly appointed with white cushions and wipe-clean surfaces, a small galley and two front cabins for overnight stays. Above deck there was outside seating towards the rear and a flying bridge large enough for a skipper and companion. Terra had been out on her a couple of times before, running errands for Briggs or Victor. They normally went out after dark.

Another vehicle parked up next to theirs and the four occupants silently unloaded weapons and canvas bags, handing them over the rail and depositing their luggage in the cockpit, to be stowed inside. Briggs and Victor were the last to arrive in a large Bentley SUV, the latest addition to his collection of luxury sports cars and 4x4s, stolen to order from the mainland. She noticed that the two of them were arguing about something or other. It was so quiet here she could hear their raised voices without quite catching their words. Briggs looked across at her and fell silent. He winked and blew a kiss. She hesitated, staring back at him, butterflies in her stomach, before reciprocating. She hoped he hadn't noticed her hesitation in the darkness.

Briggs opened the door, waiting for her to step down from the Range Rover. The gravel in the boatyard crunched noisily underfoot as they made their way across the yard. All around them, there were yachts and other craft craned out of the water for the winter. Many of their hulls remained half-painted, tarpaulins flapping in the breeze where they had come loose in the storm.

She followed the others down to the jetty and stepped on board, a rucksack over her shoulder. Briggs had told her to pack some warm clothes for an overnight trip but had been coy about the purpose of their visit to the mainland. It wasn't like Briggs to risk such a large group so far away from Carisbrooke Castle.

Terra had again been puzzling about why the Allies tolerated Briggs' presence on the island. After his attack on Osbourne, perhaps they determined it was safer to keep him in plain sight, rather than driving him and his organisation underground. It was known that he still retained a small number of hostages as a human shield. A missile attack on the castle would be unthinkable, too high a risk of collateral damage. Victor feared a hostage rescue scenario or ambush outside the safety of the castle when they were at their most vulnerable. So far, the unlikely truce had held and Victor operated under the belief that the Allies needed Briggs more than he needed them. His protection racket made him the closest thing the island had to a mafia boss. Things on the island tended to run more smoothly with Briggs around.

The Allies had learned the hard way that messing with Briggs had its consequences. Construction projects ground to a halt, food deliveries stopped arriving on time, crops got spoiled, farm animals died in mysterious circumstances. Of course, nothing that could be directly tied back to Briggs, but it was common knowledge that nothing happened on the island without his blessing. Sooner or later, Victor said, the Allies would need to deal with Briggs, but for now, they had other more pressing matters to attend to and let him come and go. He was a small nuisance to be tolerated. The Allies had bigger fish to fry.

Once everyone was on board the *Sheridan* and their belongings stowed, they cast off and cruised downriver at barely above impulse power, keeping their noise to a minimum. It was virtually pitch black and Terra strained to pick out the unlit channel markers in the darkness. A couple of the larger buoys down river were solar-powered and flashed a silent rhythm. The skipper didn't dare power up the large searchlight on the flying bridge so as to avoid attracting unwanted attention.

The Allies had spies everywhere, tracking Briggs' movements. It was a miracle they had made it this far without being spotted. Even after her eyes adjusted to the darkness, without street lights or even a moon to see by, Terra wondered that the skipper, a local man named Tom, could actually see anything. Looking over the side she could hear waterlogged objects bumping against the bow of the boat as they nudged them out of the way. From the rancid smell on the water, Terra imagined rotting animal carcasses or decomposing bodies, swirling in the eddies and backwaters. She closed her eyes. Even after all this time, the horrors of the outbreak lay all around them if you cared to look.

As they reached the mouth of the river Medina, the smell of sea air was intoxicating. It reminded Terra of her former life at Hurst, of Jack. She realised she hadn't thought about him in some time. It was surprising how quickly she had moved on. As one chapter closed, another was just beginning. She wouldn't call the team at Hurst Castle friends. No, they were acquaintances, people she had spent considerable time with, been through so much together, but at the end of the day, they had little in common. They had been thrown together by circumstance.

She had never been good at having friends. Boyfriends yes, but not friends. Most of her relationships had been purely functional, useful to stave off the boredom. Others, like Jack, had served a purpose, a stepping stone to something better.

Terra was reminded that Briggs seemed to have an unhealthy obsession with both Jack and Zed. It was more than jealousy or anything trivial like that. He blamed them for the missile attack on his motorcade a few months ago. Six of his men had died.

Despite Terra's protestations that they had nothing to do with it, Briggs blamed Jack. He kept repeating the twisted logic that the Americans had pulled the trigger but Jack had loaded the gun. She explained away his thirst for revenge as some kind of old school macho rivalry. In Briggs' underworld, a failure to show respect was inexcusable. It was illogical, but then so was much of what Briggs did. Victor claimed Briggs was ruled by animal instinct and desire, irrational in the extreme, but Terra doubted that. The man she had come to know liked people to underestimate him, it gave him an advantage. As someone who had worn many masks over the years, she recognised another master of disguise. It was something they had in common, she thought.

Briggs reached for the walkie-talkie on the *Sheridan*'s chart table, tuned the frequency to a pre-set channel and depressed the receiver three times without speaking. After a short delay, there was an acknowledgement given as one long period of silence. Victor had confided that there would be another boat running interference tonight, ready to distract the Allies when the time came. A powerful searchlight reached out towards them, sweeping past their vessel without lingering. It lit up their faces, dazzling them momentarily, then its beam was gone.

Leaving Cowes behind them, they hugged the western edge of the river mouth before picking up speed and powering across open water towards Beaulieu, surfing down a series of small waves. Staying tight to the shoreline, they rounded the headland and in to Southampton Water.

In the distance, they could see the lights of the *USS Chester* at anchor, a couple of miles away. There was some commotion, the flash of small arms fire, searchlights scanning the water. Terra imagined that the other boats Briggs had contacted were running diversionary tactics to occupy the defenders while the *Sheridan* made her escape. They had used that ruse many times.

On the opposite side of Solent Water, there were the dark shapes of several enormous container ships moored up in the docks, waiting to unload. They had been there for as long as anyone could remember. Their cargos of hand-made furniture, cars, washing machines and fridge freezers made irrelevant by the outbreak of the virus. It was said that one of the ships held thousands of brand new Toyotas and Lexus SUVs, Hondas, Hyundais and KIAs, intended for car dealerships throughout the south-east.

Following the shoreline round to the West lay the *Maersk Charlotte* at anchor, riding higher now she was unloaded. Her cargo of humanitarian aid destined for Africa had been a God-send for the Allies, yielding a treasure-trove of much needed items for Camp Wight. Smaller ships ferried supplies from the docks to the island daily, including tents, pallets of bottled water, dried goods, pop-up buildings, timber, plastic sheeting, and sanitation equipment. It had been the stroke of luck the Allies needed to kick-start the relief operation.

Over the past few weeks and months, Terra had watched from Carisbrooke Castle as the landscape around Newport had begun to change. A tent city, known as 'The Jungle', had sprung up in the fields outside of Newport. A dangerous place where desperate people traded goods and services. To Briggs, the Jungle served as a bustling market place to recruit workers, deal drugs and sell bootleg alcohol and cigarettes. Most of the people arriving had nothing to barter with except blood, sweat and tears. Anything and everyone was for sale to the highest bidder. Exploitation and prejudice went unchecked, right under the noses of the Allies.

The *Sheridan* made a final course correction and aimed for a forest of masts in the half-light at Hythe Marina. Reversing their engines at the last minute, the *Sheridan*'s forward momentum slowed as the bow nudged against the wooden jetty. Two crewmen jumped down with bow and stern mooring lines, holding her tight against the pontoon just long enough for their passengers to disembark.

In the shadow of a boat shed, four vehicles waited for them in darkness. One of the cars, a large SUV with raised wheel arches, flashed its headlights three times. Its occupants remained inside the vehicle. Victor and Briggs stepped down onto the concrete quay, keeping their distance.

Terra's mind was racing, trying to figure out who was there to meet them. After a short delay, the driver-side doors of each of the vehicles opened in turn as four men emerged. Three of them grouped together and sat back against the bonnet of the larger vehicle handing round cigarettes, their faces illuminated briefly by a Zippo lighter.

Their leader wandered over towards the jetty. He stopped a dozen paces away, shielding his eyes from the torchlight shining towards him. He wore a black uniform, his bulk accentuated by what looked like body armour. He gestured for the torch to be lowered and continued forward. It looked like he was wearing police riot gear, with shoulder pads, knee guards and a breast plate, but she couldn't be sure in the gloom. Victor stepped into his path, blocking his route to Briggs.

After a moment's delay, he outstretched his hand towards the stout figure wearing a balaclava over his head.

"You must be Copper," said Victor, inclining his head.

"And you must be Victor," nodded Copper tersely. The two men shook hands as if neither quite trusted the other.

Victor led him over to meet the other new arrivals. Briggs was trying to light a cigar, sharing a private joke with one of his henchmen whose sycophantic laugh irritated Terra. Briggs' hooded eyes were fixed on the approaching pair. He spat on the ground in between them as they came to a halt, flicking the half-burned match off the quay into the water. He looked Copper up and down with a sneer.

"You'll excuse me if I don't shake hands."

"Norman Briggs," Copper said, shaking his head. "I never thought I'd see you a free man."

"Funny old world, isn't it? I got let off for good behaviour."

"For what you did, life should mean life."

Briggs took a deep draw on the cigar and coughed, the smoke catching in his throat as he laughed.

"That was a long time ago. I've done my time."

"Don't kid yourself. The police officer you killed was a friend of mine. You shot him in cold blood. He was unarmed. He had family, three kids."

"It was nothing personal. He was in my way, that's all. Anyway, what does it matter now? Time you moved on, chum. I reckon the virus did you a favour n'all."

"How's that?"

"All those inmates your lot put away in Parkhurst Prison. Most of them are dead. They got what they deserved, eh?"

"Except you Briggs. Except you."

"Guess I'm the lucky one then," Briggs laughed, staring at his boots. He seemed to be enjoying himself.

"Still. New world, new rules. Haven't you heard? I've gone straight. And I hear you've changed your ways too."

"I didn't have a choice. We all had to change to survive. Unlike you, some of us changed for the better."

"You may not like it but right now, it would seem that we need each other. We find ourselves on the same side for a change."

"I wouldn't quite put it like that. You've got Victor to thank for putting us together. The enemy of my enemy… I help you get what you want, you help me get what I want. That's all this is, an exchange of services."

"Doesn't change anything," asserted Copper.

"Call it what you like, mate. Your predecessor and I had an understanding. We helped each other out a few times. Whatever happened to King anyway?"

"He got careless."

"Don't suppose you had anything to do with that, did you?" said Briggs knowingly.

Copper shook his head, grimacing at Briggs. "What does it matter. I'm in charge now. I say what goes. If you have a problem with that, we can go our separate ways. I don't need this," he said glancing at Victor.

Victor intervened "Gentlemen, with all due respect, time is not on our side. If we're going to do this, we need to get going now. Our enemy moves against us. For the next few hours, they are vulnerable. Their people exposed. We must seize this chance. Strike now and we gain the upper hand. We'll have leverage. The opportunity to get what we want."

Briggs continued to stare at Copper, squinting with one eye into the first light of dawn as the sun appeared behind the buildings to the East. He took another long draw from his cigar and blew a stream of smoke into the cold morning air.

Copper moved his head from side to side. "Say we help you. Go along with your plan. You get what you want. You help us get what we want. Then what?"

Victor looked across at Briggs who gave him the nod to continue.

"We all need to look at the bigger picture," suggested Victor. "Every day we wait, the Allies get stronger. Soon, our chance will be gone. On the island, they have food and power already. There's no virus to worry about. Hundreds more people arrive each week. They're building an army, restoring communications infrastructure. In time, they plan to use the island to mount a clean-up operation of the mainland, further projecting their power and influence. If Peterson gets his way, the Americans will be in charge with that puppet Armstrong by their side. We can't stand-by and let any of that happen."

"So what's the alternative?" asked Copper.

"We take the island for ourselves. Drive them away. Purge this place of their interference and politics. If today goes our way, then we'll have the upper hand."

"So aside from smuggling and trade between our groups, what's in it for us."

"Right now," continued Victor, "thousands of people are migrating south, trying to reach the island."

"Yeah, we've noticed."

"We believe that's only going to get worse. As word spreads, more and more people will come. Lymington is one of the three main embarkation points. The town is critical to the Allied plans to secure the western corridor. They need to guarantee safe passage on both sides of the Solent. If we let them, they'll turn Lymington into a fortress, place it under military control. Your freedom to operate in the local area will be eliminated. Your group will be driven out. If we work together we can stop that happening."

"So why would we work with you, rather than doing a deal with the Allies ourselves?"

"Because the Allies will view you as a threat. They'll make

you leave or wipe you out. You really think they want you on their doorstep? Sure, they'll promise peace but then crush you. Look what they did with the groups around Portsmouth. Whereas with us? You get to do whatever the hell you want. You'll have power, wealth, influence. You name it."

Copper removed the balaclava, squinting into the dawn sunlight. Terra admired the richly-coloured tattoos on his neck, steam rising from his bare head. Terra was sizing him up, listening carefully to his questions. She thought she recognised in him that inner conflict between duty and ambition. It was a condition she knew only too well. Here was a man who had devoted his former life to upholding law and order as a policeman but somehow he had been seduced by opportunity.

In the political vacuum that had ensued following the breakdown, opportunists with a thirst for power had flourished. What remained of functioning institutions struggled to regroup, licking their wounds. Men like Briggs and Copper's old boss King, had taken full advantage, seizing control, orienting communities around their own beliefs and values, ruthlessly suppressing any who stood against them. Perhaps Copper had never intended things to go this far, this fast. Yet here he was. Since his boss had been captured by the team at Hurst, he was in charge, going through the motions of leadership. He reminded Terra of Jack. Well-meaning but indecisive at best. He lacked the natural authority and intelligence that had attracted her to men like Briggs. She didn't know Copper, but she had met his kind many times. He was easily-led when one applied the right amount of pressure.

Copper was conferring with his deputy, his back turned to Victor. Terra noticed Victor and Briggs sharing a knowing look as if they knew what would happen next. Perhaps they had planned this all along. Copper looked up and nodded.

"Very well, you've got yourself a deal. But on one condition."

CHAPTER TWENTY-TWO

Riley was the last passenger into the camouflaged personnel carrier. The Sergeant had referred to their ride as an APV. The whole base seemed to run on impressive sounding acronyms. The interior of the bulky vehicle was bathed in a soft green glow that took Riley a moment to get used to. She found a seat directly opposite Zed facing inwards, in between one of the scientists and Professor Nicholas.

Once the door at the rear was closed up, it was like being stuck in a tin can, stuffy and hot. After a moment's delay, the diesel engine coughed into life and the vent above her head started blowing cool filtered air from outside. She closed her eyes and breathed in deeply, trying to dispel the rising sense of claustrophobia.

In the last forty-eight hours, she had barely seen Zed. When they ate together, he had been monosyllabic, introspective and preoccupied with his investigation. She tried her best to engage him, but it was like he was in a trance. She hadn't seen him like this before. He clearly hadn't slept much and looked haggard and gaunt, with dark circles under his eyes. Each time she had asked him about progress, he blew out his cheeks and said that they were no closer to a breakthrough. He said it might take years, that it was wrong to expect miracles. She had apologised and left him to underline passages of interest in the text on his lap.

She could hear the driver and one of the soldiers in the cab running through their final checks. He released the hand brake, revved the engine a couple of times, wrestling with the gear lever, before rolling slowly forward to join the line of vehicles in front of them. They were as well prepared as they could hope to be. Their route was planned, the team briefed for the final time. Each of their four vehicles had been meticulously checked by Porton's resident mechanic. Their fuel tanks were topped off with a jerrycan, tyres inflated. Each of their windscreens had been fitted with metal bars and wire mesh as a precautionary measure to protect the passengers against the expected hail of stones and bricks they would encounter as they left the compound. They were carrying extra fuel, water and food just in case they got held up or had to take a detour round blocked roads and fallen trees.

The squad of soldiers from Porton was split between the vehicles. They would act as local guides until they reached the coast. The APV carried their most precious cargo: the lead scientists; several hard drives; laptops loaded with research data and reams of written notes. Zed had asked to tag along with the scientists. Riley was invited to keep him company. She figured a bunch of geeks would be more likely to leave her in peace than the playful banter of the Americans. The Seal team had squeezed themselves into an armoured Land Rover at the rear of the convoy and called out to her as she walked past.

"Hey Irish girl, O'Reilly. Come sit with us. We brought some of that guacamole you like so much. What's the matter? Us grunts not good enough for you now?"

She kept walking, ignoring their jeers and whistles, keeping her eyes fixed forward. She had remembered Zed's advice: keep them onside. Anyway, she had Sergeant Jones to thank for the brand-new Glock pistol, spare clips and a flare gun packed in her rucksack, still in its case.

The soldiers from Porton Down were the only ones who really knew what lay outside the perimeter fence. Riley was reassured by their relaxed professionalism. They looked bored and lethargic as if the trip they were about to make was routine. Their squad leader, a swarthy Corporal, chewing gum, remained alert and ready, his weapon kept in front of him as if he expected trouble at any moment. It was said that a mob was lurking inside the compound, which in part determined their dawn departure. They hoped to catch them napping.

Riley looked around at the rest of her fellow travellers. They were a sorry party of socially inept scientists and lab workers. Several were peripherally aware of her staring and seemed to avoid eye contact. She imagined this was the first time they had been outside the facility for many months, their skin pale and blemished. The scientists showed little interest in their surroundings, tapping away at the laptops on their knees.

As the APV swerved and bumped over some debris in the hangar loading area, for a moment, one of them looked up irritated as if jolted awake by the violent movement. Pushing his glasses back up the ridge on his nose, he squinted through the rear panel to the outside world. She wondered whether these guys really were as smart as they were cracked up to be. They certainly didn't look like the saviours of humanity, let alone capable of inventing a vaccine.

Alongside the APV they could hear raised voices as the Staff Sergeant walked down the line of vehicles banging the flat of his hand against their doors, checking they were ready to leave the relative safety of the hangar. Engines in gear, they nudged forward so that they were all in a line.

The reinforced bay door in front of them remained sealed shut until the last minute. Riley unclipped her seat belt and crouched low behind the partition that separated the cabin so she could see out of the front windscreen. The red light above the hanger door turned green and a warning siren sounded, as the bay door slid back. Either side of the convoy walked a dozen soldiers wearing body armour and combat helmets. They would escort them to the edge of the base and clear the way of any locals who tried to get in their path.

It was first light, a pale dawn. A grey, cloudy start to the day with rain clouds threatening in the West. The APV rolled slowly forward. The central console between the front seats housed what looked like a short-wave radio transmitter, a larger version of what Jack used on the *Nipper*. Riley leaned forward, trying to listen in to the radio chatter between the base commander and the convoy. It was garbled and full of static. The co-driver twiddled one of the knobs and adjusted the gain until the interference cleared and they could hear the other vehicles reporting in and ready to head out.

Riley sat facing forward trying to see out of the windshield, but they were so close to the Humvee in front, she couldn't see much. The soldiers jogging alongside kept pace for the first few hundred meters before the convoy picked up speed on the open tarmac. Their escorts started dropping back and stopped. In the rear-view panel, she could see the Corporal's hand raised as a goodbye. She watched as the squad turned their backs on the convoy and double-timed it back to the safety of the hanger bay.

A heavy object smashed against the side of the APV, jolting her back to the here and now. It was followed by a series of smaller noises, stones most likely, as a crowd emerged from behind a grass bank.

"Here they come," shouted the driver. "Bloody hundreds of them."

A volley of shots rang out from far behind them as the turret of the Humvee provided some covering fire, scattering the mob.

The convoy slowed again as it reached the main gate. A double fence with a small chicane and speed bumps designed to slow the approach of vehicles entering the base. When the gate had been fully manned, cars and trucks would have entered a holding area inside the first fence where a pair of security guards checked the occupants' IDs and security passes under the watchful eye of CCTV cameras. Today there was no one in sight, the front gate misshapen, pushed to the side, as if hanging by a single hinge.

The compound was no longer secure, its fences repeatedly breached. Strong points and observation towers had been abandoned some time ago. Ahead of them the gates stood open. A series of speed bumps slowed their progress, followed by a narrow concrete chicane. Beyond, running alongside the perimeter fence, the tarmac of the main road beckoned.

As the convoy approached the chicane, a wine bottle with a burning rag stuffed in the end arced towards them and shattered against the Humvee. Flames engulfed the roof and right side as more people emerged from their hiding places to bombard the convoy with bricks and masonry. Riley was startled by the noise. She could feel the searing heat from inside their own vehicle. The Humvee in front braked hard and the APV almost rear-ended them.

Zed barged Riley out the way to look through the narrow gap, watching the equipment strapped to the top of the lead

Humvee smouldering, thick clouds of smoke spewing from a burning spare tyre.

"Why are they stopping? Keep going for God's sake."

The convoy picked up pace again as a voice from the lead vehicle said: "Sorry about that. Some kid just ran straight in front of us. I had to swerve to avoid hitting him."

"Don't stop for anyone or anything," said a voice over the radio.

"Copy that."

The gap with the Humvee in front grew again as they accelerated out of the front gate and alongside the fence heading for the main road. The road ahead was clear, the crowd of people beyond the perimeter ran for the tree line, leaving the APV to drive over the speed bumps, through the chicane and out on to the main road beyond the base.

"Stay alert. If the Sergeant's right, that was just the friendly send-off. We can expect plenty more interest like that along the way."

Riley sat back in her seat and sighed, reattaching her seat belt. She realised she had been holding her breath for large parts of their departure. Zed resumed his reading, forcing a smile, noticing Riley staring at him.

CHAPTER TWENTY-THREE

For the first couple of hours, the convoy stuck to narrow country roads that ran alongside lush farmland, overgrown with wild flowers and poppies. The meadows round here were some of John Constable's favourite tableaux. The landscape he had painted almost two hundred years ago was as English as you could find, unchanged and beautiful.

Catching glimpses of Salisbury Cathedral in the distance, they progressed south. Skirting the city centre, they avoided the main roads, following the meandering line of the River Avon. They passed through the picturesque village of Aldebury, its duck pond flooded and overgrown. The convoy continued on to Charlton-All-Saints and the surrounding farms and fields where cows and sheep had been left unattended for too long. They could see several beasts had fallen in the stream, unable to get themselves out, rotting carcasses infecting the water downstream. Along a barbed-wire fence, several sheep had become entangled, bleating for a farmer who never came, slowly starving to death. The smell was overpowering even now, so much so that they kept their windows closed and switched the air-conditioning over to recycled air.

Leaving the open fields behind them, they approached the

edge of the New Forest. With every mile of their uninterrupted progress, Riley allowed herself to hope. Did her travelling companions really hold the key? Zed had said that it might take years to produce a vaccine. Would generations to come know a world without the virus? Could things ever return to normal, after all this time? Looking out the window, she imagined she might see soldiers waving them forward, guarding the road. They were already way ahead of schedule. At this rate, they might even make it back to the island before nightfall.

Riley relaxed back into her seat, listening to the Professor and the scientists arguing about something to do with genetics. She found their back and forth almost impossible to follow, preferring to watch the others tapping away silently on their laptops. She tried to engage Zed in conversation to pass the time, but he was buried in another of the reports he had brought with him, scribbling notes in the margins.

The Professor looked up and caught Riley's eye. He had a kind face, greying hair and sharp eyes that betrayed a keen mind.

"Has there ever been anything like the Millennial Virus before?"

The Professor seemed initially puzzled by her question, blinking back at her. Zed looked up and gave her a knowing smile.

"Yes and no," said the Professor. "Mother Nature has been perfecting the flu virus since the dawn of time, but trying to predict the next outbreak is like trying to predict the next earthquake or tsunami. We live on a fault line and it's always been a question of when not if. Every now and again, she tries something new, something different. Just when modern medicine thinks we've got everything under control, that's when she unleashes hell. Some would say it's all part of a natural process. Homo Sapiens has been dominant on this planet for quite some time. Not quite up there with the dinosaurs, but a good run."

"So you think this could be our defining moment? Like the meteor strike they say wiped out the dinosaurs?"

"Well, a pandemic virus is nature at its most terrible. The strongest force of natural selection there is. By targeting the frail and the weak and killing them off in their hundreds of thousands, a virus has the potential to fundamentally shift social structures. Depopulation of whole regions will bring about changes in the landscape, a return to nature, not seen since medieval times. The very psychology of the country will be deeply scarred for centuries to come."

"Does that mean that history can tell us what's likely to happen next?"

"Put it this way, we already know the long-term effects of a pandemic outbreak of this size and scale. The Black Death is probably the closest precedent, albeit a bacterial infection. It wiped out nearly one third of the British population in the 14th century."

"Sorry, you've lost me there. What's the difference between a virus and a bacteria again?"

The Professor seemed amused by her question. Some of the scientists around paused whatever they were doing and stared at her.

"Sometimes, it's hard to tell them apart as their symptoms can be so very similar. At its most basic, bacteria are single-celled organisms that tend to live in the gut and help digest food. Bacteria are normally killed by antibiotics. Whereas a virus is smaller and requires a living host to survive, invading cells, reprogramming their software to produce a virus. Lots of common infections like pneumonia or diarrhoea can be caused by either bacteria or a virus, which makes them hard to distinguish sometimes."

"So if the Black Death was bacterial then I assume it was spread by rats and fleas. Where did it come from in the first place?"

"Good question. Again, there are parallels with our friend the Millennial Virus. Historians reckon that the bubonic plague originated in central Asia and arrived in mainland Europe around 1347, spreading quickly from port to port until it reached England in 1348. You will remember from your history lessons that the bubonic plague was pretty disgusting, characterised by black swellings under the arms and in the groin. Victims died quickly, typically within three days. Less well known was the fact that there was a pneumonic variant of the plague also doing the rounds. It was even more deadly. Spread by direct contact with the infected. Some say that what made this variant so devastating was its hybrid nature, combining the worst of the bubonic plague with the flu virus."

Zed had stopped his reading and was listening intently to the Professor.

"So how did people survive the Black Death? Is there anything we can learn from what worked back then?"

"Oh plenty. The rich and members of the upper classes did best. Many of them managed to avoid contact altogether by escaping to the countryside. Some even indulged in hedonistic pursuits, believing the end of the world was justification for one last party to go out on a high. But the poor and lower classes stood little chance. They lived in appallingly unhygienic conditions that allowed the plague to spread unchecked. That is, until the introduction of plague pits to dispose of the dead.

Before that, bodies were left unburied, wherever they fell."

"So how did the Black Death die out?"

"Well, unfortunately, the British climate with its long cold winters and wet summers provided the perfect conditions for the Black Death to survive for several decades, resulting in a second pandemic years later. Fortunately, the generation that had survived the first outbreak had developed increased immunity to the virus, but their children were not so lucky. Many of the victims of the second outbreak were children born without immunity. To the extent that they called that second outbreak 'The Children's Plague'."

Riley noticed that Zed was leaning forward with a far-away expression on his face, as if an idea was forming in his head, his curiosity piqued.

"But surely immunity is in part genetic, Professor?" asserted Zed. "The children of those that survived the plague would inherit their parent's immunity."

"Yes, that's most likely true. Modern science suggests that genetics plays a significant role in immune response, affecting our ability to fight off a disease. The immune system has evolved over time to provide an improved line of defence against some pathogens, even some cancers, but the flip-side is that this heightened immune response makes the body more vulnerable to autoimmune diseases, where the body produces antibodies that attack the host's own healthy cells and tissue. I'm talking about diseases such as Rheumatoid arthritis or Multiple Sclerosis."

He took a sip of water from a canteen at his feet before continuing.

"We know from analysing skeletons from medieval graveyards like the one at Winchester Cathedral not far from here, that in the aftermath of previous pandemics like the Black Death, there were actually beneficial effects to the health of subsequent generations. People tended to live longer and be healthier, with diet significantly improved by the wider availability of fresh vegetables and meat following the elimination of a third of the population."

"You can tell all that from their bones?"

"Yes, we look at the skeletal markers of physiological stress. Things like how tall they were, enamel hypoplasia, tibial periosteal lesions, that sort of thing. Or to put it more simply, people who were already in poor health had a more elevated mortality risk than their healthier peers."

"So you're saying that the next generation will not necessarily benefit from this outbreak through improved immunity but that the survivors, by their very nature, will be stronger, through a process of natural selection."

"Yes, spot on. I would wholeheartedly agree with that summary, wouldn't you?" he turned to address Doctor Hardy, who pushed his glasses up his nose and was just about to pick holes in that argument, when the driver jammed on his brakes.

The convoy slowed to a halt on a narrow lane with high hedges and trees lining the roadway on each side. The branches of ancient oaks reached high above them forming a green canopy that blocked almost all the light. Sunshine broke through ahead of them, falling on the road surface in dappled patches. The driver switched on his headlights, illuminating the rear of the Humvee in front of them.

"What's the hold up?" he shouted, leaning out the window. "Why have we stopped?"

The driver of the vehicle in front, cracked open his door, poking his head out for a better look up the road. A runner squeezed through the gap between the hedge and the wing mirror and passed the message back.

"Corporal, the road ahead is completely blocked. We've got trees down. Looks like we're going to have to back it up. What do you want us to do?"

"Go take a look will you. See if there's a way round. Williams, there was a junction about a mile or two back. Check the map and find out where that leads will you?"

After what felt like an age, one of the soldiers from the Land Rover at the front jogged back to the Humvee and leant through the open window talking to the driver before moving back down the convoy to the APV. The driver wound down his window and waited for the man to catch his breath.

"There's no way round. We need to reverse all the way up this road. There was a turning about a half mile back, an entrance to a farm. Try and turn round where you can."

"You're joking yeah? Have you tried reversing one of these things? They're not exactly built for going backwards."

"You there," he said pointing at the solider in the passenger seat, "get off your arse and walk him back. It's not difficult. Or do you want me to send the Sarge back to explain how it's done?"

The two men shook their heads. Reluctantly, the driver engaged reverse gear and checked his mirrors. With foliage either side blocking his view, he slammed the steering wheel and cursed his luck. Riley looked outside and noticed the clearance on each side was no more than a couple of feet. Reversing a half mile backwards would lose them a lot of time but they didn't have much choice.

It was slow-going but after some time they found the farm entrance to a field with a rusted gate that wasn't padlocked. They were able to lift it open, providing just enough space to manoeuvre the APV around to face the direction they'd come.

They retraced their steps to the junction, stopping at a village signpost pointing in multiple directions. The driver got out and conferred with one of the officers, checking the map and gesticulating to the right in their intended direction of travel. They hadn't gone more than another mile when the convoy ground to a halt again. The situation seemed strangely familiar to all. Two fallen trees blocked their path at right angles to the road.

"That's weird," said one of the soldiers on the radio.

"Everyone relax. It was probably just the storm. Brought down trees all over round here."

Zed was muttering something under his breath. He didn't like it. He didn't believe in coincidences. He leaned forward and spoke to the driver.

"Can you get one of the men to check whether the trees fell or were they cut? If there's saw dust, then we'll know they were cut." The driver gave Zed a filthy look as if he had just asked the dumbest question. "Go on, ask him. It's important."

The soldier relented and relayed the question. After a few seconds delay, the voice from the Land Rover came back on.

"You're right. They were cut. Someone cleared up after themselves, but there's definitely sawdust buried in the mud. Looks very recent. Last couple of hours. The sawdust is still dry. No storm brought these trees down."

"What does that mean Sarge? Are we in trouble?" asked the soldier in the passenger seat.

"Look, it's probably just a first line of defence for a survivor camp beyond here. They don't want vehicles driving straight into camp without warning. It's what we'd do too. There's likely a single route only known to them."

"Or it could mean that someone knew we were coming and blocked our route," suggested Zed.

"Don't go spreading wild theories, please. I'm sure there's a perfectly innocent explanation."

"There's probably someone watching us now," warned Zed. "Everyone keep your eyes peeled."

Riley shifted uncomfortably in her seat. She felt like a caged tiger in here. She longed to be outside, where she could see or hear an attack coming. Not stuck in here with these scientists. The forest looked so inviting. With the engine idling, the air vent was only just taking the edge off the high stench of unwashed bodies cramped together inside this tin can.

Once more they reversed up the road and set off again, this time down a different path that led them towards the M27 motorway and Cadnam junction that provided access to the main road through the New Forest.

"Didn't the Sergeant say specifically he didn't want to come this way?"

"He doesn't have much choice now, unless we want to make a big detour east towards Calmore and Southampton. It's more built up there. More cars, more people. Sarge is right, this is still the better route."

The road seemed to open out a bit with wide open spaces and sweeping views to left and right. There was gorse and grass as far as the eye could see. Wild ponies and cattle roaming free here. For Riley, it was like stepping into a dream. Unspoilt and beautiful, views stretching into the distance beyond the trees. Here there were no signs of the breakdown. Life had carried on regardless, oblivious to man's desperate struggle.

Ahead of them, the road narrowed again into a single file roadway as it funnelled through a gap in the trees where the canopy grew thicker and more enclosed. The convoy slowed to navigate some objects in the road, rocks and planks of wood, a discarded load from a truck. Either side were bushes and thick foliage that suddenly made Riley feel claustrophobic again inside this dark tunnel. She had just turned to ask Zed something when there was an enormous deafening explosion.

For a few micro-seconds their ten-tonne APV seem to lift up in the air before banking on to two wheels and sliding over on its side in a terrifying screech of metal. They slid down the wet bank until their momentum slowed and their front wheel dropped into a narrow water-filled drainage ditch.

Riley was knocked unconscious momentarily as she landed heavily on top of Zed, dimly aware of voices and smoke filling the passenger compartment.

Zed wasn't moving and she noticed a rivulet of blood streaming from a cut on his forehead. She rolled off Zed's inert body on to the cold metalwork of the upturned cabin, but found her leg was trapped, pinned underneath some heavy containers that had been stowed against the side of the cockpit. The black webbing had broken loose, spilling its contents. There were shouts from outside. As her vision began to fog, she listened with strange detachment to what sounded like a fireworks display. The last thing she heard before passing out was the wrenching of metal as someone attempted to lever open the twisted rear door. Sunlight flooded into the cabin as she gave in to the pain, lapsing into unconsciousness.

CHAPTER TWENTY-FOUR

Riley woke, disoriented. It took her a few seconds to regain her senses, piecing together the fragments of memory that had led her here. She remembered the APV on its side, the smoke. She had been dragged from the wreckage, manhandled into the back of a truck, but that was about it. The rest was blank. Where was she?

It was dark and her hands were tied behind her back. She was lying on a dirty mattress on a bare concrete floor. The room, as much as she could see, was littered with empty plastic cups and food wrappers. She listened carefully for any noises that could provide a clue to her whereabouts. A light scratching, scuffling sound suggested a mouse or rat was her only companion.

She levered herself up on to her backside. Her eyes were beginning to adjust to the gloom, taking in her surroundings. There was a narrow window not even big enough for a child to escape through. Through glass thick with grime and cobwebs came a hint of moonlight. She could make out branches with dense foliage reaching down towards her, brushing against the brickwork. Her mouth had a metallic taste to it. Coupled with the throbbing coming from her cheek, neck and shoulder, and the sticky feeling around her scalp where hair was matted together, she assumed there had been some bleeding. A towel by her side was stained with blood where someone must have staunched the flow and cared for her while she was unconscious. That was encouraging, she thought to herself. Someone wanted her alive.

She looked around the room, searching out any other discernible shapes in the shadows. She was alone in what looked like a basement room. Judging by the pipes in the ceiling, the industrial air vents, the racking against one wall, it was likely a warehouse or commercial building of some sort. The door looked solid and heavy with a simple lock and a small square window of reinforced glass.

She stretched out her legs and got circulation flowing again to her feet. Wiggling her toes, her limbs were stiff and sore. Unable to reach out, she flexed and wriggled against her bindings, checking herself for further injury. Other than a sore head and some bruising to her hip and shoulder, she seemed fine, nothing broken. She could still walk, or run, should the opportunity to escape arise.

Her memories began to return like shafts of sunlight piercing a dense fog. She remembered the explosion, the APV teetering, rolling on its side and then nothing. She didn't remember how she had got here or where she was. Leaning against the wall for support, she got herself on to her feet and hopped over to the window. It was too high to see out of, other than a sycamore tree towering over the building, framed against an overcast moonlit sky. There were no other buildings she could see. In the far corner, she tried leaning on the door handle but found it locked. Outside she could see several doors like hers and a corridor that stretched to left and right.

Riley shouted "Hello. Is there anyone there? Can anyone hear me?"

She listened for any response or movement, but there was silence. She tried again, this time banging her body and head against the door, lying down and kicking out with her feet. She put her ear to the door, hoping for an answer.

From one of the other rooms she heard what at first sounded like a pained groan. It came again, this time more distinct. It sounded like someone trying to speak, but with a sock or rag stuffed in their mouth. Riley banged again and then shouted.

"Can you hear me? Is that you Zed?"

She heard the same muffled vocalisations, more insistent this time. It was hard to say for sure, but it sounded like Zed.

She cast her mind back to the explosion. They had been on a narrow country lane. The other routes they had tried had been blocked by fallen trees. Zed had been suspicious that someone was channelling them towards something. Towards what though? A trap? Perhaps the explosion had been a road-side bomb. What did the military call those things back in Afghanistan and Iraq? IEDs. Improvised explosive devices. Set to knock out passing vehicles, including heavily armoured personnel carriers like the one she had been in. It was a miracle they were alive at all. Unless the Humvee in front had set off the charge and had simply been knocked on its side by the force of the blast or a collision with the wreckage from the Humvee. She had been looking behind her when the explosion had occurred, otherwise she would know, wouldn't she?

Why would anyone want to set an IED on a country road in the middle of nowhere? She remembered the driver saying they were somewhere near Cadnam and Lyndhurst, heading through the New Forest towards Southampton, avoiding major roads.

Perhaps Zed was right, this was planned. An ambush. A trap set for them. But why? How could anyone know about the convoy in the first place? Did they get a tip-off about their cargo? For a second Riley had an awful thought. What of the computers and data drives? There had been smoke in the cabin, a fire. What if the drives were damaged beyond repair? What if all those piles of paper printouts went up in smoke?

She reassured herself that they must have copies. They would have taken precautions, kept back-ups for something that important, back at Porton Down. The military were good at stuff like that. They would have security protocols. They would guard their data, build in redundancy, encryption, secured within vaults impervious to outside forces, computer viruses or third-party attack. Besides, the data and samples were useless unless whoever had them also had the capability to interpret and analyse. Like Zed had admitted, there were only a handful of people in the country who could understand this stuff. Then, like waking from a dream, the realisation dawned that perhaps it was the scientists they were after all along. That knowledge and expertise were irreplaceable.

Footsteps in the corridor made her stiffen and move further away from the door, towards the corner. She readied herself. Her breaths short, steeling herself for whatever came next. She heard a key turning in the lock and the door swung open as overhead strip lights flickered on. They had power here at least, which suggested a certain level of sophistication.

She could see a well-dressed woman standing outside with a clipboard under her left arm. A surly looking man entered somewhat cautiously, a handgun held nervously in front of his body, as if it might go off at any second. His paunch spilled over the waistband of his tracksuit trousers as he looked around the room, keeping his weapon trained on Riley. Finally, he checked behind the door before standing aside, making way for the woman with the clipboard. She dipped her head in gratitude and advanced assuredly towards Riley. She was petite and dark-haired. There was something clinical about her. An undertone of disinfectant permeated the stale basement air. Riley assumed she must be a doctor or nurse.

"How are you feeling?" she asked, inspecting the cut on Riley's forehead. "Looks like that wound has stopped bleeding at least. I expect you're still feeling a bit bashed-up though?"

"No thanks to you. Where am I and what am I doing here?" asked Riley tersely.

"I'm sorry, how rude of me," she smiled superciliously. "Forgetting my manners, I should have introduced myself. My name is Doctor Chengmei. We rescued you from the wreckage of your vehicle. You were involved in an accident. Not sure how much you remember."

"An accident, you say? I remember an explosion. I'd say we were hit by a road-side bomb?"

"A bomb? That all sounds a bit dramatic. Look, I'm sorry, I wasn't sure how much you'd remember."

"You can start by telling me why my hands have been tied. And where are the other people I was with? Where are you holding us?"

The Doctor raised her hands, attempting to pacify Riley. "I assure you, all your questions will be answered. But, right now, I just want to make sure you're alright. No broken bones, abdominal pain, no internal bleeding?"

"Just bumps and bruises as far as I can tell. I've had worse, I'll be fine."

"Come on, let's take you upstairs. There's someone who wants to meet you."

The guard removed a flick-knife from his shirt pocket,

reached down and cut through the cable ties securing her ankles. Riley felt the delicious sensation of warmth flooding back through into her extremities, though with her hands still tied, she couldn't massage them to relieve the pain.

Holding her roughly by the arm, she was led through the doorway into a dimly-lit corridor on their way to the stairwell, passing room after room, not dissimilar to her own. She couldn't see inside, but imagined each room had its own occupant. They climbed some metal stairs to a white tiled floor above. It looked like an office building or part of an industrial complex. There was a reception desk and seating area ahead of them where a small expectant group was gathering. They cut right at the next junction towards a door to a box storage room which had been part cleared to leave a simple white desk, with a pair of folding chairs, one on either side.

Without ceremony, they deposited her into a chair facing the entrance, stepping aside to make way for four new arrivals. She didn't recognise the first three, but to her surprise, the woman at the back was very familiar to her. She almost did a double-take seeing Terra.

Riley was confused, caught between relief and astonishment, she rose to greet Terra, yet something was wrong. Terra avoided eye contact altogether. There was no hint of recognition. Was she pretending not to know her? She decided to play along, unsure what game they were playing, but assuming it was for the best.

Riley noticed that one of the other men was studying her reaction, watching the way she was staring at Terra. A knowing smile spread across his face, seemingly enjoying their subterfuge, not giving the game away. Riley looked away from him, feeling her cheeks flush under his scrutiny. The other two were ignoring this charade, whispering conspiratorially by the door. One of them was dressed head to toe in black. He looked military or paramilitary. The other seemed more relaxed. He was well-built with a squashed nose that looked like it had been broken in several places. He wore a plain grey t-shirt that revealed a rich tapestry of tattooed colour along his arms and neck.

The door was kicked shut and Riley took a deep breath, trying to remember what Zed had taught her. Under interrogation, everyone broke in the end. It was pointless endangering your life and health unless someone else's depended on your silence. Stick to your story, don't deviate. Tell them just enough. No more, no less. Don't fight the process, resign yourself to your fate. Know that you are powerless to stop whatever happens to you. She could only hope that Terra would protect her somehow and stop things getting out of hand.

CHAPTER TWENTY-FIVE

Just when Terra thought she could stand no more, Copper stepped back from the bowed head of their captive, wiping sweat from his upper lip. The questions had been relentless. Any hesitation was punished with an open-handed slap. Twice Riley had looked up at Terra imploring her to make it stop.

Terra stepped outside the interrogation room and joined Briggs, Victor, and Copper in the corridor. They had been going at it for nearly an hour and everyone needed a break. Briggs lit a cigar and offered one to Copper, who shook his head.

"This one knows nothing. We're wasting our time with her," said Victor.

"Maybe, maybe not," suggested Briggs.

"I told you already," implored Terra. "Riley is a nobody. She's not a scientist, she's not even military. She's just along for the ride, the same as Zed."

"Well, at least she's confirmed what we already know. The convoy was en route to the island. They're being met along the way by a larger force. They're planning to evacuate Porton Down over the coming weeks. But, beyond that, Terra's right, she's not telling us anything new."

"What do you want to do with her?" asked Victor.

"She's baggage. Another mouth to feed," suggested Copper. "I say we get rid of her."

"Not yet," cautioned Victor. "Not until we get to the bottom of this. Not until we've got the Professor and the others to talk. Copper, over to you. This is your specialty isn't it? I say it's time we apply a bit of pressure, don't you?"

Copper clenched his gloved fists, nodded and went off to fetch the Professor.

Briggs didn't bother knocking and stepped back inside, leaving the door ajar for the others. Victor grabbed Terra's arm, pulling her close. He spoke in barely above a whisper.

"Why are you protecting her? Who is she really?"

"I'm not protecting her. I told you the truth Victor. She's just someone I knew from Hurst. We weren't even close. She's a nurse, a physiotherapist or something. She dealt with victims of post-traumatic stress. We spent two years together, that's all."

"Don't get sentimental on me. We don't have time for loyalty. Do what has to be done. Don't get distracted."

"Don't worry, I won't," she said, pulling her wrist free.

Terra brushed past Victor, who was still staring at her, questioning her resolve, puzzled by her squeamishness.

Back inside, Riley looked up at her as she walked in, head cocked to the side as if resigned to the role she must play. The left side of Riley's face was flush and bruised where Copper had slapped her repeatedly. Her lip was swollen and one eye bloodshot. Terra realised Riley had been crying, tears streaming down her cheek. As the others came back in, she wiped away the tears, holding her head up high, refusing to crack. She was too proud for that. Terra could feel Riley's eyes boring into her, as she stood at the back behind Briggs, casually placing her hands on his shoulders.

"Now, why don't we start again. You say you know nothing about the Professor or the scientists you were travelling with. That you'd just met them, that you hadn't spoken much. Okay, let's say that's true. Then why don't you tell me why they brought you along in the first place. You were in the APV which makes you important somehow. But from what you're telling me, it sounds like you're a bit of a fifth wheel, Riley. In which case, we don't need you either. If I was you, I'd start talking. You might live longer."

"I told you already, I was brought along as an observer. To keep an eye on the men. Most of these guys are in poor shape, they're showing classic symptoms of stress, they've been running on empty for weeks, months even. Some of them are malnourished. I've already treated cases of scurvy, diphtheria, dysentery. My job is to ensure they don't blow out, stay operational for as long as possible."

"Fair enough, so you're part-shrink, part-doc, part-physio. We used to have counsellors like you at Parkhurst. Box-tickers, form-fillers, pen-pushers. Fussing about well-being, whether we were depressed or not. Of course we were depressed. Anyone would be depressed if they had been banged up for fifteen years. It's not like talking about it once a week with a counsellor would make up for losing your freedom. Still, always did enjoy my chats with the shrink. You could always wind them up. Educated company was in short supply you see."

Briggs seemed to pause, lost in thought for a second, as a knowing smile spread across his face.

"Maybe you're not so useless after all. There might be room in my organisation for someone with your skills."

By Briggs' standards, Terra realised this was borderline flirting. She certainly didn't want Riley for competition back at the castle. She squeezed his neck, digging her thumbs underneath his shoulder blades a little harder than she'd intended. Briggs flinched and seemed to get the hint, brushing her arms away, leaning forward again.

"So tell me again about the convoy. You said there were four vehicles, two squads of soldiers. One of the groups was American, the other was from the base at Porton Down. How many men in total?"

"I don't know exactly, but I'd say twenty, maybe twenty-five."

Briggs checked his scribbled notes and made sure her story was consistent, that her version of events remained the same.

"And the scientists, you mentioned they are working on a vaccine. Did you see them loading samples of the vaccine? What else did you see in the other vehicles beside food and weapons?"

"I wasn't there when they were loading up. We were the last to arrive, the other vehicles were ready to go. I only saw what was inside the APV."

Victor jumped in. "Boss, we're getting nowhere. Let's press pause and concentrate on the others."

"Alright, maybe you're right. She's a decoy. She means nothing. Take her back to the holding cell and bring Zed back up again. Now he's been softened up a little, I suspect he might be a bit more cooperative. We can be very persuasive at times. It's just a matter of time before he spills his guts. Ain't that right Copper?"

Terra wondered what they were doing to him down there in the basement. She was dimly aware of the howls and screams in the night when she was trying to sleep. It sounded like a medieval torture chamber. The men helping Briggs who were based here seemed mildly amused as if this was entertaining for them. She knew they would be rewarded well for their cooperation. Briggs had brought two crates full of brand new assault rifles, as a gesture of goodwill.

A few minutes later Zed was dragged in and dumped roughly in the chair. He was in poor shape. Dirt and dried blood covered his face. Terra wasn't sure if the blood was from the accident or from the interrogation. His head slumped forward onto the desk, breathing hard from the exertion of climbing the stairs. Copper grabbed his head and yanked it back, his face close to Zed's.

"Remember me, do you? From the hospital in Lymington? Because I remember you," he snarled.

Doctor Chengmei intervened, her slender hand on Copper's arm.

"He's in no fit state for interrogation. This man needs rest, can't you see? He should be on a drip for God's sake."

Copper shrugged off her hand, ignoring her pleas. He leaned over Zed, enjoying his discomfort, watching his eyes struggling to focus.

"Give him a shot of adrenaline. I only need him lucid for a few minutes. Then you can do with him what you want."

The Doctor reluctantly agreed. She unzipped a small pouch with a needle and syringe filled with a colourless liquid. As Copper held him tight, she rolled up his sleeve, located a vein and injected him with the adrenaline. The effect was almost instantaneous. If it had not been for the restraints and Copper holding him down, Terra had no doubt he would have jumped out of his seat and wreaked havoc. As it was, they waited for the immediate effect to subside before subjecting him to a barrage of questions. When he didn't answer immediately, Copper slapped him hard across the face.

"Again, what do you know about the virus?"

"I told you before," said Zed blinking rapidly, sweat forming on his forehead, "you've got the wrong guy. I'm not a scientist."

"We know that. You told us already. You're an analyst," said Briggs, reading his notes again. "You worked for the MoD years ago. Special investigator. Iraq. Biological and chemical weapons. Blah blah blah."

"Who do you think we are?" added Copper, leaning a forearm against his throat until Zed started coughing and choking, struggling for air. "I warned you that if you lied to us or held something back, you would be punished. Remember?"

Copper released the pressure just long enough for Zed to catch his breath, nodding feverishly.

"I told you everything I know. The Millennial Virus, MV-27. First strain detected in Singapore 2000, highly contagious. Spread through bodily fluids. Airborne. No known cure. Immunity limited to less than ten per cent of the population."

"Yes, yes, yes. We know all that. What about this Project Wildfire? Apparently you're some kind of expert. Or did that slip your mind?"

"That was years ago. I don't see how that's relevant."

"I'll be the judge of that. The Professor seemed to think it was. That there might be a link between the virus and a secret weapons programme."

"No one knows that for sure. It's just a hunch. A theory."

"Go on. Humour us."

"Back in the Eighties and early Nineties, we were investigating the existence of an Iraq weapons programme that was trying to weaponise the flu virus. It wasn't viable. But the scientists working on it were never seen or heard of again. Some said they continued their research in America, that other countries had similar programmes, that the outbreak was no accident. Like I say, it was just a theory."

"Doctor? What do you think? Does that sound plausible or is he just telling us more crap to stay alive?"

Doctor Chengmei was standing against the wall, shaking her head. She wanted no part in this man's torture.

"I'm hardly qualified to comment. I'm a General Practitioner, not a specialist."

Briggs seemed to be weighing up his options, thinking through what he'd learned from the other occupants of the APV. Terra knew for sure that his talk with the scientists had been unsatisfactory. They had been seemingly incapable of answering simple questions without either dissolving into tears, blubbing like children, or pleading for their lives. Briggs had been frustrated that they spoke in a language no one in the room understood except perhaps the Doctor.

"Whether it's true or not. You kept that theory back didn't you? You thought Briggs didn't need to know about Project Wildfire. He wouldn't understand. He's not a scientist. Why should he care? We had to learn about it from someone else. I asked you earlier whether you'd told me everything you knew and you told me you had. In my book that makes you a liar."

Briggs started tutting to himself, shaking his head.

"You know what? I met dozens of people like you in prison. They were two a penny. People who thought they were smarter than everyone else. Jumped up wide-boys who went to college, got a degree, big job, worked in the City or wherever. They were the stupid ones. They learned nothing about how the real world works. I called it a common-sense by-pass. You see, living on your wits, starting with nothing, not having a family to give you a head-start in life, it all teaches you to look after yourself, to be independent, to be a self-starter. You know what I did? I surrounded myself with people smarter than me, taught them how to think, how to act, how to get what they wanted. People like you make me laugh. You've spent your whole life learning stuff that doesn't matter anymore. You're a wind-up toy in a digital world. The virus made all your knowledge irrelevant. The new world is made for people like me."

Zed remained silent, staring back like a trapped animal, the effects of the adrenaline beginning to subside, replaced by fatigue and fear. He struggled against his bonds, trying to get up and get out of that room. Terra thought he looked like a man on the edge of sanity, losing his grip.

"Looks like we got ourselves a fighter here. Perhaps it's time we taught him some respect eh? Copper, grab that axe thing of his will you."

Terra watched with growing alarm as Copper kicked through a pile of personal belongings in the corner of the room. The pile included various items rescued from the APV. He unhooked the double-headed axe from the backpack it was secured to. Zed had told her once that he liked to keep it about his person as a deterrent more than anything. Copper tested its weight in the palms of his hands. There was something pleasing about it. It was reassuringly solid yet light and perfectly balanced. Reluctantly, he passed the axe to Briggs who patted it affectionately.

"Hold out his arms. We need to teach this one a lesson."

"Briggs, please. You don't need to…"

"Shut it Terra, unless you want to take his place."

Copper grabbed hold of his wrists tied together and forced his arms out on the table in front of him.

"You know, in Saudi Arabia, when a thief was caught stealing, his hand would be chopped off as a deterrent to others. If a man lied then his tongue would be cut out."

Briggs stood up and switched the axe from one hand to the

other. "Adultery, well that was a hundred lashes. Witchcraft was my favourite. You lost your head for that. You Zed, I reckon you look like a bit of a sorcerer, eh?"

He lifted Zed's chin with his hand, peering deep into his eyes, flicking from one to the other. He lowered his voice, it sounded almost caring.

"You probably don't remember, but a lot of my people died because of you. That missile that took out my convoy on the island was your doing, wasn't it? You've been working with the Americans all along. Conjuring up mischief wherever you go. Well, not anymore."

"Please," said Terra, interjecting again. She'd witnessed similar punishments before and didn't want to be a party to Briggs' butchery.

Briggs leaned forward and quickly inserted the tip of the axe in between Zed's wrists, flicking through the cable tie with one twist. He splayed his two arms apart with the blade and before Zed could react or flinch, brought the axe down hard embedding itself in to the vinyl surface.

Terra screamed and covered her face, not daring to look at what was left of Zed's arm.

"I'd say your magic days are over, wouldn't you?" said Briggs, wiping a splatter of blood from his cheek. "Patch that arm up will you Doc. I want this one kept alive."

CHAPTER TWENTY-SIX

Riley couldn't stop crying. She had been standing near the window for the last few hours, craning her neck to distract herself with the dark tapestry of autumnal colours in the surrounding trees. On any other day, the festival of yellows, browns and greens would have lifted her mood, but not today. The screams she had heard from above, shook her to the core.

When she had seen with her own eyes what they had done to some of the other prisoners, she found it hard to control her anger. How could they do something like that? What could possibly have justified such brutality? She worried about Zed, that his stubbornness and refusal to cooperate would get him into deeper trouble. That those inhuman animal screams she heard had belonged to Zed.

When the Doctor had looked in on Riley the next morning, she could tell from the troubled look on her face that something was terribly wrong. It took a few minutes for the whole truth to reveal itself, for her to come clean.

At first, Riley didn't dare confront her fears, preferring to believe the Doctor's unease related to betraying her Hippocratic oath, ignoring professional medical responsibilities, or something. She was evasive in her answers, avoiding eye contact.

In the end, when Riley asked after Zed, the Doctor could contain herself no longer. She told Riley in breathless sobs what they had done to him. Riley turned away, fighting for breaths. It felt like all the air in her lungs had been squeezed out of her. Her chest was held in a vice, like the panic attacks she had suffered as a child. She remembered her mother's advice, coaxing her to slow her breaths, to regain control.

"I'm so, so sorry. I had no idea they would do that. To punish a man in that way. It was unspeakable."

"Why didn't you stop them? You're a doctor for God's sake. You're sworn to save people, not stand by and let this happen."

"There was nothing I could do," she said, shaking her head, covering her mouth with her hand in anguish. "We should never have agreed to help these people."

"Then why did you? Briggs is a monster. He'll stop at nothing to get what he wants."

"We had no idea. They came here offering gifts. They told us they needed our help to stop the convoy from Porton Down reaching the coast, to capture their leaders and send them back where they came from. They promised us weapons. They already knew how much we distrusted the soldiers after what they had done to the surrounding communities. Those bastards kidnapped two of our group. We never saw them again. Briggs told us that they infect the people they capture with the virus, to test some vaccine they're developing. They all deserve to die for what they are doing at Porton. They're the ones who are evil."

"It's lies, all lies. They're twisting the truth to suit their purpose. The team at Porton Down is trying to develop a vaccine that could save us all. Can't you see that Briggs is duping you? He's telling you what you want to hear, to gain your trust. Those men you helped capture are scientists and researchers. They might well be our last best hope of salvation."

"You really believe that there's going to be a cure? Don't kid yourself."

"Not yet, but in time, they'll find the answer."

"You forget, I was there, during the outbreak. Watching all those people die. There was nothing we could do. We tried everything. We threw the kitchen sink at that virus and it just laughed back at us. Is it true what Briggs said? That the virus was bio-engineered?"

"We don't know that. It's just a line of enquiry. No one knows that for sure."

"I wouldn't put it past those bastards at Porton Down. It beggars belief. Millions of people died, and for what?"

"You really believe our own government, or any other government for that matter, could do something like that? No way. Who would possibly gain from the mass extermination of the human race?"

"Don't be so naive, only every terrorist and extremist in the world."

"The only way we'll find out for sure is if those scientists are allowed to finish their research. What if they can figure it out? Shouldn't we give them the chance? It might be our single greatest hope. Why snuff that out, give up before we've given them every opportunity?"

"Listen. I gave up hoping a long time ago. When you lose everyone you care about, you stop believing there's someone upstairs looking out for you."

"But hope's about all we have left. It's what keeps us all going. Camp Wight, the island, it's a fresh start. Something to look forward to. The belief that we can rebuild, make a better world. That the human race isn't finished, it's just going through a painful readjustment. That we'll find a way. Can't you see, it's our duty to keep trying until we figure it out."

"Listen, I don't want to rain on your parade. Really, I admire your resolve. But getting people's hopes up like this, is wrong. Promising them false dreams, luring them to the island like they are, when the only thing waiting for them is hard labour. We've all heard the stories, the truth about what's really happening on the island. What the Americans are up to. We're much better off staying where we are, making the best of our lot, working together with the local communities, becoming self-sufficient. Not upping sticks and leaving this behind so we can start again, working for someone else. People like us, call us the disenfranchised, we don't want anything to do with those guys, the military, the government. They're the people who got us in this big mess in the first place."

"You've got this all the wrong way round. They're trying to save us."

"Who says we want to be saved? We're doing fine. We're making the best of our lot here. The sooner you give up spreading false hope, the sooner you can accept your reality."

"You're wrong if you think surviving is going to be enough. Things are only going to get worse. The last few years have been easy. It's what comes next that I worry about, a descent into savagery."

"Not here, we're good people. You brought that wickedness with you and you should take it back with you when you're gone."

"Then don't stand in our way. Open your eyes and see who these people are, what they're capable of. Briggs is an escaped convict, a career criminal. He's not one of the good guys."

"We're not taking sides here. We're just doing what we need to survive."

"Fine then, send us on our way. Give science a chance. Maybe you're right and we're all deluded, but what if you're wrong? Do you really want to be one of the people who stood in the way of progress? You're a doctor. You dedicated your life to saving people."

"But not those people. Not after what they did. They deserve whatever's coming to them."

"But what about the rest of us? Me, Zed and the Professor. We're not from Porton. Don't tar us with the same brush, please."

"When you threw your lot in with those guys, you chose sides, sealed your fate. There's nothing I can do now. It's out of my hands."

"Please, I'm not telling you to take our side. All I'm asking for is a gesture, turn a blind eye, that's all. Tell me how I get out of here."

The Doctor tilted her head and stared at Riley. She sighed and shook her head. "I can't help you Riley. They'd kill me if I tried."

She turned away and slowly walked towards the door which was locked from the outside. She knocked and waited, facing away from Riley. The guard's footsteps were heard approaching down the corridor. The Doctor turned and closed her eyes.

"Listen, I'll protect you as much as I can. I won't let them do to you what they did to Zed. Okay? Let me talk to the others. We may have underestimated you guys. But no promises."

"Thank you Doctor," said Riley, "that's all I'm asking. And Zed? Look after him, please. Tell him I'm here."

"Sure. And call me Jen. No one calls me Doctor any more," she shrugged. "I stopped trying to save people a long time ago."

"It's never too late to change," offered Riley as the Doctor smiled weakly and left.

When the door had closed again, she heard the key turn in the lock and the guard's footsteps heading away down the corridor. Riley was left to her thoughts. Every time she imagined Zed and pictured his missing hand, she burst into tears, burying her head between her legs to make the mental images go away. Eventually, she lay down on the mattress and drifted off into a restless sleep filled with strange dreams of torture and severed limbs.

She woke to a rhythmic tapping coming from the window. Riley dismissed the noise as the branches of the tree outside, swaying in the breeze. Out of the corner of her eye, she noticed a movement and there at the window was a pair of eyes looking down at her. It took her a moment to take it in. It seemed so incongruous, yet there it was. The bearded face and features of Sergeant Jones smiled down at her, waving her over so that he could speak to her.

"Been looking all over for you. Where are the others?" his voice just loud enough to be audible through the glass.

Riley shrugged her shoulders and pointed in the direction of the other makeshift cells she had noticed on her way up for interrogation.

"Stay here. We'll be back as soon as it's dark. Be ready at midnight. Try and get word to the others too."

Riley nodded excitedly and then the face was gone. She almost wondered whether she had imagined the whole episode. Sitting back on the mattress, the practicalities of the attempted rescue dawned on her. She was in the basement of a heavily-guarded building with not just Briggs and Copper's thugs to deal with, but an unknown force who were based here. It could be dozens if not hundreds of them. She knew Jones had five of his guys with them and the Porton Down team had another seven or eight. Even with luck on their side, could that possibly be enough?

Knowing Jones, they wouldn't risk an all-out assault. They would use all their skill and guile, make use of every advantage afforded by their training and equipment. That would likely mean stealth, night-vision, diversionary tactics. Whatever she might think of Jones and his men, they were professionals and she had to believe that they had done this sort of thing before. As for Briggs and Copper, they had no idea what was about to hit them.

CHAPTER TWENTY-SEVEN

Zed regained consciousness with a gasp that made his whole-body flex. The pain in his wrist exploded up his arm as if every fibre in his body was crying out. He rode the wave of nausea, staring down in horror at the stump where his left hand had been.

Blood-soaked bandages covered his lower forearm and wrist. He closed his eyes, retreating into an inner-world. His mind was playing tricks on him. He could feel sensation in his fingers as he tried to wiggle them, but there was nothing there when he opened his eyes.

His head was woozy, his thoughts jumping around as he tried to remember, to make sense of what had happened. The Doctor had given him morphine. He should be grateful for that at least. He recognised a numbness in his very sense of being, a total loss of sensation, of caring. He was experiencing a delicious disconnection with reality and the world around him, but as that protective envelope began to dissipate, pain had broken through. A rhythmic throbbing began to drown out his every thought.

He struggled for mastery of his senses, gritting his teeth. Opening his eyes, he realised it was dark again. He was back in the same bare concrete room in the basement, dimly-aware of the moans and sobbing coming from surrounding cells. Overnight, the world had been turned upside down into a place of torture. They were all now at the mercy of their executioners in chief, Briggs and Copper. Their whims would determine his fate, whether he lived or died. Nothing he said or did would change that. The sense of helplessness was disconcerting, and at the same time, disarming. His father had always told him not to worry about things outside his control. This was one of those times. He must resign himself to his situation, accept its constraints and then work with what he had. Unfortunately, that wasn't much.

His only hope was that others were in better shape than he was. He had to believe that some of their party had escaped captivity. He remembered little after the crash. He knew from the discomfort that he had been knocked out. There was nothing broken, but he was badly bruised down his left side. That pain was eclipsed by the terrifying sight of his arm, cradled tenderly in front of him. He needed to disconnect somehow, block the agony, stop it from overwhelming his senses again.

He rolled on his side, trying to stimulate his circulation again and relieve the pressure on his injured shoulder.

His private introspection was punctured by a metallic scratching coming from the door. It sounded like someone inserting a foreign object into the lock, testing the handle. Perhaps it was the Doctor coming back to check on his dressing, give him some more morphine to help him sleep. He opened his eyes wider to try and discern the source of the commotion, but the door remained closed. There was a loud thud as if someone was throwing their weight against it and then, with two loud kicks, the lock splintered and gave way, sending its chrome fitting careering across the concrete floor.

A torchlight arced round the room looking for something or someone before arriving at his face. He shielded his eyes with his good arm, squinting back. There was a flurry of movement as someone rushed over and he flinched, expecting an imminent blow. Instead, a female outline he half-recognised crouched down next to him. He gasped in pain as the woman threw her arms round him. Even with his eyes closed, he knew it was Riley. She drew back, hand over her mouth kneeling in front of him, pulling him upright. She leaned in close, supporting his weight as he tried to stand.

"Come on, we're getting you out of here," she whispered softly. It was the most delicious thing he had heard in days.

One of Jones's men joined her on his other side, and between them they got him upright and walked him out the door, propping him up against the wall. There were other torchlights further down the corridor, as the rescuers systematically checked each room for the scientists. They passed the empty cells, Zed's left foot dragging awkwardly, moving inexorably towards a rusting iron stair case at the far end that led to a fire escape. The door had been crowbarred open. Outside, in the cool dark air, Zed started to shiver uncontrollably, dressed only in a ragged t-shirt. He faltered, his last reserves of energy spent as the soldier manhandled him the rest of the way beyond a footpath and overgrown grass verge towards the tree line and the darkness beyond.

Behind them, Zed could hear voices. A floodlight powered up from high on the exterior wall, bathing the car park and landscaped garden with orange light. Zed heard the Staff Sergeant's voice shouting to shoot out the light before their pursuers could locate the escaping group. A few seconds later, a short burst of automatic fire, ricocheted off the brickwork and smashed the glass, plunging them back into darkness.

Torches to their right danced across the car park, panning round the back of the building, searching for the source of the commotion. Muffled exchanges of fire and muzzle flashes from the first floor rooms lit up the trees as bullets landed all around them. One of the soldiers to their right went down, clutching his leg. Zed paused to help him, but was dragged onwards. Looking over his shoulder, he saw the man get gingerly to his feet as he limped onwards.

As they reached the tree line, Zed felt damp leaves beneath his bare feet. The smell of wet grass and pine needles was overpowering as they pushed further into the forest, leaving the firefight far behind. Zed stumbled again and nearly fell before Riley intervened, straining against his body weight.

"Not much further. Come on Zed. You can do this big guy," she urged between gritted teeth.

Two soldiers emerged from their hiding places ahead of them, covering their escape with weapons drawn and Zed recognised the men from Porton Down. One of them took the place of the American, who seemed relieved to rejoin his team leading the last of the hostages away from the building.

"Did you get the drives and the laptops?" shouted a voice ahead of them.

"We're going back in now to search for them," said the American.

"They were in the interrogation room on the ground floor," shouted Riley. "Three rooms down from the lobby. Be careful."

The American nodded and swung the assault rifle hanging on a strap from behind his back in front of him, jogging back to find the rest of his team. The exchanges of intermittent fire seemed to intensify behind them as shots were heard from left and right, as more defenders arrived from the surrounding buildings.

They headed deeper into the forest. Zed's vision was clouding again as his head lolled against Riley's shoulder, his feet dragging behind him as the Porton man on his left struggled to keep Zed upright. His reserves spent, he begged to be set down to get his breath back. He simply couldn't go any further.

He heard voices ahead of him and a torchlight shone in their faces. Once they had been identified, the torch dipped down and they were escorted the last few meters to the back of the waiting vehicles. Two soldiers took over from Riley, manhandling Zed into the back seat of the Humvee. He flopped back against the headrest, clutching his wrist. Riley climbed in beside him, wrapping a sleeping bag round his torso, squeezing his shoulder to let him know she was there for him.

With a groan, his head slid down onto the seat, cradling his arm in renewed agony. The soldier raced round to the other side of the vehicle and Zed could hear him fiddling with a pouch on his webbing as he tore open a medical pack. Rolling up the sleeve and exposing his right arm, Zed felt a small nick as a needle found his vein and delivered a shot of morphine. He felt a numbing warmth spread slowly up his arm and once again overwhelm his senses. He smiled in spite of the pain and gave in to the delicious feeling of floating.

"Don't worry, he'll be fine. He'll be out of it for some time."

Riley's face leaned over him and the last thing he heard before slipping into unconsciousness was her soothing voice close to his ear. "Sweet dreams big guy."

CHAPTER TWENTY-EIGHT

The Humvee and the two other vehicles that remained of the original convoy from Porton Down bumped along a narrow farm track in darkness that ran parallel with the main road towards Totton and the outskirts of Southampton. Riley was nursing Zed's head in her lap, stroking his hair. The morphine shot had knocked him out and for the last couple of hours he had been blissfully unaware of their escape from Briggs' clutches. She tenderly wiped a damp cloth across his feverish brow, closing his mouth to stop him snoring.

Riley tuned into the conversation of those around her. They had sustained three additional casualties in their rescue attempt, bringing the total wounded to five, two of them serious needing urgent medical attention. They had been stabilised but one needed surgery to remove a bullet lodged in his shoulder. Another had received a knife wound to his abdomen which had been patched up by the medic from Porton Down, assisted by Riley. Out of the eight hostages, they had returned with seven. The Professor was missing. No one had seen him since the ambush. They had searched all the other holding cells in the basement without success.

Their only hope was that the Professor was being held

somewhere else, in a different building, according to his elevated status. Riley wondered why they wanted him so badly and remembered her interrogator's questions about his role on the council and the research facility he had established on the island. To her, he was simply a bumbling, wire-haired, bespectacled academic, but she was beginning to believe he could have been Briggs' target all along.

Behind them in the Land Rover and the other Humvee beyond, she could see Sergeant Jones in the passenger seat, relaxed but alert. His attention was fixed on the rear-view mirror, making sure that they were not being followed. As daylight broke, they had put several miles between Briggs and them, passing a green-painted corrugated metal church hall in the sleepy village of Bartley just south of Cadnam, sticking to minor roads, making slow but steady progress.

A voice on the radio broke the conversational lull in the Humvee.

"Newtown, this is Sea lion. Can we get an update on your ETA?"

The co-driver in the front grabbed the microphone and relayed their position with a noticeable smile. Another couple of miles and they could expect to be met by the advance party from the island, who had made the crossing to secure their designated rendezvous point. The *Chester*'s helicopter was on standby to provide air support in case of further attempts on their group.

Colonel Abrahams seemed furious. Scattered around him on the bench seat towards the back were boxes of folders and documents recovered from the APV. Many of them were soaking wet, their sheets stuck together, or worse still, burned beyond recognition.

"How bad is it Colonel?" asked Riley, turning to face him. "Did we recover everything that was taken?"

"Only what they left behind in the APV. They took the laptops and a couple of external hard drives. We've lost Terabytes of research data. Those are still missing. Our search team checked the ground floor but found nothing."

"Did they check the interrogation rooms? The box rooms nearest the lobby? That's where I saw them last."

"Briggs and his group had superior numbers. Once we'd lost the element of surprise, we were outgunned and had to retreat. There were too many of them. We got the scientists, that's the main thing."

"I'm assuming you have back-ups of all that stuff."

"We do back at Porton Down, but there's no way we're going back there now. It's too dangerous. I'm not running that gauntlet again. At least we know where they are, should we need them."

"So what happens now?"

"Our escorts are waiting for us at The Anchor Inn at Eling on the Test River. There's a shallow draft passenger ferry plus a couple of fast launches ready to take us to the island."

He checked his watch. "High tide is in just over an hour, so our window of opportunity closes quickly after that. Eling is tidal, so we have to be there within an hour of high tide or there won't be sufficient water to get us out. Corporal, how far to go?"

"Sir, it's touch and go right now We're going as fast as we can, but the roads round here aren't great. We could save some time diverting back on to the main roads. But after what happened last time, we're keen to stay off the beaten track."

"Very well, just let them know that we're on our way and to wait as long as they can. If the worst comes to the worst, we'll have to set up base at The Anchor and hold out until the next high tide. But that will mean taking our chances with the locals in broad daylight."

In Riley's lap, Zed was stirring, his head writhing from side to side. She stroked his forehead to sooth the pain, reaching for the damp cloth. His eyes flicked open suddenly, grabbing her wrist in alarm, his body tensing.

"Hey, hey, it's okay. I've got you Zed," reassured Riley.

"Where am I?" he said, straining to look out the window.

"You're safe. You're in the Humvee with me and Colonel Abrahams, heading for the coast."

Zed threw his head back and harrumphed as if that was some kind of a joke. He groped around him with his good hand. "Where's my rucksack?"

The Colonel shook his head. "We didn't find it, I'm sorry, there wasn't time," said Riley.

"Oh that's just great. That had all my notes, all the research in it. Do you have copies of the documents you shared with me?"

"Not with us, no hard copies I'm afraid. The electronic copies will be back at Porton."

Zed rolled his head back, cursing their bad luck.

"Why, what was it? Was there something specific in there?"

"Just some archive documents. The Wildfire reports I told you about."

He gestured to Riley for a drink and she handed him a plastic gallon container half-filled with water which he glugged from greedily.

"I need those documents, Colonel. There were transcripts of interviews with the Iraqi scientists we interrogated. I had underlined all references I thought might be relevant. I found a couple of mentions of a flu virus, nothing substantive though. What I wouldn't give to get five minutes with that Iraqi now. Find out what they were planning…" his voice trailed off as his eyes closed, grimacing against a surge of pain, sinking back again.

"Relax Zed. Don't work yourself up," cautioned Riley.

"For now Zed," said the Colonel, "I'd keep any discussion about Project Wildfire under wraps. The last thing we need is people getting the wrong idea, that the virus was man-made. The repercussions could be unthinkable. Any conspiracy theories could fuel discontent, potentially start a rebellion against Camp Wight and the Allies. Perhaps that's why Briggs was so keen to get his hands on the research. It would hand him a smoking gun."

Zed was mumbling, delirious again. His eyes flicked open as if remembering something. There was a look of alarm, close to panic, in his eyes.

"What is it?" asked Riley, suddenly worried.

"Briggs knows. He asked me all about Wildfire. I don't know how he found out, but he knows. I couldn't stop them. One of the scientists must have mentioned it. I tried my best to resist, to hide the truth, but they beat it out of me."

He held the stump of his left hand up as proof.

"It cost me an arm and a leg," he laughed in spite of himself.

Riley noticed the pain returning on Zed's face as he was reminded of the living proof of the injury he had sustained.

"If he has the Professor, then he could make him talk, confirm the rumours. Even without direct evidence of collusion, conspiracy theories have a habit of being believed. It could spread quickly."

"Like wildfire, you mean?" joked Riley, regretting it instantly.

"You're right. The Professor could provide legitimacy to their story, confirm the rumours. They might even be planning to use him as a puppet to foment rebellion against the Allies."

"Somehow, we have to stop the Professor from talking," said the Colonel. "He could do untold damage to our efforts to establish Camp Wight. If we can't get him back alive, then we will have to silence him," sighed the Colonel.

"You mean kill him?" checked Riley.

"If that's the only way, then yes, that's exactly what I mean."

CHAPTER TWENTY-NINE

Heather woke startled in the darkness. It took her a few seconds to get her bearings. She checked the Casio digital watch she had been given for her birthday by her father. It was barely after six-thirty. She was under canvas, in a six-person tent at the refugee camp on the island. A man's voice was shouting for the new arrivals to wake up, banging on their canvas as he strode along the line sending the rain pooling on sloping roofs cascading down on to the grass below. Heather and the other occupants emerged, bleary-eyed from their slumber.

This was their second night on the island. Heather and her newly adopted family still displayed no symptoms of the virus. In another twenty-four hours, they would be passed fit and shipped out to their future lodgings where they were told they would live and work. Today was the day they would finally be told where they were each heading.

The paraffin lights were relit in some of the tents as they dressed quickly. Each of the groups headed in turn to the canteen for a hot drink and a chunk of stale bread. Guards watched them disinterestedly, hurrying any laggards on their way with a firm shove or a kick up the backside, haranguing them with jibes and insults. No one was exempt to their personal attacks. Short and tall, thin and fat, white and black. Discrimination in all its forms. Heather wondered what gave them the right to treat people like this, as if wearing a uniform gave them some kind of licence of impunity. It was almost as if the new arrivals were an underclass, immigrants in their own country in this upside-down world. Only the timely intervention of an officer in a raised voice seemed to keep their behaviour in check.

When it came to be the turn of Heather's group they were marched to the canteen in silence. Talking was forbidden here if you wanted to avoid a rifle butt in your back. Several had found out the hard way that it didn't pay to stand out from the crowd. Heather had spent the last two years perfecting the art of keeping a low profile, putting the hood of her coat up and keeping her face hidden, her body language defeated. Rowan had taught them well, how to think, how to behave to stay alive. She had him to thank for the skills they had acquired. How she wished he was here now and the rest of their group. They would know what to do and how to find Connor again.

Her adopted family was a few steps behind her. The boys were whispering quietly to each other. Heather flipped round scornfully, putting a finger to her lips to silence them. One had a blanket round his shoulders, the other was chewing on something. They both ignored her, staring back affronted, screwing up their faces as if to say "who are you to tell us what to do?".

Heather recognised one of the soldiers from the ferry terminal and stepped out of line to speak with him. In an instant, one of the guards watching the line broke off his conversation and rushed forward, pointing in her direction, gesturing for her to get back.

She ignored him and in her most polite voice addressed the soldier.

"Excuse me, I'm trying to find my brother, Connor. He's nine years old. Brown hair, blue eyes, about so high," she gestured.

"What do I look like? A childminder? How would I know?"

"You were there at the ferry. You took him off, put him in quarantine. He had a cough and a cold, that's all."

He softened a little, remembering the pair of them. "Oh yeah, I remember. Well, if he wasn't sick, and he's still alive, he'll go to one of the camps for kids. But I wouldn't get your hopes up. Not many of the infected survive."

"He wasn't infected though."

The soldier shrugged his shoulders and turned away.

"How do I find him again? Who should I speak to?"

He ignored her questions and resumed his conversation with another. Her adopted mother was waving, imploring Heather to retake her place in the line. Out of the corner of her eye, she noticed the guard who had been advancing towards her gesticulating.

"You. Yes, you. Get back in line, now."

Heather rejoined the family who had advanced a few paces forward. The guard was distracted by something behind them. She couldn't see but perhaps someone else had dared disobey orders. Heather escaped with a passing glare as he raced on, policing the line.

They shuffled forward until they reached the stairs that led inside a farm building which had been set up as a field kitchen, with large boiling cauldrons of water set on top of fire pits. A small team of women were handing out polystyrene cups with a hot milky liquid that passed for tea, poured from large metal catering pots. The bread was flat and hard and difficult to eat with a dry mouth and parched throat. Heather put hers in her pocket for later and drank the tea on the move while it was hot.

The line continued forward into a barn with a farmyard beyond where several hundred people were waiting, huddled together for warmth. Several hay bales had been stacked next to the wall as a makeshift stage and Heather could see a group of uniformed men welcoming someone who looked important. She couldn't make out his face from this distance. There was a swagger about him, a coolness towards others that made her think he did not belong. Something about his stance reminded her of a gunslinger in a western, with a pistol on his hip. She assumed he must be American. The other soldiers were deferential towards him and she noticed him shaking hands with another, giving him a box that looked like a carton of cigarettes. A vicar joined the group, wearing black with a starched white collar. He had greying hair and glasses, but his shoulders were broad and his frame athletic, like someone who might have played football for the local team on Sundays. He shook hands with the soldiers and was introduced to the American.

As the last of the refugees shuffled into the barn and they closed the doors behind them to keep out the wind, an officer clapped his hands and appealed for quiet.

"Good morning and welcome to Camp Wight. My name is Captain Armstrong, I trust you have been well looked after. I know many of you will have come a long way and suffered unbelievable hardship just to reach the island. Your presence is hugely appreciated."

His accent was British, educated, slightly affected. Posh, thought Heather. It reminded her of the Vice Principal at her old school whose life-time in academia had made his language awkward, institutionalised somehow. Despite his best intentions, the Vice Principal had become an instant figure of fun for the children. Much imitated and derided, in equal measures. She wondered whether the officer standing on the hay bales had suffered the same ignominy.

"Father Davy will be coming round to talk to each of your groups later to formally welcome you to the island and to answer any questions you have. I'm sure you have plenty right now."

There was a murmur from the crowd as if that was the biggest understatement of the year.

"We're all keen that you clear quarantine and head to your new homes. First thing you should know is that, here on the island, everybody works. No exceptions. You've all been interviewed and assessed. Those with qualifications and trades will be put to good use. Those without will join work parties and construction crews. You'll all be assigned to teams based on your skills and knowledge. We try our best to keep families and groups together, but as I'm sure you can understand, that's not always possible. Any unaccompanied minors without their parents will be taken to Ryde Boarding School not far from here."

Heather's newly adopted mother patted her shoulders and gave her an encouraging squeeze. Heather had expected something similar so wasn't entirely surprised. In some ways, being placed with other children her age, was the best to be hoped for. After the last few months of scraping a living, fending for themselves, the idea of living in a boarding house, protected and warm, with enough to eat, almost sounded too good to be true.

There was a commotion at the front as a man who had been quietly mumbling his dissent, openly heckled the officer. Despite those around him encouraging him to be quiet, he erupted into a tirade of abuse. Two of the soldiers approached him, fending off his punches and kicks before wrestling him to the ground and dragging him away, blood streaming from his nose. The vicar interceded on behalf of the man, cautioning the soldiers against further violence. Heather could hear the heckler shouting in defiance. "I'm not working for you. I'm not working for any of you bastards."

The officer standing on the hay bale platform tried awkwardly to laugh the interruption away, before being joined by the American who took over.

"Listen up. My name is Lieutenant Peterson from the United States warship the *Chester* anchored there in the Solent. I'm here to tell you that not everyone is going to agree with the way we do things round here. If you don't like it, you can leave. There's a ferry waiting to take you back to the mainland any time you like."

The American paused, surveying the crowd, enjoying their shakes of the head.

"No, I didn't think you wanted to leave so soon. Well, life is different now, the rules have changed. You don't get something for nothing. You either work, or you leave. It's that simple."

The British officer took over with a nod, now that the mood in the crowd had calmed down a little after the American's intervention.

"We're building a new community here at Camp Wight. There can be no passengers, no bystanders. Unless you agree to these terms, there can be no room for you here," he warned.

"We each have a duty to educate ourselves, to put our skills to full use. Every man, woman and child must continue their education and keep learning. Not just about the world or traditional subjects like maths, geography, religion, but also practical skills like first aid, medicine, animal husbandry, how to fix a car, hunt and fish. In short, survival skills."

A voice from the front shouted out again.

"But what use is algebra or trigonometry now? Why waste time learning about things with no relevance any more?"

"It may not be so important now, but think to the future. We are the new custodians of human knowledge. We have a duty to our children and our children's children to acquire and share the skills and knowledge we need not just to survive but to thrive. In years to come we'll need to rebuild, to make this place what it once was, maybe even to build a better world.

"But what if we don't know any of those things? Who's going to teach us?"

The officer smiled and turned to the vicar, sharing a private joke.

"It is a foolish form of vanity," smiled the vicar, "to think we are above the skills we need or that we are incapable of learning. Ignorance is not a sin, but remaining so, certainly is. Through God's grace, we all enter this world knowing nothing. As of today, you are each reborn."

Armstrong nodded and took over.

"Spread the word. Starting today, let it be known throughout this land that Camp Wight is open for business. We are recruiting. We need to train doctors, nurses, soldiers, fishermen, farmers, engineers. So if you've always worked in an office, now's the time to retrain and learn a trade."

"Time is not on our side," continued the American. "Winter is coming. We're going to need enough food and supplies to last out. As we speak, crops lie withering in the fields, needing to be harvested. There won't always be these inexhaustible stores. In time, the shelves will be emptied, the warehouses full of dried goods and tinned food will be used up, then what? How will we survive? Or the generations to come? That legacy will be short-lived. We must fend for ourselves, become self-sufficient. If we don't maintain the vehicles and machinery we need, then we'll quickly return to a pre-industrial age, reliant on horse and cart for transport. We'll look back on these first five years as the easiest. What comes next will be the harder, believe you me. We need to dig in fast to avoid a slippery slope to savagery."

Captain Armstrong stepped forward again, surveying the crowd. Their words seemed practiced as if they had used the same speech many times to successive groups.

"The last few months have been a much-needed pause for breath. What comes next will be far worse. We have a moment of respite to collect ourselves, to prepare. If we don't do that, then the danger is that we embark on mankind's last stand. Let me tell you that the threat of the virus remains very real, even here on the island. If the virus jumps again, if a new strain appears, more resistant than before, then God help us. We can't let that happen. We have to take steps now, to protect ourselves, to build the defences to prevent that happening. We are not helpless, nor should we behave so."

"In the morning, those that are passed fit will go forward to their new lives. I encourage you to make the most of this opportunity, seize it with both hands. This is a fresh start. With your help we can make Camp Wight a beacon to the country and to the rest of the world."

There was a ripple of half-hearted applause as Lieutenant Peterson and the other officer shook hands and congratulated each other. Heather puffed out her cheeks. Were these just more words or did they reveal a renewed purpose?

Could she allow herself to believe things would really be better now? Or was this just someone else peddling hope to the desperate? She shook her head, refusing to accept that hard work alone could fix the world. She had seen with her own eyes that the virus was an irresistible force. Even if they could ensure the island was virus free, it would take more than that for man to prevail again. As her father liked to say, to the disapproval of those who bothered to listen, mother nature had a habit of disrupting man's best laid plans.

The officers at the front of the room stood and watched as the barn began to empty. The mother of her adopted family shepherded the children towards the exit, keeping them close together. Joey leaned in to his brother and whispered: "What a load of happy clappy crap" and the two boys sniggered. "Joey," shouted his mother. "Mind your language, young man."

Heather smiled to herself, sincerely hoping the American's speech wasn't just another set of platitudes.

CHAPTER THIRTY

Saying goodbye to her adopted family had been harder than Heather had expected. The mother hugged her and wished her good luck. The father had meekly patted her shoulder like a faithful dog. The boys couldn't have cared less, until their mother nudged them in the back and they managed a forced "Good luck".

They had all been rechecked that morning by a medic for any symptoms of infection before being cleared for departure from the compound. She was to be taken to the boarding school in Ryde, where all the other unaccompanied minors were being placed. Perhaps her brother would already be there. She hoped she might find other kids from Hayling Island who had made the crossing. She wouldn't be alone, she thought, but being around other kids would feel weird after all this time.

There was an old school mini-bus waiting at the end of the compound, near the farmhouse. One of the guards collected Heather from her tent and walked her over, making sure she actually boarded the bus. Her name was ticked off a list and with a final look behind her, she climbed the steps. Inside, there were a dozen or so kids of all ages. The two youngest children at the front were no more than five or six years old. Their faces dirty.

They looked forlorn and lost. She imagined they had already been passed from pillar to post, only to be displaced once more. Heather wondered how they had made it this far and what had happened to the families who had brought them here.

Towards the back were older children, boisterous and excitable. Clearly, leaving the refugee camp and heading to their new home was a big deal for them, like going on holiday. To Heather, she felt nothing. She was punch-drunk. Refusing to believe she was going to a better place. In a moment of cynicism she admitted to herself that there were no better places, just more of the same.

She took her seat and used her sleeve to wipe some condensation from the window to see outside. The lines of green canvas stretched as far as the trees in the distance, as a low mist hung above the fields. It was still early and there was a bleak beauty to the place that she would remember. Those that progressed from this stepping stone, would start a new life on the island, cleansed and passed fit. They were being handed a passport to something better.

The bus bumped along the heavily rutted road, splattering mud up the lower side of the windows, making slow but steady progress to avoid getting stuck. They had seen so many other vehicles before this one get bogged down and towed out by the farmer's tractor. The driver showed some considerable skill in avoiding the deeper furrows and water-filled potholes, weaving along the road ahead.

At the junction, they rejoined the main road, back on to a hard-top tarmac surface, picking up speed. In the morning daylight, Heather had the chance to look around the countryside and notice other camps like hers in the distance. A forest of canvas, interspersed with portacabins and temporary structures.

There must be hundreds, if not thousands of refugees already here on the island with more arriving every day.

They passed convoys heading away from the ferry terminal, heavy earth-moving equipment and a low-loader with something that looked like a combine-harvester. Military vehicles were also heading inland. She recognised Humvees and personnel carriers, a light armoured tank, a rocket launcher, and Toyota pick-up trucks mounted with machine guns. Heather wondered why on earth they needed so many weapons on the island.

After a half-hour on the road, they turned off and headed towards Ryde town centre. Compared to the mainland, Ryde had escaped relatively unscathed by the chaos that followed the outbreak. Most of the buildings were intact, with their roof tiles in place. Here and there were burned-out shells of houses, some had been abandoned with smashed windows and boarded-up doorways. Parks and graveyards were overgrown, reclaimed by nature. On the whole, the town still looked like a town. Roadways were kept clear, vehicles had been towed or were pushed to the side to allow traffic to pass through unhindered.

What Heather noticed most were the people. Normal-looking people going about their daily business. Cyclists with parcels strapped to their baskets, shopping trolleys being wheeled along, brim-full with books and other assorted items. She saw men and women on horseback. There was a street market with dozens of people lining up to trade items they had scavenged. Life had returned to a loose imitation of normality. Of course, there was a military presence, the same as everywhere else on the island. On each corner, and down side streets, camouflaged army trucks lay in wait, maintaining a visible deterrent against lawlessness. She noticed civilians with red armbands, the same as they had at the refugee camp. It must signify some position of responsibility, she thought. At the camp it had been a licence to bully and harry the new arrivals without censure. Rounding a corner, she snatched a glimpse of open water, of Spitbank Fort, of Portsmouth far away in the distance, with a ferry emerging from the harbour, bringing more refugees to the island.

Finally, they reached a grand-looking building with an impressive frontage where a group of adults were waiting outside to greet them. One by one, they shuffled down the steps and stepped off the school bus onto a tarmac surface, tinged with green. They gathered all the children together, separating them into two groups by age, keeping the youngest together, before leading them off inside.

The building still had the look and feel of a school, although many of the classrooms had been cleared and converted to dormitories for the many children now living here. There were still posters of upcoming school events on the walls. Concerts and art competitions, photos and trophies still in their cabinets. It was enough to make Heather believe that life might just be different living here. Two officers were talking to a smartly dressed woman who might have been the school principal.

Heather was shown in to a girls' dormitory where sixteen camp beds and mattresses were laid out in rows against the walls. Someone had hung sheets down the middle of the room, creating a separation into two rooms. Most of the other girls were of a similar age to Heather, eyeing each other suspiciously in silence. So this was going to be her new home, thought Heather. It was warm and dry at least. Better than roughing it or spending any more time in the caravan. She picked one of the three beds that were still spare nearest the door and set her rucksack against the wall. Lying down, she gave in to her exhaustion, using her backpack as a pillow and closed her eyes.

What felt like a few seconds later, she felt a firm hand on her shoulder, shaking her awake. Looking around her, she realised that the room had emptied and a teacher was standing over her, not looking best pleased.

"Didn't you hear the bell? Everyone else is in the hall. Come on, let's be having you. Leave your things here, you don't need your backpack."

Heather hurried down the hall with the teacher behind her, passing classroom after classroom, rows of lockers and doorways to changing rooms, before finally arriving at some double doors that led into the main hall. They were already closed and she could hear a large body of people inside. The teacher arrived behind her and waved her in with some impatience.

A hundred faces simultaneously turned to stare at Heather as the principal at the lectern paused mid-sentence to look her up and down. She pointed at a space on the floor in front of her. Heather apologised, feeling her face flush as she took her place on the wooden floor right under the nose of the speaker.

"For the benefit of our late arrivals," she peered down at Heather to reinforce her point, "here at Ryde, your days will consist of classroom work in the morning, where you will resume your school education in core subjects such as English, Mathematics, History, and Science. We have a hot lunch at midday here in the hall. In the afternoons, you will learn practical skills such as carpentry, plumbing and heating, electrical engineering and car maintenance, as well as many other everyday design and technology tasks."

"Our goal is to equip you with a hands-on knowledge of the world so that you may serve your community. In the evenings and on the weekends you will join volunteer groups assigned to clear houses for accommodation for the new arrivals, repair vehicles, and work in our vegetable gardens or on our farms here at the school. Through the hard work of our community, we aim to be self-sufficient, but with winter nearly upon us, we need to redouble our efforts so that we have enough stores to last us through."

"Right, do any of you have any questions, before we send you off to orientation?"

A forest of arms went up, including Heather's. One by one, her fellow arrivals asked everything from how long they would be here, when they would have new clothes, whether they played any sport at Ryde, whether they could swap rooms to be with a friend, on and on until Heather could detect the Principal's tolerance and patience, wearing thin.

"Miss, why do we have to study geography? It's not like any of us will get to travel abroad again."

"That's no reason to limit the scope of our learning. Who knows, one day very soon, I hope many of you will venture beyond these shores. Explore new countries. Yes, you there with your hand up. Blue jumper. Yes, you."

Finally, she noticed Heather's hand still raised underneath the lectern.

"Miss, I came to the island with my younger brother but we got separated. Will he be sent here when he clears quarantine?"

"Right, I'm sure there are plenty of you with friends, brothers and sisters who got separated. If they are unaccompanied minors like you, then they will eventually find their way here to Ryde. But there's a chance that they could have initially been sent to one of the other schools. There are several not far from here in Newport, Cowes, Yarmouth, Shanklin, Sandown, and Ventnor that he might have been taken to. Don't worry, they'll get everyone where they're meant to be, one way or another."

Heather nodded in gratitude, but didn't feel overly reassured. If Connor had been cleared of the virus, he could have been sent anywhere. How on earth was she going to find him? She didn't imagine she would be allowed to just wander the island unsupervised, looking for him. Her only hope was that he would be sent here. In which case, why wasn't he here already? Perhaps, those suspected of infection had a more rigorous process to pass before they were released.

A sharp kick from behind, just below her ribs, made her wince in pain and nearly cry out. She whipped her head round and recognised the mean girl from her tent at the refugee camp. For reasons known only to her, she had taken an instant dislike to Heather. Just her luck to be stuck with her again. She rubbed her back to soothe the throbbing pain, staring back at the older girl. She glared back, nudging the person next to her and sniggering at Heather's expense. The girl drew a line across her throat, tilting her head to one side as she held her stare, until Heather looked away again. Out of the frying pan, into the fire, thought Heather. She patted the penknife hidden deep inside her trouser pocket. It was the one Rowan had given her. She had refused to give it up at the checkpoint back in Portsmouth. She hoped she would not need to teach that girl a lesson and prove to her that she was not to be trifled with.

CHAPTER THIRTY-ONE

"We're running out of time, sir," said the co-driver of the Humvee, nervously looking at his watch. What remained of the convoy of vehicles from Porton Down threaded its way through a series of obstacles and abandoned cars. Debris blocked their route, forcing the convoy to pause while two soldiers jumped down and lifted a man-made barricade out of the way. They were already well behind schedule. At the Anchor Inn at Eling, the two R.I.Bs and a shallow-draught passenger ferry from the island would be waiting for them on a falling tide.

For the last two hours they had managed no better than walking pace. Riley shifted anxiously in her seat watching the soldiers lift the last of the cut timber and crates, pushing an SUV with flat tyres out of their path. They ran back and moved off, leaving a cloud of diesel smoke behind them.

A few hundred meters further down the roadway, they turned the next corner to find a low-loader positioned to block the road. It was impassable, they would have to find another way round to reach the RV point. Two figures in camouflaged fatigues emerged from behind the blockade, their arms raised, walking slowly towards the convoy. In his right hand, one of them held a rifle high above his head in a gesture of amnesty.

"Thank God. They're Royal Marines from Portsmouth naval base," said the Colonel, to Riley's immense relief.

He jumped down to greet them and stood listening, hands on hips, as the soldier pointed back the way they had come, directing them towards a narrow lane to their right.

The two Royal Marines walked the convoy back until they were able to mount the pavement and turn around. After a small detour through a car park, in between two warehouse buildings, they bumped back onto the main road, two hundred meters beyond the barricade.

The Colour Sergeant came on the radio to relay the message that had been received while the Colonel was out of the vehicle.

"Colonel, the pilot radioed to say we have less than fifteen minutes before the tide drops far enough that the boats get grounded where they are. I've told them to stay afloat whatever happens. If worst comes to the worst, they can come back on the next tide and we'll have to make camp where we can," said the Sergeant.

"You tell that pilot that it's a matter of life and death. He's to wait in the channel until we get there. We'll swim to the boats if we have to."

"Copy that sir. He's going nowhere."

"It should be just up ahead sir," said the driver. "Providing we don't encounter any last-minute hitches, we'll make it."

"We better do, Private. The last thing we need is to get marooned on the quayside. If we don't get those casualties to a hospital, they won't last the night."

Round the next corner they were met with a hail of gunfire from a building to their left, that left its mark against the bullet-proof windshield.

"Keep going," shouted the Colonel, crouching down low. "Corporal, I thought you said you cleared these buildings already. Any chance of some covering fire?"

Behind them, the gunner on the other Humvee opened up, swinging the machine gun round and raking the second floor, as broken glass and masonry rained down on to the pavement below. At the sound of gunfire, Zed's eyes flicked open and he sat up to see what was going on.

"Don't worry, it's just some half-arsed locals giving us a send-off," reassured Riley.

From their right-hand side, a man ran forward holding a bottle stuffed with a flaming rag. He hurled it towards the windscreen of the lead Land Rover. It shattered on the bonnet, engulfing the vehicle in a fireball. The driver kept going as best he could, but misjudged the next corner, ploughing straight into the back of a parked car. By the time the gunner had swung round, the assailant was gone, disappeared into an alleyway that ran between a row of council houses.

The Land Rover reversed out, its windscreen shattered but unbroken. They limped on with one of their front tyres smouldering, as the flames licked the blackened paintwork.

"Another hundred yards and we'll have eyes on the quay sir. We still have five minutes before they run out of water."

"Don't let me down now. We might still get out of this."

Ahead of them, two soldiers emerged from their firing positions behind a low wall, waving the convoy onwards on its final leg. As they approached the last corner, they could see the quay and small flotilla waiting to take them to the island.

"Don't slow down till we get there. Get everyone ready. I want a fast turnaround here," said the Staff Sergeant's voice on the radio.

"Please tell me you have the quay secure, Sergeant?" asked the Colonel wearily.

"Yes sir, we have the whole landing area surrounded."

The convoy rounded the final bend, tyres screeching on tarmac. The driver braked hard as he brought the Humvee alongside the passenger ferry. The doors of the three vehicles flew open and their occupants jumped down, helping out the wounded and those unable to walk unassisted. Riley supported Zed towards the larger of the rigid inflatable boats with a gun mounted on the bow, where Sergeant Jones and the Americans were heading. Two of Jones's men had taken up firing positions to left and right, covering the roadway.

"Riley, stick with us. We're going to detour to the *Chester*. We can get the Doc to patch Zed's arm up if you like, once he's treated these gunshot wounds."

Riley glanced at Zed and nodded back. "Thanks Jones."

Behind them in the distance, there was the unmistakable sound of a motorbike revving its engine, going through the gears as it accelerated towards them, zig-zagging through the obstacles littering the surrounding streets. They all turned towards the sound.

There was a bend in the road some two hundred meters behind them that obscured the approaching rider. Jones put his fingers to his lips and whistled to get the squad's attention. With rapid hand signals, he split his team to provide covering fire whilst they finished loading the rest of the injured on to the waiting boats. The soldier helping Zed broke off and hurried over to join the rest of his squad. Riley noticed he had a different type of gun with a longer barrel and a telescopic sight that Riley assumed was a sniper rifle. He knelt behind the low brick wall and took up a firing position, looking back the way they had just come.

"Everyone get down," shouted Jones. "Kavanagh, talk to me. What have we got?"

"Single motor cycle. Rider is wearing a helmet, can't see their face," he said peering down his scope. "Looks like they're carrying a package."

"Colonel, anyone expecting visitors today?"

"Negative, assume it's hostile. Could be carrying a bomb or anything."

"Confirm, Kavanagh, if they don't slow down, you take the shot."

"Male or female?" asked the Colonel.

"Hard to say, sir. Probably female."

The bike showed no sign of slowing down, rounding the corner and accelerating again towards the landing area. The rider's head seemed to come up from its hunched position seeing the group in the distance, one hand on the handle bars, the other gripping a canvas holdall with an oversized shape sticking out the top. The bike was no more than a hundred meters away making straight for them.

Without warning, the sniper fired and the rider lost control, lurching to the left before being thrown over the handle bars and skidding to a halt next to the pavement on their side. The bike lay twisted and broken, its wheels still spinning. Riley could still make out the deep throb of the engine, stuck in gear. For some reason it hadn't cut out when it crashed. Jones and one of the others double-timed it up towards the bike and crouched down next to the body, leaning close to the helmet to raise the visor and see whose face lay within.

Riley was too far away to see what was happening, but noticed Jones stand upright suddenly and start waving towards Riley, shouting her name. She ran up the roadway towards them, wondering why on earth they needed her. She wasn't qualified to treat this type of injury. She wondered why Jones hadn't asked for the Porton medic instead. She was terrified it might be someone she knew. Why else would they ask for her?

"I'm sorry, we had no idea. She didn't slow down, we had no choice," said Jones as Riley approached the injured rider with some trepidation.

"I don't understand. Who is it? Is it Terra?" trying to reconcile the shape of the person lying prone with what she remembered of Terra. This person was wearing a black leather jacket zipped up to the top, biker boots and blue jeans. Nothing she recognised immediately. There was a black canvas holdall a few meters away that the rider was reaching for.

"She asked for you by name Riley. Said her name's Jenny."

Riley saw the pained expression in the eyes within the visor for the first time and recognised Doctor Chengmei from the forest camp. Her breaths were coming in short gasps, clutching at her midriff, as her body convulsed again. They rolled her onto her back and lifted up the jacket to expose an entry wound from the sniper's bullet that was oozing dark blood, staining the top of her jeans. The soldier felt behind her back and found where the bullet had passed clean through her. They could only hope that it had missed her vital organs. The medic arrived out of breath, unpacking some field dressings to staunch the flow of blood that was already pooling on the ground. He looked up at Jones and shook his head.

Riley crouched beside the Doctor's inert body, cradling the helmet with her hand, not daring to remove it unless her neck or back were broken. They made her as comfortable as possible, glancing at each other, fearful of their chances of saving her. She had sustained multiple injuries, her left leg and ankle lay awkwardly at an impossible angle.

"Riley," she whispered, blinking for her attention. "You were right."

"Don't try and talk Jen. Save your energy."

"You were right, about everything. We should never have helped Briggs," she gasped, gritting her teeth against a wave of pain. "As soon as you left, he took it out on us. He blamed us. It was a massacre. I barely got away with my life."

Her body was racked by coughing, her back arching as her mouth filled with blood. The medic rotated her head to the side, fighting to clear her airway.

"I'm so sorry Jen. They had no idea it was you. I should have guessed, I should have known you would come."

The Doctor nodded, trying to smile, her teeth stained with blood. "I brought you something," she gulped, reaching for the holdall. "They left it, left it behind. You were right."

She gripped Riley's hand and seemed to lapse out of consciousness, her eyes beginning to close.

"Isn't there something we can do for her?"

The medic grimaced, shaking his head. She was too far gone. With one final heave, the Doctor's chest rose and then slowly fell, her eyes fixed on Riley.

"I'm so sorry," said Jones. "There's nothing we could have done."

"Sergeant, if we don't get going, we're going to get stuck here too."

Riley was still holding the Doctor's hand as the colour began to drain from her face. Jones helped Riley up and she reluctantly released her grasp before jogging back to the boats, where everyone else was now loaded and ready to leave. The helm was lying flat on the quay, looking underneath the boat, where they were grounding with the added weight.

The Staff Sergeant positioned two armed soldiers at the stern of the small passenger ferry to ride shotgun, just in case any of the locals wanted a final potshot at their party. Riley could hear the pilot ram the engine full ahead trying to get off the mudflat, watching over the side as they inched forward, leaving a trail of mud and seaweed in their wake. He was mumbling something about shallows ahead of them, worried about getting stuck again on the falling tide. He shouted towards Riley's R.I.B to stay close just in case they needed towing off again.

They stayed tight with the channel, watching the water visibly draining around them, as submerged objects, shopping carts and tyres, started appearing further out into the river. Sure enough, a few hundred meters further on, the bow of the vessel rode up suddenly, as the keel grounded abruptly on soft mud.

They could see from the R.I.B that the larger boat was well and truly aground, tipping to starboard in the shallow water. The pilot threw his hands in the air, cursing under his breath. He rammed the inboard engine in reverse and a torrent of bubbles and dirt churned out behind them. They were wedged in place.

The two R.I.Bs had shallow V-shaped hulls for planing and speed, but were heavily laden with men and equipment. They coasted back towards the stricken ferry, raised their outboard engines so that they were at a forty-five degree angle, careful not to damage their propellors. Coming alongside, they each threw towing lines that were made fast to two cleats at the stern. On the count of three, slowly and then with more urgency, the helmsmen pushed their throttles forward and the lines went taut as they attempted to tow the ferry clear.

At first, she stubbornly refused to budge, but then slowly, little by little, the boat slid backwards until they were back on an even keel, sending a small bow wave towards the river bank.

Away to their right Riley saw a flurry of activity as three locals broke cover, firing wildly in their direction. They ran towards them over open ground, heading for the quayside nearest them. Two were hurriedly reloading. They were still too far away to do any damage but closing the gap quickly.

As soon as the flotilla was back in the main channel, they threw caution to the wind and put their engines ahead full, surging towards deeper water. The R.I.Bs overtook the ferry, powering away down river. Riley watched nervously over her shoulder as the locals ran to intercept around the next bend. This time they would be in range.

The soldiers shouted for everyone to keep their heads down as the two men knelt down and took aim at the approaching boats, failing to notice that by exposing themselves, they would provide a target for the sniper. Riley saw Jones's man take careful aim, adjusting for the movement of the boat, but his head came up again. He didn't have a clear shot, gesturing for the helm to veer right.

The first shotgun volley splattered in the water all around the stern of the boat, but the second found its mark, shattering one of the cabin windows and leaving pellets embedded in the woodwork and fibreglass. Riley stayed low, conscious that the inflatable seat of the R.I.B would offer poor protection if they targeted their boat. The sniper fired but the combination of distance and bouncing on the water ensured his aim was wide. Before they rounded the corner out of sight, she saw one of the men shaking his fist at them.

She turned round, laughing in relief at the good fortune of their escape.

"That was close."

She noticed one of the Seal team to her left clutching his forehead, where a deep graze in his scalp was oozing blood down his face. He smiled back at her and the expression of relief froze, regretting her words.

"Just a flesh wound. I've had worse, believe you me," he grimaced. Riley turned away before he launched into another story about some tour of duty in Afghanistan or Iraq.

"Yes, I'm sure you have, Corporal," she sighed. She had heard her fair share already on this trip.

At the mouth of the river, the other R.I.B accelerated away towards Cowes on the island, trailed at a growing distance by the larger vessel. Their own R.I.B turned to port, passing the entrance to the Hamble River and set course for the *Chester* a couple of miles away. They radioed ahead to prep the medical team for the arrival of the casualties. One of them had lost a lot of blood and there were concerned looks exchanged between those caring for him. The heavily overloaded R.I.B started to roll uncomfortably with each wave and the helm eased back the throttle so that they rode the swell a little better.

Little by little, the American destroyer grew larger until she towered over them. The *Chester* was much longer than Riley had imagined. Over one hundred and fifty meters end to end with two funnel stacks split into two, where wisps of smoke or steam were just visible. Her bow rose up at the front where her anchor chain plunged towards the sea bed in an eastward flowing tide.

Running alongside, approaching amidships, Riley noticed torpedo tubes, deck-mounted machine guns and her main armament of a five-inch gun that the Americans boasted could hit any target up to thirty miles away. Her mast and double cross-trees were a thicket of sensors and aerials.

By way of welcome, Riley could see the walkway being lowered and a team hurried down the ramp to a small landing platform ready with stretchers to help the wounded to the medical bay. They threw their lines and Riley helped to fend off against the high-sided hull of the *Chester*, preventing the R.I.B from riding up and scraping against the lowered walkway. Finally, when her turn came, Jones grabbed her hand and hauled her up. Between them they supported Zed to a seat in the medical centre where one of the kitchen staff handed them each a steaming hot cup of cocoa.

CHAPTER THIRTY-TWO

The arrival of the wounded from Porton Down had prompted a flurry of activity on the *Chester*. The ship's doctor and his team were already dressed in green surgical gowns, scrubbing for surgery outside the operating theatre. Riley deposited Zed on a bench seat outside the medical centre, resting his head back against the wall. He was cradling his arm where the field dressing had come loose with itching. She noticed a whiteboard with four names written in block capitals, letters and numbers alongside each denoting their injury and blood type. Zed's name was at the bottom of the priority list.

"This here's our Chief Medical Officer, but you can call him Doc," said Jones disarmingly. "He doesn't stand on ceremony. He'll take care of Zed."

"We've met before actually," corrected Riley. "He's been to see us a few times. Things we couldn't deal with ourselves - blood poisoning, multiple fractures, gunshot wounds, that sort of thing."

"How is Toby by the way?" added Doc, listening in to their conversation. His mouth was covered by a surgical mask, so she couldn't read his expression.

"Oh he's fine, thanks to you. The cast came off last week and he's already running around with his mates again."

"Well, you tell him from me to take it easy. We don't want him falling off walls again. I apologise. I've got my hands full here, perhaps we can grab a coffee when we're done."

"I'd like that. I appreciate you seeing Zed like this. Second time in six months he's darkened your doors."

"Between him and Jack, we're beginning to think you Hurst folks are a little accident prone. Can't stay out of trouble eh, Zed?"

One of the female members of his team added: "Now the hospital on the island is back up and running, they're picking up most of the slack. We're getting fewer non-military emergencies now. This is rare excitement for us."

The Doctor finished prepping, holding both his gloved hands in the air, waiting for his team to wheel through the first heavily-sedated patient into the operating theatre through some double swing doors. A male nurse in scrubs poked his head out, holding the door open.

"Colonel, if you wouldn't mind coming back in a couple of hours, I'd like to talk some more in private," requested the Doctor to a silent nod. "And Riley, it would be good to fill you in about Adele. She's quite the talk of the town right now."

"Sure," she replied a little hesitantly. "I'd be happy to. We'll pop back later."

Riley wondered what the Doctor could possibly want with Adele this time. It was common knowledge that Adele had immunity to the virus. The blood tests had suggested high levels of an antibody consistent with the Porton Down team's findings. The child had been hooked up to more medical apparatus than she could remember. She had given more blood than Riley thought was possible for a girl of her age.

Riley had taken her for overnight trips to see the Professor's labs twice in the last few weeks alone. Perhaps they had made a breakthrough in the meantime, though why had the Professor not mentioned it to the Porton Down team. She wondered whether the Professor had kept anything else back and whether the reciprocity had been genuinely embraced on both sides.

Sergeant Jones escorted Riley and the Colonel through a maze of walkways and corridors up to the Combat Information Centre where they found Peterson and his team in a state of high anxiety. It took Riley a moment to adjust to the dim lighting in the room. Rows of screens displayed radar, tactical information systems and live aerial feeds from what looked like a drone. Each of their operator's faces was lit by a ghostly pale glow, accentuated by the soft red lighting from above. There was something almost demonic and disturbing about the place.

"Is now a bad time or is it always like this?" whispered Riley to Jones, trying to stay out of the way, keeping a low profile.

"No, it's normally like this. This is where it all happens. Operation Overwatch for Camp Wight. Twenty-four hour surveillance of every waterway and approach in the Solent. They average something like thirty separate incidents every day. Everything from intercept missions for small craft trying to make unauthorised trips to the island, then there's escort duty for the ferry crossings and finally transporting personnel back and forth. The guys in here are the eyes and ears. This is mission control for the whole of central south of England."

"So I see," she said, looking over the shoulder of the operator nearest her, whose digital map showed the Isle of Wight and mainland coastline stretching from Bournemouth in the West to Brighton in the East.

Any larger ships or vessels were marked with an identifier

showing course and speed, like an air traffic controller's screen. There was minimal activity for what used to be a busy waterway. The operator tapped on one of the vessels and zoomed in on a boat that was leaving Hythe.

"Sir," his voice was raised, trying to attract the attention of the officer of the watch who looked up from a screen opposite. "We have two tangos heading south out of Hythe at approx fifteen knots."

"Do we have any assets that can intercept?"

"Affirmative, retasking Alpha Seven now.

"I had no idea it was such a sophisticated operation," whispered Riley. "Been a while since I saw a computer and all this tech you have here."

"Yes, I imagine it's a bit different from Hurst."

"We still do things the old-fashioned way. Pair of binoculars, sextant, compass, searchlights. That's about as high-tech as we get over there. Vigilance is our watch word."

"Don't get me wrong. The old ways are still the best. You start relying on technology, sometime soon it's going to let you down. That's why we learn to navigate by the stars and the sun. Live off the land. Keep fit and healthy. That's how we stay alive."

"Your team is an inspiration to the rest of us," flattered the Colonel, listening to their conversation with a strange detachment, surveying the war room as if he was at home in this environment, surrounded by intelligence feeds. "I wish we had more like you."

"Thank you sir, that's certainly our plan. We are working hand in hand with our counterparts in the Royal Marines as part of the new corps command training centre just outside Cowes. We have our first intake of new recruits being trained up."

"Yes, I've seen it. Very impressive. I hear there's been an arm-wrestle of sorts between British and American training methods."

"Guess we all think we're the best. We've found a happy medium. Taken the best of both programmes and condensed it down to six weeks. Basic military training, weapons, fitness, survival skills."

"Sounds like you're building an army?" suggested Riley.

"No, it's strictly small scale," replied the Colonel. "First intake is fifty men and women. Second intake is slightly larger. Look, it's a start. But with the security situation deteriorating, we're still just scratching the surface. We'll need hundreds more recruits if we're to keep the Portsmouth, Southampton and Lymington corridors open for refugees."

"So what happens to all the people you catch illegally trying to make the crossing?"

"Well," sighed the Sergeant. "In the beginning, our orders were to intercept them, explain the error of their ways. Sometimes it was just some harsh language. Others more determined got a shot across their bows. But over time, we found the same people trying again and again. Any other time we'd arrest them, lock them up. Unfortunately, we have no way to incarcerate them. So if they refuse to comply, we sink their boats. Make sure they can't try again."

"What do you do with the passengers. Please tell me you take them back to the mainland?" said Riley opening her eyes wider waiting for a response. "You don't just let them swim home?"

The Sergeant grimaced but didn't duck the question.

"We can't risk infection. Many of these guys trying to make the crossing have been turned away before. They failed the test, Riley. Picking them up and taking them back would be an unacceptable risk for the coastguard teams."

"That would explain why we see so many bodies washed up

on the beaches. Surely there's another way? It's barbaric to let men, women and children drown."

"If there is, I don't know what it is. They know the risks they're taking. They know what will happen to them if they get caught."

"Why is it always so black and white with you people?" lambasted Riley, her frustration boiling over. "These guys are desperate. They're not evil, they're just trying to survive. Colonel, you do realise this heavy handedness gives the Allies a bad name? You're turning a humanitarian crisis into a disaster."

"There you go getting all high and mighty on me again, Riley."

"Don't tell me Sergeant, you're just doing your job. Following orders?"

Jones shrugged, looking for support from the Colonel, who seemed amused by Riley's bravado. She glared at them both before remembering Zed's cautionary words about keeping the Americans on side. She never knew when she might need them again. She feigned a smile and Jones frowned back at her, visibly surprised to see her backing down, as if he was relishing the prospect of another fight. He reminded her of Zed.

From across the room, Peterson had been watching the group, interpreting their body language, curious about the topic of conversation. Riley had heard it said that Peterson was proficient at lip-reading and always seemed to know what people were thinking, adept at following conversations from a distance. Their group was standing awkwardly by the door and he wandered over to greet them.

"Good to have you back, Colonel, Riley." he nodded, his hands behind his back. "I hear you got the Porton scientists back safely. Sergeant, what's this I hear about the Professor being MIA?"

"Yes, sir. Our convoy was attacked on the way back. An IED

took out the APV with the Professor inside. We were ambushed by a superior force, caught in a crossfire. Nine of the Porton team, including the Professor and Zed and Riley, were captured and taken to a forest camp a couple of miles away. The rest of us were cut-off, in danger of being surrounded. We were forced to retreat, barely got everyone else out alive. We waited until nightfall and mounted a rescue operation. Unfortunately, we were unable to locate the Professor or the laptops and drives."

"I look forward to reading the debriefing report."

"Yessir, I'll have that to you by 1700 hours."

"What about Briggs? I heard he was involved?"

"That's correct. Briggs and some of the team from Lymington hospital were there. A man they called Copper. They were working together by all accounts."

"They have taken to calling themselves freedom fighters," added the Colonel. "Trying to rally support to their cause from the forest camps. They seemed very interested in Porton's virus research and knew all about Project Wildfire. Tortured the scientists and Zed until they talked. Briggs now has it in his head that there is a conspiracy."

"So you're telling me that we have a major leak on our hands. That the ambush and delay in hostage rescue may have serious repercussions. What's your assessment Colonel?"

"Well, with the Professor, they have a credible spokesperson who can legitimise any claims they make about the Allies."

Lieutenant Peterson was scratching his chin, taking this all in. He looked puzzled: "I'm not sure I'm following you. What sort of claims could they make?"

"That the Allies are complicit in the outbreak, that somehow the government was involved in bioengineering a virus. That we caused all this."

"And, I'm guessing that, as ridiculous as his theory sounds, it doesn't matter if it's not true. It's a lie that would easily be believed."

The Lieutenant stiffened, placing his clenched fists down on the desktop. The muscles in his neck tightened, the frustration clear for all to see. "Colonel, I don't like the sound of this."

"Without the Professor, it's just a wild rumour," suggested the Colonel. "No one would believe them."

"Then we need to get the Professor back or take him out. Sergeant Jones, sounds like you have a mess to clean up."

"Sir?"

Riley had been listening patiently and wondered why no one had mentioned Terra.

"Lieutenant, are you also aware that Terra, one of the hostages taken from Osborne House, was part of Briggs' group? It was hard to say, we didn't get to speak, but she seemed to be collaborating with them."

"I wondered when she might show up. I wouldn't judge her Riley. She's a smart lady. She'll be doing what she can to survive. Being in captivity makes you do strange things. Who knows, she may be collaborating. She may even have developed Stockholm Syndrome."

Riley half-remembered the term from her counselling training. It was used to describe the behaviour of prisoners in captivity, where, in some extreme cases, they develop an attachment to their captors.

"You mean she might have romantic feelings towards Briggs?"

"That's right. It's more common than you might imagine. Very well. Jones, if you get the chance, you find a way to get her out too. Now, if you'll excuse me, we have a few pressing matters to attend to."

"What's all the commotion? Anything we should know about?" asked the Colonel.

Peterson paused, as if trying to decide whether or not he should share.

"We have a situation developing in the West. Our pilot reported a huge number of refugees massing north of Lymington and we're monitoring another large group approaching from further West heading towards New Milton and Milford along the coastal road. We've let the team at Hurst know to be on their guard and we're sending more troops to secure the ferry crossing from Lymington. But if numbers carry on building as they are, we'll have to close the western corridor, divert those migrants to Southampton where they'll be better able to handle that volume of people. We just don't have the manpower to split our forces between three sites."

"The other Council members are aware of this?"

"Yes, the situation is being managed. It's all blown-up since you've been away in Porton."

"Understood. Thank you for the heads up. It's vital we keep lines of communication open. We all depend on Operation Overwatch as our eyes and ears. The moment we lose that coordination, things will fall apart quickly. We can't risk that."

"Agreed Colonel. You have my word."

"What will happen to the team at Hurst if that group moves on their position?" asked Riley, concerned for her friends.

"Well, Hurst has been refortified and part-militarised. With the reinforcements, they now have two squads there and enough firepower to handle whatever comes their way. Those walls are thirty-feet high. They'll be fine," he reassured her.

"What if the castle gets cut-off and they try to starve them out?"

"I wouldn't be overly concerned, they've got months of supplies, enough water to drink. If it came to it, we could resupply by boat. They could survive for a long time."

"The alternative we are pursuing is that we evacuate all non-military personnel quicker than planned and get everyone over to the island."

"We're not at that point yet, Lieutenant," suggested the Colonel. "Let's keep monitoring the situation. They may by-pass Milford and head inland towards Lymington and Southampton. Let's just make sure we're ready to get them out if that time comes. No point worrying about something that may never happen."

CHAPTER THIRTY-THREE

After they had finished up in the war room, Jones led Riley back down to the medical centre where a female nurse was finishing up, applying a new dressing to Zed's wrist. The wound had been meticulously cleaned to eradicate any chance of infection. The Doctor had initially been concerned about blood poisoning, but after a cursory investigation he stepped away, pleased with how he said it would heal.

"In time," said the nurse, "we can fix you up with a prosthetic arm. You'll have some limited movement, be able to pick things up, that sort of thing."

Noticing the sadness in Zed's eyes she added: "Don't worry, I know it seems like the end of the world, but I've worked with plenty of combat veterans with similar injuries. They can do amazing things these days. You'd be surprised."

The clean bandages had filled the whole room with a faint scent of liniment and disinfectant. It was a smell that evoked so many memories for Riley. The death of her father, the birth of a niece, caring for her mother's long-term illness. It had been some time since she had thought of her family.

Zed held up his arm and rotated the stump, inspecting the bandages.

"We'll need to keep you on a low-level painkiller till it heals," continued the nurse. "You're right-handed, so just be grateful, it was your left."

"Be grateful?" said Zed outraged, "This wasn't an accident you know? I didn't just stick my arm in a wood chipper, someone chopped my hand off with an axe."

"I'm sorry, I didn't mean to upset you. I had no idea, I just assumed it was..."

"Right, you assumed..." repeated Zed through gritted teeth.

Riley put her arm on Zed's shoulder. "Take it easy big guy. She's only trying to help you."

"Well, your bedside manner could do with some work there, nurse."

The nurse stood, her cheeks flushed with embarrassment and excused herself, leaving Riley and Zed alone. He looked up at her with a pained expression, mortified by his outburst.

"Sorry, I guess I'm still coming to terms with what happened. This thing won't just grow back," he said holding up his left arm, managing a weary smile. "Listen Riley, thanks for getting me out back there. That's the second time you've saved my life."

"Don't mention it. You'd have done the same for me. It's the Americans you should be thanking, they were the ones who got you out. Who knows what would have happened to us all if we'd been left there at the mercy of those butchers?"

"I can't help blaming Terra. I know you think she was trying to protect us, but there's no way they knew all that without Terra spilling her guts. Briggs seemed to think I was holding something back, that I was lying to him about Project Wildfire."

"I know, I had that same conversation, but they quickly realised I knew very little of value, which was fortunately true."

"So now they have the Professor which means they must

know everything we know. The Colonel thinks they'll somehow use him to foment rebellion, to spread the lie that Porton Down had something to do with the virus. With all the thousands of desperate people heading towards the island, he might just be able to recruit an army to his cause."

"Particularly if they can convince the new arrivals that the Allies are responsible for everything bad that's happened," added Riley. She paused as if remembering something that had been troubling her. Her sharp intake of breath drew Zed's attention.

"What is it?"

"I forgot to mention. We were just in the operations centre upstairs where all the radar screens and feeds come in. Peterson happened to mention that they're monitoring huge crowds of people heading towards Lymington along the coast road from the West."

"And you're worried they'll head for Hurst. I doubt it. If they're following the main road, then they'd need to swing south to reach Milford and the castle. I can't see them walking a mile and a half out of their way up a shingle spit. The castle is heavily defended, it would be crazy to try anything."

"I know, but after what happened last time, I need to be there. Remember, we thought the castle was impregnable once before."

"It's different now with all the military there. Plus, who knows? If we had been there last time, things might have been very different. For a start, we could have been killed."

"Maybe, but if there's even the slightest risk, I want to be there for Mila and Adele. Make sure they get out safely in good time."

"Look, I'd volunteer to come with you, but they need me here. The Colonel and the others are heading on to the island first thing tomorrow. I'm going to tag along, check out the new research facility they're building at St Mary's hospital. I'm sure your new friend Jones can fix you up with a ride back."

Riley's cheeks flushed a little. "He's not so bad."

"Developing a soft spot for him, are we?"

"Hardly, he's still a red-neck. Not exactly my type."

"Hey, I don't suppose they found my rucksack? I lost everything, all my notes and papers."

"Not that I've heard. The Colonel told me they have a back-up of most of those folders on the drive. We have Jenny to thank for that. If she hadn't driven the laptop and drives out to us, they were talking about having to fly back up there again."

"I think that's inevitable, don't you?"

"Don't say that. Jenny did that for us. I just hope it was worth it."

The Doctor knocked and stuck his head round the door.

"Sorry to interrupt. Mind if I borrow Riley for a bit?"

"Be my guest, Doc. I think we're all done here," he said raising his bandaged arm. "I'm going to try and find the Colonel. Make myself useful."

Riley followed the Chief Medical Officer back along the narrow corridor, stepping over a water-tight hatchway, passing the operating theatre she had seen earlier. They arrived outside a small office set up with a desk and computer, with personnel files and folders secured inside a bookcase with a wooden slat across the front to stop them falling out when they were at sea.

"Have a seat, please," he said, easing back into a comfortable leather swivel chair that was bolted to the floor. "I wanted to give you a quick update about Adele. How is she doing?"

"Yes, so you said. She's fine thank you. She's nervous about leaving Hurst behind, but I think everyone's slowly coming round to that idea. Other than that, she's just a normal little eleven year old, or as normal as you can be after the trauma of losing your entire family and everyone you knew and loved. Why the interest? Is there something wrong, Doctor?"

"Based on the fact that you're the nearest thing she has to a guardian now, I thought you should be the first to know," he said shuffling a pile of patient folders, looking for the right sheet of paper. "We found something unexpected in her blood tests."

Riley's weary smile froze as her mind searched for an explanation. As he located the test results and started reading through them again, she could feel her heartbeat racing. There was an acute sense of déjà vu, as if this scene had played out so many times in her life.

"We were trying to understand more about the source of her immunity and why the team at Lymington hospital had been so intrigued by her and the other girl you mentioned, Stella was it? Well, we think we may have found a clue. You see, Adele has quite a rare form of blood cancer called acute lymphoblastic leukaemia."

The Doctor's words made her stomach begin to cramp, fearing the worst. Her father had been diagnosed with lung cancer when he was fifty-three. The thought of nursing an eleven year old through long-term care was too painful to imagine.

"Oh God, how long has she got?"

"Hold on Riley, I'll get to that. How much do you know about ALL and leukaemia?"

"Not much, but I nursed my father through chemotherapy and lung cancer. I'm assuming ALL is similar."

"Fortunately, leukaemia is extremely rare in children. It was only blind luck that we spotted it when we did. It's where the body produces a high number of abnormal white blood cells. As you know, the immune system needs to make lymphocytes to fight infection and, in patients with ALL, the process stops working properly. Without boring you with all the detail, the lymphocytes grow too quickly to be effective and they start clogging up the bone marrow and preventing it from making other blood cells."

"I'm not sure I'm following, so you're saying it would affect her immune system? How does that relate to the virus?"

"Well, that was the bit that made our team curious. The defective immune system could be one important clue to her immunity."

"That's interesting Doctor, but surely that would only relate to Adele. You're not suggesting that all the survivors have defective immune systems are you?"

"No, but it's often these outlier cases that help shed light on all the rest. It's just a theory at this stage, but one we want to discuss with the scientists from Porton Down who are the real experts in all this."

"So what does all this mean for Adele? What are her chances of survival?"

"I'm afraid the outlook is not good. Normally, we would put her on a course of chemotherapy and she would go on a waiting list for a bone marrow transplant. But, that was before the outbreak. Right now, the best we can hope for is that the symptoms develop slowly and with a bit of luck she might have six months, maybe a full year. I'm sorry, I wish I had better news."

Riley looked at her shoes under the table and tried hard to master her emotions. She wiped a tear away from her cheek.

"Doctor, I appreciate you telling me," she said putting a brave face on it. "If it's OK with you, I'd like to be the one who breaks the news to her. She's a tough cookie, but she's way too young to understand something like this."

"Of course, that's why I wanted you to be the first to know Riley."

"Now Doctor, is there any way you can get me a ride back to Hurst Castle? What with the evacuation to the island and now the news about Adele, I feel my place should be back there."

"Let me see what I can do for you," he smiled weakly as they both stood and shook hands. He opened the door for her and they set off in silence towards the canteen to find Sergeant Jones.

CHAPTER THIRTY-FOUR

One of the crew led Zed through a maze of passageways and stairwells looking for the Colonel. The ship seemed virtually deserted with so many transferred to the island or the refugee processing centres on either side of the Solent.

They arrived outside the closed door to the Officer's Mess where Zed could see the scientists from Porton Down through a Perspex viewing window being entertained by Peterson. The crewman knocked and showed Zed in. Peterson finished what he was saying before welcoming Zed with a curt nod.

The scientists were sat either side of a dining table, with bottles of ketchup and mustard in the middle, enjoying a plate of spaghetti with tomato sauce. Looking around the room, Zed was surprised to notice the politician he had met at Hurst a few days earlier. David Woods had his head lowered, scribbling furiously in a black-lined note book.

When Peterson finished his briefing, he asked the scientists a series of detailed questions about the specialised equipment they would need for the laboratories they were prepping for their arrival on the island. As they listed off the technical specifications, the Colonel moved chairs to be next to Zed and spoke in barely above a whisper.

"The good news is that the laptop Doctor Chengmei delivered to us actually belonged to the Professor. We're not quite sure how but one of the scientists managed to guess his password," he said staring at the man responsible who shrugged his shoulders, "so we now have access to the Professor's notes and the reports he was working on."

"What about the rest of the stuff from the APV? I don't suppose anyone found my rucksack?" asked Zed.

"I'm afraid not, but the majority of the documents and folders we brought with us survived the fire and the rest seem to have dried-out well enough. So all in all, it's a setback, but by no means the end of the world," his voice died away, instantly regretting his poor choice of words.

"What about the Professor?" asked Zed pointedly. The rest of the room fell silent, hearing his voice.

"Losing the Professor is a blow, no question," said the Colonel addressing the whole room now. "There's no one who knows more about pandemic viruses than him."

Zed noticed the incredulous expression on Doctor Hardy's face, remembering how he had pointedly disputed the extent of the Professor's knowledge. It would appear there was some professional rivalry between the two men.

"There's no question that, as an academic and a historian, the Professor is a world expert," continued the Colonel, feeling he had to justify himself. "He advised the Cabinet for a number of years on government policy."

"With all due respect, Colonel, the Professor is a generalist. I can assure you that the people round this table are the very best this country has to offer."

The Colonel relented, trying to patch things up after his faux pas.

"I apologise, what I should have said is that we are extremely fortunate to have Doctor Hardy and his team from Porton Down assisting our efforts. Each of them are experts in their field."

"We'll do whatever we can to get the Professor back, but in the meantime, the show must go on," said Peterson.

The room fell silent as the scientists seemed satisfied with the Colonel's olive branch. Zed sat forward, resting his good arm on the table.

"Assuming now is the right time, there are some questions I've been meaning to ask."

The Colonel encouraged Zed with a wave of his hand.

"Please, be my guest."

"Mr Woods?" said Zed leaning across the table and addressing the politician who was still immersed in his notebook. His head snapped up as if surprised that Zed should be asking him a direct question.

"Reading the reports prior to the outbreak, when the virus was first detected, it would seem that there was forewarning of what was to come. So why were the authorities in this country so poorly prepared?

"Yes, of course. It's an important question," he said, clearing his throat and removing his spectacles. "In all honesty, it was a shambles. At first the Ministry of Health incorrectly assumed that the outbreak was simply a seasonal spike. The media were partly to blame. The winter flu crisis had become somewhat of an annual scandal at the NHS and that familiarity led to an undeniable complacency which made everyone slow to react."

He half-laughed as if remembering something: "I was actually part of the cross-party committee that reviewed the pandemic preparedness plan a couple of years ago, so I know a little more than most. I can assure you that the plans were very carefully thought-through with four robust lines of defence: surveillance, vaccines, containment measures and medical treatments."

"I'm not sure the UK did any better or worse than anywhere else," said Doctor Hardy supportively. "The WHO's Sentinel Programme was set up as an early warning system. They had something like one hundred and ten influenza centres in eighty-three countries. It was state of the art. Incredibly sophisticated, massively resourced. They had antigenic maps tracking over five thousand strains of the virus, collaborating internationally. Their job was to analyse each strain against different antibodies to see how the immune system reacted. Their focus was mostly on Asia as the likely source of an outbreak."

"Why Asia?" asked Zed.

"Because in Asia, particularly in rural areas, many villagers live in close proximity with chickens, ducks and geese, which are so often the hosts for influenza viruses," he answered.

"There's no question that the WHO early warning system failed," admitted the politician. "It was too porous and slow. We were warned that if an outbreak could not be contained within the first thirty days, there would be little chance of stopping its spread. The delays in inter-agency co-operation proved devastating. It was always assumed we would have more time when the first outbreak was detected…" his voice trailed off.

"You see the flu virus has such a short incubation period," added Doctor Hardy, "it moves at frightening speed. Air travel and densely populated urban areas would do the rest."

"What about all the hype around Google Flu Trends speeding up detection?"

"Yes, we all read that. The theory was sound, that by tracking key search phrases related to the virus and treatment, we could identify outbreaks much faster and deploy our resources appropriately. It was fast and cheap and by all accounts it worked as a public health service, but it was still early days for the system. Our response was always too slow."

"Mr Woods, you mentioned vaccinations as the second line of defence. The Professor told me that the UK government had an annual immunisation programme in place to protect key workers, doctors, nurses, politicians," said Zed, raising his eyebrows. "He mentioned two million doses stored in strategic locations around the country. Can you explain what happened to those and why they weren't deployed?"

"Because it all happened so fast. The Professor was right. This country invested huge resources in stockpiling antiviral drugs for just such an outbreak. From what I understand, those drugs simply didn't work for the Millennial Virus."

"That's not entirely correct," countered Doctor Hardy. "It's true that the government and military kept large stocks of Tamiflu and Relenza. Both proved somewhat effective in boosting immunity, perhaps by as much as thirty percent. At best, that helped to slow the outbreak and keep critical services functional that little bit longer, but certainly not sufficiently to be of lasting value against MV-27. In the past, we've employed what we call plasmid-based reverse genetics to create a seed strain for a human vaccine. Essentially, we home in on the hemagglutinin, the protein that triggers the immune response, and develop a vaccine based on a weakened form of the virus. That worked previously against H1N1 and H5N1, but as soon as the virus evolves, it can quickly elude the vaccine and enter the body undetected by the immune system."

"And based on the Porton team's research and clinical trials so far," said the politician, "are we confident that a prototype vaccine is close at hand?"

"I wish that were so," regretted Doctor Hardy. "It could take several years and synthesising a vaccine is just the start. In all likelihood, large-scale vaccination would require the production of millions of shots, enough for multiple doses per person. Setting up the production line alone could take years."

"We're already working on it," assured the Colonel. "We have two sites just outside Newtown which we expect to be operational in nine months' time. In the interim, we have transferred limited stocks of Tamiflu and Relenza to the island."

"Well, the longer we wait, the more manageable that problem becomes. Fewer people to treat," scowled Zed.

"Quite, although we expect population numbers to stabilise now the initial outbreak has subsided," said the Colonel, frowning. "Doctor, for the benefit of Mr Woods, perhaps you can recap on your analysis of the virus and its origin?"

"Certainly, we completed analyses of three of MV-27's eight RNA segments some time ago, which placed them within the human and swine families, certainly outside the avian virus group and H5N1 variants. The team discovered many parallels with the Spanish flu pandemic in the aftermath of World War I. We were lucky enough to exchange data sets with the US Armed Forces Institute of Pathology's historical archive, which contained more than three million autopsy samples including many victims of the Spanish flu pandemic. We were also able to cross-reference our findings against Royal London Hospital's collections of tissue samples from 1918-19."

"I'm sorry Doctor, I'm not sure I'm following you. I thought you said the Millennial Virus was a variant of avian flu? Is that no longer the case?"

"Most flu strains originate from an avian host. With the Spanish flu, after nearly one hundred years of study, we're still a little sketchy on how the process works and how the virus mutates to acquire novel genes. Most experts agree that, in order to become capable of affecting both birds and humans, an avian flu virus must first undertake a prolonged incubation period in pigs. This allows the virus to exchange genetic material with human flu strains. Mutations are fairly common, producing new viruses capable of rapid infection."

"So you're convinced that this virus evolved naturally without human interference?" asked the politician.

"Absolutely," said Doctor Hardy. "Right now, any suggestion that the virus was genetically altered as some sort of bio-weapon is preposterous and unsubstantiated by any evidence I've seen."

"Well, hold on," cautioned Zed. "That's certainly not the impression I had from the Professor. He seemed convinced there was a chance that MV-27 was man-made."

"Convinced is a strong word," corrected the Colonel. "I'd say it was a line of inquiry he believed was worthy of further exploration. I think it's fair to say that Doctor Hardy's team is skeptical."

"In my view, it's simply not credible," confirmed Doctor Hardy.

"Regardless of whether there's any truth to it," said the politician, "we need to be very careful. Any conspiracy theory like that would spread like wildfire. Right now we have no way of countering it. If people start to believe that the government failed in some way, that this whole disaster was avoidable, then we'll lose control quickly."

"The vaccine is everything," asserted the Colonel. "The people have to believe that we are close to a solution. In the meantime, we can accelerate the deployment of our Tamiflu stocks and get everyone on the island vaccinated. That should buy us some time and build trust and confidence."

"If Tamiflu shots are limited, I recommend we keep them in reserve for key personnel only at this time," suggested Peterson.

"That would be contrary to the UK government's guidelines we just discussed," said the politician. "The best way to defend the island against a fresh outbreak is to vaccinate as many as possible. Build up the herd's levels of immunity."

"We've learned the hard way that we can't save everybody. As the highest-ranking officer, it's the Colonel's decision to make. Colonel, unless I'm mistaken, this operation remains under military jurisdiction?"

"Lieutenant Peterson is correct. Until we can locate additional supplies of Tamiflu or Relenza, we hold what we have in reserve. I'm not ignoring the guidelines on this, but right now, we don't know what's coming. We need to keep our powder dry."

"I can't emphasise enough," said the politician in a display of displeasure, "that the limited efficacy of available vaccines, not to mention the delay in producing something that will be effective against the virus, is going to have to be kept totally secret. If I'm going to be out there telling people that they're safe on the island and that a vaccine is imminent, we as a collective, need to lock this down. If people even get a whiff of the truth, then this house of cards will come crashing down quickly."

"Very well," said the Colonel rising out of his seat and leaning forward over the table. "I need everyone in this room to commit to a code of silence. This information does not leave the room."

The meeting finished rather abruptly and the scientists were led back to their sleeping quarters where a movie had been laid on for their evening entertainment. Peterson grabbed Zed's arm as he was leaving.

"The Colonel and I are having a night cap, care to join us?"

"Thank you, but it's been a long day for me and I've lined up a date with one of the Doc's sleeping tablets."

"It won't take long, but it's important," fixing him with a Hollywood smile that would have made him millions in another lifetime. Zed reluctantly agreed and followed him towards the Captain's suite underneath the ship's conning tower.

The suite was furnished with several armchairs and a low sofa with armrests. On almost every inch of wall were photos of military personnel, past presidents, home ports and family members. Through a narrow doorway was a bed and a small bathroom beyond. Peterson approached a walnut-veneered side-cabinet with two decanters and four crystal glasses set on top.

"Have a seat gentlemen. Let's see," he said picking up one of the decanters. "I've got brandy or whiskey. No ice though, sorry about that."

It had been some time since Zed had tasted either, but chose whiskey. He swilled the amber liquid around the glass, inhaling deeply with his eyes closed. The fumes alone were intoxicating enough and caught in his throat. He took a sip and allowed the whiskey to slide around his mouth, before swallowing greedily. It tasted like pure nectar.

"I know, right?" grinned Peterson. "Twelve-year old, single malt. I nearly promoted the guy who found me this."

He took a sip in mild reverie, before putting down the tumbler on a U.S. Navy branded coaster. He perched on the side of the desk and leaned forward with his arms crossed.

"What I'm about to tell you is highly classified. I need your word, both of you, that this goes no further."

The two men straightened in their chairs and nodded.

"One of the mission profiles the *Chester* was designed to fulfil was responding to a nuclear, biological or chemical attack. We were equipped with enough NBC suits for an entire crew, along with a fully functioning lab to analyse any samples we collected."

Peterson sat down in a brown leather arm chair opposite the two men, inspecting the liquid in his glass.

"Before the *Chester* sailed from our home port in Coronado Island, San Diego, the Captain and XO were briefed on a full spectrum of current threats in the Middle East and Asia based on the latest intelligence reports. I wasn't party to those briefings, but as acting commanding officer of this vessel I have since read everything. I found something that I think would interest you both greatly."

He walked over to a wall safe and dialled the combination before reaching in and extracting a thin brown folder with three sheets of paper stapled together in one corner. He handed the document to the Colonel who scanned the front page, trying to make sense of what he was being shown.

"This report is eyes-only. Any mention of its existence will be flatly denied."

Zed was trying to read what was written on the page, but the angle was reflecting the light in such a way that all he could make out was the heading "US Navy Intelligence - CIA Briefing".

"That's the last report we received, dated more than two years ago. It basically lends a lot of credibility to your theory, Zed. One of our CIA operatives in Jakarta, Indonesia intercepted an encrypted communiqué between North Korea and what we believed to be Russia that, once decoded, referenced project 'Chuma'. Now that had our intel guys jumping around for a while as Chuma is apparently the Russian word for plague or pestilence. We believe a rogue faction in the Russian military was providing technical assistance to Pyongyang. The communiqué suggested that they were working on a flu virus. Of course, that report was an advisory note only, no one seriously considered this a credible threat to national security."

"Hindsight is a wonderful thing," said the Colonel.

"But even if they had succeeded in their research, there's no way to prove any of this, is there?"

"Well, that all depends on the team from Porton Down. If they were able to further sequence the virus, find some link or genetic marker, then we'd have something."

"And the reason you're not trusting the others with this information is because…?" asked Zed.

"This document could be the smoking gun that legitimises any conspiracy theory. Until we have some semblance of proof, this stays between the three of us, am I clear?"

Reluctantly, Zed and the Colonel nodded their agreement.

CHAPTER THIRTY-FIVE

Shortly after dawn had broken, Jack became the last to arrive outside the castle entrance. The work party of some fifteen people stood shivering in temperatures that had barely risen above freezing this morning. Over their shoulders and leaning against their thighs were a variety of gardening implements including chainsaws, shovels, rakes and various tools to maintain the farm machinery.

They were on their way out to the fields around Keyhaven to attend to their daily duties. A group of three were heading to the waterfront fields that overlooked Hurst, with views towards Yarmouth and the island. Each day they would gather their herd of dairy cows inside the large shed to be fed and milked. After a recent night-time raid the previous week when one of the cows had been found dead, its carcass butchered for meat, they took it in turns to leave a volunteer on site to watch over the animals. It was a boring job, but some liked it for the peace and quiet away from the castle.

Once the three were done with the cows, they would move on to tend to the resident flock of pedigree Zwartbles sheep that they had maintained since the outbreak. They were a curious sight, with black or brown fleeces, white socks and tails. They had proven surprisingly good company and followed the team around, bleating and nudging against the thighs of workers as they put out feed or mucked out the pens. Some of the crew thought of the Zwartbles as pets rather than beasts. Their numbers had swollen after another successful lambing season providing new additions to the flock. Jack resisted any talk of killing the animals, they were worth more to Hurst alive than dead. Their fleeces and wool were coveted and worn by many to insulate them against the cold winters.

Another party was heading to the two fields nearest the marshland that had been turned over to vegetable production. This year had been their best yet and their winter crops included leeks, parsnips, sprouting broccoli, squash, turnips, carrots, and cabbages. Most of their production was bartered with other local groups in the village or further afield.

Three of Corporal Ballard's squad came with the group to keep watch over them as they worked. The area around Milford-on-sea had been sparsely populated for some time now, but in the last few weeks that was changing as more and more migrants moved East towards the embarkation points at Lymington or Southampton.

There were half a dozen smaller groups that lived in the village, occupying some of the bigger properties, but they mostly kept themselves to themselves. They were no trouble. They traded with Hurst from time to time and cooperated where mutual interests overlapped. Any new arrivals were looked on with suspicion and encouraged to move on, not to linger where they were not wanted.

Jack pulled his dirty yellow oilskin jacket tighter around his shoulders, zipping up the front until it was snug under his chin. He surveyed the rest of the group, standing waiting for him.

They were in good spirits this morning. He did a quick head count, checking that Joe, Will, Tommy, Sam and Scottie were all present and accounted for, before moving off slowly up the shingle back towards Milford.

Joe caught up with Jack: "Has Sister Imelda left yet or is she still here?" he asked.

Jack paused mid-step and studied Joe. Jack had spent half the night tossing and turning, pondering the question of what to do. He was placed in an impossible position. Do the right thing or remain loyal to his team? He had a good mind to refuse the Sister's request for Jean and Joe to stand trial, but his scruples were getting in the way.

"My hands are tied," said Jack. "She says she won't leave without Jean."

"What are you going to do then?" said Joe, looking understandably anxious, like he hadn't slept much either worrying about what would happen next.

"Well, if Jean refuses to go, there's no way the Sister can remove her by force. So I'd say we're at an impasse. Listen Joe, I'm trying to do the right thing but I don't have much room to manoeuvre. Someone or something is going to have to budge."

"Please Jack. There's no way she'll get a fair trial. They already think she's guilty and if I go with her to protect her, now I will have to stand trial too. It's impossible."

"Well, the only solution I can see is that we hold the hearing, or trial, whatever you want to call it, here at Hurst. That way, it's fairer for everyone. We can even get someone independent to decide."

"You're seriously going to allow the pair of us to go on trial?"

"If you're both innocent then you have nothing to worry about."

"You know we're both innocent Jack."

"Well then. I'm sorry Joe, I think that's the best to hope for. I will suggest that to the Sister as a compromise when we get back."

Jack made clear that was an end to the matter and trudged on, looking out over the sea towards Mudeford in the distance. It was a clear morning as the sun rose slowly behind them, casting long shadows from the castle walls. Joe dropped back to fall in line with the others, shaking his head. It was hard going on the shingle with Jack's heavy boots slipping with each step, displacing the stones underfoot.

Jack cast his eyes further west and south beyond Christchurch Bay towards Old Harry Rocks and Studland Head. He remembered taking his young nephew to see Anvil Point lighthouse, taking in tea and a walk at Durlston Country Park. The views back towards the island and his home at the time just outside Barton on Sea had been stunning on a Spring day. He used to love to hike along the coastal paths on his own when he wasn't fishing or maintaining the boat. Chesil Beach was a long drive but worth it, Lulworth Cove, fossil hunting on the Jurassic Coast. He wondered whether it was still the same, whether he would ever get to free camp in the dunes again or visit his favourite camp site near Swanage.

"Look Jack," said Will, pointing into the distance. Ahead of them where the shingle joined up with the roadway at the edge of Milford village someone had lit a bonfire. They must have dragged branches and logs up from the woodland a few hundred meters away. The first smoke was curling up into the morning sky.

The party stopped in its tracks as Jack grabbed his binoculars trying to make out the faces of the two figures standing warming their hands.

"Can you see who it is Jack?" asked Sam.

"Not from here. There are two men by the looks of things. They certainly don't look familiar."

He passed the binoculars to Will who squinted into the distance. "These things are filthy, I don't know how you see anything through them."

"Terra used to clean the lenses for me. Probably a bit overdue now. Listen Will, Sam, Tommy, let's go and talk to them, find out what they want. The rest of you carry on to the farm and get started."

One of the soldiers stepped forward, grabbing the walkie-talkie from his belt. He was assigned for their protection and was taking his responsibilities seriously for a fresh faced young man, no older than Sam.

"I should call this in, see what Sergeant Flynn wants us to do," said the young soldier.

"Good idea. Wouldn't hurt to have a little back-up, just in case."

The party split at the bridge that led over the waterway that ran alongside the remainder of the raised sea defences towards Milford. With a wave, Scottie led the rest of them onwards towards the open fields and farm beyond.

Jack and the others stopped a couple of hundred meters from the bonfire, watching the flames and smoke leap higher into the air now the damp wood had finally caught properly. At either end, the men had fashioned two fork-shaped branches and rammed them into the stones. They were in the process of skinning and gutting an animal ready to be roasted on the spit.

"I'll do the talking," said Jack. "The rest of you just back me up. I don't want any trouble, so let's take it easy."

The two soldiers weren't used to taking instructions from

civilians and exchanged glances before nodding their agreement. The group of five men spread out in a line as they continued up the remainder of the dirt roadway. The two men finally noticed their approach, one nudging the other. They appeared to be unarmed, or made no attempt to reach for their guns. One of them continued skinning what looked like a lamb.

"Morning," shouted Jack, keeping his distance, unwilling to get too close, his arms crossed in front of his paunch. "What are you doing here?"

The two men seemed to find that funny and sniggered into their sleeves. They were an odd-looking pair whose appearance suggested they had been sleeping rough for some time, unshaven and filthy. One wore a camouflaged fishing jacket that reached down to his knees with hooks and tied fishing flies attached to his breast pocket. The other wore a full-zip track suit with a bright orange beanie. They were both of them no older than twenty. Their joviality quickly passed and was replaced by dead-eyed stares, seemingly unintimidated by the five of them.

"Maybe you missed the signs or can't read, but this here's our land. That's our place up the beach there," Jack said pointing to the castle. He gestured towards the fire and the dead animal. "That's our firewood you're burning and by the looks of things, that's one of our lambs you just killed."

The two men nodded but seemed unfazed, shrugging their shoulders.

"You don't own this land. No one owns it. It ain't stealing, anyhow."

"What's that supposed to mean?" threatened Will with unapologetic menace, before Jack cautioned him with a stare.

"We're just passing through, that's all. So I wouldn't go making trouble. We're on our way to the island."

"Just the two of you?"

"No, we're just the first. There are plenty more behind us."

"Where have you come from?"

"Here and there. Bournemouth mostly, but there are other groups from Weymouth and Poole too."

As he was talking he inserted the butcher's knife deep into the lamb's throat and sawed through the muscle and tendons until the skull fell with a disturbing crunch on to a rock, blood splashing across his boots, though he didn't seem to notice. He took the long stick which had already been sharpened to a spear and thrust it through the neck cavity, ramming it through its body until with a sharp twist, it emerged at the other end. Grabbing both ends, he placed the skewered animal on to the spit, watching the flames begin to lick the carcass, turning the flesh a charred black.

"I like it round here. Good view of the island. Reckon we could stick around here and wait for our friends to arrive," said one man to the other, ignoring Jack. "Those your fields over there, are they?" said the man in the track suit, pointing towards Scottie's group in the distance.

"That's right. They're our fields," insisted Jack.

"Got any eggs? Any chickens?"

"Enough for us, yes, but not enough to share."

"That's a shame. It doesn't have to be like this you know. You give us what we want and we'll leave you alone. We don't want to hurt anyone."

Will and the others looked at each other, dumbstruck by their bravado. Jack was in no hurry to start a fight, but these men needed to understand where the line was drawn.

"Listen, I'll tell you what. Finish your fire, warm your hands, eat your meal, then be on your way. You're not welcome here. I want you gone by the time we get back. Okay? Do we understand each other?"

"Oh I think we understand each other," smiled the man in the fishing jacket.

With a final stare, the Hurst group turned on their heels and strode back towards the bridge and the fields beyond.

"What was all that about?" asked Sam.

"Beats me," said Jack. "They must have a screw loose. They're lucky we didn't shoot them where they stood."

"Something tells me they're still going to be there when we get back," warned Will.

"And I doubt they'll be alone by then," added Sam. "Didn't he say they were the first. I wonder how many more of them there are? Perhaps the fire is to guide the rest in."

"I doubt it Sam," said Will. "We've had plenty of people passing through here in the last few weeks. News travels fast. There will be dozens more groups on their way West towards Lymington and the island."

"Private, call it in. I want everyone back to the castle by lunchtime. Tell Sergeant Flynn we need to double the guard and get some more men out to keep watch on the workers."

The Private grabbed his walkie-talkie and turned his back on the group, trying to reach Flynn.

"Will, can you get after Scottie and tell him to bring the animals back to the castle this afternoon? We can put them in the field behind the lighthouse for now. They'll be safer there. I don't want them so far away from us if things kick off."

Will nodded and set off after Scottie at a slow jog. The group were already far along the tidal road that flooded from time to time, dodging between puddles to keep their boots dry. In the distance Jack noticed another plume of smoke rising above the wood. It was definitely time to get everyone back to the safety of the spit.

CHAPTER THIRTY-SIX

Riley had been up since dawn waiting for the first boat heading west she could locate. It was a routine personnel transfer run up from Portsmouth to Lymington, so only required a small detour to the *USS Chester* anchored in the main channel and then on to the castle.

Riley was down in the canteen, saying goodbye to those already assembled at this early hour, devouring a hearty buffet-style breakfast with fresh eggs delivered from the island the day before, cooked any style, something that tasted like bacon but was likely a substitute, fried tomatoes, fresh bread rolls, frozen sausages, and pancakes with Canadian maple syrup. She had never seen such a feast.

Zed seemed to be labouring, hunched over his plate with one good hand. He was having some trouble cutting his sausages but was too proud to ask for help. Despite his initial protest, she leaned over his shoulder and grabbed the knife and fork, making short work of slicing everything up into bite-size pieces.

Jones paused mid-mouthful watching Zed's indignation across the table, a mischievous smile spreading across his lips. "Looks like you need a hand."

There a moment of silence as Riley cringed, wondering

whether Zed was quite ready for jokes at his expense. Zed looked up into the Sergeant's eyes.

"I'm glad you find my injury amusing," rebuked Zed dead-pan.

"It's not like you're completely armless, I know," continued Jones, to a snigger from one of his team.

"Very funny Sergeant. Very funny," he smiled. "Your jokes are about as hilarious as the scientist's flu jokes I've had to listen to."

"Really? I didn't know they had a sense of humour."

"They don't. Only lame one-liners."

"Try me."

"Oh stuff like 'man walks into a doctor's surgery with a runny nose. 'Flu?' asks the doctor. 'No, came by bicycle'."

"You're right, that is terrible. What else you got?"

"Don't encourage him," groaned Riley.

"Last one I promise. What's the difference between bird flu and swine flu?"

"Don't tell me, I heard this one already. Something about tweetment and oink-ment."

"With all this swine flu talk, it's like the 'snoutbreak of the aporkalypse'. Next we'll all be waking up with apples in our mouths."

"Right, when pigs fly…"

"Enough already," shouted Riley, "that's terrible."

"I tried to warn you. Never ask that man to tell jokes."

There was a knock at the door and Riley turned to see a crewman in a survival suit breathing heavily.

"Mam, just to let you know your ride is two minutes out."

"Thanks, I'll be right there."

Riley felt a tightness in her chest, all of a sudden feeling emotional about leaving her new friends behind. She hugged Zed's back and affectionately kissed him on the head, ruffling his hair. She waved goodbye to the rest of them and headed out the door. Jones got to his feet and followed her out. Outside the doorway, Riley paused, waiting for him to catch up, noticing the other men exchanging knowing looks.

"Wait up Riley. I just wanted to say that if you need anything, and I mean anything, just call. One of my team is always listening in on channel 9. They know where to find me," he smiled awkwardly. "Listen, it's been fun hanging out."

She blushed at his attentions, tucking a lock of hair behind her left ear. She hadn't allowed herself to actually care about anyone for too long. It had been her self-defence mechanism. Besides, no one had asked her out on a date for quite some time, if that's where this conversation was heading.

"Me too," she said. "Sorry I was such a hard-ass back at Porton. I appreciate what you've done for me, for all of us. Not sure what would have happened if you hadn't shown up when you did."

"Oh, it was nothing, just doing my job. So listen, if it's okay with you, I might pop on over and see you at the castle sometime next week."

"I'd like that. Thanks," she smiled, looking at her hands. "Okay, I better be going, that boat won't wait for me."

"Be seeing you," he said, touching her arm.

"You too."

She turned with a wave and headed left towards a watertight door nearest them that led on deck where they were loading up a small Royal Navy fast launch. Two large crates were being winched up to the *Chester* as two other men climbed down the rope ladder. A crewman helped her down onto the smaller vessel.

She took the hand offered by the Royal Navy officer below. She had mixed feelings about leaving Zed and the team. She desperately wanted to get back to the castle and Adele, but felt torn. Yet there was nothing more she could do here on the *Chester*. Her place was back at Hurst.

The crew cast off the mooring lines and they headed away from the *Chester* against the incoming tide. As soon as they were clear, the helm throttled up the powerful diesel engines and Riley watched the churned-up waters and diesel fumes curling into the morning air behind them. They headed up towards the bow of the enormous destroyer, watching their wake slam against the *Chester*'s steep-sided hull.

Out in the main channel to the East, they were dazzled by the morning sunshine breaking through scattered clouds. Behind them, she could make out the Isle of Wight ferry in the distance leaving Portsmouth harbour with a Royal Naval escort holding course alongside. She wondered how many more of the refugees would be on their way to a new life on the island. It was said that there were now several hundred new arrivals per day. She wondered where they all lived and worked. It must be a massive logistical operation. She'd like to see it for herself one day.

She was enjoying the sensation of speed as they bumped over the waves heading back West, feeling the wind in her hair, ducking against a shroud of salt spray as they caught a wave. As they neared the entrance to the Lymington river, the pitch of the engine dropped and their speed slowed, their bow returning to a shallower incline.

They reached the outer markers to the river entrance passing marshland and mudflats on either side of the narrow channel that was lined with wooden posts and buoys. She was surprised to notice two soldiers occupying a small race committee platform at the head of the river, exposed to the elements. As they passed close by, she saw there was a small shelter with a radio set and GPMG machine gun set up to cover the river entrance. In worse weather, she imagined it would be untenable or at the very least a torrid guard duty for the men posted there.

In the distance Riley could see a forest of masts and boats moored up in Yachthaven and Berthon marinas to their left. Compared to peak season, the marinas were virtually deserted. During the first outbreak, so many locals had taken to their boats to escape the mainland and either head to sea or to the island in the hope of finding refuge from the virus. There had been talk of people setting course for the Channel Islands, where it was believed there was no virus. Several of the vessels tied up in the main channel had broken free in the storms and littered the shoreline, holed and wrecked.

The navy launch weaved a path through the tight river channel between moorings. The passage had not been dredged in some time and was said to be impassable to larger vessels, though the flat-bottomed ferry seemed to have no trouble operating here. She could see the Lymington ferry port now ahead of them opposite the main town. Even from this distance, you could hear the buzz of activity carried on the wind.

The whole of the river front around the port was lined with hundreds of people. Everywhere she looked she could see hunched figures huddling together in shelters and tents. Long lines of refugees snaked towards the fortified entrance to the port. There was a large military presence here, barriers and metal fences set up to limit access to the embarkation and quarantine zones. The whole area around the port was unrecognisable to her; she had only heard second-hand stories of its transformation under military occupation.

The navy launch cruised slowly against the morning tide towards a landing jetty nearest the ferry, which towered over them. She could hear the unsettling screech of grinding metalwork as they loaded vehicles, hand carts and successive groups of people. A hundred dirty faces watched their approach. Many looked beaten, young and old, barely able to stay awake, leaning over the railing. All their fight was gone as if every ounce of energy had been used up to reach the ferry port from whichever Godforsaken place they had come. These were the lucky ones, those that were virus free, passed fit to make the crossing. Looking up at their faces, Riley couldn't help but feel a tremendous sadness descending on her. There was simply no way to help this number of desperate people. The island would be a fresh start for many, a chance to rebuild, but for those turned away, there could be no hope. They would not survive another winter like the last.

The launch did not linger. They dropped off six soldiers who were on rotation, picking up several others who would head back to the barracks at Portsmouth, their time in Lymington over for now. The soldiers tended to work seven days on the front line and seven days back at base. In total, nearly two thousand personnel were now tasked with the security and reconstruction of the Solent area. Their numbers were swelling every day as the Allies neared critical mass.

They retraced their steps back along the channel towards open water, turning west towards Hurst Castle, outlined against the skyline. Its dark shape looked unfamiliar from here. The shingle spit on which the castle perched stretched inland towards Keyhaven, its white lighthouse towering over the castle walls. Each roll of the launch took Riley one step closer to home. She wondered what she had missed in the time they had been away in Porton Down.

They set course directly for the eastwards facing jetty and unloading area not far away. It had been reconstructed so that larger vessels could reach the castle at all tides without having to navigate the shallows and tidal mudflats of the inner passage that led to Keyhaven. Ahead of them, Riley could see the shape of a young man, puzzling at who would be waiting for her. She wasn't expected, unless Jones or Peterson had called ahead to let them know. She recognised the friendly face of Sam waiting for her, his hand raised in welcome. He helped fend off their bow as Riley jumped down on to the wooden platform.

"Hello stranger," she said as Sam embraced her warmly.

"Jack's waiting for you in the lighthouse. He asked me to take you straight there."

"That sounds ominous. I thought it would be a surprise."

"Nothing surprises Jack. He knows everything that goes on round here. You know what he's like."

Riley raised her eyebrows and fell into step alongside Sam with a cursory wave to the guys on the launch who were pulling away, heading back towards Portsmouth. They walked alongside the narrow-gauge railway track that ran along the walls of the castle, laid in years gone by for unloading stores from visiting ships. Some said the castle had been a home for smugglers when contraband was landed here and other places to avoid paying duty. It seemed to Riley that this would be an ideal spot, away from prying eyes and official interferences. This had always been a wild unholy place where natural law re-asserted itself over man's attempts at control.

The door to the lighthouse was open and Riley could see Jack sitting at his kitchen table cradling a hot cup of tea.

"There you are. Our traveller returns eh? How did you get on in Porton Down? Sorry to hear about the trouble you had getting back."

"How did you hear already? Who told you?"

"Oh, I had a call with some of the council members last night. Colonel Abrahams shared the bad news about the Professor and what happened to Zed's arm. Hear he's been patched up and is helping the scientists."

"Wow. There goes my currency. So what have I missed here, Jack?"

"All going to plan, thanks. The handover is going fine, we've got another party heading to Yarmouth today. By the end of the week, we'll be a skeletal civilian crew here. More soldiers arriving today."

"Have they found us somewhere suitable to live yet?"

"Yes, didn't you hear? We've been billeted to Freshwater Bay Hotel on the southern side of the island, so the advance party is getting it ready. It sounds ideal, there's a golf course nearby which has been turned over to farmland. Good soil and excellent climate for all manner of plants and vegetables. What else? There's a beach, beautiful views over the cliffs and rocks. Really, it's more than we could have expected."

"Sounds great, but it won't be the same though, Jack. You know that, right?"

"Listen Riley," he said with a heavy sigh, "I need your support on this one. There's no point fighting what's about to happen. It's the 'least worst' option for us. Besides, things are changing here quickly. The sooner we get everyone out the better."

"What's this I hear about all these refugees moving through the area causing problems? The Americans seemed concerned."

"Yes, it's not great. We've got people passing through every day, stripping Milford and Keyhaven bare. We've had to bring all the animals back on to the spit where we can watch over them. Several were disappearing each night. Milford village and

Keyhaven are becoming no-go places for us. I've had to suspend scavenging teams for now. All stores are coming in by sea from the island. It's putting a huge strain on our resources already."

"Can't the soldiers protect us?" asked Riley confused.

"They could if we could get our vehicles out."

"I don't understand. Why can't they just drive along the spit like normal?"

"Because those travellers have barricaded the roadway, blocked us in. I think they're trying to starve us out."

"What? Why would they do that?"

"It's the Sisters, Riley. I think they're behind all this."

CHAPTER THIRTY-SEVEN

The journey back from the forest camp had been uneventful thus far. Terra was sat in the back of the people carrier behind the Professor. She was removing the brown nail polish from her finger tips and trying to choose between 'Hot Tub Pink' and 'Miami Red' from her makeup bag. She decided the pink might be a bit over the top for today, tutting as the vehicle bounced over a pot hole.

In front of her, the Professor was sandwiched between two of Briggs' men. He looked like he hadn't slept much but was otherwise unharmed. Unlike the treatment of the other prisoners they had captured, the Professor had been well treated. Briggs had been respectful, even deferential towards the academic. He had interrogated him several times, before rotating through the scientists and then Zed and Riley. He played one off against the other, probing for inconsistencies. Perhaps it was on account of his age or willingness to co-operate, Terra wasn't sure, but Briggs had behaved almost reverentially towards the Professor.

At one point, she noticed Briggs smoothing down the academic's collar, patting his shoulders affectionately when he spoke with him. She suspected that the Professor reminded him of someone. She imagined some boyhood male role model, perhaps a priest or benevolent Uncle. He had never once mentioned his father. In fact, other than a few anecdotes about juvenile detention and playing truant, Briggs never talked much about his childhood at all.

Briggs had been furious when the Americans had attacked in the night. He was seething that for a second time they had crashed his party and stolen his prize from right under their noses. It had been blind luck that they had not found the Professor. The leaders of the forest group had invited them to a dinner in their honour, toasting the new alliance into the early hours. The Professor had been quizzed about the island. Everyone seemed hot under the collar at the Allies' complacency. They had underestimated the scale of the combined threats posed by the rebellion. More and more groups were rallying to the cause. They wanted to take back what belonged to them and banish the military from the region once and for all. The island was theirs, wasn't it?

Terra was amused by their growing confidence. She exchanged furtive glances with Victor when he caught her eye, wondering what he made of all this. Surely, the more allies Briggs secured, the bigger the task they would have in overthrowing his control. She marvelled at Victor's ingenuity. He was always so busy, thinking two or three moves ahead. Playing one side against the other. It was a dangerous game. All she had to do was mention his duplicity to Briggs and Victor would be gone in an instant, but she knew the same could be said of her. It would be a zero-sum game. They would both be finished. Briggs would have no tolerance for treachery. She had found that out the hard way, early on. The scar on her wrist was testament to that. When it came to beatings, he avoided her face, preferring to leave his mark below the neckline. He needed her to look good.

Briggs had blamed his hosts for the attack. They had lost almost everything. The scientists, Zed, Riley, many of the computers and external drives. Two of his men were dead and another badly injured in the ensuing firefight. Terra had stood by terrified as Briggs vented his fury on the forest group. Their failure to ensure adequate protection, their blatant incompetency, would not stand. They had been afraid of him. They told him to leave, tried to threaten him with what would happen if he tried anything. Briggs had lost his temper, shot their leader in the head at point-blank range. They had gunned down the others in the room in cold blood. They left no one alive, even those unarmed. Terra remembered the feeling of helplessness, shaking uncontrollably as Briggs' men laughed, kicking the inert bodies to check they were dead.

"Come on, that's enough excitement for one day," he said trying to comfort her, wiping the blood from her face with a clean white handkerchief. "We've still got the Professor. That's what matters."

He put his coat around her shoulders steering her towards the back of a waiting car. They collected the men's weapons and some stores for the journey and set off before the rest of the group could return to discover their leaders massacred.

After three hours of driving, they finally emerged from the forest and the tree canopy opened up to reveal farmland and chocolate-box houses, picturesque villages in the approach to Lymington. Most of these places looked occupied again with smoke curling from their chimneys in the late afternoon chill. It was said that hundreds of people were moving through this area, stripping it bare like locusts. The locals had mostly moved out, some of the first to relocate to the island. They had been warned that the ferry port at Lymington would become a beacon to refugees from all over the region and beyond. Their safety could only be guaranteed on the island itself. They didn't need asking twice. Those that had taken their place used the houses nearest the road as temporary accommodation. On walls and road signs, they noticed graffiti, spray painted messages left for surviving friends or family they hoped would pass this way.

At the bottom of the hill, they followed Copper's men in the car in front and turned left towards Lymington's New Forest Hospital. The road here was barricaded with concrete barriers positioned to force approaching vehicles through a narrow chicane, sand-bagged firing positions on either side.

The guard recognised their vehicles and pushed back the mesh fence on small wheels to allow the convoy of three vehicles to pass. They parked near the front entrance and went inside.

Several of the hospital group emerged to welcome them before noticing the strangers amongst them.

"Who's this then?" asked a short balding man with a moustache that called to mind the lead detective from a British murder mystery series Terra had enjoyed as a teenager. She couldn't recall the title.

"This is the man I was telling you about, Charlie meet Briggs." said Copper, introducing his right-hand man. Briggs nodded, but made clear his continued displeasure at finding himself collaborating with former members of her Majesty's constabulary.

"So, you're Reginald Briggs? I never thought I'd see the day..."

"Not this again. I did my time. Don't you people ever give up?"

"Listen, Charlie, can you get everyone together?"

"Sure, what's on your mind?"

"I'll tell you later. We're moving out in the morning. It's time we got on the front foot."

"Yes, boss. About time," encouraged his subordinate with a grin.

***

That evening, Copper, Briggs, Charlie and the Professor stood at the front of the large atrium near the hospital reception desk. Nearly two hundred people were packed in here, craning their necks, trying to see the two strangers waiting for their turn to speak. Terra stood towards the side, casting her eyes across the sea of faces, wondering if she would recognise anyone here.

"Can I have your attention please?" shouted Copper. "Everyone, listen up."

Charlie put his fingers to his lips and whistled loudly as the conversations finished abruptly and the room fell silent.

"As some of you know, me and the fellas have just got back from a little trip. Our mission was to intercept a military convoy heading to the island from a research facility at Porton Down, which many of you will have heard of," he paused, watching a few of those nearest him nodding or trying to figure out where they had heard that name before.

"Porton Down is an old MoD base near Salisbury, where they did all the testing of viruses and biological weapons. Turns out they know quite a lot about the Millennial Virus. That's one of the places where the government was storing massive stock piles of the vaccine which could have stopped the outbreak and saved millions of lives, but they chose to keep it for themselves."

There was a murmur of discontent as people digested what they were being told. Many seemed skeptical to Terra, as if they doubted the veracity of the statements, refusing to believe that the government would knowingly withhold a vaccine which could have saved lives. Copper gestured towards the Professor who was shaking his head at the last statement.

"This man here is Professor Nichols. He was the government's go-to expert on pandemic viruses. He was the person who advised them that the population should be vaccinated. There's not much the Professor doesn't know about the virus. He told me...he told us," he corrected himself, casting a sweeping arm around the others standing nearby, "that Porton Down was conducting secret tests that might even have caused the outbreak itself."

"Now hold on," interrupted the Professor before Charlie grabbed hold of his arm to silence him.

"You'll get your turn to speak in a minute," said Copper, silencing the Professor. "First I want you to hear from our new friends who live on the island. I know a lot of you have been talking. Talking about upping sticks and heading over there. Well, before you make a big mistake, I want you to listen to this man. Briggs is here to tell us what's really going on over there and why going there would be a really bad idea."

Briggs stepped forward and surveyed the room disdainfully for a few seconds.

"All you lot think the island is some kind of utopia. You might even believe all the lies that they're spreading about how they have food, water, electricity, phones. Well, I'm here to tell you that the truth is very different. I should know, we live there. The fact is, Camp Wight is a forced labour camp. And whilst they don't make everyone shave their heads and wear sack cloth, everyone who goes there is made to work. Those people don't get to eat unless they've done a day's work. I'm not talking about office work, sitting at a desk all day. I'm talking labouring, morning, noon and night, digging ditches, putting up walls, clearing bodies. Little kids are split up from their families and sent to special prison camps where they get re-educated, taught to believe more lies."

He paused, nodding at a few of the crowd who were shaking their heads at him, refusing to accept his version.

"Everyone in this room has probably lost people to the virus, people they were close to. You've probably heard that everyone on the island gets given the vaccine, that they don't have to worry about the virus anymore. It's lies, all lies. The Professor here will tell you that there is no vaccine. The only thing they have is that Tamiflu and the other stuff they mass-produced before the outbreak. It's useless, barely makes any difference."

"Anyone who thinks they'll be safer on the island is kidding themselves. You're better off staying here."

"What about the people who are immune?" shouted one of the women at the front of the room.

"There's no such thing as immune," corrected Copper. "Some of you have increased resistance to the virus, but virtually no-one is immune. The virus will mutate again and when it does very few of us will escape. Even if they could find a vaccine, by the time they've produced it in sufficient quantities, chances are the virus will have changed again. Isn't that right Professor?"

"Well yes, that's the nature of viruses, they are constantly changing. It's like trying to hit a moving target, but that doesn't mean that an effective vaccine couldn't..."

"Thank you, Professor," he said cutting him off as Charlie yanked him back into place, pinching his bicep painfully.

"Then there's the Americans," added Briggs, laughing sarcastically. "They arrived out of the blue and started ordering us around, telling us what to do and what not to do. They've found a puppet in Captain Armstrong who does their bidding. There they are parked out in the Solent with all their guns and missiles pointing at our heads, threatening us if we don't toe the line. Well, on the island, we've all had quite enough of their interference. We need to deliver the message that they are not welcome around here anymore, to move on and find some other corner of the globe to make their home. This place belongs to us."

Briggs smiled as a small cheer arose from part of the crowd. "That's right. I've seen for myself. Whilst we're all starving, fighting over scraps, them lot over at Osbourne House are feasting on roast duck, pork chops, fine wine, champagne, caviar. They have the best of everything. Well, let me tell you, they've had their fun. It's high time we drove them out, for good."

There was muted agreement and encouraging grunts from those at the front. Copper patted an impassioned Briggs on the shoulder and took over.

"First things first, tomorrow night we're planning two raids. The first will target the ferry port at Lymington. The second will drive to Hurst Castle. As you know, they're illegally holding our leader, Damian King there. They still refuse to give him up, despite us asking nicely. We'll be joining forces with Briggs here and his men, plus there are a few other groups heading this way from Christchurch and Bournemouth who support the cause."

"So pack your stuff, get some rest, because as of tomorrow, it's time we start a revolution."

CHAPTER THIRTY-EIGHT

Heather was next in line to see the Doctor. She waited outside the Principal's office where the draught from the front entrance howled down the corridor from time to time. In her lap she had open an old red-jacket hardback recommended to her from the school library. She had reread the same page several times now as her mind was elsewhere. She was thinking about her brother, wondering how he was coping without her.

In her peripheral vision she was paying attention to the group of soldiers down the hall, who were trying to look busy. She pointedly avoided eye contact with the taller one in particular, Jonny, they called him. Yesterday, he had accosted her in the passageway, forcefully grabbing her arm as he leaned in close. If she closed her eyes, she could recall every detail of their brief encounter. The booze on his breath, the mole on his cheek, the three-day stubble, the two stripes on the arm of his uniform, holding her firmly against the wall, towering over her. The approach of footsteps had made him look away and she had taken the opportunity to kick him in the shins and wriggle away from his grasp.

The scrape of a chair on the linoleum floor made her close her eyes and exhale quietly. She knew what was coming next, but kept her breathing steady, her muscles tensed. His large frame part-blocked the pale light from the window to her right. She folded the corner of her page to mark her place and closed her book.

"In trouble again are you, Heather? Come to see the Principal?"

Heather ignored his pathetic attempt to provoke her.

"Don't be like that," he said, pretending to be wounded by her indifference. "Hey, what are you reading?" he continued, noticing the book in her lap.

"Nothing you'd have heard of, Jonny."

"Oh so you know my name, eh?" he smiled, emboldened by her familiarity. "Go on try me, I like a good read."

He glanced over his shoulder and winked at his co-conspirators back down the corridor. They were watching his efforts with knowing smiles as if this was a game they played often. No doubt they had a bet on the outcome. They seemed to gamble on everything. She had seen them exchanging cigarettes, coins and jewellery, probably looted from the refugees they were tasked with protecting, in return for special treatment, whatever that meant.

Heather sighed and held up her book, revealing gold lettering with the words *Pride and Prejudice* on the cover.

"You wouldn't like it. No pictures. Full of big words."

She fixed him with a stare that would have sent most people packing, but not Jonny. He clenched his fists and leaned closer. Heather noticed his left eyelid twitching involuntarily.

"You know what? You kids should show us a bit more respect. We're here to protect you. But you people don't seem to realise or appreciate that. A little bit of gratitude wouldn't go amiss."

"Protect us? The only thing we need protecting from are men like you."

Jonny bristled with indignation, knowing his subordinates were watching his clumsy advances. He leaned over her, jabbing his finger in her face. He had just opened his mouth to vent, when the door to the Principal's office opened and the Doctor stepped outside. He was dressed in military fatigues with an American flag on his sleeve. He seemed surprised to see Jonny there, leaning over his quarry.

"Corporal Aldrove, is it?" he said reading the name on his chest. "Your job is to guard these minors, not harass them. If you need something to do, then go and fetch those medicine crates stacked outside."

Heather smiled sarcastically as Jonny acknowledged the Doctor's instruction and sloped away, taking the other two men with him. She followed the Doctor in to the office and closed the door behind them.

"Right, take a seat. So," he said, reading the handwritten sheet on a clipboard passed to him by one of the teachers who was assisting him, "Heather, if you can roll up your sleeve, what we're going to do this morning is take some blood and give you your first flu shot. Have you given blood before?" his tone was professional but light-hearted.

Heather looked at the American suspiciously, wondering why they would need an American doctor to do this kind of stuff. Didn't we even have our own doctors any more, she thought?

"I don't remember. What do you need my blood for anyway?"

"It's nothing to worry about. We're taking blood from all the new arrivals at the school. We're hoping that your blood can teach us more about the virus and how we can develop a vaccine," he smiled, writing her name on the vial and preparing the sterilised needle.

She winced and looked away as he inserted the needle into the prominent vein on her left arm. "There we go, that didn't hurt now, did it?"

She noticed the Doctor was staring at her and met his gaze. He looked away, realising he was making her feel awkward.

"You look awfully familiar. Are you sure we haven't met before?"

"I don't think so. I would remember you," she said with a heavy dose of sarcasm.

He seemed to find that funny and exchanged a look with the teacher. "You got any brothers or sisters? Maybe I've met one of them?"

Heather seemed to perk up suddenly. "I have a brother. His name is Connor. He's nine years old. He was quarantined when we first arrived. He was sick but it wasn't the virus, I'm sure of it."

"Well then, he'll be just fine. Listen, if he was really sick and got pneumonia or something, they'd have taken him to St. Mary's Hospital. As soon as he gets the all-clear, he'll likely be sent here. Maybe that's why you look familiar. It's possible I could have met him," he said, but didn't seem entirely sure.

He finished with the blood sample, securing the lid tight and placing it in a plastic grid with all the others. Once she had been given her flu shot, he stood up and patted her on the shoulder.

"Okay, Heather, that's all for today. Can you send the next person in please?"

She thanked him and wandered outside to the corridor, avoiding eye contact with Jonny who was still standing in the lobby with his hands on his hips. She could hear the brakes of the school mini-bus screech to a halt by the main entrance and ran out excitedly, hopeful that her brother would be amongst the latest to arrive from the refugee camp. One by one, she watched the dirty faces and hunched shoulders of a dozen boys and girls of all ages, as they were sorted into two age groups. When the last of them had got down, Heather approached the driver, who shook his head.

"Sorry Heather. Not this time. I'm keeping an eye out for him. Don't give up hope, will you?"

"Thanks Cyrus. I'm sure he'll turn up sooner or later," she said, feeling deflated.

The school bell was ringing inside which meant lessons were restarting after the morning break. Heather checked the handwritten schedule in her back pocket and ran inside to grab her text book and pencil from an otherwise empty locker. She was one of the last to arrive in the Principal's classroom on the second floor. For some reason, she still found the layout of the school confusing.

"Good morning class. Today we're going to be looking at the book of Genesis and the Old Testament story of Noah's Ark and what it can teach us about our current predicament. I trust you have all done your homework and familiarised yourselves with the text," she said looking round the room to note the nods from the thirty or so in the class. Heather remembered the Bible story well and her hand shot up to the scorn of those around her.

"Yes, Heather. What's your question?"

"Miss, is it true that God sent the flood to punish mankind for his wickedness and cleanse the world so we could start again?"

"That's certainly one theory, that the flood was a reversal of creation. But I'm more interested in hearing what the class thinks."

Another hand shot up at the back, an older boy that Heather had never noticed before. "If God was angry at us, why didn't he just kill all the bad people and let the good ones live? Surely the virus killed good people too. I don't get it."

"That's a very good point. The virus kills indiscriminately, doesn't it? It doesn't sound very fair, but certainly consistent with the Old Testament which is full of stories of a vengeful God, full of wrath. You'll notice it's a very different God from the beneficent father figure of the New Testament. Does anyone remember the book of Exodus and the ten plagues that were unleashed on the people of Egypt?"

"Miss, why do we have to learn about the Bible? Some of us don't even believe in God."

"Thank you Thomas. We'll be studying all religions, not just Christianity, to learn what religion, including atheism can teach us about the world around us," she smiled.

"Miss," said another girl about Heather's age, sat near the front, "is it true that we're all going to die, like in the great flood?"

The other children laughed at this and the girl flushed, shrinking into her chair. The teacher hushed them and answered her question with the seriousness she felt it deserved.

"I'm sure this is not the end. We're here now on the island, aren't we? We're the lucky ones. I suppose if we were all just to give up, then perhaps you're right, things would be different. Like Noah, we've all been given a fresh start, so we need to seize that opportunity with both hands. We are free to choose our own destiny."

Heather was looking out the window, pondering the Principal's words. It reminded her of the speech she had heard at the refugee camp when she'd first arrived. It was almost as if they were scripted to have consistent messaging, to inspire hope and purpose. She wondered what was really going on, behind the smokescreen and propaganda. Her father had taught her to be dispassionate, to scrutinise the evidence, to be skeptical in the absence of facts. It was a mantra that he said would serve her well in life.

CHAPTER THIRTY-NINE

From her raised position, Riley was watching the sun sink lower towards the horizon as it seemed to dip its toes in the ocean. She held on tight to the strap above her head, bracing herself against the violent lurches to left and right. Jack's Land Rover Defender bumped along the narrow shingle roadway that ran along the top of the sea defences linking the castle to Milford village. He was driving her out towards the barricades to see for herself what was going on.

They stopped a couple of hundred meters away and studied the small group gathered around a camp fire, near a footbridge that crossed over the narrow ribbon of water that divided the shingle strip from the tidal road to Keyhaven. There were half a dozen men gathered here, weapons leaning against rocks, warming their hands against a cold wind. She could see one man wrestling to free one of the broken wooden slats from the bridge for firewood. Three cars were positioned on the shingle side of the roadway to block any vehicles from leaving Hurst castle. Back towards Milford itself, she could make out a second barricade of items dragged from nearby houses and cafes.

"I count six," said Riley, squinting through Jack's Zeiss binoculars.

"That sounds about right. There were two of them yesterday, then dozens more of them arrived and occupied the houses along the front."

"Why stop here? Why not just carry on to Lymington or wherever they're trying to get to?"

"Most of their group kept going, but these ones stayed put."

"Why? Have you tried to talk to them?"

"Several times. They're not very forthcoming."

"So what makes you think the Sisters have something to do with this?"

"Oh it was something Sister Imelda said. She didn't seem altogether surprised when I told her that the road had been barricaded, as if it was only a matter of time before Sister Theodora would come to 'sort things out'."

"What did she mean by that?"

"Well, she wanted to take Jean and Joe back to stand trial. She'd probably take you too if we let her. I offered to hold the trial here at Hurst as a compromise, but she refused. She's been making quite a nuisance of herself since she arrived. Keeps calling us heathens and refers to the castle as a den of iniquity."

"She should get out more. Compared to the rest of the places I've seen, this is a model community. At least we're not raping and pillaging. What does she expect?"

"Beats me. She disapproves of our so-called 'abominable standards of immorality'. Mixed dormitories, relationships outside of wedlock, that sort of thing."

"Sounds about right. Listen, why don't we go and just talk to these guys? See if we can reason with them. If it's only the two of us, then maybe they'll listen."

"It's worth a try," said Jack, shrugging his shoulders. "They got a bit jumpy last time when the soldiers started brandishing their guns. Maybe it'll be different with you here."

They parked the Land Rover, leaving the beam of their headlights switched on to illuminate their path and to announce their presence to the group on the beach. They set off at a brisk pace towards the camp fire which they could see flaring in the dying light. They were still a hundred meters away when the men turned and noticed them. One of the men stood quickly, grabbing his rifle, and took aim at Jack's chest.

They froze, holding their hands in the air to let the defenders know they were unarmed, they resumed their approach.

"I'm telling you Riley," whispered Jack between gritted teeth, affecting his most disarming smile, "they're not friendly. You sure you want to do this?"

"Come on Jack, what are you afraid of?"

They took another few steps before a warning shot rang out above their heads. They stopped again as the man silhouetted by the flames took aim at Jack's head.

"That's far enough, Riley. You want to go any further, you're on your own."

"Come on, I just want to talk to them."

"I know, but people like them only respect force. We'll try again in the morning with an armed escort."

They retraced their steps towards the Land Rover in the dying light. Their shadows stretched out in front of them across the shingle as they walked. Riley's arms and legs looked elongated, almost alien. The sun sank below a band of cloud as darkness fell abruptly, closing in around them. Riley felt a shiver pass down her spine. It was a coldness and sense of foreboding she had not felt for some time.

Upon reaching the relative warmth of the vehicle's cabin, Jack decided to reverse up the roadway. It was too narrow to make the turn. It meant Riley could keep an eye on the group round the camp fire and make sure they were not stupid enough to follow them. Jack was parking near the main gate when Sergeant Flynn came running out to meet them.

"What happened? I heard the shot."

"Oh it was nothing, just a warning. We got a bit too close to their camp fire and they didn't like it."

"They're just kids. I wouldn't go exciting them. Sooner or later, they'll get bored and move on. There's nothing here for them."

"I wouldn't be so sure about that, Sergeant. Will seems convinced that they are here to stay. He thinks they're scouts or an advance guard."

"I doubt that. They'll know full well that this whole place is under military control. They're only here so long as we tolerate their presence. If we wanted to, we could smash our way through, no problem. No, I don't believe they'll try anything stupid."

"I hope you're right, Sergeant," sighed Jack. "In my experience, it pays to be careful."

They followed Jack through the main gate to the castle. Inside, there was already a palpable sense of unease. The sound of heavy boots running towards them revealed two soldiers carrying a heavy load. Riley watched them struggle towards the walls at the western end where they were keeping watch on the camp fire.

"What's going on Corporal?" shouted Sergeant Flynn.

"We just heard on the radio that they've been picking up a lot of activity today on the New Milton and Pennington approach roads to Lymington. We had reports of a huge convoy of vehicles heading along this way and now one of the lookouts says he can see lights in the distance."

"Sergeant," said Jack, grabbing Flynn's sleeve, "it could be the Sisters. We shouldn't take any chances."

"Very well," said Flynn raising his eyebrows, "sound the general alarm and get everyone to their posts. Like you say Jack, we can't be too careful."

***

Jack and Tommy passed the binoculars between them, straining to see the camp fire and line of vehicles beyond. The reports had been correct. Every time he checked, the headlights seemed to have got a little closer to the spit, advancing at walking pace along the coastal road that ran alongside Milford beach. Beside them, on the castle's ramparts, a pair of guards crouched behind a stack of sandbags, shivering against the cold. They were responsible for a tripod-mounted machine gun set up to have a wide arc of fire over the castle approaches.

There was a commotion in the courtyard behind them as Sergeant Flynn and Corporal Ballard shouted instructions, making their final preparations. They had posted men to the fortified positions around the castle walls, covering the roadway leading to the front gate. Flynn and Ballard were arguing about something, gesticulating wildly.

"What's going on, Tommy?" asked Jack, leaning in closer, keeping his voice low. The two civilians were spectators only and their offers of help had been refused by Flynn. They had been told the military would handle this, whatever that meant.

"Oh, Flynn and Ballard are all in a flap. They can't get hold of command and need to know what their rules of engagement are. They are only authorised to monitor the situation and report back."

"How many of them do they think there are?"

"At the barricade we saw six men, but I heard one of the guards say there were more than a dozen vehicles heading this way. Where the hell have they all come from?"

"Well if they're the same group as the guys manning the barricade, they'll most likely be heading east from Bournemouth and Poole."

"What do they want with us though?"

"That's what I'm worried about. I can't believe the Sisters could rally this big a group. It doesn't make any sense."

Tommy shrugged his shoulders. The two of them took one last cursory look at the unfolding scene behind them and descended the wooden staircase to the courtyard below.

Flynn had ordered the castle to lock down. The interior was bathed in an eerie orange glow from the powerful floodlights set on the walls. Jack could hear the generator rumbling gently as they passed, his trouser legs ruffled by the stream of warm air from the outlet vents. It was already pitch black around the castle, which made the arrival of such a large group in the darkness even more curious. The shingle spit was a dead end, it wasn't like it was on the way to someplace else.

They had seen large groups moving along the coastal road before now, but why would they come along the spit towards the castle? There was no sense to it. What possible purpose could they have in coming here? They must have known there was a heavy military presence, mustn't they?

"Everyone back inside," shouted Flynn, "close the gates, raise the drawbridge. I want everything locked down just in case they try anything tonight."

There was a raised voice from the ramparts and a runner descended the steps two at a time and hurtled towards them.

"Sarge, they're coming. The convoy just passed the first

barricade and they're heading onto the spit. They're definitely coming this way. What do you want us to do?"

"Get command on the radio. We need those rules of engagement. No one fires until we are fired upon."

The private acknowledged the order and ran back to pass the instruction to the radio operator sat in the guardroom. From the front entrance, Jack could hear two men cranking shut the small drawbridge by hand. He walked round and watched as the two men wrestled with the chain mechanism. The gap above the drawbridge reduced inch by inch. The drawbridge was welded with metal plates to ensure no opposing group could force entry as they had done before. They had also dug out the original moat that surrounded the Tudor castle facing Keyhaven and the water was said to be several feet deep to deter a direct assault with ladders over the wall.

They could hear mechanical noises now, carried by the wind. The sounds of engines straining in first gear. A hundred sets of footsteps displacing stones and rocks, advancing slowly towards them. Jack ran back to the stairway and climbed up to see for himself. The sight took his breath away.

As far as the eye could see there were hundreds of people carrying torchlights dancing in the darkness, walking alongside the convoy. At its head was a Toyota pick-up truck with the silhouettes of a group of people standing up in the back.

"You sure we're not expecting visitors today?" shouted Flynn, an edge to his voice.

"None that I'm aware of," replied Jack, his voice thin and brittle.

"What do they want?"

"I don't know for sure but I have a pretty good idea why they've come here," sighed Jack. His hand had begun to shake, so he thrust it into his pocket before anyone could notice.

CHAPTER FORTY

On board the *Chester*, Zed was in the state room with Doctor Hardy and the Colonel. They were surrounded by paperwork, studying printouts of reports. For the last two hours, they had been arguing about how best to deploy their precious stocks of Tamiflu.

The Professor had given instruction that each new arrival on the island, particularly those under eighteen years of age, should be given a flu shot at the earliest convenience to boost the collective immunity of the refugees. Doctor Hardy disagreed, siding with Lieutenant Peterson. Their reserves were limited and should be held back for key workers, military and medical personnel only.

Zed was doing his best to ignore them and focus on his reading pile. He could not stop thinking about the confidential CIA briefing document Peterson had shown him. It proved that his theory about Project Wildfire was at least viable. The mysterious circumstances in which the project was shut down and mothballed had always made him deeply suspicious.

His curiosity was piqued by one of the WHO reports detailing an H1N1 outbreak in the Seventies, which referred to an avian strain known as "Russian flu". What made this incidence of H1N1 notable was its near twenty-year absence. It was almost as if the flu strain had been frozen in time from the Fifties and accidentally released as the result of a laboratory accident. It confirmed, in Zed's mind, that the Russians had been running their own clandestine programme.

Each government had always known that this type of bioweapon research project was akin to opening a Pandora's Box. In order to prepare their country against attack, they had to create a vaccine based on a weakened version of a virus, capable of spreading terrifyingly quickly. When you thought about it, it was kind of back to front and upside down. Attack was the best form of defence, or something. Despite the mandatory level four biohazard containment protocols, everyone knew that a breach would be terminal. One mistake and they could unleash a pandemic of Biblical proportions.

Zed shook his head at the sheer stupidity of the whole thing. He stretched his arms wide in a yawn, rubbing at his tired eyes. The others stared at him with some amusement.

"Why don't you take a break, Zed?" said the Colonel.

"I think it's time we all took a break," agreed Peterson. "We're getting nowhere. Let's meet back here in half an hour. Zed, you want to join me on deck, clear the cobwebs?"

"Sure," said Zed, getting awkwardly to his feet. His left foot had gone to sleep.

He followed Peterson through a doorway and out towards the water-tight door to a narrow walkway that ran alongside the ship's bridge. After the stuffy warmth of the stateroom, up here it was freezing cold. A biting wind swept in across the Solent.

It was a clear night and a crescent moon cast a pale light across the island. A faint shimmer of scattered lights danced on the water from the towns of Ryde and Cowes. To Zed, since they had restored limited electrical power to the island, it remained an unfamiliar sight. The warm glow from living rooms and the occasional street light in town centres were somehow reassuring and comforting. It was a sign that things were slowly returning to normal, or at least an approximation of normal. Nothing would ever quite be normal again, he mused.

Peterson joined him at the rail. Both men looked out across the water in silence.

"This is where I come to get peace and quiet. The crew knows that when I'm out here, I'm not to be disturbed unless the ship is sinking or under attack."

Zed smiled and nodded. "I know what you mean. There's something so peaceful and relaxing about the sea. It's what I love about Hurst, being surrounded by water, listening to the waves and the wind. It's my little slice of heaven."

"I hear the place you're moving to on the island is every bit as special."

"Ah, but it won't be the same. It could never be quite the same."

"I don't know, I envy you. Being able to settle down, relax, grow vegetables, that sort of thing. Deep down, I'm just a farm boy from Idaho. I miss the fields of corn, riding horses, that simple life. Hey," he said pointing to Zed's arm, "your fighting days are over my friend. You can take it easy on the island, let others take up the slack."

"Not really my style. I'm not really the settling down type. I'm like a shark. If I stop swimming, I'd probably die. Besides, after you showed me that report, my brain went into overdrive. My place is with the research team."

"You really think there's a link between the Millennial Virus and the project you worked on all those years ago, Project Wildfire?" he asked incredulously.

"After what you showed me, I'd say it's definitely possible. Doctor Hardy pulled down all the archived reports from the Porton Down servers before we left. I'm slowly working my way through the folders. There are thousands of scanned documents covering the last thirty years. Right now, working on my own, it's like looking for a needle in a haystack, but if I keep looking, I know I'll find something. I could do with a team. Don't suppose you have anyone you can lend me?"

"Not without compromising security. Like I said, that report stays between the three of us. If the Porton team discovers a link, a genetic marker that proves the virus was bioengineered, so be it, we come clean and share the intelligence report, but until then, you're on your own."

"I don't understand why you wouldn't want to vaccinate everyone on the island. Even if it's only twenty per cent effective, it's better than nothing."

"Because the illusion of immunity is a dangerous thing. The quarantine protocols are designed to keep the island virus free. If people start thinking that the virus is no longer a threat, we risk a fresh outbreak. This way, we use that fear, channel it towards vigilance and a heightened sense of preparedness."

"Do you remember the war on terror?" continued Peterson. "The US government went to great lengths to ensure that the American people were always vigilant, aware of the threat. It was critical that they supported the war effort, that they were prepared to sacrifice a degree of privacy for the greater good. The idea of a virus and the threat of an outbreak is similar. It's an awfully effective way of instilling discipline and exercising control in a potentially chaotic situation."

Something about Peterson's language troubled Zed. His desire to control others, to manipulate the truth to his own ends, struck him as Machiavellian. He started to shiver uncontrollably. He was only wearing a t-shirt and thin sweater and the temperature had plummeted quickly now the sun had set. They were just turning to head inside when Jones appeared at the doorway. He waited inside, making way for them.

"Sorry to disturb you sir. I've got Captain Armstrong on the radio. He's getting reports that there's been a firefight at Lymington, that the detachment there are under attack again. He's requesting air support, a show of force."

"It's the same as we've seen at Southampton over the past few days. These people are desperate. They're coming in greater numbers than we can possibly process with the resources we have right now. I don't think a show of force is going to do anything other than stir things up. Anyway, the Brits need to take care of their own dirty work, we've got our hands full at Southampton."

"Is there any update from Hurst?" asked Zed. "Riley mentioned before she left that you're monitoring huge numbers of people in the area."

"So I heard. Captain Armstrong didn't mention anything about Hurst. We've got our own problems to deal with," he sighed before noticing Zed's concern. "Listen, why don't we get the drone airborne and see what we can find out. What do you say?"

"I'd really appreciate that. Thanks Lieutenant."

"Not knowing is the worst, right? Jones, put your team on standby just in case. So much for a quiet night eh?"

Peterson set off towards the Command Centre as Zed and Jones exchanged worried looks.

"Don't worry Zed, if things turn nasty, I'll get her out. I promise. She's got my number if she needs to reach me," he winked.

***

Back in the Command Centre, Zed was looking over the shoulder of the drone operator with his arms crossed. The video feed showed an infrared outline of the Lymington river estuary, as the drone flew on at an altitude of around one thousand feet towards the ferry port. The heat differential between the water and the land showed as shades of grey on the screen. Zed was admiring the mastery of the pilot who had a simple joystick that reminded him of the Atari games console he had grown up with all those years ago, playing Mission Control and Asteroids.

"What kind of weaponry does this thing have?" asked Zed.

The drone pilot looked up from his screen and pushed the headphones to the side so he could hear better. "None sir, this is a surveillance quadcopter model, no armaments. It just gives us eyes on the situation and targeting capability for the ship's weapon systems."

"So you could launch a missile at them or something?"

The pilot stifled a laugh. "We could do that, yes sir. My job would be to relay the target coordinates and the fire team would make that call."

"Ever had to do that?"

"No sir, not yet. But there's a first for everything."

The pilot slipped the headphones back into place and resumed his vigil on the flight systems, which were displayed as an array of on-screen data showing course, speed and altitude. The drone was passing over the top of outlines of pleasure craft, yachts, day fishing boats and larger power boats of all shapes and sizes. The enormous shape of the Isle of Wight ferry came into view and the ferry port beyond.

On the infrared display, a large number of heat signatures was evident inside the compound. Nearest the ferry, furthest away from the entrance, were what looked like several groups of men, women and children huddling together, sheltering behind a building. It quickly became clear why.

The drone came into a hover overhead and showed scattered defenders manning the barricades and fortified positions overlooking the road. Rammed against the perimeter fence was a truck that was on fire and several shapes lay on the ground around it where they had fallen. The bodies showed as a dim grey as if their life force had already ebbed away. They could see muzzle flashes and a firefight in progress. The pilot relayed his report into his microphone and Peterson and another officer joined them at his station, looking over his shoulder.

"Have we made contact with Lymington yet?"

"No, sir."

"Well, keep trying. Any sign of a perimeter breach?"

"Not that we've seen so far. Looks like they tried to ram-raid the front gate, but the line is holding. They are still under attack from the first group here in the tree line and beyond these buildings on the far side of the main road," he said, pointing to indistinct shapes on the screen. "There's a second group approaching the river side of the enclosure, four vehicles, one of them looks armoured, possibly equipped with a heavy weapon."

"Where the hell did that come from? Okay, relay those coordinates to the fire control team."

"How do you know they're the bad guys? Couldn't they be reinforcements or something?" asked Zed innocently, despite the disparaging looks of those around him.

"Sir?" interrupted one of the operators from another station, "we've just heard from the team at Lymington. Commander Jackson confirms that they are under attack by a superior force, one heavy machine gun, mortars, small arms. Requesting fire support from the *Chester*."

"Very well. Fire control?"

"Fire control aye. GFCS has the co-ordinates locked in. Five-inch ready to fire."

"Clear to fire."

"Firing now."

Zed heard a distant thump as the five-inch gun mounted on the Forecastle of the ship fired a single round. His eyes flicked back to the screen as they waited a few seconds for the projectile to cover the five miles or so to its intended target. The corner of the screen where the cluster of attacking vehicles had taken up position erupted in a fireball, showing as a white-out on their screen. When the contrast returned, there was smoke and a large crater surrounded by twisted metalwork and fragmented heat signatures.

"Target destroyed, sir. And looks like the second group are having second thoughts."

"Good job, gunner. I think we're done here. Check in with Commander Jackson and make sure he's got the situation back under control. Pilot, let's get that drone returned to base."

"Lieutenant," Zed intervened, "can we continue on to Hurst and see what's going on there?"

"Pilot, how much flight time do you have left?"

"I'm showing twenty-six minutes of remaining flight time. Say ten minutes to return to the ship, so sixteen to spare, sir."

"Very well. When you're ready then, let's take a look at Hurst Castle please."

The drone banked round and set off across the river, passing houses and boatyards underneath as it skirted Lymington town and headed south-west towards Keyhaven over the mudflats and marshland below. After a few minutes, the far edge of the spit came into view.

Along the castle walls, they could see body shapes occupying defensive positions and a flurry of activity in the courtyard. Zed wondered which of these heat signatures belonged to Riley. Knowing her, she would be in the thick of the action, making a nuisance of herself.

The drone continued on its course towards the far end of the castle enclosure and up the spit towards Milford. Zed suddenly saw what all the commotion was about.

Stretched out for several hundred yards was a convoy of vehicles and crowds of people walking slowly up the narrow ribbon of land.

"Where the hell did these guys come from?" said Zed in surprise. "There's got to be several hundred there."

"I don't know where they came from or where they think they're going. But if they think they can just bust their way in to the castle, they have another think coming," said the Colonel dismissively.

"Let's hope they just want to talk, not fight," yawned Zed.

"Jones, can you fix this man up with a bed for tonight?" said Peterson looking round and noticing how tired Zed looked gripping on to the chair in front of him to stop himself falling over. "By the looks of things, it'll take them a while to reach the castle. Why don't you get your head down for a while? It could be a long night. We'll wake you if there are any developments. Go get some rest."

Reluctantly, Zed realised he was right. He needed another shot of morphine to take away the pain in his arm which had returned. He would be out of action for a while at least. He just had to hope that the convoy was there for another reason. He just couldn't figure out what that could be, other than to attack.

CHAPTER FORTY-ONE

Riley was with Jack and Sergeant Flynn on top of the Gun Tower at the centre of the Hurst castle complex. It gave them a panoramic view of the approaches and the long line of people and vehicles heading their way. The exterior sodium floodlights set up along the castle walls revealed a sorry procession of men and women.

On the refugees' feet, many of them wore shoes wrapped in plastic and strips of blankets to shield them against the worst of the weather. Others were hooded, carrying duvets, sleeping bags and waterproof sheeting. It was like a moving conveyor belt of human detritus, transported by the last vestiges of hope. Though several carried weapons, this wasn't an army in any conventional sense. They were refugees on their way to the island. So why on earth, wondered Riley, were they taking the time and trouble to visit the castle?

The Toyota pick-up truck at the head of the convoy turned front on to face them, parking near the main entrance to the Tudor castle. The vehicle behind pulled in alongside in full view of the figures on top of the Gun Tower.

Riley was trying to make out the faces of the five people sitting in the back of the truck. One of the men stood up as if on cue, leaning over the truck's cabin to angle a powerful light towards his face so he could be seen. He certainly didn't look familiar.

He reached down into the belly of the truck and pulled out what appeared to be a loud hailer, like they used in public meetings and protests she had attended on NHS picket lines. He fiddled with the switch and was met by dissonant feedback, echoing round the castle walls. He adjusted the volume, apologising to those around him who were clutching their hands over their ears. He pointed the megaphone away from his body and tried again. He depressed the button and blew into it a couple of times to check it was working and then cleared his throat.

"People of Hurst, people of Hurst," he repeated, seemingly self-consciously at the sound of his booming voice reverberating round the brick and stone. "We come to you in peace as your allies and friends."

"Where have we heard that before?" whispered Riley.

"Many of us have walked a long way to join you today. We are in urgent need of food and shelter for the night."

"Why are you here?" shouted one of Flynn's men from above the gate.

"We're on our way to the island and were told you would be able to give us shelter."

"There are too many of you," shouted Flynn's man, before he was hushed by the soldier next to him.

"Please, we have women and children, senior citizens who will die if they stay out in the open."

"It's a trick," said Riley under her breath. "Don't trust them."

There was a silence as both sides seem to take stock.

"I understand that Hurst is now under military command,"

he continued with growing authority, "with a humanitarian obligation to provide assistance to those who request it. May I ask who is in charge here?"

Riley glanced at Jack who seemed unsure how to answer. Technically, Hurst was under military control and Sergeant Flynn was the highest-ranking soldier, but he seemed reluctant to step forward. Flynn was no politician, that was for sure. He gestured Jack forward, encouraging him to respond on Hurst's behalf.

"I am Jack, may I know who you are?"

"Jack?" he sounded surprise, "I was led to believe that you had already left for the island. My name is not important, but you can call me David. There are others amongst us that know you better than I."

With that, he stepped aside and handed the loudhailer to the hooded figure behind him. The figure rose from the shadow cast by the truck's cabin. The woman theatrically threw back her hood so that her features caught the light for the first time. It was a face Riley would never forget.

"Jack, we have not met though I feel we know each other well. My name is Sister Theodora. I sent my emissary, Sister Imelda, to you several days ago and she is still not returned. Am I to believe that she is being held captive here?"

"On the contrary, the Sister is alive and well. She is our guest, not our prisoner. I will fetch her for you, so she can speak for herself."

Jack passed the instruction to Tommy who set off in search of the Sister.

"I have heard it said that you hold several prisoners here and that anyone who stands against you is swiftly dealt with. Is this what Hurst has become, a lawless enclave?"

"Not while I live and breathe. Hurst is a beacon of freedom and fraternity."

"Then how do you explain that she was sent here to plea for help and has been so poorly treated? My request was that you hand over Jean and Joe to us so that they may stand trial for their crimes. We maintain that both of them were responsible for the fire that killed many innocent people from my group."

"They deny what you are accusing them of and I believe them. Even so, I offered to hold the hearing here at Hurst on neutral ground, but Sister Imelda refused. She insisted they be tried by their peers back at the Chewton Glen. I disagreed. Considering you claim they are guilty, I don't see how they could get a fair trial."

"If that's your final decision, then so be it. You have sealed your own fate. Harbouring known criminals makes you and all who reside here accomplices."

"My offer stands. I believe it is fair and right. We would guarantee an independent and fair trial, free of prejudice, conducted by those with no affiliation to the people you accuse. Sister Imelda was adamant that any such claims of independence were false. It now seems clear that she came here with no intention of compromise or settlement. Let's be clear what this is about: revenge, not justice."

"Sometimes, they are one and the same."

"Only if you believe in a natural law and a violent justice, red in tooth and claw."

"I assure you, sir, we are God-fearing folk, not vigilantes. We simply want to see those responsible held to account for what they did."

Tommy appeared through the roof top entrance with Sister Imelda trailing behind. She was brought to the edge of the Gun

Tower roof so that those below could see her.

"Are you well Sister? Why did you not return?"

"Because they refused my request outright, as you rightly predicted. Sister, I knew that if I waited, eventually you would come."

"And here I am," she replied, throwing her arms wide. "Now perhaps you can make them see sense before this situation deteriorates further."

With that the Sister sat back down and the man next to her clicked off the beam of light illuminating the party in the pick-up truck. In the silence that followed, a hubbub of conversation could be heard throughout the castle and the crowd outside.

***

At the heart of the Tudor castle, Sister Imelda pleaded with Jack and Sergeant Flynn to come to their senses. She turned to Riley.

"Riley please, you know what Sister Theodora is capable of. Once she's set her mind to something, she doesn't back down."

"And the people she's come here with, who are they?"

"Some of them I recognise, local groups we worked with, but there are too many to explain this great a number. They must have come from far and wide. Bournemouth, Christchurch, Weymouth, Poole, who knows? We know there are a lot of people trying to reach the island."

"Do they not see the military presence here? The decisions here are no longer mine to make," said Jack with a heavy heart. "Sergeant Flynn is in command."

"Then Sergeant I beg you. Give her what she wants. Throw open your gates and give them shelter for the night."

"We all have orders Sister. This isn't some refugee centre. We're not set up to dispense humanitarian aid. This is a military outpost charged with the defence of the Solent. The only thing I can do is call this in and see if we can get dispensation to release food and bedding, but we're not opening those gates."

"May I remind you Sergeant that you have a humanitarian duty to provide assistance to civilians in distress?"

"Not when they issue threats," countered Jack. "Don't be fooled Flynn, this is an attacking force. They intend to occupy the spit and force a settlement. Be sure to relay that to headquarters. The only thing bullies respect is force."

"These are civilians, Jack, not soldiers," reassured the Sister. "Surely you don't intend to fire your weapons at unarmed men, women and children?"

Riley was listening to the Sister's attempts to twist and distort with increasing frustration. "You really are a piece of work. Don't come over all innocent. You know full well that this whole crusade is a charade. How do you explain the large number of heavily armed men flanking the refugees? Do you really think we wouldn't notice them quietly occupying the spit over the last few hours, surrounding the castle and posting lookouts to spy on us?"

"I assure you…" started the Sister, playing the innocent.

She was interrupted by a commotion outside. Riley could hear the repeated beeping of car horns as two vehicles attempted to barge their way through. The crowds in between them and the gate were pressed closer together and they had to physically ease people aside. They were playing what sounded like Mozart's *The Marriage of Figaro* at top volume.

Racing back up to the roof of the Gun Tower, Riley could see an expensive looking Range Rover and what looked like a Humvee. Rounding the far corner of the castle, they were flashing their headlights urgently, nudging people aside as they progressed towards the main gate. The two vehicles both screeched to a halt, scattering stones at the shins and ankles of those around them. The doors flew open and Riley recognised the swagger and self-importance of Briggs and his entourage. Last but not least emerged the Professor and Copper.

Riley could scarcely believe her eyes. She hurried back towards the stairwell, taking the steps two at a time, stumbling and grabbing at the rail to keep herself upright. She ran across the courtyard, through the Tudor gate towards the gatehouse. Inside, two of Flynn's men looked surprised by the interruption. One of them was trying to raise headquarters on the communications equipment set up on the desk.

"Can I help you?" asked one of them as if she was interrupting something important.

"I need to get an urgent message to Sergeant Jones on board the *Chester.*"

"I'm sorry, if you come back in the morning, I'd be happy to help get a message to your boyfriend, but with what's going on outside, now's not really the time," he said with heavy sarcasm.

"What? No, look, it's important. I've just come from the *Chester*. I'm one of the team that just returned from Porton Down. I need to tell Jones that those men outside are the same ones that ambushed us."

"Now look, I don't care who you are or where you've come from. I take my orders from Sergeant Flynn, not you, so if you don't mind..." he said rising from his chair.

Riley looked him up and down dismissively, her blood boiling at his petty bureaucracy and male chauvinism. "We're wasting time. Please don't make me go get the Sergeant. I promise you, you'll regret it."

"Last warning. Either you get out or I'll have you thrown out. Private Lester, show this lady out would you?"

"Yes, Corporal."

Riley clenched her fist and thought about ramming him up against the wall, but thought better of it. "You idiot. You've probably just got us all killed. I'll be back, God help me, I'll be back."

CHAPTER FORTY-TWO

Riley stormed out of the radio room and headed back up the stairs to find Flynn. Her mind was churning. Briggs and Copper must be supremely confident. They were taking a mighty big risk coming here. She wondered whether the presence of the Sister lent an air of respectability to their mission tonight.

She found Flynn on the roof top scanning the convoy with a pair of binoculars.

'Sergeant, can I have a word please," asked Riley impatiently.

The Sergeant seemed distracted, as if he had just spotted something in the distance he didn't like the look of. He ignored her and relayed further instructions to Corporal Ballard who was on the walkway below him, keeping his voice low to avoid alarming others. Riley turned to Jack in despair.

"Jack, please. This is important. Why won't anyone listen to me?" she said physically stamping her foot in anger.

"What is it, Riley?" asked Jack, noticing her frustration for the first time.

"We have to get a message to Lieutenant Peterson. You do realise who those men are?"

"Never seen them before. Don't tell me, friends of the Sisters?"

"No, much worse. The man on the right, the tall one there," she said pointing at the figure striding around purposefully shouting at his men, "is Briggs, and the shorter, stouter one next to him is Copper."

"You mean *the* Copper who led the attack on Hurst? Why didn't you say anything before?"

"I've been trying to tell you for the last twenty minutes but no one's listening."

"Sergeant," interrupted Jack to no effect. "Sergeant," he shouted, more insistent this time. The Sergeant looked up flustered.

"What is it Jack?" he replied with some irritation. "Look, I'm sorry, I appreciate your help, but this is now a military matter."

"You do realise who we're dealing with? That man out there is Briggs," he paused waiting for a reaction, but Flynn seemed not to recognise the name. "You know, public enemy number one, the man who attacked the convoy from Porton Down?" he said pointing towards the figure now staring at them, as if he could hear every word. "And the other guy there led the attack on Hurst a few months back."

"Rings a bell, but so what? Why are you telling me this?"

"Because now it all makes sense. I know why they're really here."

"Weren't you listening Jack? They've already told us their reasons."

"Don't be fooled Sergeant. That's all a smoke screen. The real reason they're here is Damian King."

"What makes you think that?"

"It's obvious, isn't it?" he said, increasingly frustrated with Flynn's refusal to take their concerns seriously. "They want him back. He's been held prisoner here for months. I've always refused requests to hand him over. If anyone should stand trial for what they've done, it's him."

"Slow down, you're not making any sense."

"What I'm saying is that, not only do they want us to hand over Joe and Jean, but they're also here for Damian King. They're using the Sister as a patsy, a smokescreen."

"Jack's right," Riley leaned in supportively. "Sergeant, if you give an inch, they'll take a mile. This whole place could fall like a house of cards."

"Trust me," continued Jack. "They're out for revenge. They want to finish what they started when they first attacked this place."

"But listen," cautioned Flynn. "I don't have a whole lot of choice. I appreciate what you're saying, but at the end of the day, they're right, we do have a duty to provide humanitarian assistance."

"Has everyone lost their heads around here?" implored Riley throwing her hands in the air. "No offence Sergeant, but this is above your pay grade. Call it in to command. Let Colonel Abrahams decide what should be done."

Flynn bristled at Riley's condescension. "I take my orders from Captain Armstrong, not the Colonel or the Americans."

"But you said yourself that the Captain is not answering, so what are you going to do Flynn?"

"There's not much more I can do. Without authorisation, all I can do is wait."

"Unbelievable," raged Riley. "Every minute we delay they're surrounding this place. Then what?"

"If you'll excuse me, I have a base to organise," shrugged Flynn to Riley's thinly-concealed annoyance. He walked away to find Corporal Ballard for an update.

"Jack," said Riley conspiratorially, "we can't wait around for them to get their act together. We need to take steps right now. There must be another way of contacting the Colonel and Peterson. They need to know this. Do we have any other way of getting the word out? What happened to all our old walkie talkies?"

"Follow me Riley. Don't worry," he winked, "we've still got a few tricks up our sleeves."

***

Riley followed Jack through the corridors of the castle to a store cupboard where he had stowed some of his gear ready for transfer to the island. Inside a grey canvas bag was his service revolver and a black walkie talkie with a charger cable. He checked the safety and tucked the revolver in his belt, along with a handful of bullets. Grabbing the radio, he powered it up and was relieved to find that it still held a charge.

"It's short range Riley, so they may not hear anything we say, but it's worth a try."

She snatched it from his hand and turned the dial till the digital read-out showed 'Channel Nine'. She closed her eyes, composing her thoughts for what she wanted to say. She had to assume that others less friendly to their cause would be listening.

"This is an urgent message for Jones, this is Irish girl. The men from the Forest are here now. Repeat, they are here now."

There was a crackle of static as she released the transmit button and then silence.

"Jones said that one of his guys monitored this channel day and night, just in case," said Riley anxiously.

She looked at the handset and twisted the volume button to make sure it was working. There was a reassuring green light on the top by the on/off switch that suggested there was still power. Riley was just about to try again when an American voice answered: "Standby."

They exchanged excited looks and waited. She gnawed at her fingernails, hoping that the message had been received and understood. She trusted Jones's team that it would be treated with the urgency it deserved.

"Go ahead Irish girl. This is Guardian Angel. What can we do for you? I hear you have some visitors?"

"Thank God you guys were listening. The Brits here are dithering, they're cut-off from their chain of command and seem incapable of making a decision for themselves."

"We have an asset overhead right now. Looks like you have quite a party in progress."

"We thought we heard something. I wondered if that was you."

"Always keeping an eye on you. You know me."

"That's so sweet," she said as Jack gave her a quizzical look that made her feel self-conscious.

"What do you have in mind? We need some guidance here. It seems like quite a confused situation you got there. Good guys and bad guys all mixed up."

Jack grabbed the handset and took over. "We need to evacuate the civilians before things turn ugly here. If you can get some transportation up here nice and quiet, we might be able to get the civilians out without them noticing."

Riley was gesticulating at him, but it was too late. Now anyone listening in would know their plan.

"It's risky. I might be able to get my hands on a couple of R.I.Bs, but not enough for forty five. The other option is you find a secure location, like a basement, and barricade yourself in till the morning when we can get some reinforcements to you."

"We don't think we can last out that long. The last thing I want to do is get trapped in a basement with no food, water, or radio reception."

"Understood, then let's keep that as a last resort."

"Listen Guardian Angel, we don't have much battery left. I'll power it up again in half an hour and see what you've come up with. In the meantime, we'll get everyone ready just in case you can get us out."

"Copy that. Will come back to you when I know more."

***

Outside the castle gates, in the warmth of the pick-up truck's cabin, Terra was sitting next to Briggs with the air-con turned up, flexing her gloved fingers next to the heater vent. Copper and Victor were huddled together in the cramped back seat alongside two others. A voice came over the handheld radio lying on the dashboard and Briggs grabbed it impatiently.

"Boss, we just intercepted a series of transmissions we believe to have come from Flynn's men inside the castle. Sounds like they are experiencing some communication issues. They can't raise their Captain and they don't know what to do."

"Excellent. Victor, your jamming device seems to be worth the price we paid for it," said Copper with a smug grin spreading across his face. Victor nodded. He looked relieved more than anything else.

"They're cut-off," he mumbled, "they'll have to make their own decisions now."

"I'm sorry I doubted you," conceded Briggs.

"By the way, we also intercepted another call on an insecure channel. They were talking in code. An American and a woman's voice. Sounds like they're trying to organise a rescue."

"How romantic," mocked Briggs. "Make sure we're ready for them. So Terra, how is it to be back at your former home? I told you I had a surprise for you."

"I love it darling," she enthused. "Seems different to the last time I was here. They've fortified the whole place. I don't remember those machine gun nests around the walls or the steel panels welded to the front gate. Seems like they've learned a thing or two from the last time someone tried to break in."

"It won't make any difference," shrugged Victor.

"We didn't try to break in," corrected Copper, "we ransacked this place. Nearly burned it to the ground."

"If that's true then why the hell are we back here cleaning up your mess? If you'd have done your job properly and not left a certain someone behind, we wouldn't need to be here."

"Last time, we underestimated them. It won't happen again."

"And tell me again, what's the deal with the Sister?" asked Briggs, turning towards Copper.

"She's the veil of respectability we talked about. She makes this whole thing legitimate."

"Who is she though?"

"She runs a women-only group we worked with a while back. Based in a hotel near New Milton up until a fire ripped through the place. They moved out of the area and we lost contact. We had an arrangement. Quid pro quo."

"Now I am curious," said Briggs. "What sort of arrangement?"

"Protection, food, that sort of thing. Plus they had some weird breeding programme."

"Breeding programme?"

"Yeah, it proved very popular with the men back at the hospital. I used to get a lot of volunteers. Something to look forward to on a cold winter night."

"All makes sense now. If they're going to start repopulating the place, they'll need a massive baby boom," mused Victor. "It's no wonder they're crying out for young women of child-rearing age on the island. I heard they have a maternity unit set up near Newtown with line after line of empty beds and infant cots. The Sisterhood will get VIP treatment."

"The Professor mentioned something about a wide-scale vaccination programme. In time, he said that they would be able to inoculate at birth, or genetically alter the embryos before they're born or something."

"I wouldn't believe everything he tells us. The scientists told us there is no vaccine, that they're still learning about the virus. It could be decades before they can move beyond the theory."

Their conversation petered out for a few seconds as they noticed some activity on the castle walls. A soldier was carrying a box of something towards the machine gun nest covering the entrance to the castle.

Terra remained puzzled by Briggs' confidence. She felt a little nervous sat directly in the firing line. They were virtually staring down the barrel of the machine gun. It wasn't just the threat of violence, she was also distinctly uncomfortable being this close to her old home and Jack. She knew most of the other people she had spent time with would already have left. After all this time, she wondered what she would say to Jack.

The last time she had seen Zed and Riley, it was under impossible circumstances. She had watched helpless as they were interrogated and beaten. She had tried to intercede on their behalf but Victor had told her not to get involved. She thought back to what Briggs had done to Zed's arm and shuddered in horror.

The sheer brutality had been unforgivable. He was inhuman,

barbaric, almost medieval in his despicable use of torture. Yet, hadn't she allowed it to happen? She could have spoken up, appealed to Briggs' mercy, but she had remained silent. That sat heavily on her conscience. In a funny way, had Zed been killed outright, at least there would have been closure. Like this, her discomfort and guilt remained raw. They would assume she was guilty by association.

All these unsettling thoughts were still buzzing around her head when she realised with a slight jolt that she had completely missed what Briggs had said to her and noticed him staring. He didn't like to be ignored.

"I said, do you know where they'll be holding Damian King?"

"Well, not for certain, but really there are only two likely places," she replied animatedly, thinking through the various options. "There are a couple of dry storage rooms with lockable doors, where they have kept people before. They're in the bowels of the castle. He'll be in there, I'd imagine."

"I reckon it's time to stir up the hornet's nest and see if we can't get inside. Copper, have a word with the Sister can you? Let's keep pushing Jack's buttons. Sooner or later, they're going to let their guard down. Let's keep our wits about us. Tonight could still be full of surprises."

CHAPTER FORTY-THREE

The crew quarters on board the *Chester* were a little basic for Zed's liking. Even after more than two years of sleeping in a draughty castle on an assortment of threadbare mattresses and shared rooms, this was a new low. The bunk he had been assigned to for the night was in a bunk room that smelled musty and lived-in. His guide had apologised and explained that all the officer quarters were occupied so this was the best they could do at short notice.

He was issued with a blanket with a residual stench of damp and sweat masked by fabric conditioner or possibly air freshener, he couldn't tell. The foam pillow offered little support and was heavily stained with an oily residue from what he assumed was Brylcream or some other hair product. It was at least warm, but with the air conditioning turned off on this level to conserve power, it was stifling and airless down here. He was sharing the room with half a dozen others who seemed to come and go at all hours as they rotated through different watches.

He was woken by a firm nudge in the back which he shrugged off as the clumsy actions of another transient room mate. The hand on his shoulder was more insistent the second time.

"Zed, wake up."

It was a voice he recognised but he felt so exhausted that he tried to ignore it, hoping they would go away.

"Zed, you need to wake up. We've just heard from Riley and Jack. Briggs and Copper have just showed up at the castle. I thought you'd want to know."

His eyes flickered open, suddenly wide awake. He sat up too quickly, smashing his head against the bunk above. Swinging his legs over the edge, he clutched his forehead, still seeing double. He remembered the pills the Doctor had given him which must explain why he felt so groggy and disoriented. He hoped it would pass quickly but knew from experience it would take several cups of strong coffee.

"What time is it anyway? It felt like I just dropped off."

"It's about midnight. Come on, we don't have much time. Here are your clothes."

Zed slid into his jeans and finished getting dressed on their way to the Ops Centre. Jones filled him in en route, relaying the bones of his conversation with Riley.

"So what's the plan? Can you get that many out?"

"Unlikely, not without anyone noticing. If I was Briggs, I'd have the whole castle surrounded, all landing areas patrolled. From the thermal imaging we got from the drone, we assume they're using the civilians as human shields, trying to stop us launching a surgical attack. It's smart. We can't touch Briggs and Copper without collateral damage. And if we did try and mount a rescue, it's uncertain how the crowd would react. They could turn on us. It's more complicated than it sounds."

They passed the medical centre on their way, passing room after room of men sleeping or keeping watch over their stations throughout the night.

"What do the Colonel and Lieutenant Peterson suggest?"

"Well, there's the rub. Hurst is under the command of the Royal Navy, so technically, Captain Armstrong is in charge. Officially we can offer assistance only when it's been asked for."

"And unofficially?"

"Unofficially," he winked, "we can do whatever the hell we like. As long as no one finds out."

"You mean 'ask for forgiveness not permission'?"

"Something like that. I still need to get sign off from the CO. I can't just take my team out on personal crusades and vendettas you know. If Peterson gives this the green light, then we'll go get Riley and as many of the others as we can get out."

"And if we get the chance, what about Briggs?"

"This is a rescue mission, not an assassination attempt."

"Fair enough, so what are we waiting for? When do we leave?"

"Wait a minute. I never said anything about you. My team are specialists at this type of operation. It's what we do. Having a civilian along is not advisable. Especially one with only one arm."

"Listen Jones, no one knows that place like I do. If you're going to get in there without anyone knowing, then I'm the only person who can help. You need me."

Jones tilted his head, weighing up the options, playing it out in his mind. He didn't seem overly convinced, but shook on it anyway.

"This is a bad idea, but I don't have a better one. You're going to need some kit," he said looking him up and down, "can't have you tagging along looking like that."

***

The two R.I.Bs loaded with four men each were slowly lowered one by one down the steep sided hull of the destroyer. They swung out over the water underneath the davits whose pulleys and ropes whirred with electrical efficiency. With a small splash, they touched down in the light swell. One of Jones's men released the cables and they revved their twin outboard engines and headed out to join the other R.I.B which was waiting for them off the *Chester*'s bow.

Zed looked around at Jones and his two other companions on the R.I.B. They were dressed head to toe in black, with webbing and pouches accentuating their bulk. They wore black helmets with night vision goggles secured at the front and balaclavas that covered their faces. He found it hard to distinguish one from the other. From spending time with these guys during the trip to Porton Down, he knew they were professionals. They looked relaxed but alert. They kept conversation to an absolute minimum, facing outwards, eyes on the shoreline and surrounding water for any unexpected contact.

The sea state was relatively calm compared with the storms of the previous week. At night fall, the wind had dropped to barely above a whisper, so there was a residual swell only. It made for a comfortable half-hour sprint up to the castle in the darkness, surfing across the waves at nearly thirty knots.

Zed had been kitted out with the same uniform as the soldiers. Unlike the others who seemed to be bristling with knives and weapons, he had been given a matt black Heckler and Koch Colt pistol which he had secured to a chest holster integrated with his body armour. Jones had been clear, it was for emergencies only. He was their guide. If they encountered any resistance, he was to sit tight and let them deal with it. With a shrug, he was content to go along with the plan. He was in no position to argue on this occasion.

When they got to within a half mile of the castle they cut

their speed to avoid any unnecessary noise. There was a westerly wind which would help mask their approach, but they needed surprise on their side if their plan had any hope of working.

Jones unclipped the handheld radio and raised it to his mouth.

"Irish girl, this is Guardian Angel. E.T.A ten minutes."

"Copy."

Zed had briefed them carefully before they left. There were several landing areas accessible to small craft that lay between the sea defences and groynes, hidden from view from all but those on the castle walls or waiting on the shingle beach. Ironically, it was the same route that Copper's men had used to attack the castle, though this time, the plan was to break out, not in.

There were scattered clouds and a thin crescent moon. Unless Briggs' men had infrared gear, it was very unlikely they would see the R.I.Bs as they drifted in silently on the waves.

Jones gestured for Zed and the other men in the R.I.B to crouch low as they cut the engine and grabbed a single paddle to steer the remaining hundred meters to the beach. Zed lowered the night vision goggles into place and it took a few seconds for his eyes to adjust. What he saw made his eyes nearly pop-out on stalks.

***

Jack and Riley gathered the remaining civilians in the Hurst canteen where he had quietly briefed them about their planned escape. On the sides were stacked unwashed dishes and pans from the evening's dinner which had been cut short by the approach of the convoy.

"Listen, we've only got one shot at this," said Jack. "We need to be ready on top of the roof by the back wall in ten minutes' time. Space on the boats will be tight, so don't bring any bags. Just wear warm clothes and meet back here as quickly as you can."

"What do we say to the soldiers if they ask?"

"Say nothing. If they find out what we're doing, they'll try and stop us. Okay, off you go, time is of the essence."

A few minutes later the first of them arrived back wearing heavy woollen coats, hats, waterproof trousers, whatever they could find at short notice. Jack surveyed the motley crew and removed items they were carrying that were superfluous: children's toys, keepsakes, weapons.

"You won't need any of that. We'll come back and get your stuff another time," he lied, knowing full well that for many of them, this would be a one-way trip to the island, possibly never to return. They would be leaving all of their worldly possessions behind. Jack knew that, for Scottie in particular, it would be hard. He had spent the last couple of years curating a vast library of rare books and first editions gathered from the local area. Hurst's museum cabinets displayed curiosities from a by-gone age. Vinyl records, games consoles, computers, mobile phones and expensive wrist watches. Posters from rock concerts, gold disks, paintings, and sculptures. It was a treasure trove of memorabilia. A time-capsule of what life had been like before the outbreak.

For the rest of them, they would not look back. Moving to the island would be a fresh start, their slate wiped clean.

Riley led the first group out on to the roof, keeping them low and hidden in the shadows, in case anyone was scanning the building for movement. Jack joined her and uncoiled the long mooring line which Sam had been splicing with a new eye. The rope was dry and warm, covered in crusted green algae and seaweed that crumbled in his hands. He looped it through the new eye and secured the end round the post of a rusted railing and tested the line. It would hold, Jack was fairly sure, but only if they went one at a time.

He looked over the edge and scanned the shoreline, searching for Jones. Even from this elevated position, he couldn't see anything but knew they were close. Directly below them, he heard displaced stones and a cough that betrayed the presence of one of Briggs' men. Jack shuffled back into the shadows away from the edge, gesturing to the others to stay low and keep quiet.

***

Through Zed's night-vision goggles, he could see three heat signatures standing separately along the beach. One appeared to be smoking which would render his ability to see in the dark as virtually nil. Another was hiding in the shadows, trying to warm himself, alternately throwing his arms wide before clutching his sides, panting heavily. The other further up the beach was looking in the wrong direction, out towards Christchurch Bay. One of Jones's men had a longer barrel weapon and took up a firing position, aiming towards the first of the guards.

Jones gave the instruction and allocated the remaining two targets to the men on the other R.I.B. He counted down from three and with a light pop, Zed noticed the figure in the distance crumple and fall. As he scanned the beach for the other targets, he saw all three were down.

Jones grabbed the radio and whispered: "Now, now, now."

***

Jack heard the dull impact as the man below them sank to his knees, clutching his chest. There were similar thuds from left and right, so that when he looked over the edge, he noted all three men on the beach were down. They waited impatiently for the 'go' call from the Americans over the radio. Liz went first, helping the children down on to the beach and shepherding them back into the shadows, pressing a finger to her lips. Jack kept watch on them from above, anxiously glancing at his watch. Everything was taking too long. They might only have a few minutes before they were discovered.

"Where are they?" whispered Riley in his ear, clutching the radio to her chest to muffle any unexpected noise.

"There," exclaimed Jack, spotting the two dark shapes on the water as a chink of moonlight reflected off a PVC paddle as it dipped silently in to the waves. Jack checked left and right down the beach, but satisfied himself they had the beach to themselves, for now.

One by one, the figures clambered down until all the women and children stood huddled together, crouching behind a buttress, keeping away from the dead body and blood soaked pebbles in front of them. Riley had volunteered to stay behind.

***

After a few seconds delay, Zed could see a rope thrown over the castle wall and the first of several figures lowered themselves over the lip and clambered awkwardly down on to the beach. In a couple of minutes there were eight people huddling against the wall.

The first of the R.I.Bs coasted the rest of the way in and bumped against the shingle beach. One of Jones's men stepped down in to the breaking waves and waded in, holding the bow of the R.I.B from grounding.

The men in the boat met them halfway up the beach and waved them forward, one at a time. The first of the passengers, a young boy with his arm in a sling, ran down and was helped on board. It took Zed a couple of seconds to recognise each of them and they seemed surprised to see him. First Toby, then two of the other children were lifted onto the boat.

When the first R.I.B could take no more they pushed off again and paddled back out to open water, allowing the second boat to make its approach. All told, they managed thirteen in the first trip and shuttled them the half kilometre or so over to the small beach to the south of Cliff End Battery on the island.

They deposited their load and raced back towards the island. There had been no sign so far of Jack or Riley, but the children had said they were organising the extraction and would be the last to go across. That sounded like the Riley he knew.

They took the same precautions with their second approach, scanning the beach for any new arrivals. They figured it would not be long before the guards were missed or failed to report in. They had no time to lose. They cut the engines again and paddled the last few metres. This time there was a small group already waiting for them on the beach and they made it in and out quicker. Jones's men stood guard, scanning the beach for movement.

By the time they returned for their third approach, there were already twenty-one people safely transferred to the island, but at best, they were only halfway there. Another twenty-four to go meant at least three more trips. Their window was quickly closing. It would take a miracle for them to avoid detection.

***

It took what seemed like an age for the R.I.Bs to make it over to the island and back. By the time they were ready for the next group, Jack became aware of faint voices rounding the eastern edge of the castle coming to investigate why the men on the beach were not answering the radio calls. The discarded radio next to the dead man's body had chirped from time to time with increasing urgency. Jack had considered answering the call, but thought better of it.

Below them, the beam of a powerful hand-held torch arced across the water, searching out their man guarding the beach. Jack was out of time. Their luck had just run out.

CHAPTER FORTY-FOUR

The boats were half-way back towards Hurst spit when a powerful searchlight reached out across the water hunting for the R.I.Bs. Through his goggles, Zed was momentarily blinded, but as the concentrated beam moved past them, he could make out a flurry of activity as a dozen men rounded the corner of the castle wall from the eastern end of the spit racing round to the landing area. On top of the wall, he could see those inside hastily pulling up their rope ladder.

"Game's up," said Jones. "I count a dozen armed men. There's no way we can risk another approach without a firefight."

"But Jack and Riley are still in there. How are we going to get them out?"

"I don't know Zed. Is there any another way? Judging by the drone sweep, the whole of the front of the castle is swarming with people. Don't suppose there are any tunnels or secret passages you want to tell me about?"

"Afraid not. This is the only way in and out."

"I suggest we lie low for a bit and report in. Maybe try again later?"

"We're having trouble contacting HQ sir. Seems like someone is blocking our transmissions."

"Really? That's pretty sophisticated for some half-arsed locals."

"But how come we can still contact Riley?" puzzled Zed. "Does that mean normal marine wavebands are still working?"

"You're right. That would make sense. It wouldn't be secure, but we can still speak to them. Let's give it a try."

***

Hand over hand, Jack hurriedly pulled up the rope, letting it fall at his feet. He ushered them away from the edge again before leading the waiting group back inside. Sergeant Flynn was waiting for him at the doorway, hands on hips, shaking his head.

"What the hell's going on Jack?"

"Nothing you need to know about Flynn. We're doing what you should have done a long time ago, getting these civilians out of here."

"I've told you. You're all perfectly safe. You're getting everyone worked up about nothing," said Flynn, addressing the group.

"You don't know Briggs and Copper. You don't know what they're capable of."

"Listen, I have thirty of my men here. I've got machine guns covering every entrance and approach. I'm telling you, if we all stay calm, nothing's going to happen. In fact, by your actions, you're putting lives at risk. I don't want to provoke them."

"It's a bit late for that don't you think?"

"What do you mean?"

"Well, there are three dead bodies on the beach for starters, maybe more."

"Goddamit, Jack. You're putting us all in danger. If you're not careful, you're going to start a war."

"You had your chance, Flynn. Someone needed to act. We're taking matters into our own hands. I've just taken twenty-one hostages off the table."

"Hostages? Don't be so dramatic. This isn't some siege, I've told you, these people are refugees. One of their leaders is a nun, for goodness sake."

"That's what they want you to think, Flynn. You're playing into their hands."

"Sergeant," said a voice behind them, trying to catch his breath. "They're demanding to speak with you again. They want to know why you're saying one thing to their faces whilst others are escaping behind their backs."

"This is exactly what I wanted to avoid," spat Flynn. "You've just made my job a damn sight harder."

***

Flynn and Jack stood on top of the Gun Tower looking down at the huge crowd of faces staring up at them from below. Their numbers had swollen again as more and more arrived from their route march down the shingle beach.

Jack noticed an older man with wiry grey hair being helped up on to the back of the Toyota truck, which they were using as an improvised speaking platform. He realised it must be the Professor, struggling to make out his features in the long shadows cast from the sodium floodlights positioned every fifty meters.

The Professor shook hands with Sister Theodora and took his place next to Briggs and Copper, with Victor sat behind them, orchestrating events.

"Sergeant, we demand to know why you insist on deceiving us."

The Sister's voice, amplified by the loud hailer, echoed round the walls.

"To our faces, you reassure us with platitudes about your good intentions. But behind our backs, you conspire to murder our people and disappear into the night. How can we trust anything you tell us now?"

Her tone was measured and calm as if she was delivering a Sunday sermon to her congregation. The Sister's words appeared to be as much for the crowd around her as they were for Flynn. Her delivery was such that she was rewarded with a few gasps and murmured agreement.

"We will add that to the list of wrongs you've done us so far," she continued, casting her free hand around her in a sweeping gesture.

"What about the dozens of our people murdered by the man standing beside you?" shouted Jack above the hubbub.

"This man?" said the Sister with feigned surprise, gesturing towards Copper. "The man you're accusing of murder is a decorated police officer. He served this very community for nearly ten years. You're trying to tell all of us that an officer of the law attacked you? I don't know about anyone else, but I find that a little hard to swallow."

"It's true. That's exactly what happened."

"Why should we believe you now, when all you've told us so far are lies? Sergeant Flynn, why do you continue to let this man speak on your behalf? He is discredited and dishonoured and you should no longer harbour such a man."

All Jack could do was shake his head. He knew now that whatever he said in his defence would be twisted to their purpose.

"As for all you others, you soldiers hiding behind sandbags, I see you scratching your heads and wondering who to believe. Well, let me tell you. The truth is that the people who have been occupying this castle till now are the real thieves and murderers.

They were the ones who attacked the hospital in Lymington, and burned down the hotel my group was living in. There is no end to their depravity. This very night, they have killed three more of our men for daring to stand against them."

The Sister shook her head reproachfully, pausing to glance at Victor, who seemed to be enjoying his plan playing out.

"Let's not have any further bloodshed tonight. I appeal to you all to come to your senses and throw out these disabusers. Cast them out in to the night. Hand them over to face justice for what they've done, what they've all done. And please, let these poor hungry folk have food and shelter for the night, I beg you."

Jack almost laughed, it was so ridiculous, yet when he turned round Sergeant Flynn and Corporal Ballard were looking him up and down like their eyes had been opened.

"You realise that's all just a pack of lies? That man there pulling the strings," he said pointing accusingly at Briggs, "is a career criminal. You realise he was serving a life sentence at Parkhurst Prison. And Copper, the so-called decorated officer, is no such thing. He may have been years ago, but not any more. He was the man who led the attack on Hurst that killed dozens of my men. He shot them dead in cold blood, executed them against that wall just down there," his voice faltered remembering the atrocity that was committed right here during his absence.

"And Sister Theodora is the same person who imprisoned members of my team and accused them of starting a fire they had nothing to do with."

"I don't know about you Ballard," said Flynn, shaking his head disapprovingly, "but I reckon they're all as bad as each other. I don't know who to believe any more."

"That's right, Sarge. They're all as bad as each other," repeated his subordinate like an automaton.

"No, that's where you're wrong," countered Jack with growing animation, throwing his hands wide in supplication. "Flynn, please. You know me, we've been here for weeks together. My people are not thieves and murderers, come on. Come to your senses, man, and see this for what it is."

"I'm sorry Jack. Right now, it seems like you're part of the problem rather than the solution."

"You're joking," sneered Jack, half-laughing, "We made this place what it is. Before we got here, this was just a museum and coffee shop. Look at it now, it's a fortress. Don't forget, I was the first to arrive here after the outbreak. I gave these people a home, a fresh start. Everything you see around here is down to me and my team. Look at it now."

"That's right, look at it now. Hurst Castle is no longer under your control. I'm in charge."

Flynn nervously shuffled his weight from foot to foot. He seemed to relent for a moment, unsure how to proceed. He was way outside his comfort zone.

"Listen Jack. Believe me, I'm trying to do the right thing here. My orders are to keep this place safe and secure. No one said anything about dispensing humanitarian aid to passing groups, but now they're here, I don't see how we can refuse to help them. The things they're saying about you? I don't know, I want to believe you, but it's not my job to decide who's right or wrong. Without Captain Armstrong's orders, my hands are tied."

"I say we hand them all over and be done with it," suggested Ballard coldly.

"I always said you were an idiot," spat Riley. Ballard towered over her slender frame, but said nothing, puffing out his chest and giving her a dead-eyed stare.

"The least you could do for us is buy us some time," said Jack.

"Give us a chance to get the hell out of here."

Flynn seemed to consider that for a second, weighing up his options.

"I could do that but your exit routes are blocked. You might be better off hiding this out."

"We'll think of something," said Jack confidently, but inside he was beginning to think that Flynn was right, they should surrender themselves before someone else got killed.

***

"What are we going to do Jack?" asked Riley when the two of them were alone again. She was worried about him. He looked exhausted by the last few hours. He would never have agreed, but she secretly wished she had persuaded him to leave earlier. His pride and continued presence at Hurst could complicate matters, even make things worse.

"If we could get the *Chester* to send its helicopter up here, we could get another dozen men out, but I doubt they'd risk it. It's too dangerous," said Jack. "Like Flynn said, this whole area is under British control. Armstrong won't take kindly to American interference. Imagine what would happen if there was a friendly-fire incident or some locals got gunned down. It would be a PR disaster."

"I think it's a bit late for public relations, don't you? We're on the verge of widespread civil unrest. You didn't see what we saw at Porton Down and in the New Forest. The rebellion against the Allies is real. Briggs is trying to start a war, can't you see?"

Jack seemed distracted, his brain overloaded by events. His first thoughts were probably concern for his team and getting them out. Politics would have to wait for the morning.

"Where are Jones and Zed now? Can we get them on the radio?"

"Knowing Jones, he'll be close, lying low somewhere out in the channel."

"Or else, they're over at Cliff End Battery wrapped up in blankets having a cup of cocoa."

"I doubt it, they won't rest till we're all safe."

Jack seemed to brighten, straightening up as if emboldened by an idea.

"Perhaps we can get Zed to pass on a message to the *Chester*. If they won't risk a rescue, perhaps there's another way."

"You're not making sense. What do you have in mind?"

"A diversion. If they can distract Briggs, we might just be able to escape. Pass me that radio."

"Just be careful what you say. If I know Briggs, he'll be listening to every word we say."

"Trust me," said Jack with a thin smile. "I know just what to do."

CHAPTER FORTY-FIVE

"I'm not sure Peterson would go for it," said Sergeant Jones, struggling to hear against the engine noise and rushing wind as they bashed back across the swell towards Hurst, the Needles rocks visible to their left. "It's a bit heavy-handed, high risk of collateral damage, but it might work."

"We owe it to Riley and Jack to at least try. Look, if we leave them at the mercy of Briggs and Copper, we know what's going to happen," continued Zed, holding up the stump of his arm. "You know they'd murder those people in cold blood, just like they did at the Forest camp."

"But not with Flynn and his men there. Those soldiers are not going to stand by and let that happen."

"Listen, once they get those gates open, they may not be able to stop Briggs."

"They'd be crazy to open those gates. If they sit tight, they're in no danger."

Jones turned around and addressed the radio man sheltering at the back of the boat. He was staying low, keeping out of the wind and spray. He had his hand clutched to the side of his head.

"Corporal, any luck getting hold of the *Chester*?"

"Not yet. We're still being blocked by whatever jamming

equipment they're using. It's killing our signal."

"Why don't we try heading a bit further east and see if we can't get out of its range?"

"Good idea."

Jones tapped the helm on the shoulder and pointed down the Solent towards Southampton.

The swell was larger out in the main channel, and they pitched violently between the waves, trying to put more distance between them and the men on the beach. Zed began to feel the tension in his shoulders relax a little. For the last few minutes, he had been gripping the strap next to him as they were thrown around. He was beginning to feel decidedly queasy, leaning his head over the side.

"If you're going to vomit, make sure you do it downwind, can you?" shouted Jones, leaning in next to him.

"I'm not a complete lightweight. Just give me a minute," he replied, gulping air to try and regain control.

"Good signal sir," said the man on the radio. "Trying again now. *Chester*, *Chester*, this is Guardian Angel."

"Reading you loud and clear Guardian Angel. Go ahead."

"Requesting fire support mission. Target coordinates," he said flicking his head torch on and double-checking the map reference in the plastic pouch on his lap, "Zulu One-Seven, Charlie One-Two." The radio operator flicked his head back at Jones who nodded in agreement to confirm the order.

"Copy. Target co-ordinates are Zulu One-Seven, Charlie One-Two," repeated the voice of the radio. There was a small delay before he continued, "Guardian Angel, that's showing on my screen as a friendly target."

"Confirm, we have eyes on the target. No civilians in these zones. Request non-lethal rounds only. Smoke and phosphorous."

"Copy, Guardian Angel. Will need clearance from the CO. Hold in position."

***

Terra was bored and tired. They had been cooped up in front of the castle for the last two hours. The driver had turned the engine off to conserve fuel which meant the temperature inside the truck had plummeted. Despite Briggs' bravado, there was no sign of progress. She was beginning to think she should just curl up and try to get some sleep. The driver and passenger door opened simultaneously and Briggs and Copper got back in, bringing with them an icy blast of freezing night air.

"Are we going to be here much longer?" asked Terra, unable to resist a yawn.

"Let's hope not," replied Victor contemptuously. "We've left them no option. They're surrounded, cut-off from their chain of command. They'll come to their senses and agree terms."

"Not if Jack and his team have anything to do with it," cautioned Copper.

Terra sat up hearing Jack's name, suddenly spying an opportunity.

"Why don't you let me speak to Jack? I could talk him round. He'd listen to me."

The three men turned to face Terra, with obvious suspicion.

"I bet she could as well," said Briggs with a knowing smile, before seeming to dismiss the idea. "No, we'll keep you in reserve for now. I reckon they're ready to throw in the towel. They don't want a fight."

Just then, from behind them came a terrifying sound that seemed to split the air. There was a ground-shaking explosion towards the end of the spit that lit up the castle and the interior of the vehicle, dazzling all of them.

"What the hell was that?"

"That was no mortar round. That was a round from the *Chester*. What the hell are they doing? Victor, you said they wouldn't risk collateral damage."

"Looks like we underestimated them," said Victor, cowering in the back.

"Any casualties?" asked Copper winding down his window and speaking to one of his men from the hospital.

"Maybe it was a warning shot. It was way down the spit, beyond where those animals are. There was no impact, perhaps it was a dummy round."

"They're not targeting us, they're trying to start a panic, a stampede."

With a deafening screech, another round landed near the East jetty in a fireball that they felt as well as heard, so close to them. This time, debris rained down around them on the roofs of cars, sending the refugees running screaming for cover. The bombardment was closer this time, perhaps designed to scatter the crowds further away from the castle.

Above the screams of those outside running in all directions, Terra could hear something else. Terrified animals were whinnying and lowing, desperate to escape the small enclosure behind the lighthouse. She noticed many of the refugees were surging closer to the castle walls. Others were already running headlong back towards the spit and the safety of Milford village, leaving behind everything they had brought with them.

Another explosion landed even closer, no more than a hundred yards from the lighthouse, smoke spreading out towards them before dissipating in the night breeze.

The next round seemed to land in the surf, sending spray high into the air. Terra didn't know what to think. There was widespread panic all around them. Their driver jumped back into the vehicle and started the engine, slamming the gear stick into reverse.

"Hey, where are we going?" asked Briggs.

"If we stay here, we're going to get hit. They're getting closer. We need to pull out."

"We're not leaving. That's exactly what they want us to do. Get in closer to the walls. They're not going to risk hitting the castle."

"The rest of them are scattering."

"Fools. It's a diversion, nothing more. They're trying to drive us away. Get the men back to their stations. Keep watching the beach."

"They're all running away boss."

"Fine, I'll do it myself. Copper, bring your men."

***

When the first round landed behind the castle, Zed stood up and cheered, almost losing his balance before sitting down again. It was a magnificent sight. The sky lit up in a blinding explosion that framed the castle and the lighthouse, like a grand fireworks display.

As they got closer, through the scope fixed to his helmet, Zed could make out half a dozen men on the beach looking around them nervously, their focus gone. The sniper beside him fired two shots, no longer worried about stealth or surprise, taking out two of the armed men. The rest looked around in panic trying to locate the R.I.Bs in the darkness. They didn't have long to wait.

The two assault craft raced in at twenty knots as the two men kneeling on the bow of each boat opened up with their HK MP5 submachine guns, raking the beach and scattering the defenders. By the time they cut their engines and surfed the last few meters in, most of the defenders had run away or were lying wounded in the breaking waves.

The first boat bumped aground and Zed saw the men on the bow jump down scanning left and right covering the beach. The rest of the civilians were already waiting their turn at the top of the rope. As soon as they got the all-clear, the first of them lowered themselves over the side of the wall. Zed couldn't tell who it was from below. They waved them down one after another until the first boat was full.

The second R.I.B had just landed when the water around the boat seemed to come alive as bullets landed all around them. There was a hiss of air escaping from one of the inflatable panels near the stern. It had narrowly missed one of the engines. Looking east, Zed could now see a small group of Briggs' men taking up positions, firing blindly towards them.

Jones's men returned fire, keeping their heads down as they waved three more down the shingle and into the waiting boat. A hail of bullets ripped up the beach, ricocheting off the brickwork and sparking off the pebbles. Zed was still looking up anxiously for Riley when, to his relief, he recognised a female shape coming down the rope. It had to be her. She was the only woman left in the place. He watched nervously as she lowered herself over the edge. In her haste, her boot seemed to lose grip and slip from a protruding stone. Her body rotated round and crashed against the wall. She fell the last ten feet, landing awkwardly, twisting her ankle and falling painfully on her hip.

One of the soldiers stumbled up the beach to help her but went down clutching his shoulder, just above the Kevlar body armour he was wearing. Jones was waving them on, shouting at one of his men to go help. There were now shots coming from the other boat which was safely away and providing covering fire to the men on the beach. Copper's men were well dug in, advancing from cover towards them, diving behind groynes and rocks as they fought their way closer.

"Keep firing," shouted Briggs. "Keep their heads down."

Seeing Riley lying prone on the ground, shielding her head from the bullets, something in Zed snapped. He was tired of feeling like a spare wheel.

He threw himself over the side. Misjudging the depth of the water, he found himself immersed up to his chest. The cold stole his breath away. He steadied himself, holding on tightly to the side of the R.I.B as his feet slipped on the shingle, trying to gain purchase.

His good hand reached for the Colt pistol, wrestling with the Velcro loop securing it to the holster in the Kevlar chest plate. He lowered the night vision scope again and scanned for targets. It took a moment for his eyes to adjust.

He was suddenly knocked off balance. A bullet seemed to glance off his helmet, dislodging his scope, which clattered on the ground next to him. He ripped the helmet from his head and was relieved to find he was unharmed. When he looked up again, Riley was right in front of him, flattening herself to the wall.

He levered her up with his stump and helped her down the beach towards the waiting boat. Another volley of bullets ripped up the shingle around them and she stumbled again, clutching her calf in agony.

"Come on, Riley. I can't carry you."

She was crying, gasping in pain. She could barely walk and limping heavily, supported by Zed. With only one good hand, he found it impossible to keep the weapon raised and pointed towards the muzzle flashes along the beach.

As they approached the boat, Jones's men seemed to intensify their covering fire, seeing their struggle. Zed deposited Riley with her back against the side of the boat, raising his weapon again, scanning for targets.

Without his support, she tumbled backwards over the side of the boat and onto the rigid fibreglass floor. For a second, she disappeared from view and Zed threw himself in on top of her as bullets tore up the rubber surround of the R.I.B.

"Time to go, time to go," shouted Jones.

They pushed off and accelerated backwards against the breaking surf. Waves swamped over the back of the boat and covered Zed and Riley in freezing cold seawater before they could lever themselves up on their knees.

As they reversed away from the beach, Zed could see more figures lowering themselves down the rope but they were too late. Briggs' men were advancing up the beach towards their landing area. He took stock of those around him in the boat. Jones was breathing heavily but seemed to be unharmed. They had three additional male passengers who all looked terrified and soaking wet. In all the confusion, Zed realised that Jack was not amongst them. He was still back on the beach.

CHAPTER FORTY-SIX

Jack cursed his luck, watching the R.I.B reverse away from the beach. He heaved his large frame up the rope, hand over hand, until, to his surprise, he came face to face with Flynn. Flynn had his arms crossed, dumbfounded to see Jack and the others still here.

Flynn reached down and helped him the rest of the way, until he flopped over, exhausted, trying to catch his breath.

"What are you doing still here?"

"There was no time. Riley and the rest of them made it out though."

Once Jack had mastered his breathing, he sat up and counted heads. There were still twelve of them left behind, stuck at the castle, waiting to be rescued.

He smiled at Sam and Nathan, grateful for their loyalty. Will and Scottie had also volunteered to stay behind, along with a few others closest to Jack.

"Joe got away, so that's one less thing to worry about. Sister Theodora can sing for her supper now."

"She won't give up you know," warned Tommy. "She'll blame the rest of you for," he waved his hands, searching for the right expression, "obstructing justice, or something."

"She can try," shrugged Jack. "Have you managed to get hold of Captain Armstrong yet?"

"We're still trying, but all we're getting's static. We've tested all the equipment. There are no problems this end."

"Could something have happened in Portsmouth?"

"Maybe Lymington and Southampton are under attack too?"

"I doubt it. It would take a massive coordinated effort for an attack of that scale. I'm not convinced Briggs has that kind of clout, or not yet anyway. Besides, I've never known Armstrong not to maintain radio contact. They just installed that new transmitter in Southampton the other week to boost the signal."

"It doesn't make any sense. Nothing seems to be getting through."

"Could someone be jamming our signal?" asked Will.

"Unlikely, I don't see how, unless…"

"Go on Sergeant."

"You mentioned that some of these guys used to be CID and local law enforcement. Some of those anti-terrorist teams might have access to fairly sophisticated tech that could disrupt mobile signals. It's possible that someone with a bit of hardware and programming skills could modify the frequencies and disrupt our military communications, but I'd say it's unlikely."

"Anything we can do about it?"

"Well, those hand-held walkie talkies should still work. They use traditional maritime frequencies, so if we have the range we might be able to relay a message via the Americans. It's worth a try. But remember, we're on an open channel. They'll hear every word. Be careful."

"Even if we can get a message through, what can Armstrong do? It would take hours to get another team up here by boat. Lymington is closer but they're a small detachment, like us. I'd say we're on our own for now."

"We're in your hands, Flynn."

"If you're right Jack, the prisoner is what this is really all about. They're here for him. So really, there are only two things we can do. Hold out till the morning or hand him over before anyone else gets killed. That's probably the least worst solution."

"We open those gates and we're all dead, you realise that?"

"Don't be so dramatic Will," reassured Jack. "The Sergeant's right. Let's just give them what they want. It's the only way," he shrugged.

***

Briggs was growing impatient. It was well after two in the morning and Victor's whole plan seemed to be unravelling. The firefight on the beach had closed off Hurst's escape route once more, but had come at a heavy cost. Two of Copper's men were badly injured and another two boatloads had got away, from right under their noses.

Terra could tell he was fuming. Someone would pay before the night was out, that was certain. For some reason, they had underestimated the Allied response. They had never foreseen the intervention of the Americans. The bombardment of the beach and landing area had taken them all by surprise. Terra's ears were still ringing. Her left hand was still trembling from the explosions so close at hand. She imagined this was what American military planners meant by "shock and awe".

"Stay as close to the castle walls as you can. They won't risk killing their own people," reassured Briggs.

As they walked back from the beach towards the waiting vehicles, an old man wrapped in a threadbare blanket had the audacity to stand in their path and address Briggs.

"How much longer do we have to wait for them to open the gates?"

Briggs stopped mid-stride, with a look of undisguised disgust. He slapped the old man hard across the side of his face.

"They will be open when I say they're open. Didn't I promise you food and shelter? Then that's what you'll get. Now get out of my way."

The old man shrunk back, stepping aside, clutching at his reddening cheek. The crowd parted to let Briggs and his men through. Terra spotted Victor and the Sister talking animatedly. It looked like he was trying to placate her about something. The Sister caught sight of Briggs over his shoulder as he approached, pushing Victor out of the way.

"No one said anything about killing," said the Sister reproachfully. "This whole operation has been shambolic. I would never have agreed to be a part of this if I'd known."

"Sister, with respect, they shot first. We were not the aggressor," defended Victor.

"Nevertheless, I refuse to condone murder. You either agree to resolve this peacefully or I walk away right now."

"I assure you we're all here for the same reason: to see justice done."

"Well, you promised me, you promised all of us, that this would be a bloodless coup. I want no more bloodshed and certainly not in my name."

With a look of disdain, she turned on her heels and walked back to her group who were waiting a short distance away, huddling together in the shadow of the castle walls.

Briggs watched her leave and kicked at a stone at his feet in frustration.

"I'm warning you Victor. Sort this mess out. I've had about enough of amateur hour."

Victor resolutely met Briggs' stare, the sparkle in his eyes undimmed.

"Terra, remember the story I told you about how Agamemnon finally ended the siege of Troy?"

Terra looked confused for a second and then remembered.

"I assumed you were joking."

"It's time we used our secret weapon. Don't you see? Jack trusts you. It's the only way."

Terra was unconvinced, blinking back at him, wishing there was another way.

"But they haven't seen me for nearly six months. They may not even remember me."

"Of course Jack still remembers you. Don't be so coy. He probably still loves you," sneered Briggs. "He'd do anything for you, isn't that what you told me?"

Terra straightened the folds of her coat and shrugged. Perhaps he was right. Jack had always had a weakness for her. With the right degree of pressure, she could always twist him around her little finger, couldn't she?

How could he forget the times they had spent together? Even Terra remembered fondly the many nights she had been invited back to the lighthouse. Sharing the tiny bedroom, waking up to stunning views of the island and the Solent. Those times had meant something to both of them, hadn't they?

She would never describe what they had as love, but they both got what they wanted out of the relationship. The only difference was that she was the one who left to start a new life with Briggs, albeit under strained circumstances. For Jack, there had been no such closure. He was sure to still have feelings for her. She knew it was wrong to take advantage, but perhaps this was the way to resolve this situation without further loss of life. Plus, Victor was counting on her, she couldn't let him down.

She let out a deep sigh and turned to face Briggs, looking him squarely between the eyes.

"If I agree to go along with this, I want your word that you're not going to do anything to Jack."

"You have my word," nodded Briggs with a wry smile, "I won't do anything to him."

"Very well, then I'll be your Trojan horse."

"Good," said Victor, exchanging a knowing look with Briggs.

The crescent moon appeared from behind a cloud and she studied it absent-mindedly. She shuddered realising what she would have to do. Victor had convinced her it would all be worth it. Talking about it was one thing, but now it came time to act, she hesitated. Whichever way she turned, there would be consequences. That was for certain.

CHAPTER FORTY-SEVEN

Jack descended the cold grey steps to the passageways that ran beneath the castle. Outside the makeshift cell where they were holding the prisoner, he found Tommy looking flustered at the sound of unknown footsteps hurrying his way.

"Thank God it's you," he said, clutching his chest in relief. "What's going on up there? I've been going half-crazy. First I heard the convoy heading this way and then those explosions shook the whole place."

"How long have you been down here?"

"Sam was meant to come and take over about an hour ago. I'll murder him when I find him."

"It's not his fault, he's been helping Riley and the others. Sorry, I think everyone forgot all about you. Listen, go and take a look for yourself. Copper is back with a whole army this time, making all kinds of demands."

"Bloody hell. What about the prisoner? Don't you want me to stick around?"

"I'll be fine, you go right along. I'd like a word with him alone."

Tommy shrugged his shoulders, impatient to go outside. It was freezing and dark down here, with only a paraffin lamp for company. He handed Jack the set of oversized keys, took one last look around the damp corridor and left, pleased to be rid of the place.

Jack shuffled through the keys till he found the intricately tooled bronze one that he imagined must be as old as the Tudor castle itself. Inserting it into the lock, he took a deep breath and threw open the door.

Inside Damian King was sat cross-legged on the bed with his reading lamp lit. In his left hand, angled to catch the light was a hard-cover biography of Benito Mussolini. He raised a finger to acknowledge Jack's presence, making him wait until he had finished his page. Picking up his book marker, he thrust it deep into the folds of the book.

"Is it time already?"

"Your friends are outside."

"Well then, we shouldn't keep them waiting."

He got quickly to his feet and Jack naturally took a step back, maintaining the distance between them. Damian King noticed his caution and laughed.

"Do you really think I'd try anything now?"

"I know what you're capable of."

"Clearly, you don't know me very well then. I think I'll actually miss our little chats. I consider them a sort of therapy," he said with a mock flourish.

"I'll be sure to tell your friends Copper and Briggs how cooperative you've been."

"Be my guest. Don't flatter yourself Jack. I told you what I wanted you to know. Nothing more, nothing less. They'll no more believe I helped you, than if you told them I'd found God."

Jack looked around the cell at all the drawings and hand-written notes stuck to the wall with sticky tape.

"Don't you want to take any of this stuff with you?"

"It's all up here Jack," he said tapping his forehead. "You know what? I think all this thinking time has done me the power of good. I was so angry about the world when I came here, now I feel nothing."

"I'm glad to hear that some good has come of your stay."

King stared back, his eyebrow raised quizzically, unsure whether Jack was being serious or not.

"You really don't get it, do you?" he derided. "You really believe all that psychobabble you told me about mindfulness and neurolinguistic programming. About everyone being born good, nature versus nurture. You think that you can talk anyone round to your way of thinking?"

"This isn't the first time I've counselled someone you know. I've met plenty of troubled souls in my time. Oh, but that's right, I forgot, they broke the mould when they made you."

"No one made me. I made myself. People like you think that monsters are made and can be unmade. I disagree. People like me choose the path they take and no amount of talking is going to make them change their ways. We don't want to change. We've having too much fun," he smiled. "Who wants to be like you anyway?"

He shook his head, laughing openly at Jack's disapproval.

"You know what, Jack? You're so arrogant you could never understand someone like me. Arrogance is your weakness. That, and not listening. Didn't anyone ever tell you that God gave you two ears and one mouth so you could use them in proportion? You're so busy waiting for your chance to speak that you miss the point."

"Well then, thank goodness I don't have to listen to any more of your nonsense." He pushed the door open. "You're free to leave."

The prisoner made no attempt to move.

"Oh, but I'm not finished yet. Something's broken in that thick skull of yours, isn't it?" he said tapping his forehead again. "I always said to myself, Damian, don't be so hard on him, he's probably got salt in his ears from a lifetime alone on that fishing boat of his, all at sea."

He sniggered to himself, adopting an almost demonic smile.

"Well, there's a storm coming, Jack, and you're directly in its path."

"After all this time, it saddens me that you really have learned nothing. You're still the sad, bitter person with a chip on his shoulder who arrived here, believing the world was against him."

"That's right. You wasted all that time and for what? Nothing."

Jack shook his head. There were so many things he wanted to say, but King was right, it didn't matter anymore. He deserved to be in a lunatic asylum, perhaps they both did. Men like King were incapable of seeing the world as it really was. He had no respect for the things Jack valued and had worked so hard for. Men like King thought the world owed them something. After today, he was likely never to see him again. He wasn't worth the effort.

Jack stepped outside waiting for King to follow him. The prisoner took one last look around his cell and blew out the lamp, plunging the room into darkness. In the narrow passageway, the prisoner stretched his legs and rolled his shoulders, flexing muscles he had not used in some time, enjoying the space and freedom after the cramped confines of his cell.

Jack held the revolver in front of him and gestured towards the stairs at the end of the passageway. King looked at the gun and sneered, limping away as the circulation started flooding back to his extremities. He seemed to be growing in mobility and confidence with each step.

They climbed the stone stairwell and paused at the covered entrance to the courtyard. King took a deep breath of sea air. He closed his eyes and let the breath out slowly, his senses alert, listening to the sounds of the crowd outside the castle walls.

"So many have come."

"They're not here for you, King. They're here for a meal. Someone told them we had food."

It didn't seem to matter to King. He looked suitably gratified that he would soon be free.

Flynn appeared on the stairs above them and seemed surprised to see King out of his cell. Jack could have sworn there was an exchange of nods between the two men. He had always suspected Flynn of harbouring certain sympathies towards the prisoner, though he never for a moment believed him capable of outright collaboration.

"Jack, there you are," said the Sergeant, composing himself. "Can I borrow you for a minute? There's something you need to hear over at the guardhouse. Ballard, can you get someone to watch the prisoner for me?"

Jack followed Flynn and Sam through the Tudor gate towards the front entrance. Ahead of them dozens of men were busy erecting barricades and setting up firing positions behind overturned tables and heavy water barrels. This would be their last line of defence.

Inside the guardhouse, the castle's former gift shop, one of Flynn's men was shaking his head in frustration. A pair of headphones sat lop-sidedly on his head as he adjusted the dials on a radio set.

"Still nothing from Armstrong?"

"Just static on military channels."

"So tell us again what you heard on maritime frequencies."

"That's right. Every few minutes, we've been getting a woman's voice on channel sixteen, asking for Jack. She sounds scared. Judging by the signal strength, it must be very close range."

Jack's mind was racing. "What did she want?"

"She didn't say. We thought it might be one of your people who made it across to the island trying to reach you."

As if on cue, the radio crackled into life and a voice Jack recognised instantly called his name. It had to be Terra. He snatched the microphone from the soldier's hand.

"Terra, is that you? Where are you?"

"Jack, thank God. I'm right here, just outside the lighthouse. If you go up to the top of the Gun Tower you'll see me."

"How did you...I can't believe it's really you..."

"Listen, there's no time Jack. I'll tell you all about it, but first, please there are a lot of desperate, hungry people out here who need your help."

"What about Briggs?"

"All he wants is your prisoner, Damian King. He won't cause you any trouble. Just give him what he wants and he'll leave, I'm sure of it. Anyway, most of the refugees who came here have gone. They were scared away by the fighting. Please Jack, you need to open the gates. Come see for yourself if you don't believe me."

He stepped back from the radio, trying to digest what she had told him. Could it be true? He so wanted to believe her. Despite everything he knew about what had gone before, his rational thoughts were being swamped by waves of emotion. His hand was shaking so much, he gripped the back of the chair to steady himself. Jack gathered himself, noticing Flynn staring at him as if he had lost his marbles.

"It's your call, Jack. Why don't we do as she suggests and head up to the roof, take a look?"

Jack nodded, suddenly finding it hard to breath. It was as if his heart was beating out of his chest. So many times he had longed for this day, when his Terra would come back to him. After all this time, giving in to his hopes felt like a release.

He took the stone stairs two at a time to the roof of the Gun Tower. What he saw reminded him of a war zone.

Beyond the lighthouse, he could see smoke rising from craters along the beach. The dark shapes of several animal carcasses littered the ground. Looking out over the front entrance, he was relieved to find most of the crowd had gone. Along the shingle spit, heading back towards the safety of Milford village, he could see hundreds of people now scurrying away in terror, empty-handed.

"See over there," said Flynn peering through binoculars, pointing into the darkness towards the lighthouse. He passed them to Jack who pushed his glasses up onto his forehead, squinting through the eye pieces. He located the white outline of the lighthouse against the dark landscape and there huddled in the doorway was a dark shape.

If it was Terra, then she was barely recognisable, dressed in rags, with a headscarf shrouding her face.

"Are you sure it's her? This isn't some kind of trick?"

"It's got to be her," said Jack, looking again, daring to believe.

The months of worry he had endured were seemingly at an end. The sense of relief was palpable. Grabbing at the wall, he slumped forwards, his legs shaking so much he could barely stand. Sam was there in an instant, shouldering his weight and patting him on the back. The more Jack looked, the more he convinced himself it had to be her.

"Can we get her into the castle without anyone noticing?"

"I don't see how. If we let her in, we'll have to let them all in."

"But most of the others who came here seem to have legged it. There are only a few stragglers left."

"They're waiting for the handouts they were promised."

As if on cue, Sister Theodora's voice echoed around the castle over the megaphone.

"There has been enough bloodshed here for one night. I appeal to all of you, on both sides, to lay down your arms and call a truce so that these poor people can be given food and water. There are many amongst them, young and elderly, who won't last the night. They'll freeze to death without your help. Do you really want that on your conscience? I beg you, please, open your gates and let them in. I give you my word that they will not bite the hand that feeds them."

Jack closed his eyes. It had come to this. Was he really prepared to put his own interests above those of others? His altruism towards the refugees was one thing, but wasn't he forgetting Zed and Riley's warnings about Briggs and Copper?

He wanted so badly to see Terra again. Every fibre of his being was crying out for their reunion. He shook his head and determined that, for once in his life, he would dismiss logic and reason. Briggs would need to be an idiot to try anything with all these soldiers around.

"Listen Flynn. Sooner or later we're going to have to come to some kind of agreement. We can't risk a prolonged siege. Now that most of the civilians are away, I don't think it makes sense waiting any longer. I suggest we give Briggs what he came here for. If we hand over the prisoner, he might just leave. The Sister's right, those people need our help. We can't just sit here and watch them die on our doorstep."

"You've changed your tune haven't you?" puzzled Flynn. "Very well. That settles it," said Flynn, his mind made up. He turned to address Ballard. "Get everyone you can spare to the front gate. Now that the refugee numbers are a bit more manageable, let's get ready to receive groups of thirty at a time, women and children only. I just hope you're right about this Jack."

Looking out across the black waters of the Solent, Jack could see lights in the distance over at Cliff End Battery and Fort Albert. The majority of his team had been safely evacuated. He imagined the rest of his group drinking tea and laughing in relief, looking back at the castle with mixed emotions. Perhaps they were looking back at him this very moment.

"I just hope I'm right too," he whispered with a grimace.

CHAPTER FORTY-EIGHT

Terra was waiting next to the lighthouse as Victor had instructed. The filthy coat and scarf she had been handed stank of sweat and piss. She held her breath to avoid inhaling the stench.

Being so close to the lighthouse again where they had shared so many memories was proving uncomfortable. Remembering her time with Jack felt like opening a long-forgotten photo album. Moments frozen in time that she could picture if she tried. Revisiting their happier memories was indulgent, she knew that. She couldn't allow herself to dwell, to linger. She had moved on. The whole episode was history. He had been a stepping stone in her life, no more, no less.

She almost laughed remembering their first time together; his awkwardness and apologies. The loose leathery skin around his neck, weathered from a lifetime at sea. How repulsed she had been, almost disgusted with herself.

Between the lighthouse and the front gate, the crowd had thinned. In the distance, she could see the taillights of several of the vehicles bumping away along the shingle roadway. The refugees who had stayed were huddled expectantly out of sight near the drawbridge.

From inside the castle she could just make out a commotion,

as voices and footsteps echoed from the covered entrance. It suggested the soldiers were preparing to open the drawbridge. She tried to imagine what would be waiting for them on the other side.

If Victor was right, they would be poorly prepared. By the time they realised their mistake, it would be too late. Disguised amongst the helpless refugees were Briggs' men, heavily armed and spoiling for a fight.

Victor led her over to join those nearest the gate. He pressed up against her back, urging her forward, sensing her reluctance. His head was covered by a dark blue hoodie to hide his features. There was a tartan blanket thrown around his shoulders, masking the outline of a rifle he carried slung over his shoulder.

"Once we get inside, all you need to do is point Jack out to us and we'll do the rest. Agreed?"

"You promised me you won't hurt him."

He slapped her hard across the face. "Don't get sentimental on me Terra. You know what has to be done."

She nodded in reluctant agreement, tears streaming down her face as she winced against the stinging pain. She hated being used like this, but an inner voice reminded her that it was no worse than she deserved. The two of them merged with the waiting crowd, shrinking lower so as to blend in with those around them.

Beyond the gate, they could hear scuffed footsteps again and the grinding of metal on metal as the defenders wrestled with the lever to release the chains that would lower the draw bridge over the small ditch that ran around the castle walls.

Victor cautioned those around him to stand back to avoid being crushed. Terra looked around her, aware of others pressing forward with a darker purpose. Amongst the shivering shapes of mothers and children, hugging each other in expectation, she noticed Briggs grinning back at her. His men were dressed as refugees, with thick winter coats and hats grabbed from members of the crowd.

Inch by inch, the gap above the drawbridge widened as they saw light coming from inside. They stepped back further, making room. People behind jostled against each other, eager to be first inside. The leading edge of the drawbridge passed their eye-line. Inside Terra could see the two men operating the mechanism with three others anxiously pointing weapons towards the sea of faces now staring at them, waiting for the divide to be bridged. The drawbridge clanged down into place sending a cloud of dust dancing at their feet as they surged forwards.

The soldiers directly in their path appealed for calm, surprised by the sheer numbers of people funnelling through the narrow entrance. They retreated towards the barricades. An officer stepped out gesturing for the refugees to slow down as they ran.

"Women and children only," shouted the officer. His voice was lost amongst the shouts and excitement of those who advanced without pause.

More and more people swarmed into the gap, heading over the drawbridge into the castle. Terra saw the officer shake his head in despair, struggling to be heard. He unholstered his side arm and fired two shots into the night sky.

Those at the front paused momentarily, suddenly unsure, before resuming their advance.

The officer fired again over their heads. Then he lowered his arm, pointing directly at the man closest to him. Before he could fire, he was barged aside and enveloped by the crowd.

Oblivious to the threat, the refugees ran on, ignoring the

barrels of various weapons poking over the sandbags and upturned tables. The soldiers were waiting for the order to open fire, glancing wide-eyed at each other, unsure what to do. They hesitated a moment too long and they too were overtaken by a tide of humanity.

Terra headed left, Victor at her side. The soldiers were distracted, no one was watching them, their faces hidden, darting into the shadows. Behind her a flurry of shots rang out in the confused melee. She glanced over her shoulder, her breaths short as adrenaline coursed through her veins. It wasn't clear who was firing, but the soldiers above them on the wall were pointing at something, a shape in the crowd. Another volley of shots rang out as two of the soldiers fell from their elevated position, tumbling into the crowd, then were trampled underfoot.

The soldiers nearest the gate hugged the wall, pushing and shoving to force their way forward. The officer was shouting for the soldiers to form a human barrier, to stem the flow of refugees surging forward. She could hear someone trying to crank shut the drawbridge again, but knew it would be a wasted effort. They kept coming, dozens more would be returning from the spit, cramming towards the entrance, surging inside.

Terra ran on towards the Tudor gate just as the two soldiers guarding the inner castle slammed the heavy doors shut, wrestling with the keys to lock the door. Briggs and Copper threw their weight against the doorway and one side cracked open an inch but closed again immediately as more bodies jammed against it from within. The key turned and then it was done.

She could hear raised voices from within and the sound of the wooden brace heaved into place to secure the double doors. Despite their renewed efforts to force their way in, the path was blocked. They stepped back and looked up at the wall above. It was too high to climb. This was a medieval fortress built to repel invaders. However, Terra knew well that it was no longer impregnable, not by any stretch of the imagination. With the Victorian modifications and extensions, you could access the rooftop via the seaward-facing bastions.

Victor had other ideas and Terra was bundled out of the way as a large covered contraption on wheels was brought up behind them. They removed the tarpaulin to reveal what looked like a battering ram. A tree trunk crudely sharpened to a point had been covered with metal, hammered into shape.

She stood aside as several of Copper's men took up positions at each hand-hold, six of them in total. On the count of three, they threw their weight against the contraption, picking up momentum before slamming into the resolute oak. The whole frame of the door seemed to vibrate and shake, raining dust and debris down on to the paved stone flooring, but it held firm. They rolled the battering ram back a dozen yards and tried again with renewed vigour. The collision with the woodwork splintered the lower half, as the gap widened between the join in the doors, burying its metal head into the weathered oak. There was a chorus of alarm from within.

As Briggs' men rolled the contraption back, a volley of shots rang out from above, trying to target the men below. One of them fell as the others dived forward into the shadows, out of sight. Briggs cursed and shouted at Copper's men to get back to their posts for another try. He urged them forward, volunteering another to take the place of the wounded man.

This time, they shortened their run-up and avoided making themselves a target. The defenders above no longer had an angle of fire, leaning forward and firing blind.

Copper grabbed hold, corralling them once more. The ram left its mark, bursting through and holing one side of the door so that when they heaved it back, they could see terrified faces within.

Briggs inserted his prized silver SIG Sauer pistol into the gap and squeezed off deafening shots in all directions until his clip was empty. He stepped aside to reload while the battering ram was wheeled back for another try.

Terra took one look and realised that the oak doors had no resistance left and could hold them no longer. She secretly hoped that Jack and the others would have had sufficient time to escape, to barricade themselves somewhere safe. There were only a few places left to hide and Terra had a good idea where those would be.

***

From the roof of the Gun Tower at the centre of the castle complex, Jack listened with increasing alarm to the repeated assaults on the Tudor gate. In the main courtyard of the western wing of the castle, hundreds of people were roaming around, searching every corner and cupboard for food or anything else they could scrounge.

The soldiers were helpless to prevent them. They had at least restored some semblance of order. Pressed against the doorway to the canteen, they were now handing out various items to the outstretched hands of a hungry crowd.

It was only a matter of time before they would burst through their last line of defence, then what? Once they were within the Tudor fortress, the whole castle would be quickly overrun and those who remained here would be trapped.

Jack's mind was racing, running through the various options.

Will and Tommy were by his side waiting for his instruction. Both had grabbed shotguns and rifles from the armoury which they handed out to the others. They stood ready for whatever came through those doors, checking their weapons. Jack seemed to come to his senses, listening to the shots fired from above.

"Listen up, I think our best chance will be to get out now through the disused gate in the north-east bastion."

"Jack, they'll be watching the beach like hawks. They won't make the same mistake again," warned Will soberly.

"What about Terra?" said Sam.

"There's no way to find her now. She couldn't have known Briggs would attack."

"What about Riley and the Americans? Are you still in contact with them?"

"Not for the last hour or so. With any luck Riley and the others will have made it across to the island now. We're all that's left," said Jack, shaking with adrenaline, looking round at the sullen faces of his team.

"Whatever you're going to do, you need to do it now. That gate won't hold much longer," shouted Will.

"What happened to the prisoner?"

"I handed him over to Flynn and his men. They'll have him now. He's no longer our concern."

"Then, you're right," said Will. "There's nothing left for us here, we need to get out while we still can."

"Is the *Nipper* still tied up on the eastern jetty?"

"She was last time I looked. Are you thinking what I'm thinking?"

"It's our best chance. Right, here's what we're going to do."

***

Outside the gate, Copper's men readied themselves for a final charge.

"This time boys. It won't hold much longer. On the count of three."

They charged the few meters, picking up momentum and with a deafening crash, the oak rendered, splitting apart on one side, sending metalwork clanging across the courtyard. When they withdrew the battering ram, a narrow space remained, large enough for a child to fit through. Briggs reached through the gap and forced up the wooden bar securing the two doors. The locking mechanism was badly damaged and with a final nudge from two of his men, the whole left hand door rocked to the side, held by one set of remaining hinges.

Briggs waved Victor and the others through, glancing behind them to check they were not being followed. In the main courtyard, the soldiers were fully occupied with crowd control, too busy to see what was going on at the Tudor gate.

Stepping inside the inner castle, Terra heard voices from above, echoing off the stone enclosure. Victor gestured for her to keep to the shadows, to avoid offering themselves up as targets. She could see faces pressed against the windows of the first floor of the Gun Tower trying to make them out in the darkness below.

Briggs shouted to the defenders. "We're here for Damian King. We've not come to fight."

In the distance they could hear footsteps running away from them in the darkness. With a nod of his head, two of Briggs' men ran to investigate. Briggs seemed more concerned with negotiating with the soldiers, now their fight was lost. The remaining defenders were trapped, there was nowhere to run. Terra leaned in close to Victor and whispered.

"Victor, they must be making for the eastern gate, the one I told you about."

"You told me it was disused."

"It was in my day, but perhaps it's been repaired."

He wolf whistled to get Copper and the rest of the group's attention. They were readying themselves at the bottom of the stairwell, preparing for a final assault. Victor pointed towards the entrance and set off towards the far gate.

"Copper, you go," shouted Briggs, "Don't wait for me."

Copper pointed at four of his men who followed Victor and Terra towards the east gate and the darkness beyond.

***

Jack and the others advanced through the wide courtyard of the eastern wing of the castle, where several military vehicles had been stationed after ferrying supplies from Lymington. The group threaded their way through, sticking to the shadows, keeping out of sight. Jack waited for the last of them to catch up before throwing caution to the wind and running the remaining meters.

They found two of Flynn's men still guarding the entrance. They sounded alarmed by the hurried footsteps of so many, calling out to each other and drawing their weapons at the silhouetted shapes racing towards them in the half-light.

"Who goes there?" they shouted nervously.

"It's Jack. Sergeant Flynn sent us here. The castle is being overrun by refugees. They need you back at the front entrance."

"We can't leave our posts without Flynn's say so."

"Not this again," said Jack rolling his eyes. "Listen, we need you to open this gate, right now, and let us out," he said forcefully. "We're the last civilians, there's a boat waiting for us."

"Like I said, we can't do anything without a direct order."

"Oh for goodness sake. What is it with you lot and following orders?" shouted Scottie. "Why can't you think for yourself for a change and just do the right thing?"

"We don't have time for this," said Will shaking his head, looking around the group.

"Either you let us out," insisted Jack, "or I won't be held responsible for what these men do to you."

"Are you threatening us?" the younger man warned impotently, brandishing his weapon, stubbornly refusing to concede. He glanced at his older partner who discouraged him from doing anything rash. They were outnumbered six-to-one.

Whilst the two soldiers were distracted, Will and Sam began flanking them and with a sudden lunge, Will grabbed the barrel of the man's rifle and wrestled it free. The older soldier gave up his weapon without a fight.

"There's a good chap. Now give me the keys," demanded Jack.

The soldier fumbled in his pockets and removed a black metal key which he offered out in front of him. Will gestured for the soldier to unlock the door. Behind them they heard voices and footsteps advancing through the gap towards them. It was now or never.

With a loud groan, the left-hand side of the gate swung open on its rusted hinges. Outside it was pitch black and they hurried beyond the narrow bridge that ran over a ditch, half-full of water. One by one, they jumped down into the freezing water, hugging the side of the castle to stay out of sight, heading towards the eastern dock where they hoped the *Nipper* was moored. Sam ran ahead to get her ready to cast off and start the engines but Jack called him back.

"Sam, stay with us. They'll be watching the dock, don't get separated."

They could hear raised noises not fifty meters behind, close to the East gate. They pushed on, staying low and hidden from view. As they approached the jetty, Jack realised something was wrong. The *Nipper* was nowhere to be seen.

CHAPTER FORTY-NINE

Zed helped Riley over the side of the R.I.B and half-carried her through the surf. Her injured leg dragged awkwardly behind. They staggered up the small beach towards Cliff End Battery at the far end of Colwell Bay. At the top of the slope, Zed could just make out the row of holiday bungalows that overlooked the Solent, facing back towards Hurst Castle.

He lowered her down as gently as he could behind a large rock covered in seaweed and fumbled in the Velcro pockets of his webbing till he found the small penlight Jones had given him earlier. Getting down onto his hands and knees, he inspected the wound in her calf. It was much worse than he was expecting.

Riley's lower trouser leg, sock and boot were soaked in blood. The bullet had passed clean through the flesh. Feeling round to the other side he confirmed there was an exit wound. It should heal well enough. There were no signs of bullet fragmentation or injury to any bones.

Riley arched her back trying to see the wound for herself.

"Don't look, it'll be fine," he reassured, easing her back down against the rock. He borrowed a blanket from one of the others and made her comfortable, applying pressure to stem the bleeding.

"We've got to go back for Jack and the others," winced Riley.

"You're not going anywhere with that leg."

She groaned as Zed ripped off a strip of his t-shirt and wrapped it around her thigh, just above the knee, pulling it taut with his teeth. It was awkward with just one good arm, but through sheer grit and determination, the tourniquet held. Ignoring her pain, he applied a bandage to the ankle, as tight as he dared. He stood back, admiring his handiwork, noticing a dark red stain growing larger by the second. It was the best he could do in the circumstances. When the wave of agony had subsided, she opened her eyes and pleaded with him.

"Please Zed. You've got to get Jones up here. I need to talk to him."

"Take it easy. You're not the only one who got shot, you know. Two of his men are badly wounded. He's got his hands full."

"Someone needs to get back over there now before it's too late."

"If it wasn't for him, you'd still be stuck on that beach. You could start by thanking him."

"There will be plenty of time for thank yous later. Right now, Jack needs us. Please, you've got to get back over there. I'd never forgive myself if something happens to them. Don't leave them at the mercy of that butcher Briggs."

"Okay, Okay. I'm going. But listen, you stay put and get that properly looked at." He leant forward and gave her a kiss on the forehead. She reached up and stroked his face.

Zed called Liz over. She was handing out some biscuits to the other new arrivals, gulping water greedily from a plastic bottle.

"Can you keep an eye on Riley for me? She's in a lot of pain, keep her company can you?"

He caught sight of Jones, striding up the beach, speaking animatedly into his radio. Perhaps there had been news from the *Chester*. He patted Liz on the shoulder and ran after Jones.

A flash in the darkness caught his eye as he looked back across the water towards Hurst Castle, its outline just visible in the distance. With the floodlights and the pre-dawn mist, there was a strange halo about the place which made it look somehow ethereal, like it was rising up out of the darkness. He smiled to himself. Perhaps it was divine intervention.

He let out a deep sigh, remembering that he was on the island now. He was safe, whatever that meant. Yet here he was preparing to go back into the fray again to save Jack. Hadn't he risked his life enough times for one night? He would be heading back into the lion's den, yet the prospect of a reunion with Briggs and Copper made him cast aside all thoughts of personal safety. He longed for five minutes alone with one or both of them, his lip curling at the thought.

Jones was organising what remained of his team. To make room for all remaining twelve civilians in the two boats, they would leave three of Jones's men here to tend to the wounded. Zed patted him on the shoulder and the American looked up at him wearily.

"How's Riley doing?"

"She'll be fine. It was just a flesh wound. No broken bones. Clean exit. How about your guys?"

"One's pretty shot up, but the Kevlar armour saved his life. The other took a bullet to his throat, missed the artery. He's lucky to be alive."

"Apparently there's a doctor lives just up there, at the Battery," said Zed, pointing towards the imposing structure up the beach. "We've sent a runner to find him and bring a stretcher."

"Listen, Zed, I need you to stay with them..."

"I don't want to hear it Jones. I'm coming along, that's all there is to it."

"Look, I don't want any more casualties on my watch. Things could get pretty nasty. This time, they'll know we're coming. We may not even be able to make a landing."

"We've got to at least try, Sergeant. We can't leave Jack and the others there."

"You know, if it was one of my guys over there, I wouldn't hesitate. Believe me, I understand how you're feeling. I've been in your shoes before."

Jones threw his hands in the air. "What do I know? Don't make me regret this, okay? Let's go before I change my mind."

They collected all spare ammunition from the wounded team members and reloaded the R.I.Bs ready to leave. As Zed climbed aboard, one of the men walked them back into the surf, holding them steady until they lowered the outboards into the water and started the engines. The remaining two climbed in and they reversed off the beach back towards the castle one last time.

***

Back on Hurst spit, Jack was kneeling painfully on the shingle looking out to sea, staying hidden from view. Where the hell was the *Nipper*?

It had been tied up earlier that day which meant that someone must have cut the mooring lines. It was nearly high tide and still flowing eastwards. If she had been cut loose in the last two or three hours, she couldn't have drifted far. With any luck, she would have been blown along the shingle towards Keyhaven and become grounded on one of the mudflats.

He scanned the darkness with his binoculars. There was

something. A shape in the water not one hundred meters away from the shore, back towards Keyhaven. He nudged Sam and pointed towards it, passing him the binoculars.

"That's got to be the *Nipper*, right? What else could it be?"

"It's her alright Jack. Reckon I could swim over and bring her back, pick you lot up. What do you think?"

"Take Will with you, he's a strong swimmer. Don't go alone in case you get into difficulties. I'll stay here with the rest of them."

Sam stood and kicked off his boots. In five seconds flat, he had removed his bulky clothing, stripping to a t-shirt and boxer shorts. Will did the same and together they hobbled down the beach across the sharp stones and shingle towards the water's edge. Lowering themselves gingerly into the water as silently as possible, they set off towards the *Nipper*, keeping their heads above water.

Jack watched them swim slowly almost parallel to the beach, heading towards deeper water. The current sweeping past the end of the shingle should help push them closer.

He looked at his watch. Its digital display glowed in the darkness. It was past three in the morning. He reckoned it would take them five minutes to swim there, a further five to get her ready and perhaps another five to get back. In the meantime, they had to hope that they could stay hidden and undiscovered.

CHAPTER FIFTY

Zed kept low to avoid the spray as the assault craft powered back the short distance towards Hurst spit. Jones was scanning the castle and surrounding water with his night vision goggles. They slowed again as they were halfway across the narrow channel that ran between the island up towards the Needles rocks.

Jones's hand went up and the helm slowed the engine in response. They all looked in the direction he was pointing, at the outline of a boat in the distance. Zed had discarded his helmet when he had been hit by the stray round during their rescue of Riley. He tapped Jones on the arm, eager to know what he was drawing attention to. Without looking round Jones fished into his breast pocket and removed a spare night-vision scope. Zed grabbed it firmly, squinting through it with one eye, until the castle came into focus.

To the right of the spit, beyond the eastern extent of the castle and the lighthouse towering over it, he saw a fishing boat drifting in the current towards Keyhaven.

"Once you've found the boat, check out the two men in the water."

Zed took a moment to locate two swimmers splashing towards their intended target. One of them was powering through the water, his head submerged, while the other trailed behind doing what looked like breast-stroke.

"Can we pick them up?"

"They'll make it to the fishing boat before we get near them."

"So, where are the rest of them?"

"There," he said pointing at two shapes sheltering near the castle walls, keeping out of sight. "Looks like they're going to try and take the boat in and pick up the others."

"They'll never make it. They'll hear the fishing boat coming long before they get close."

"Then we'll have to help them. If we can get in close, we can pick them up ourselves. The question is, where are the rest of them? There should be more."

***

It was taking too long. Perhaps the tide had changed or it was slack water by now which meant the swimmers' progress towards the *Nipper* was taking longer than expected. The sea temperature would likely be several degrees above freezing. In another few minutes, the body temperatures of the swimmers could crash and leave them disoriented or even incapacitated.

Back towards the castle complex, they could hear voices outside the gate. If they mounted a search in this direction, they would be quickly discovered. There was nowhere to hide except right here in the shadows. Jack took a chance and raced beyond the castle walls towards the site of a World War II gun emplacement with a low wall and hiding places beneath. The others followed him over, within a stone's throw of the East dock.

Just as the last man hurried towards Jack, a powerful searchlight swept across the base of the castle walls, scouring the shingle, flashing above the heads of the larger group still hiding in the ditch. It lingered around the cluster of buildings nearest the lighthouse, trying to locate them. From the seaward side of the castle they could see torchlights dancing across the water, footsteps in the darkness. In a few more minutes, they would be caught in a pincer movement. One way or the other, they would be discovered.

Jack ran back to the others and panted breathlessly: "We have to go now. Dump anything bulky and make a run for the water's edge. Don't wait for me, start swimming."

"What about you Jack?" asked Scottie concerned.

"I was never much of a swimmer. I'll create a distraction."

"No Jack, you've got to at least try. It's not that far, we'll help you."

Jack swallowed hard. Scottie was right, he had to try to get away. The prospect of capture was far worse than drowning or hypothermia.

"Come on then. We'll stay together."

They tore off their outer clothing and heavy boots. One by one, the group ran forward, staying low, keeping as quiet as possible.

Jack waded into the water up to his waist and the cold took his breath away. As the others continued down the steep shelving beach up to their chests, he watched them push off and start swimming. Jack lingered, taking a moment to adjust to the temperature, feeling the freezing stones slip beneath his bare feet. For a man who had spent his life at sea, he had always hated swimming. He only learned to swim at the age of twelve.

Torchlight behind them zeroed in on the noises at the water's edge as Copper's men ran up the beach towards them.

Jack flung himself forward into the water, submerging his

head for a moment before resurfacing, spluttering. He swam as best he could, but was quickly out of his depth floundering for a foothold. He struggled to regulate his breathing or keep his head above water, gulping down successive mouthfuls, choking on the seawater. He angled back towards the shingle a few meters further down the beach. He was relieved to find he could stand again.

Jack flung himself forward, half swimming, half walking, his progress laboured. When he broke the surface again, blinking away the salt water, the torchlight zeroed in on him and the water in front of him seemed to erupt with gunfire.

He raised his arms above his head, turning around awkwardly to see how close they were. To his surprise there was a man standing not ten meters away, training his weapon at Jack's head. The game was up.

***

"Woah!" exclaimed Jones, watching the scene unfolding on the beach, from the R.I.B.

"What just happened?" asked Zed, struggling to see anything with the spare night scope he had been handed.

"First we had these two men in the water swimming for the fishing boat over there. Then looks like the rest of them gave up waiting and went swimming. Next this guy here," he said pointing, "he just shot up the water nearest the beach and now the last swimmer is getting out again."

"What about the rest of them? Are they still making for the boat, or heading back?"

"Looks like they're still swimming, but they're parallel to the beach so all those bad guys have to do is walk down the shingle and it'll be a turkey shoot."

"Get us over there now," shouted Jones. The helmsman threw the throttle forward and the bow of the R.I.B responded, rising up as they picked up speed, covering the few hundred meters towards where Jack and his team were in the water in about twenty-seconds.

"Give those men some covering fire, Daniels."

They were too far out and going way too fast for accuracy, but the hail of gunfire tore up the beach. Briggs' men ducked down, looking around them startled, trying to locate the source of the new threat racing their way. Zed noticed that the swimmers were diving down and swimming under water to confuse the men on the beach.

Another burst from the American's HK submachine gun scattered Briggs' men as they dived for cover.

"Get us between the swimmers and the boat," shouted Jones.

"Sir?"

"Just do it, will you?"

The helm came right in close to the shingle beach, much closer than was sensible in any other circumstances. Jones and the other soldiers raked the beach again with machine gun fire, attempting to keep the attackers' heads down to prevent them from returning fire.

Zed looked up and saw two half-naked men already on board the fishing boat. One was in the wheelhouse, trying to start the engines, while the other was pulling ropes out of the water so they wouldn't get tangled up in the propellors. He reached down and tried to help up the next man to arrive at the stern quarter, waving him away from the propellors which were now churning up the water. If they were going to save the men in the water, they had to close the gap and use the fishing boat as a shield.

From behind the assault craft, a volley of shots raked the

water, puncturing one of the inflatable panels on their port bow. Zed scanned for targets but Briggs' men had ducked out of sight and were lying prone on the shingle.

Momentarily, their boat was caught in a cross-fire as Briggs' men to their right opened up with an automatic weapon. The R.I.B surged forward, jinking left, placing them in harm's way in between the shooters and the men in the water. They shepherded the last of the men towards the boat. Another burst of fire tore into their boat, the plastic cover of the outboard disintegrated as the engine spluttered and died. Smoke began billowing out of the housing, shrouding them in choking fumes as a small fire broke out. Jones reached down to cut the fuel to the starboard engine before the fire could spread and engulf them.

"We're losing power."

"Goddamit, get us out of here. We're sitting ducks."

"Look, the fishing boat."

In the *Nipper's* wheelhouse, Zed could see Sam clearly now, gripping the wheel, urging the boat towards them. Their bow swept past them and turned hard right to bring her alongside the crippled assault craft, shielding them from harm.

"Get aboard," shouted Will, reaching down to grab Jones's arm, as another burst of fire shattered the windows in the wheelhouse and splintered the fibreglass below.

Zed waited his turn as the others scrambled over the side, up and into the fishing boat. The buoyancy at the back of the R.I.B was compromised, with two or three sections deflated where they had been punctured. At Zed's feet, he could see black sea water swirling around the bottom of the boat, getting deeper every moment.

The fire in the engine broke through the housing and flames

erupted, searing Zed's good hand gripping the strap nearest him, lighting up the hull of the *Nipper* as it shadowed them alongside.

Zed reached up and grabbed Will's soaking wet shirt sleeve, getting a good hold. Will strained to lift him and called Tommy over to help. Between them they hauled Zed over the side until he flopped onto the deck.

Sticking his head within the wheelhouse as his men sprayed the beach in a hail of bullets, Jones shouted: "That's everyone, get us out of here."

Zed looked around the shivering faces of the men from Hurst, cowering beneath the gunwale, searching out Jack. He was nowhere to be seen.

"Where's Jack?"

"He was right behind us. He must have turned back," said Scottie, shaking his head.

"What? And you left him there?"

"He's not a great swimmer," sighed Will.

"God help him. There's nothing more we can do for him now."

Looking back through the night scope over the stern of the *Nipper*, Zed thought he could see a half-naked shape being dragged up the beach towards the castle.

"Did you hear, Terra made it back to the castle? She's alive," said Will cheerily.

Zed nodded, but something about the timing of her return made him suspicious. He had never trusted that woman.

CHAPTER FIFTY-ONE

Terra watched in horror as they dragged the half-naked man through the gates and back within the confines of the castle. His head was bowed in defeat. He seemed barely conscious. His shirt and underwear were soaking wet, almost translucent in the stark light of the torch.

She hurried after them, terrified that this was someone she knew. Copper shone the torch in his face and Terra put her hand to her mouth, recognising Jack's battered face. He had a large swelling above his right eye where he had been struck, perhaps by the butt of a rifle.

He was barely recognisable from the man she had once known. The man she remembered had seemed younger, more vibrant. He had been a leader, an inspiration to all those who knew him. The person in front of her was a shadow of his former self, half-drowned, vulnerable, and cowering in defeat.

Jack was dumped unceremoniously in a corner of the courtyard, tucking his knees under his chin like a child. His whole body was racked with bouts of shivering. Terra shrank back towards the shadows, ashamed of her part in all this. He had not yet noticed her presence.

The soldier she had seen earlier with three stripes on his arm led a prisoner through the Tudor gate. The captive had his hands secured in front of him with what appeared to be cable ties.

"I take it this is who you came here for," said the Sergeant, shoving the prisoner towards Briggs.

"Amongst other things," nodded Briggs. He fished in his pocket for a pocket knife and freed the prisoner's hands, who began massaging his fingers and rubbing his palms together to get the circulation going again.

"Good to see you again King. It's been a while."

"Six months, four days, three hours, give or take."

The two men embraced heartily, slapping each other's backs and laughing. King turned his attention to Copper who was looking a little sheepish, like a scolded child.

"Copper, what took you so long?"

"Sorry boss. Took us a bit longer than we expected to get you out. We were trying to organise a prisoner exchange but Jack was having none of it."

"Well, I haven't forgiven you lot for leaving me behind in the first place."

"You didn't leave us much choice. You'd lost it. You would have got us all killed."

"Lost it? You're joking. I was enjoying myself. You really think a moment of exuberance justified mutiny? Six months I've been stuck here."

"Six months is nothing. I did six years. Quit whinging," joked Briggs, trying to defuse the hostility.

"I only did what I thought was best," repeated Copper, his voice trailing off weakly.

"I'm sure you did, Copper. We'll let bygones be bygones, eh? You came back to get me out, that's the main thing. Better late than never," said King, inclining his head in conciliation.

Copper nodded, shuffling uneasily under the glare of his former boss. Briggs was enjoying the drama with a wry smile.

The Sergeant stepped forward, impatient to get back to his men.

"Right, you got what you came here for. As soon as those people have had something to eat, I want them out, am I clear? There's nothing more for you here."

"We'll all be gone by dawn, don't you worry. I don't want to stay in this dump a moment longer than we have to."

The Sergeant was eying Briggs warily as if he didn't trust him any further than he could throw him. Copper awkwardly extended his hand towards the soldier and the two men shook hands. As the Sergeant headed for the main gate, he stepped aside to make way for Sister Theodora and her entourage as they swept towards Briggs.

There was something totally incongruous to Terra about the Sisters' being here. The veil of respectability she had leant Briggs' operation had only ever been paper thin. She studied the other two women who shadowed the formidable presence of the nun. One of them was much younger and wore a papoose slung across her chest, that bulged with the plump body of an infant, arms and legs sticking out of its sides.

The Sister was clearly in a rage about something.

"You assured me that there would be no further loss of life…" she started to say.

"Not you again," interrupted Briggs, before Victor could open his mouth. "There's nothing here for you now. It's time your people moved on, Sister."

"Victor, you owe me an explanation."

"Turns out the people you came looking for have already escaped. This is the only one left," Victor apologised, pointing at Jack's half-naked shape in the darkness.

"Why was I not told this earlier?"

Briggs mimicked her voice and laughed. "It will be light in a couple of hours. If I was you I'd make sure you're the first out of here. Lymington's still five miles away. That dawn ferry to the island won't wait, you know."

The Sister refused to engage with Briggs as if he was unworthy of her attention. She addressed her next question to Copper, appealing to his better nature.

"What are you going to do with their leader? By all accounts he is a good man, he deserves to be treated with respect," she said pointing at Jack in the corner, who seemed grateful for her intervention.

"As the sole surviving Hurst gang member," said Copper in a voice that reminded Terra of a policeman's court deposition in a trial she had attended, "he will face justice for what his people did. That's only right and proper. Now, if you'll excuse us, Sisters, we have business to attend to."

The two Sisters seemed satisfied with Copper's answer and turned to leave, but the young woman with the infant in a sling stayed rooted to the spot. She was cradling her baby, tenderly stroking its head. She looked around the group and addressed her question to all of them: "I was looking for Riley, I hoped she would still be here."

Briggs shrugged his shoulders and turned to leave, ignoring the question. Terra looked the girl up and down trying to place her. She noticed Copper take a step forward.

"Don't I know you?" he suggested, as if not trusting his eyes.

"I don't think so."

"Weren't you one of the girls who escaped from Lymington hospital?"

Sister Imelda grabbed hold of the girl's arm and encouraged

her to leave, but she resisted, holding her ground. King strode over and grabbed hold of the girl's chin, rotating her face slowly to catch the light, as the baby stirred against her chest, as if sensing its mother's anxiety.

"You're Stella aren't you? You're the reason we came here in the first place. We came looking for you and that other girl, Adele. If you had done what you were told, none of this would have happened."

Stella seemed emboldened, refusing to back down. There was a defiance about her as if she had just come face to face with her abuser. Terra could only imagine the torment this poor girl had suffered at the hands of King and his men. Perhaps the infant was a living link to that past.

"I'm never going back with you," spat Stella. "You bastards. What you did to us was inhuman, you treated us like animals, the experiments, the torture. People like you deserve to die."

Sister Theodora intervened, standing between them. "This girl is under my protection now."

"So this is the baby everyone's been talking about," said Briggs, lifting up the corner of the sling, as Stella cradled his head protectively.

"His name's Adam."

"Well, well, well. Baby Adam," said Briggs tenderly. "If she's immune, then chances are, so's he. You realise that don't you?"

Stella shrugged, "I guess we're both lucky then."

Terra noticed Briggs exchange a nod with King as if that meant something to both of them. She knew from the interrogations of the scientists that the source of people's resistance to the virus was a subject of great debate. Perhaps Adam was the first of a new generation with enhanced immunity.

"Come along Stella," said Sister Imelda, shepherding her

away from King. "Let's do as this man suggests. There's nothing left for us here."

Terra stepped forward, curious.

"I'm an old friend of Riley's. I can pass her a message when I next see her. How do you know her?"

"She rescued me from the hospital. If you see her, can you tell her she's a Godparent, please?"

"I'll be sure to tell her."

"Don't forget, will you. I'll be looking for her," repeated Stella over her shoulder as Sister Imelda pulled her away. Stella kept her eyes fixed on Terra until she nodded in reply.

***

Terra heard Briggs' raised voice behind her. He was towering over Jack like a predator straddling his prey. One of Briggs' men raised his right boot and stamped on Jack's rib cage to wake him up. Jack was so cold, he was lapsing in and out of consciousness.

Terra took off the coat she had borrowed and barged past Briggs, draping it around Jack's cowering frame. He looked up at her gratefully with a distant expression. She smiled back at him, though she was not entirely sure he recognised her.

"So this is Jumping Jack, the man I've heard so much about. You don't look much to me, wearing your underpants and a lady's coat, you look like a drowned rat. Now what are we going to do with you, eh?"

"Jack's been my tormenter in chief for the last few months, haven't you Jack?" snarled King.

"I say he deserves a taste of his own medicine," laughed Briggs.

"We need to make an example of him. It's the least he should get for dragging us all out here in this cold weather."

Terra stepped forward, trembling, her fists clenched. "You promised me Jack wouldn't be harmed."

"Who's this then?" sneered King, looking Terra up and down. "Are you the woman that Jack's been pining for all this time? I thought you'd be better looking."

"That's enough," cautioned Briggs. "Terra's with me now. Watch your mouth."

"My mistake," he said, holding his hands up. "She's feisty, I'll give her that. I'm sure you'll be perfect for each other," he smiled.

King leaned across and snatched Briggs' silver pistol, feeling its weight in his hand, stroking the contours of its barrel, as Briggs' men looked on in alarm. "You don't mind if I borrow this do you?"

"Be my guest."

"So Copper, come closer. Stop sulking in the shadows. Come on, come and say hello properly, don't be shy. Still, I suppose you've every reason to be embarrassed after abandoning me here."

Copper sidled towards him guiltily, unsure what he was intending to do next. King put his arm round his shoulder and pulled him closer. Copper was breathing heavily, recognising a crazed look he had seen many times before.

"It's alright Copper, I'm not going to hurt you," he said, patting his cheek. "No, I don't blame you," he laughed scornfully, tapping the barrel of the pistol against Copper's forehead.

"But I do blame Charlie here," he said pointing to Copper's right hand man, who looked bemused, turning to Copper and the others for support. Without hesitation or explanation, he fired point-blank into the man's chest. The gunshot startled Terra and for the next few seconds she could hear nothing but ringing in her right ear. She watched in disbelief as the man clutched at his chest and sank to his knees.

"Packs quite a punch that thing doesn't it," he said calmly, handing the smoking gun back to Briggs. "Now that score's all settled, what about you, Jack?" he said.

"Briggs," Terra whispered forcefully, tugging at his sleeve.

"You're right babe, I did give you my word that I wouldn't harm him," he said nodding sympathetically. "But then I can hardly be held responsible for the actions of others, can I?" he winked at King.

"Come on Jackie-boy, let's get you up on your feet before you catch your death of cold. We can't be having that now, can we?"

King helped Jack up. He fell against the wall before steadying himself. Terra noticed Jack's lips were almost blue with cold, pinching the coat tighter under his chin with both hands. Terra's coat was much too small to fit round his girth, leaving a six-inch strip of exposed flesh where it wouldn't quite close. King straightened the collar of Jack's coat and smoothed down the grey hair in a side-parting, patting him playfully on the cheeks.

"We're going to make an example of you, Jack. That's what you always wanted, isn't it? To inspire others and show them the error of their ways? I've got just the idea. This can be your legacy to all those who visit the place."

With that he picked up the coil of rope that Riley and the others had used to climb down the castle walls. He looped one end through the eye and pulled it taught leaving a short noose which he placed over Jack's head and pulled tight, leading him through the Tudor gate and back to the front entrance. The others followed out of curiosity.

***

Terra followed a few paces behind Jack as he laboured painfully across the yard in his bare feet, the rope round his neck stretching taut before King yanked him back into step. There were hundreds of people in the main courtyard, standing room only, pressed together, waiting to have their turn at the door of the canteen where they were handing out hunks of bread and soup. Jack grabbed at Corporal Ballard who was standing close by, but the soldier lowered his eyes, shamed into silence by his complicity.

King barged a group of refugees out of the way, pushing one man's head roughly to clear their path. The man whipped his head round ready to strike him before he noticed Briggs entourage and stepped back.

They paused on the drawbridge as King scanned above him, searching for something he might have seen earlier. Fixed to the stone walls above the front entrance was an iron bracket for a lantern. He threw the free end of the rope over the mounting and pulled it taut, until it strained against Jack's neck.

Terra pulled at Briggs' sleeve and whispered: "Please, babe. You don't have to do this.

He squinted back at her, puzzled by her sentimentality, as if this was another test of her loyalty. He hesitated for a second, looking around the faces of his men. There was an expectation about them, as if this was a natural conclusion, a fitting end to the evening's entertainment. Terra realised with horror that this was all just a game to Briggs.

"Give me a hand could you, there's a good chap?" said King, waving him over to help with the rope.

Briggs frowned at Terra and wrestled his arm free. He stood by King's side, a smile on his face, watching his actions with some amusement. King passed him the rope and they took up the slack, ready to heave Jack off his feet.

"Any last words?" he paused.

"I've got nothing to say to you," rebuked Jack with a look of resignation.

"How disappointing. Not even, I don't know, a last cry for freedom or a cautionary word about karma?"

"I wouldn't give you the satisfaction."

"Fair enough, I was never one for long goodbyes either. Let's get this over with. When you're ready Briggs, take the strain."

The two men pulled with all their might and Jack's whole body was lifted off the ground. The noose tightened around his neck as he began to choke, fighting to get his fingers underneath the rope as it bit into his windpipe.

Terra ran to Copper and stood in front of him, desperate for someone to wake from the trance that seemed to have overtaken Briggs' men like a spell. She shook his shoulders.

"Copper, please. Do something. You were a policeman for God's sake. How can you stand by and let them do this?" she stuttered.

"That part of me died a long time ago," he replied flatly.

She raced over to Jack, whose legs were dangling a couple of feet off the ground. She grabbed hold of his knees and tried to support his weight and relieve the pressure on his throat. He stared down at her, his eyes bulging out of his face, as his whole body convulsed, making the bracket above them rattle and shake.

Victor hurried forward and tore her hands away, pulling her back against the wall. She buried her head in his shoulder, tears coming quickly now, unable to watch this gruesome scene play out.

When she turned around, Jack's feet were still twitching, his face contorted in horrible asphyxia. It was an image she would never forget, or forgive.

CHAPTER FIFTY-TWO

Just before dawn, the *Sheridan* met Briggs and his party at the eastern dock to take them back to the island before daybreak. Terra had not spoken since leaving the castle. She was still in a state of shock.

She lingered at every opportunity, looking over her shoulder at the outline of the castle in the distance. The image of Jack's lifeless body swinging above the entrance was seared into her mind.

On board the well-appointed powerboat, Victor handed Terra his jacket. She curled up in the corner of the cockpit with her knees tucked up under her chin. The tears flowed freely down her cheeks and her breath came in sobs. Victor sat down next to her and tried to put his arm around her, but she pushed him away.

"I never should have trusted you."

"Believe me, I had no idea King would do that. It was unconscionable," he said looking out towards the island. After a moment's reflection, he continued. "We always knew that we would need to make sacrifices."

"I don't see you making sacrifices, Victor. You always seem to come out smelling of roses."

"That is not true, Terra. If you only knew what I had given up," he said leaning in closer and lowering his voice, checking round to make sure no one could hear them over the engine noise and light breeze. "We are so close. Now that Hurst is under military control and the rest of your people are safely transferred to the island, we are one step closer."

"They're not my people. I told you. It was only Jack I had any feelings for, the rest of them meant nothing to me."

She turned her head away from him and pulled her arm free from where he was holding on to her. To her relief, he got to his feet. He thought about saying something else, but decided against it and went to join Briggs in the main cabin where they were heating up some coffee on the gas stove.

It was already getting brighter in the East. Dawn was still an hour away but it seemed lighter somehow, unless that was light from the island. She could see the town of Cowes ahead of them, scattered street lights along the front, marking their way. There were no signs of other maritime activity at this ungodly hour, yet she knew from past experience that this stretch of waterway was monitored day and night. The Americans were ever vigilant, sending fast launches to intercept any boats attempting unauthorised crossings of the Solent, so where were they?

After what had happened tonight, Terra half-hoped they would be caught. Despite his fine words and denial, Briggs had been fully complicit with what happened to Jack. He had allowed this to happen. It was almost as if the two men had dared each other to go further, to commit ever more barbaric acts. A bizarre game of one-upmanship that would lead to savagery.

Over the last few months, she had grown desensitised to Briggs' violence. She knew now what he was capable of. He no longer held the power to shock her. She had suppressed her emotions for so long, she felt tremendous release in her tears, purged by her grief. Her eyes had been opened to the depths of her own complicity and its consequences.

The *Sheridan* entered the mouth of the river Medina, passing the burned-out wreck of what had once been the Royal Yacht Squadron. Its two-hundred-year history as one of the world's finest yacht clubs destroyed by looters and trophy seekers in search of memorabilia and metal.

All the buildings on the right were dark and lifeless. Streetlights along the front seemed oddly out of place in this ghostly pre-dawn world. To their left, the giant hangar doors of the boatyard at Venture Quays still proudly displayed the red, white and blue colours of the Union Jack flag, first painted to celebrate the Queen's Silver Jubilee. The yard had been a hub of innovation in years gone by, building hovercrafts, seaplanes, as well as world-record breaking powerboats. The hangar had been cleared during the outbreak to act as a huge mortuary for the disposal of the thousands of victims of the Millennial Virus. It was said bodies had filled all available floor space then left to rot when the clean-up crews abandoned the site. A secondary outbreak of typhoid had decimated those who survived the virus. No one came here any more. It was a tomb to the fallen. Instinctively, Terra shielded her face, in case the stench could still reach them as they passed by.

They cruised silently up river, passing the chain-link ferry, which sat shackled to the shore. Its hull was covered in graffiti. The same tags and stylised words you saw throughout this area suggested rival gangs marking their territory, warning others away.

At the bend in the river, their progress seemed to slow momentarily against the fast-flowing tide running against them.

Keeping their engine noise to a minimum, Terra took comfort in the tranquility of the morning. It would not be long before the island would again resume this twisted version of existence. Each day another ferry load of refugees was deposited here from Southampton to begin a new life.

Briggs' motorcade was waiting for them at the quayside at Newtown and they were driven the short distance back to their adopted home in the austere surroundings of Carisbrooke Castle just south of the town.

The fields surrounding the castle had been turned over to farmland and refugee camps. The view from the ancient keep was now blighted by the construction of so many hastily erected buildings and warehouses to store all of the equipment and materials being shipped across on a daily basis.

As they drove up the narrow lane that led to the castle, the barricades were lifted out of the way as the guards waved the convoy through. The ancient motte and bailey stone entrance was nearly one thousand years old, much too narrow for vehicles to pass through. They parked up outside, facing the crumbling castle walls.

Terra had grown to love this place, so steeped in history. Harry, an amateur historian and one of Briggs' more educated associates, was full of colourful stories of the castle through the ages. He regaled the others with accounts of attacks dating from Roman times and the Spanish Armada. By all accounts, the castle had been home to significant figures from English history from Thomas Cromwell, the Duke of Salisbury, to the Bishop of Winchester. The list went on. It had even served as a prison for King Charles I after his transfer from Hurst Castle.

Of course, the place was much changed these days. The museum had been cleared of artefacts and historical displays to make way for accommodation for Briggs and his men. Some two hundred men and women now occupied Carisbrooke Castle.

Terra followed Briggs and Victor through the main gate across the courtyard towards the main building ahead of them. There was an unusual amount of activity for this early hour and it took her a few seconds to realise why.

To their right was the unmistakable dark shape of a helicopter. It seemed so utterly incongruous surrounded by the high walls of the castle. The juxtaposition of old and modern made Terra stop and stare.

"Looks like we have visitors," said Victor as he hurried on to catch up with Briggs.

She puzzled at the sight, lost in thought. The last time she had seen the helicopter was at Hurst Castle all those months ago. It had to be American, but why on earth would they be here? It made no sense to her.

She ran after Victor, eager to discover more about their visitors. Victor was conferring with Briggs about something in the vestibule, handing his coat to one of the men. Briggs nodded and they went inside, followed by Terra and the others. They had set a roaring fire, stacked with logs and broken furniture. On the far side of the room was a group of seven soldiers, dressed in full combat gear. As Terra entered, they looked up calmly, weapons lowered. To her surprise, she recognised Lieutenant Peterson, who had his boots off, drying his socks next to the fire.

"Make yourself at home, why don't you?" said Briggs with a heavy hint of sarcasm, "I thought we agreed never to meet in person."

"We did, but in the circumstances, I thought a visit was warranted."

Peterson noticed Terra standing behind the others and nodded in her direction. "Good to see you're alive and well, Terra."

"What do you want Peterson?" continued Briggs impatiently.

"Your antics have been causing me no end of headaches over the last forty-eight hours. Gallivanting around the countryside attacking my guys. You seem to have completely forgotten our agreement."

"Not before you did," said Briggs to a look of bemusement. "When were you going to tell me about Porton Down?"

"That's none of your business."

"So you planned to just keep us in the dark? Do you think we're stupid or something?"

"You got what you wanted. We agreed that you would stay out of the way."

"Not when you go behind my back and smuggle scientists on to the island, that changes everything."

"What have you done with the Professor?"

"He's safe. Somewhere out of harm's way."

"Back at the hospital?"

"I wouldn't like to say."

"Look, it doesn't matter now. He's no longer my concern. You can keep him."

"Please yourself," he shrugged.

"I have some more clean-up work coming your way."

"I'm done with your dirty work. Who is it this time?"

"Just the crew of a tanker we picked up. They'll arrive tomorrow. If you can make them disappear, like the other lot I sent you."

"What's so important about the crew of a tanker?" puzzled Victor.

"What do you think? They're from the outside world. They know too much. I can't risk them talking, spreading rumours about what's really going on out there."

"They'll find out soon enough. How long do you think you can keep people in the dark?"

"Now you listen here, Briggs, and you listen good. How I do things is my business. I control the flow of information round here, not you. You're only alive so long as I allow you to be."

"I'm not your lapdog, Peterson."

"No Briggs, you're much more important than that. Your job is to create fear, true fear," he said theatrically. "Fear that strikes terror in to the hearts of everyone on this pathetic God-forsaken island. Without fear, there can be no control, you hear me? People coming here need to believe there's a credible threat to their security."

"You've got a screw loose if you think you're in control. You need to get out more, see what's really going on."

"You don't get it, do you? Every alliance needs a unifying cause. A common enemy, and you're it. As far as I'm concerned, you're public enemy number one. You're the Boogeyman, the evil mastermind behind everything, leading a faceless organisation that strikes fear into the hearts of every living soul. You're the rebellion, the luddites, the fifth columnists, the counter-revolutionaries we all loathe and fear."

"Your pantomime is all very well, but the virus is the real threat. If there's a vaccine, that changes everything."

"Don't kid yourself. There's never going to be a vaccine. It'll take years, maybe decades. All the stocks of Tamiflu and Relenza are under my control."

"That's not what the Professor told me."

"That guy," he snorted. "He's an academic, a historian. He knows nothing."

"I wouldn't be so sure, he told me the virus could have been bio-engineered."

"And you believed him? The virus was a natural disaster, nothing more. Maybe we brought this thing on ourselves. We weren't as well prepared as we should have been. It was an accident waiting to happen."

"If the Professor is so unimportant, then why did you need him in the first place?"

"Who says I did?"

"Somehow I don't believe you."

"I don't care whether you believe me or not, it doesn't matter," he said getting out of his chair and approaching Briggs, drawing his sidearm. Briggs stood his ground, unintimidated by this show of force. Peterson pressed the cold barrel of his black revolver to Briggs' forehead, leaning in close.

"You, my friend, are going to learn to play by the rules. My rules. You do what we agreed and I'll leave you in peace. You get to come and go as you please, visit the mainland as many times as you like. But if you step out of line one more time, I'll bomb this place back to the stone age. You got that?"

Briggs stared back at Peterson, letting him have his moment of theatre, aware of all those watching. After a few moments, Briggs raised his eyebrows, with a hint of a smile.

"If I was you, friend, I wouldn't go barging into people's homes and threatening them. In case you hadn't noticed, you're a long way from Kansas, or wherever you come from. If you want things to run like clockwork on the island, you need me."

Briggs pushed his forehead against the barrel, leaning forward until Peterson lowered his weapon.

"Now, me and my men are hungry. I don't know about you, but it's been a long night, and I'm ready for a cup of coffee and some breakfast. So why don't you and your men get out before we fall out."

Peterson glared back at Briggs, eye-balling the warlord, blinking silently.

Peterson let out a long sigh, shaking his head disapprovingly. He sat down heavily opposite the fire, lacing up his boots with a forced smile on his face.

"You better tell those friends of yours at the hospital to keep their noses clean. No more chances."

Peterson zipped up his jacket, took one last look at the fire and turned to leave. Outside the window, dozens more of Briggs' men had gathered to see what all the commotion was about and the marine guard was uneasy with such a large force assembling.

Terra followed Briggs outside to watch them leave. The helicopter was already going into its start-up cycle, the whine of its engines building slowly as they wandered over. Its sliding door was open, ready to receive its passengers for the return trip to the *Chester*. As Peterson reached the helicopter, he turned and shouted back towards the waiting party, struggling to make himself heard over the rotors which were beginning to turn faster and faster.

"I'll be seeing you Briggs. Don't forget what I told you."

Briggs looked enigmatically across at Victor, his expression hard to read. Terra wondered how much longer he would put up with being treated like a naughty schoolboy.

No one spoke to Briggs like that and got away with it, at least, not for long. To a man like Briggs, respect was everything. There would be repercussions, that would be certain. Terra recognised Victor's unmistakable influence over the last few weeks. He was more patient, biding his time for the opportunities that would present themselves all too soon as the Allies let down their guard.

Terra could only guess at the cards Briggs held up his sleeve. Their game plan was entering its final chapter. If Victor was right, it would change everything. But if he was wrong, they would all be wiped out. The end of everything she had worked so hard for. She alone could be the heir to Briggs' empire.

CHAPTER FIFTY-THREE

A pale sun appeared over the island as the *Nipper* picked up the rest of the Hurst survivors from Cliff End Battery and motored the short distance to Yarmouth Harbour. Like Lymington on the mainland, Yarmouth looked quite different from the seaside town that had once drawn huge numbers of day-trippers in previous summers.

The whole ferry port and harbour area were fully militarised with high fences topped with coils of razor wire along the jetty and wall to prevent unauthorised landings. Two lookout posts were set up on top of Yarmouth Castle where a sand-bagged position revealed the barrel of a machine gun. The lookouts covered the *Nipper*'s approach as it bounced over the swell towards the harbour wall, where a group of soldiers stood waiting for them.

"Tell me again why we have to pass quarantine?" asked Tommy sheltering behind the wheelhouse.

"Because everyone has to, that's why. They can't bend the rules for anyone. That's how they'll keep the virus out, dummy," said Sam, who had a blanket round his shoulders and a pair of oilskin trousers stained with dried-on fish guts, the only clothing he could find on board. The others were huddling together for warmth below deck.

"Will you two please stop bickering? It's like being stuck with two little children. If I could walk, I'd come over there and knock some sense into the pair of you," reprimanded Riley, who was perched in the corner of the cramped wheelhouse next to the depth sounder.

"Sam, that bloke is pointing you over there," said Riley, noticing a soldier directing them towards the vacant pontoon. Sam turned the wheel and put the engine into neutral as they coasted towards the jetty. Tommy grabbed the bow line and got ready to jump.

As soon as they landed and made the *Nipper* fast, Zed helped Riley up the ramp on to the hard. She winced with each step, leaning heavily against Zed for support. Her trouser leg was rolled up to the knee, exposing the pristine crepe bandage applied by a nurse at Cliff End Battery.

The parting with Sergeant Jones had been awkward to say the least. Despite her obvious shyness, she had hugged him and allowed a kiss on the cheek in front of all of them. She had later shrugged off their taunts as the American adopting "European" ways, but in her heart she realised their new friendship meant more to him than it did to her. The last few days had confirmed that she had feelings for another, though the subject of her affections seemed entirely oblivious.

Jones' team had said their goodbyes and headed back to the *Chester*. They were being recalled as a matter of urgency, although Jones wouldn't tell her what it was all about. It had come straight from the top, Lieutenant Peterson had been very insistent. She suspected there was another attack under way in Southampton or perhaps there were more attempts to cross the Solent. She had seen for herself how busy they were monitoring all of that activity in the sector.

The soldier on the jetty directed them towards a medical station where they would each be assessed for symptoms of the virus. Zed looked strangely nervous as they waited for their turn.

"You're not having another irrational attack of survivor guilt, are you?"

"Back off Riley. We all deal with it in our own way. Unlike you, I never forgave myself for leaving my family to face the outbreak on their own. I need to live with the consequences of my actions."

"Let it go, Zed. We're your family now. Anyway, what's done is done."

"Don't get me started," he groaned, shaking his head.

One by one they were cleared into a quarantine zone where three army trucks were waiting to take them south towards their new home in Freshwater Bay at the south-western tip of the island. Captain Armstrong had provided personal assurances that the team would be quarantined on site at their final destination, rather than face the ignominy of the mandatory forty-eight hours in the squalid conditions of the refugee camps.

The convoy of trucks crossed the river estuary and wound their way south-west through Norton Green on the Colwell Road before turning east towards Freshwater. Everything was so green on the island. The houses and shops they passed looked untouched by the lawlessness of the outbreak. It was almost as if the chaos and descent into civil unrest had never happened here.

She remembered Zed saying something about lower population density and the abundance of natural resources making a difference for the islanders. It seemed too good to be true, if that was the case. Perhaps everything she had heard about the island was real. Her skeptical nature had made her cautious and she still expected each corner they turned to reveal the true scale of the humanitarian crisis unfolding all around them.

It was still early in the morning, which might explain the tranquility they discovered once they had left Yarmouth. The quiet rumble of the diesel engine was the only sound as they progressed through deserted streets. There were very few people around. She checked her watch. It was nearly eight-thirty, nearly an hour and a half after daylight, so where was everyone?

They drove down tree-lined roads with overgrown hedges and well-proportioned houses on either side. The previous week's storms had left a carpet of leaves and fallen branches on the pavements, littering the roadway. Many of the ditches were filled with water and part-submerged vehicles had been pushed off the road by tractors and diggers to keep the path clear for convoys like theirs.

The horizon seemed to open up as they approached the sea, turning right at the old lifeboat station on the beach at Freshwater Bay. Sam pointed ahead of them towards a large white hotel that dominated the headland above steep chalk cliffs. There was a barrier set up in the road, blocking the entrance to the hotel beyond with the cautionary notice 'Do not enter - Trespassers will be shot'. Bumping up the track towards the building on the cliff top, they passed sloping fields on their right scattered with cows and sheep that reminded Riley of the farmland they managed at Keyhaven.

Riley had never been here, but it was said that Freshwater Bay was a spot every bit as beautiful as Hurst spit, with panoramic views of the English Channel, where steep chalk cliffs met the sea. She was not disappointed. Looking back behind the truck she could see a small beach and rocks standing proud of the water, where south-westerly Atlantic storm systems had smashed against a coastline prone to erosion.

In the distance she could make out the wreck of a coastal steamer smashed against the rocks, its bottom ripped out, lying broken against an outcrop. Beyond were rolling hills dropping away to the sea as far as the eye could see towards St Catherine's point, the southern-most tip of the island. There was nothing south of here for seventy miles until you hit France. It was as far south as you could get, without going all the way west towards Cornwall. To Riley this seemed like the end of the world.

The convoy pulled up in front of the hotel buildings and one by one, they jumped down from the trucks, looking around them excitedly at their new home. Several of the advance party emerged to welcome the new arrivals from Hurst, asking anxiously about their journey and whether everyone had made it across. News about Jack's absence spread quickly and there was a subdued air of melancholy.

Sam and Tommy ran inside to explore, eager to grab the best room for themselves. From the outside, the hotel looked tired but habitable. So exposed to the elements, the outside walls needed a lick of paint. The roof seemed in good condition with most of the tiles still in place. Back in the day, this had been a luxury retreat so would be well appointed, with beds for all, a dining room, kitchen and generous living quarters.

From the looks of the place, its remote location had ensured it had survived intact, barring a few looted items. None of the latest arrivals had any luggage, just the clothes they were standing up in. The others would have items they could borrow until they found their feet and scavenged new gear from the surrounding properties.

Zed wandered away towards the cliff edge and, despite the pain, Riley hobbled after him past the patio area with what would have been a swimming pool with a view. The pool was half-full and green with algae. There was a rusting iron bench set just back from the cliff. Zed collapsed in a state of exhaustion. Riley joined him, standing behind him with her hands on his shoulders. She shifted her weight to her good leg, enjoying being upright once more.

The view was breathtaking and the breeze was steady and uninterrupted, unpolluted by the stench of decay you so often got downwind of human habitation. Despite the best efforts of the survivors to eliminate the threat of cholera and other diseases by clearing cottages of the dead, the smell was often unmistakable. It turned Riley's stomach just to imagine it, but here on the island, there was nothing. She took a deep breath revelling in its purity.

"Don't know about you, but I'm tired, tired of all this running around and fighting. I think we deserve a rest, don't you?"

"There's no rest for people like you and me."

"I don't know, this place doesn't look so bad. It's kind of sleepy, but that's probably not a bad thing. We've been in the wars for too long."

Zed's eyes were fixed on the shipwreck in the distance, watching the waves crash against its superstructure and sweep over its foredeck, before spilling back over the side again to be drawn out to sea in a never-ending cycle.

"I'm not staying. I need to get back to Newtown. My place is with those scientists. As soon as we've cleared quarantine, I'm out of here."

"Just rest up one week, Zed? Stay with me, please."

She patted his shoulder affectionately, leaving her hand resting there. They didn't speak for a few seconds, enjoying the silence.

"Things are going to get worse before they get better, you know that. Winter is coming and there's a lot of hard work to get this place ready, find supplies, food. We're starting again from scratch. It will take time to re-establish ourselves."

"But take a look around you. Don't you see, it's different here?"

"For now, but the war will follow us here. The only thing different about this place is that there's a strip of water between us and them. It's only a matter of time Riley. In the end it will be the same everywhere you go. Only the strong will survive."

"I know Zed, but just for once, let someone else worry about it. We could be happy here. Maybe settle down, live a simple life. I don't know, start a family, raise kids, grow vegetables, look after some sheep and cows."

Zed leaned back, resting his head against her puffer jacket. She stroked his face tenderly and he looked up at her and smiled.

"Until I find out what happened to my family, I'm still married Riley," he said twirling his wedding ring with a grimace. "Anyway, that life may be enough for normal people, but not me. You know me better than anyone Riley. I'm not capable of settling down, I'm a restless soul, a nomad. I was never good at being tied down."

He paused, as if replaying the events of the previous night in his mind. He straightened, remembering something.

"You know we had Briggs in our sights and we let him slip away. We could have ended him right there. Maybe that would have changed things. Next time, he won't be so lucky."

"He'll keep. Sometime soon, he'll get his comeuppance. I just worry what they'll do to Jack."

"We can only hope the soldiers stepped in. It was his own fault. He was so stubborn and proud. He failed to adapt. Jack still clung to the belief that good would prevail. Real life is not like that anymore. People like Briggs will rule this land. Anyone who stands in their way will fall."

"Well, revenge is a dish best served cold. He won't know when it's coming, but by God, he'll get his."

"You can say that again, Karma has a warped sense of humour," laughed Zed.

"Sometimes, before I open my eyes in the morning, just for a second, I think I might have imagined this whole thing, that I'll be back in my own bed in my city flat with my cat purring at my feet, living my own quiet little life. Then, when I do wake up, it takes me a few minutes to gather myself. There are days when I don't think I can go on. If it hadn't been for you and Jack, I probably would have done something stupid, taken my life, I don't know."

"You can't think like that Riley. None of us can afford to think like that."

"I know. I'm sorry. I guess we all have moments of weakness and self-pity. We're only human. Sometimes I find it unsettling to think that God could have allowed this terrible situation to happen. I prefer to think that the virus is in some way our own creation, an experiment gone horribly wrong. Isn't that somehow more palatable?"

Zed sighed but didn't respond for a few seconds, looking out into the distance as a lone pair of seagulls swooped towards the cliff edge, before soaring high on the wind.

"I'm fairly certain it wasn't an accident. This all happened for a reason. I just can't figure out why or who was responsible. Who could have possibly gained from the death of hundreds of millions of people, maybe even billions? Trust me, someone somewhere must know what happened. If I can find hard evidence of a link with a bio-weapons programme, then we'll have our answer. In the meantime, the important thing is that we develop an effective vaccine."

"I trust you Zed. I know a lot of people think you're crazy and they're probably right, but I believe you."

"Thanks, sometimes I don't know what I think any more. Part of me thinks that this was just a natural disaster that no one could have foreseen or done anything about. I hope I'm wrong, I really do. The thought that some organisation was responsible for this genocide, it does my head in."

Behind them, someone was ringing a handbell and calling them into the hotel.

"Must be breakfast time," said Riley looking over her shoulder. "Come on, give me a hand would you, this leg is killing me."

Zed got gingerly to his feet, stretching his arms out wide. He looked tired, thought Riley. A tiredness that sleep would never wash away. She inserted her arm under his shoulder and around his back. She gave him an affectionate squeeze, as he supported her back towards their new home. As they approached the terrace, Sam was coming down to meet them holding in his hand what looked like a letter.

Sam stopped beside the pool and waited for Zed to deposit Riley in an iron-framed chair set round an outdoor table. He handed Zed the letter.

"We found this on the counter. It's addressed to you, care of the Freshwater Bay Hotel. They knew we were coming, but don't know how long it's been there."

He took the letter and turned it over, unsure what to do with it. It had been a long time since any of them had seen a letter, let alone been the recipient of one.

"Go on, aren't you going to open it?" implored Riley impatiently.

He lifted the flap and inserted his index finger, tearing it open.

Inside was a plain-white card with an address at the top. He read the note quickly, looking up at Riley with a puzzled expression.

"Come on. What does it say?"

"It's unbelievable..." he stammered, "read it for yourself."

Riley snatched the card and read it aloud:

Ryde School, Queen's Road, Ryde, Isle of Wight.

Dear Mr Samuels,

I am delighted to let you know that your daughter Heather is alive and well.

She is being looked after by the staff at Ryde School along with all the other unaccompanied minors who arrived here over the last few weeks.

It was only by chance that we were alerted to your presence on the island. All new arrivals are subject to medical tests and we just found out that Heather shares the same rare blood type, AB minus, with you, her father. I am told there are only four others with that type on the whole island.

I would be extremely grateful if you can come and collect her at your earliest convenience. As I'm sure you can understand, we have not let Heather know that her father is still alive. So many of the children we see here are orphaned and we wanted to be one hundred per cent sure before we tell her the good news.

I look forward to meeting you.

Sincerely,
Principal Jane Shirley,
Ryde School.

"My God, that's incredible, Zed, I'm so happy for you."

"I don't know what to say or think. I can scarcely believe it. I'm numb," he said flatly.

"It's the best news ever," laughed Riley, but her thoughts were going in a dozen different directions all at once.

Zed grabbed the card and reread it quickly.

"It doesn't say anything about the rest of them, just Heather."

Riley sighed, suddenly realising why she felt so conflicted. If his daughter was still alive, then why not his wife and son? It meant that the one person Riley had allowed herself to care for, might still belong to another. It was another cruel twist of fate that seemed to make a habit of puncturing her hopes and dreams.

Sam and Zed got to their feet. She closed her eyes, cursing her luck. She had promised herself she would not get upset and yet tears started streaming down her face. As Zed stooped to pick her up and carry her the rest of the way to their new home, he noticed her crying softly. She buried her head into his shoulder, hugging him tighter.

"I'm just so happy for you, that's all," she smiled as he lifted her off her feet. There was a bounce in his step for the first time Riley could remember. At least one of them would have a chance of happiness. She would never give up hope that her turn would come.

***

The next morning, just before dawn, a commotion outside the hotel woke Riley from a restless sleep. The painkillers she had taken in the night had only succeeded in taking the edge off the throbbing in her calf. By the time she dressed and hobbled down the sweeping staircase to the lobby, there were already raised voices from below. She pushed open the swing doors to a well-appointed drawing room and was surprised to recognise Colonel Abrams and the disheveled grey hair of Doctor Hardy. The Colonel was remonstrating with Will and Tommy.

"What's going on?" asked Riley, rubbing the sleep from her eyes.

"These men are demanding to see Zed," postured Will, his arms crossed. "I've told them that he's not to be disturbed. Perhaps you can make them see sense."

"It's alright Will, I've got this," she said, stroking his arm. Zed appeared at the doorway and the group fell silent.

"Finally," sighed the Colonel, with some relief. "Can we have a word?"

"Good to see you Colonel, what's got you out of bed in the middle of the night?"

"Is there somewhere more private we could talk?"

Riley gestured for Tommy and Will to leave them and the Colonel closed the door, leaning his body against it, composing his thoughts.

"We heard what happened at the castle. I'm so sorry. I came as soon as I could."

Zed looked at the ground and then back at the Colonel. "We were lucky to get the team out when we did. We have the Americans to thank for that."

"Is there any news about Jack? He was the only one who didn't make it out," asked Riley.

The Colonel hesitated. "I'm sorry, no. There's still some confusion about his whereabouts. We've been trying to raise Sergeant Flynn all night, but the comms are still out. I fear Jack may have been captured. We'll send news as soon as we know more."

There was something about the way he avoided eye contact that made Riley suspicious. From what she knew first-hand of

Briggs, she was understandably concerned but didn't want to give voice to her fears.

"There are a lot of worried people here who would appreciate that. Last night's dinner was like a wake," admitted Zed. "So Doctor, what brings you all the way out here?"

"It would seem that the Doctor owes you an apology."

"Really? I'm not sure I'm following you."

"Perhaps you can tell Zed what you told me earlier."

Doctor Hardy seemed more awkward than usual. Riley noticed him wringing his hands and scratching at some dry skin on his wrist.

"The team has been working around the clock for the last seventy-two hours. Look, I won't beat around the bush. We've found evidence of genetic markers that could suggest some level of human interference."

"You're saying someone did bio-engineer the virus?"

"We're not one hundred per cent sure, but it looks increasingly likely."

Zed ran his fingers through ruffled hair and blinked back at them as if he could scarcely believe what he had just heard. He frowned and shook his head, trying to make sense of this revelation. His thoughts raced in a dozen different directions.

"There's a team waiting for you at St Mary's," continued the Colonel, "I suggest we continue this conversation on the way."

"What about quarantine? We're confined to quarters until further notice."

"You've both had your flu shots at Porton. I'm sure that we can dispense with the formalities. I'll vouch for you."

Riley seemed to come to her senses as if she had been numbed by what she was hearing. A single thought clamoured for her attention. "What about your daughter?"

Zed clasped his hand to his mouth. He appeared to have forgotten all about the letter.

"That's right Colonel, they found my daughter. She's safe at some boarding school near Ryde," he said fishing the envelope from his back pocket.

"I could go," suggested Riley. "Right now, she doesn't even know you're still alive, so a few more days won't make too much of a difference. If you can lay on some transport, Colonel," she said pointing to her bandaged calf with the trouser leg rolled up, "I could go collect her and bring her to you in Newtown later this week."

"Perfect," said Zed, shrugging his shoulders. "Then, what are we waiting for?"

The Colonel smiled, pushing back the sleeve of his uniform to reveal an expensive looking diver's watch.

"With any luck, we can be back at the lab by dawn."

Zed nodded excitedly and the three of them turned to leave. Riley laboured after them, out into the hotel lobby and through the double doors into the darkness beyond. There was a military vehicle waiting for them near the front porch with its engine running. Zed stopped in his tracks as if remembering something. It was clear that his mind was already elsewhere. He turned and hugged her tightly, squeezing the breath out of her lungs and lifting her off her feet before noticing her wincing from the pain in her leg. He lowered her gently and without a word climbed into the back seat and slammed the door.

Riley was left all alone standing outside the hotel as the car manoeuvred round. She angled her head to catch one last glimpse of Zed's face through the window, but he didn't look round. She wrapped her arms around her slender frame, shivering against the pre-dawn chill. The vehicle's tyres crunched round on the gravel driveway and rolled slowly back down the hill before picking up speed and disappearing off down the lane into the darkness. In the silence that followed, she could just make out waves breaking gently against the rocks in Freshwater Bay. With a heavy sigh, she hobbled back inside to find the others.

Acknowledgements

Writing a book is a lot like starting and running a business. It takes a whole village! Thank you to the small army of people who supported me and generously gave up their time to read successive drafts of *Sentinel*. You all know who you are. I won't attempt to mention all of you. No Gwyneth Paltrow Oscar acceptance speech here. But as anyone who's been involved in writing will know, it's a long and iterative process. It takes hard work, dedication and an unfaltering belief that it's all going to be worthwhile in the end. So, a big thank you to all the friends and family who helped: Tor, Jake, Bea, Rose, Tom, Bobbie, Ems, Katy, CC, Pete, Dan, Jess, Bertie, Ed, Janet, Andrew, Serena, H, Sarah, Mark, Tina, Adrienne, Chris, Shona, Jim, Jane, Darren, Cameron, Derek, Raoul, Howie, Linda and Marlene.

Disclaimer

Stay in touch

Join the Hurst Chronicles Readers' Group and be the first to hear about upcoming books in the series, news and offers.

Website: HurstChronicles.com
Twitter: @HurstChronicles
Facebook: Facebook.com/HurstChronicles

Printed in Great Britain
by Amazon

41606990R00271